HEX APPEAL

KATE JOHNSON

One More Chapter
a division of HarperCollins*Publishers* Ltd
1 London Bridge Street
London SE1 9GF
www.harpercollins.co.uk
HarperCollins*Publishers*
1st Floor, Watermarque Building, Ringsend Road
Dublin 4, Ireland

This paperback edition 2022
1
First published in Great Britain in ebook format
by HarperCollins*Publishers* 2022

A catalogue record of this book is available from the British Library

UK ISBN: 978-0-00-855113-1
Canada ISBN: 978-0-00-859778-8

Printed and bound in the UK using 100% Renewable Electricity
by CPI Group (UK) Ltd

Kate Johnson was born in the 1980s in Yorkshire and now lives in Essex, where she belongs to a small pride of cats. [illegible] Guinness Book of Records for brewing the world's strongest beer and she also once ran over herself with a Segway scooter. These two things are not related.

Kate has worked in an airport, a lab, and various shops, but much prefers writing because mornings are definitely not her best friend. In 2017 she won Paranormal Romantic Novel of the Year from the Romantic Novelists' Association with her novel *Max Seventeen*.

katejohnson.co.uk

twitter.com/K8JohnsonAuthor
tiktok.com/k8johnsonauthor
facebook.com/catmarsters

To Alysia, who would have loved this book. You taught me spells, you made me brave, you were the best of friends. Rest in peace, witch.

Chapter One

Essie Winterscale was on her way home from the village shop with two bottles of wine and a pint of ice cream when she saw the vision that would almost change the world for ever.

Like most witch premonitions it was neither clear nor helpful, consisting mostly of 'a really weird feeling about that minicab driving past' overlaid with 'oh so that's how we're all going to die'.

The shopping bag hit the footpath, and a sudden heat stole over Essie, as if the world was suddenly burning. 'But it's September,' she said out loud. There were Michaelmas daisies growing in clumps around the duck pond, and that meant summer was basically over.

She turned to look at the flowers, and as she did so the tall purple daisies grew long forked tongues.

'That's new,' she said.

She shook her head, and the flowers returned to normal. It was late September in the village of Good Winter: no more summer tourists around the duck pond, all the children back at school, the odd plume of woodsmoke coming from the older chimneys. There was a nip in the air, and the cool promise of autumn, and the calm Essie always felt as the Earth began to slow down for winter.

The minicab had disappeared.

Essie swiped sweat from her forehead. The day simply wasn't that warm.

'You all right, love?' said a voice, and Essie looked round into a face made of bones topped by violet hair. 'Essie, isn't it?'

She blinked, and the violet hair belonged to Mrs Sockburn the cleaning lady, who had never got the hang of a blue rinse. Her skin was lined and powdery, with not a hint of bone showing now.

Essie stared at the flowers, which were normal, and at the Common, which was normal, and Mrs Sockburn, who was… well, as normal as she'd ever been.

'Uh yeah. Yes. Fine. How are you, Mrs Sockburn? How's your son getting on with his twins?'

'Well, I tell you what, love, a phone call now and then wouldn't go amiss. He wants to do some zoomy thing, with a computer-pad or something. I'm sure I don't know.'

Essie considered explaining video calls, and decided that even if she lived for another thousand years she wouldn't have the time.

'Oh, and I tell you what. Remember old Agatha Cropley?'

Essie brought to mind a frail woman who had spent the last months of her life in a care home, where the only name in the visitor's book was Essie's. 'Of course. Lovely service for her,' she lied, because there had hardly been anyone but Essie and her coven at the soulless crematorium.

'Wasn't it,' said Mrs Sockburn, who definitely hadn't been there. 'Well, anyway, her house has been sold or rented or something. There's a new fella there.' She sniffed, and patted her hair, which had the rigidity of carbon fibre. 'I can't see him staying. Place is in a shocking state.'

'I thought you were doing the housekeeping there?' Essie said.

'I do a lot of things, love,' said Mrs Sockburn hurriedly. 'Well, I'll let you get on,' she added, and as she turned away, 'You've spilt something there.'

Essie looked down to see the melting ice cream leaking through the fabric of the shopping bag. 'Oh, bums.'

Essie picked up the shopping, put the lid back on the ice cream, and frowned. She'd only come out of the shop five minutes ago, and the day really wasn't that warm. It shouldn't be melting so fast.

Her hand casually hidden inside the bag, Essie concentrated, and the ice cream refroze under her hand. As a side thought, she chilled the wine, too.

Then she set off for home, trying not to think about mutant giant daisies.

Josh Henderson climbed out of the minicab, juggling three jumbo tubs of paint and a large packet of brushes, trying to wave his thanks to the driver, who ignored him and screamed away in a spray of loose stones. The drive was meant to be gravelled, but most of it seemed to have worn away and the rest was being eroded daily by the sole local cab firm.

He winced as a pebble hit the kitchen window. A tiny chip that would invariably grow and grow… He wondered how much it would cost to get the driveway re-gravelled. Probably a small fortune, and he'd have to use some special heritage gravel because of all the stupid regulations in this country.

He glanced again at the quote from the roofing company. Not a normal roofing company, but a special heritage one. Josh was beginning to learn that 'heritage' was an expensive word in England.

He looked around the kitchen in despair. 'Kitchen' was in and of itself an optimistic word for the room, which comprised a short section of Formica units that were probably older than Josh, a large wooden table that definitely was, and an ancient primeval stove that was probably older than his home country.

He'd cleaned up here as much as he could, sweeping and mopping and bleaching quite heavily. The fridge and microwave were brand new and looked very out of place against the scuffed and faded worktops. He half expected them to trigger an electrical fire, but the wiring at least seemed sound enough. Underneath the cracked and peeling linoleum, he'd found a rather fine tiled floor, and with not much else to do, had scrubbed it until it gleamed.

The kitchen could probably be quite nice if it had some

decent fixtures and fittings. The rest of the house, on the other hand…

A crash from upstairs made him jump. Shit, don't say that was another window. They were all original features, complete with wobbly panes and rotting wood frames, and he knew without asking that replacing any of them would be way out of his budget.

'Move to England,' he muttered. 'It'll be like Miss Marple before all the murders. They don't tell you,' he passed his hand over a gap in the handrail, 'about the damp, and the birds in the roof, and the goddamn heritage gravel.'

Yesterday he'd smiled at the woman in the village shop as she handed him his change and wished her a nice day. She'd looked at him as if he'd cursed her to the very pits of Hell. This village was weird. All of England was weird.

He could go back to Seattle. He could probably get another job in corporate law. Rent a new apartment. In a new district. Where Maya wouldn't find him.

Maybe not Seattle. Maybe the East Coast…

He trudged up the stairs, which creaked like the dying of a thousand souls, and poked his head into one of the many spare bedrooms. They had been mostly empty when he moved in, and had gotten even emptier since. The only thing left in the bedroom that faced over the front drive was the large glass ball hanging in a string net in the window. He didn't know what it was for, but the patterns it reflected on the floorboards looked cool, so he'd left it—

'God*dammit*,' he said, staring at the broken string and smashed glass on the floor. A couple of small brown shapes darted along the skirting boards, because of course the damn place had mice. Of course it did. And now one of them appeared to have chewed through the string, and all that was left of the globe of greenish glass was a mess on the floor.

And some... wait, was that a roll of paper? Josh crunched over to it and crouched down, pushing aside the shards of glass with the sleeve of his plaid shirt before picking it up.

It was a sheet of lined paper, the kind torn from a notebook, folded into quarters and then over at the edges, like a kid trying to pass a secret note at school. He unfolded it carefully, to see spidery writing in faded green ink and another wad of paper folded inside it, which fell to the floor amongst the glass.

'Of course it's green,' he muttered. He knew nothing about the extremely distant relative who'd lived here last, apart from her liking for cheap chintzy furniture and disinterest in updating any features of the house that were within fifty per cent of their working parameters. But maybe she'd been an eccentric old lady who'd... well, maybe she'd hidden a fortune in the cellar – somewhere Josh had not been brave enough to venture – and this was the start of a treasure hunt?

He peered at the writing, but could make out only a few words. 'Stuff and nonsense' appeared to be some of them, and at the bottom was a signature that began with an A and then meandered off through what appeared to be the rest of the English alphabet and several others, too.

Josh shrugged, and picked up the second packet of

paper, swearing quietly as a shard of glass pierced his thumb. This paper was much older, and—

'Ew! Ugh!'

What fell out of the folded packet seemed to be bits of hair and – ugh, were those nail clippings? What the hell?

'So, this is disgusting,' he said, and turned to go downstairs and wash his hands before he caught some kind of ancient infection, but something stopped him, and he never ever knew what it was.

His fingers smoothed out the ancient piece of parchment, which was torn at the creases and stained around the edges. Here and there were dark smudges, like fingerprints. The writing was crabbed with age and so looped as to be unreadable.

And yet he could read it.

I, thee right and goodlye Hopkins, do swear withall to abjure thee Devil and all who worshipe him and more I will see clearlye those beldams who are so ungoodlye and they never will cross this threshold or seat at my hearthe and never will I fall prey to they tricks and knavery this I swear.

All the dust floating in the air seemed to go still as he spoke, and then Josh blinked, and the motes swirled in the morning sunshine and the piece of paper he held was once again just an old sheet of vellum covered with unreadable handwriting.

'Weird,' he said, and put it down on the low windowsill while he went downstairs to fetch a broom.

He'd just washed his hands when his laptop chimed

with a video call. He hesitated. The only person who ever called him like that was his sister.

He'd been just about to put a dressing on the little cut on his thumb – but it had already stopped bleeding and was almost healed. The broken glass could wait, and it would be nice to see a semi-familiar face.

'Hey, dork,' breezed Siena, who appeared to be at an airport somewhere. Half her face was hidden behind huge sunglasses and she wore a massive hat. 'Why so grumpy?'

'This house is a money pit,' said Josh.

She shrugged, entirely unconcerned. 'If you need money, just ask.'

'We've been over this.' The house had been left to him, not his sister. It was pretty much the only thing he had been granted in his father's immense and complicated will, and Josh figured there had to be a reason for that. He had some savings, he'd done some contracting work while he was at college, and the house and its estate was supposed to generate an income, according to the local solicitor.

'Apparently the rents are due,' he said, as Siena peered at her picture on the screen and primped her immaculate hair.

Josh was pretty sure nobody would ever figure out he and Siena were related. She had expensively blonde hair and a perfect tan, year-round, her wardrobe was designer and tailored and she went everywhere in heels. Josh had unruly dark hair, burned easily, and would be delighted if he never had to wear anything remotely tailored ever again.

'I thought you owned the house?' said Siena, who owned seven, and three yachts.

'No, not the rent on this house. The rents from my tenants. I have tenants.' He had tenants. Josh had *been* a tenant all his life. The world was upside down.

'Cool, then why are you worrying about money?'

Josh sighed and sat down at the kitchen table. It had been here when he arrived, somewhat dusty and worm-eaten, but it was large and solid and he didn't exactly have a lot of furniture to ship over to fill the house. He'd bought a bed, and knew he ought to do something about a sofa because he was pretty sure the one in the living room had fleas.

'Well,' he said, gesturing to the paperwork the solicitor had sent him. 'First up, a lady called Mrs Sockburn, who was supposed to be taking care of this place.'

Siena peered doubtfully into the recesses of the kitchen behind him, where cupboard doors were missing and Josh had only just scrubbed the mildew out of the dresser. 'She didn't do a very good job.'

Josh tried to think of something fair to say to that, and failed. In the years the house had been empty, Mrs Sockburn had vacuumed and dusted occasionally, and totally failed to report the missing tiles on the roof, the bats in the attic, or the leaking sink in the scullery.

Holy cannoli, how do I own a house with a scullery?

'Well, in return for her services she gets a reduced rate of rent on her cottage in the village. Apparently this arrangement has been in place for years and is her right in perpetuity.'

'So you can't change it?'

'That's what in perpetuity means,' said Josh patiently.

Siena shrugged, and touched up her lipstick. 'Not all of us went to law school, Josh.'

'It's a pretty common – you know what, never mind. The rent she pays is – and trust me I read this several times and called the solicitor before I believed it – five pounds a month.'

Siena looked blank. To her, money was something other people managed on her behalf. She simply didn't even notice the amounts charged to her at point of sale.

'The market rate for a cottage like hers is probably a thousand, maybe fifteen hundred a month,' Josh said. He'd looked it up. Good Winter was a desirable place to live and character cottages were at a premium.

'Whoa. So she's totally stiffing you? Can't you sue her or something?'

This was a fairly standard response from Siena. To be fair, she'd learned it from her father.

'No,' said Josh, 'partly because she is a penniless old lady who cleans houses for a living, and partly because the agreement is, as I said, in perpetuity.'

'Well, that sucks. Who else?'

He sorted through the names on the list. 'Three of the cottages are derelict. I went around looking for them this morning. There's a barn on the drive up here that has a hole in its roof you could fly a plane through. Technically they owe me fourteen shillings a month.'

'Fourteen shillings?' Siena laughed. 'That's hilarious.'

Josh gave her a dark look. 'There's Mr Humble, who pays seven pounds a month in return for scything the grass in the long meadow, and the Ditchbourne family, who pay me a tithe from their "farm".'

She perked up at that. 'What's a tithe? Is it a profitable farm?'

'A tithe is one tenth of annual income,' Josh explained, 'and since no farming has gone on there since 1974, no, it is not. I guess I could argue that Mr Ditchbourne owes me a tenth of his earnings as an IT consultant but, seriously, Siena, this is insane. How did the old woman live like this?'

Siena shrugged. Neither of them had ever met Great-aunt Agatha, who in any case wasn't even their great-aunt but something more distant than that. Apparently the house had been left to their father when she died years ago, and he'd thought it of so little consequence he hadn't even visited the place. He'd just left it to Josh, for reasons they'd never know.

'Unsolved mystery. Look, why don't you just flip the place and sell it for a profit? Or rent it out. People would pay top dollar for a vacation cottage like this. Oh, we could fix up the barns and stables too, and put yurts in the garden? It could be so cute!'

'There you go with the "we",' said Josh, stacking the papers in order. He went through them again just to be sure he hadn't missed anything. The two peppercorn rents from the maintenance staff who didn't do any maintenance, the three derelict buildings and the tithe from the farm that wasn't a farm. And—

'Well, I thought… maybe, Josh…'

Wait, what was this one? He hadn't noticed it before, which was weird since he'd been through these papers quite a few times. And this wasn't just one page, but several stuck together, with notes and crossings out and faded ink he couldn't make out.

Beldam House, read the top typed page. Typed on a typewriter, not a computer, and there was a note attached that said it was replacing an older document that had fallen apart. He glanced at the top date. 1954, and this was the newer version?

Beldam…

'Josh?'

Josh read the top page, then reread it, and didn't realise his mouth had fallen open until Siena said, 'You look like a goldfish. And you're not listening to me.'

He reread the page, the ink brown on the yellowing paper. 'Beldam House, on Gallows Lane, Good Winter. Listed in the rent book as a guinea quarterly in… 1746? That can't be right.'

'I knew you weren't listening to me. What's a guinea?'

Josh could only shrug helplessly. 'It says attempts have been made to collect the rent several times since then, and the rate has been adjusted for inflation…' He peered at the lines of text. 'Several times, including for decimalisation, and is now expected to stand at…' He flipped over the page, where a new note had been appended.

He flipped back. He read it again.

'Josh, this is boring,' said Siena, turning her head as an announcement was made in what sounded like French.

'It says the rent should be in the region of ten thousand pounds a month.'

That got her attention. 'You said that old woman's house was worth fifteen hundred, tops.'

'Yeah. Ten grand a month?' He read it over, but the calculations were the kind that would have given his math teacher a heart attack, with absolutely no workings shown. 'It can't be right. Must be a misplaced decimal.'

'Even a grand a month would be good, right? For the…' she waved her hand, 'roof or whatever.'

'Yeah.' Josh stared off at the distance. Well, really he was staring at the wall next to the fireplace, which needed re-plastering. Why had no one managed to collect the rent in nearly three hundred years? What attempts had been made? For an amount that substantial?

'Okay,' he said, 'I've got to find this house.'

There was a letterbox at one end of Gallows Lane. Nobody ever really questioned why it was there, or which house it belonged to. In more recent years, Essie had installed a parcel drop box too, because trying to get Amazon to deliver was a nightmare when your house didn't officially exist.

She'd walked home through the woods, which was faster than going by road, and all the way back her head had been pounding.

The minicab. The demonic daisies. The heat of the end of the world.

'You all right?' said Blessing, as Essie put the ice cream in the freezer. 'You don't half look peaky.'

'Headache,' Essie said shortly. 'Weird vision.'

'Ah.' Whilst, like all witches, Blessing also occasionally had premonitions about the future, or was at least unsurprised by certain events, she had no particular affinity with precognition. Blessing made things blossom and grow. The furthest she ever had to think ahead was about nine months. 'You should tell Maude. She might be able to help.'

Essie rolled her eyes, which hurt. Maude would nod, make gnomic pronouncements, then knit something out of twine or wire wool or Essie's own hair and tell her to read the stitches, as if that was the blindest bit of use to anyone.

Maude knitted the future. Blessing nurtured and brought things to fruition. Avery manifested ideas into reality. Lilith… well, she tried not think about Lilith too much. The point was, everyone had a talent they could employ in a useful way.

Except for Essie. Essie had one thing she was good at, one day a year. And the rest of the time, she had nothing to do but try to stop her background magic leaking out and causing more havoc than a supervillain on speed.

And cold. Oh yes. She could always make things cold. She could make things very, dangerously cold.

'Don't let Maude knit my hair,' she said. She frowned. Maude had been a bit… off lately. Quieter than usual. She was still knitting constantly, but if the patterns in the yarn told her anything, she was keeping it to herself. She hadn't even asked Essie to go down the bookies for her in ages.

'Is Maude all right?' she Essie asked.

Blessing's forehead wrinkled just a little. 'Now you

mention it, she didn't touch the *Racing Post* yesterday,' she said.

The two women shared a glance. Maude had been here longer than either of them. Probably the only person who predated Maude was Prudence, and she'd technically been dead for three hundred years.

Witches got old, just like anyone else. They just tended to do it much, much more slowly than anyone else. And Maude looked old, which must mean she was positively ancient.

'I'll ask Avery to make her something,' Blessing said. 'By the way, do you know who this is?'

She held up a small doll. Essie knew exactly what it was: a poppet, a small doll made to protect and defend a person. The house was full of them, some made of straw, some of cloth, some of wax. Some were so ancient Essie had no idea who had made them, let alone who they represented.

Like most of Blessing's poppets, it was made out of little bits of fabric, sewn together into a rough approximation of a human being, then decorated and dressed to represent someone in particular. This one had lots of pale-blonde hair and a rounded stomach under a little red dress and leather jacket. It wore knee-high boots, which must have taken Blessing some time.

'One of your patients?' Essie said.

Blessing shrugged. She examined the little doll with a slight frown. 'No. I don't know why I made it.'

Essie sighed and rubbed her temples. There must be something portentous going on if Blessing was making poppets of people she didn't know. 'Well, I'm sure they'll turn up. I'm going for a nap.'

Essie liked naps. When you had no job for 364 days of the year, naps were a useful way of filling the time.

'Cool. Oh, someone phoned from some window company? They said you'd asked for a quote?'

Essie paused halfway across the kitchen. 'Because of the hole in the conservatory roof?'

Blessing shrugged. 'Apparently.'

Essie waited, just in case Blessing was about to apologise for encouraging her Venus flytraps to grow so large they broke the damn roof, but she simply inspected her nails, which she'd just had redone with floral symbols.

Essie gave up. 'And?'

'And he said he'd be in the area and might pop round this afternoon. I did say to call when he got to the letterbox,' she said, before Essie could remind her. 'Isn't it time we removed the perception spell?'

Essie moved back towards the door. 'Firstly, would anyone here know how?' she said. 'And, secondly, no.'

'Who died and made you the boss?' Blessing called as Essie made for the stairs.

'That's a complicated question and you know it,' Essie yelled back.

She got halfway up the stairs, paused to count the phases of the moon on her fingers and jumped the second-to-last step, opened the door into her bedroom, waited two seconds then opened the *other* door into her bedroom, and collapsed on her bed.

Her bedroom was always very cold. Essie pressed her

hand to her aching head, her fingers icy, and moaned softly. Maybe she was coming down with something? Except she never came down with anything. If she felt in the slightest bit peaky, a cup of Avery's famous soup usually did the trick. It was probably just the sunshine. Summer's last hurrah before the blessed cool dark days of winter arrived to give her some relief.

Sleep would help. She could dream out the premonition, write it down, and then even if it was no help at least the headache would go away.

Her eyes had just closed when she remembered that a witch could rarely see anything involving her own destiny.

Chapter Two

Essie's dreams rarely made sense to her at the time. Thirty years ago, she'd woken up screaming that the house was on fire and the subjects would save the objects. A couple of months later, fire broke out at Windsor Palace, and ordinary people helped save the priceless artworks it contained.

In her teens it had been all about magic apples. Her mother had told her to forget about Snow White, and concentrate on her herbals, and Essie had insisted that one day everyone would have witchcraft in their pockets. No one understood that one until the iPhone was released.

She'd once woken up obsessed with the number twelve, the colour blue, and large spotted cats that brought a tragedy. It was years before Mrs Finchley at no.12, the High Street, was hit by a speeding blue Jaguar and killed.

Every time, she tried to piece them into a premonition that could actually be useful, and every time she failed. So when she went to sleep that September day, she wasn't expecting to wake up with anything useful apart from maybe the cessation of her headache.

Three hours later she screamed, 'The lawyer, son of Hob!' so loudly the bats nesting in the roof fled in a large shrieking cloud.

Shadows were lengthening when Josh made it to Gallows Lane. He was pretty sure he'd walked this way several times already, but he never seemed to find the turning. He kept stopping to ask people, who pointed vaguely and said things like, 'Oh, you know where the Star Inn used to be? It's just past there.'

Finally, just as he was beginning to think it was all some kind of joke on behalf of the solicitors, he saw a large mailbox, the kind that people had at the end of their driveways in America but he'd never seen over here. A woman was checking it.

The sign next to the mailbox said Gallows Lane.

'Finally,' said Josh out loud. He strolled over and said, 'Excuse me, ma'am, do you know where Beldam House is?'

She straightened, a handful of mail in her hand, and looked him over. 'You're looking for Beldam House?' she said slowly.

'Yes! Do you know it?'

'I do.' The sun was behind her and he couldn't make out her features. She wore dungarees and she had… hair. Basically, all he could tell was that she wore clothes and had hair. And that she was annoyed. That radiated off her in waves. 'Are you on foot?'

'Yes?' Josh didn't think this was weird. Everyone walked around here. It was a village. Nothing was very far away from anywhere and besides, the bus only came once a day. 'I didn't come far. Brook Manor Farm?'

'Oh.' She shrugged. 'Yes, I heard someone new moved in. Getting the windows fixed there too, huh? I heard it was in a shocking state.'

'Yeah. It was a real mess.' Josh began to follow her as she marched off along Gallows Lane at the sort of pace usually kept up by characters in Aaron Sorkin shows. It was thickly lined on both sides with trees, arching over the sunken lane to create a dark green tunnel. 'So you didn't know the previous owner?'

He couldn't exactly tell her age in the sudden gloom. Not particularly old, was about all he could tell, given her voice. Not particularly young, either. If she were to suddenly mug him, he'd have nothing to tell the police.

'Agatha Cropley? A little. You're American,' she said, accusingly.

'Guilty as charged.' Josh considered telling her he was only half American, but he didn't really want to bring up the old man any more than he had to.

'Well, someone has to be. Look, I'm sorry, I'm in a rotten mood, it's been a hell of a day.'

As she spoke, they turned up a path to the left that hadn't seemed to be there a minute ago. The light woodland seemed to thicken into forest, and the quality of light seemed to change.

'I… uh, I'm sorry, what were you saying? Bad day?'

Something flew past his head, fast and silent and suddenly shocking. Josh was afraid he yelped.

'Fucking bats!' shouted the woman beside him. 'It's too early for you! Go back to sleep!'

He watched in amazement as the bat flapped off into the trees. 'That was a bat? I didn't think… you have bats here?'

'There's a colony of them in the roof. I'm afraid I woke them up earlier.'

'Oh. Should you have done that?'

She sighed. 'Probably not. It wasn't on purpose,' she added defensively. 'I was just having a bad…' She trailed off, and suddenly pinned him with a look. And Josh definitely felt pinned. Like a butterfly.

'What did you say your name was?' she demanded.

Her eyes were very large behind her glasses. In the low light, they seemed to glow like emeralds.

'Uh, Josh,' he said. 'Josh Henderson.'

'Henderson.' She appeared to roll that around in her mouth a bit. 'Good. And you're not a…' She looked him over, his jeans and plaid shirt and baseball cap, and said, 'No. Never mind. What was your father's name?'

'Uh,' said Josh, scratching the back of his neck. 'Why?' She couldn't possibly know who he was. He had zero public profile. Even his Facebook picture was a cartoon.

'Was his name Hob? Rob? Anything like that?'

'Uh, no. Definitely not that.'

She visibly relaxed. 'Well, welcome to Beldam House, Josh Henderson.'

She gestured, and as if it had always been there, a large

house appeared in the edge of his vision. It proved to be a very effective distraction from her weird-ass questions.

Josh would never, ever be able to describe Beldam House. It was large, and if he was pressed, he might use a descriptor like 'gothic' or 'scary as hell'. The roofs were high and steep, and there were definitely multiple roofs. Thickets of chimneys. Turrets, too. Gabled windows, black beams, those leaning top storeys that some of the older houses had around here.

It looked like a fairy-tale palace drawn by a drunk depressive.

Crows gathered on the roof and the trees around the house. He heard a dog barking, a big, deep bark, and then something growled at it and all the hackles on Josh's neck stood up.

'Marley!' the woman snapped. 'Cut it out. I'm sorry, the animals are all at each other's throats at the moment. The bats woke up the parrots, and now none of us can get a minute's peace. I tell you,' she said as she led him up the brick path to the front door, 'supper tonight is going to be like eating old boots.'

'Uh-huh,' said Josh, as he followed her up an unnecessarily long flight of steps to the looming front door. It was one of those massive, thick, dark oak numbers, the kind he'd only seen on medieval cathedrals, the wood tough as stone and studded with iron.

Hanging from a large bracket by the door was a metal cauldron on a chain. The rusted metal creaked and moaned faintly as it swung in the breeze.

The woman paused with her hand on the massive latch.

'It's not always like this,' she said. 'Sometimes it's quite nice. You've just caught us…'

'On a bad day. Right. Listen, Ms…?'

She looked him over again, in a way he didn't quite like. Here was a woman of a kind that seemed peculiar to England. They could be incredibly forthright without saying a single word, and bustled around the place Getting Things Done as if the world might end if they didn't. Kind, but not boundlessly so, and with a limited supply of patience. And possessed of a terrifying array of facial expressions that were as subtle as they were intense, and could freeze the balls off a man at thirty paces.

English women were not like American women. Josh didn't know that this made them any less terrifying.

But she *was* a woman very much unlike Maya. That much was completely obvious. And he couldn't go around distrusting every woman with an ounce of confidence, could he?

He could see her more clearly here at any rate. There was a lantern by the door that gave off quite a lot of light. She was of average height, filled out her dungarees well, and had red hair that didn't seem to want to stay in the plaits she'd imposed on it. Glasses. Blue eyes.

Wait, blue?

'Essie,' she said. 'You may call me Essie.'

Josh blinked. 'Essie?'

'Family name,' she said shortly. 'Come on, then.'

She pushed open the massive door as if it was made of cardboard, and Josh screwed his courage to the sticking place and followed her inside.

Into a madhouse.

'Ignore the parrots, they're just riled up, they'll stop if they don't get any attention,' she shouted.

Josh looked around. He could see…

…a magnificently twisted staircase that wound around an open fire, gloomy tapestries shrouded in dust, antlers and horns in the shadows. Teetering towers of furniture, cupboards and books and clocks and glass domes containing things he didn't want to look very closely at. Little doors in the panelling from behind which strange noises came. What appeared to be a live tree growing halfway up the stairs, in which several bats hung, watched by a large tabby cat with a calculating expression and a goat who was eating the foliage…

…but no parrots.

He could hear them though, in the cacophony of noise created by cats and bats and chiming clocks and a goat – a frigging *goat* – that filled the entryway.

'For the love of—' Essie muttered. 'I leave the house for five minutes and – Bob! Leave the bats alone. Go and harass the mice in the scullery.'

She pointed sternly, and the cat gave her a resentful look. Then, to Josh's amazement, it leapt over the edge of the stairs onto a chair, and from there through a half-open door.

'Did you just tell that cat what to—' he began.

'And you! Stop eating the willow, you get perfectly enough food, you're being greedy. Go. Go, or I'll cook you with rice and peas.'

The goat turned its alien eyes on her and bleated.

'Rice and peas,' she warned, hands on hips. Her hair blazed red in the light from the fire.

A woman wandered out of a door he hadn't noticed before, and said, 'Essie, don't shout at her. She's very sensitive.'

The goat glared at them in the mad, calculating way of goats everywhere. Josh took a step back.

Essie snorted. 'It's still no excuse to eat my willow tree.'

'It isn't your willow tree, it's our willow tree,' said the other woman languidly.

'She's eating the leaves.'

'Perhaps she has a headache.' The other woman sauntered up the stairs and put out a hand to stroke the goat, who ceased nibbling to nuzzle against her like a cat or dog. She crooned soothing sounds to it.

Josh could only stare. She had curves everywhere a woman should have curves, and a long fall of braids down her back. Long lashes, red lips, and the sort of swaying hips that a man would follow off a cliff.

A clicking sound in front of him brought his attention back to Essie, as she snapped her fingers at him. She gave him a wry look. 'Do you want your eyeballs back?' She pretended to hold them out to him.

Josh felt his cheeks get hot. He had been staring.

'That's Blessing. Don't worry, she has that effect on everyone.'

Blessing's eyes were large and beautiful. She said, 'Only the handsome ones,' and Josh swallowed.

'Put him down, Bless, or we'll never get anything done.'

Blessing rolled her eyes. 'Fine. Come on, kid. Auntie

Essie is in a bad mood.' She swayed away, followed obediently by the goat. Josh physically couldn't stop himself watching her.

'I'm not in a bad mood, I just live in a mad house,' muttered Essie. Then, to Josh, 'Follow me and don't wander off. The house is unpredictable today.'

'Sorry, what?' said Josh, rushing to keep up as she swept up the stairs. 'The *house* is unpredictable?'

'Yes. It reacts to our moods. I woke up in a right one, and it set everything else off. Usually,' she turned left halfway up the stairs, which hadn't appeared to have a left when Josh was standing at the bottom of them, 'we can go through the drawing room on a Wednesday. But today, it doesn't seem to want us to do that. I think the dogs are fighting in there.' She cocked her head. 'Or maybe shagging. Blessing always gets like this when the house is playing up. Creating peace and lurve by means of making all the animals super horny.'

She banged on a large wooden door. 'Knock it off, you two!' To Josh, she added, 'You don't want a puppy, do you? I tried having the little buggers neutered, but it had no bleeding effect.'

'A puppy? Uh, no, I have…' Josh looked around the hallway he found himself in, 'uh, enough to deal with. That's a hell of a painting.'

It was huge, the top of the frame barely even visible in the gloom. It filled one wall of the stairwell, and depicted a woman in period costume, seated and leaning forward as if to confront the viewer. She had red hair cascading over her shoulder and a very direct gaze.

'Oh, yes.' Essie came to stand beside him. 'When would you say that was? Regency, maybe?'

Josh was no judge of this, but there was a hint of Bridgerton about the lady's high-waisted bodice. She wore it with a red sash, and a matching red ribbon around her neck, and some memory from a history class surfaced in his mind.

'No, wait,' he said, and pointed at the background. 'That's a guillotine. That's Revolutionary France. The choker there, that's what women wore to symbolise execution, right?'

Essie peered at it, and sighed. 'If you say so,' she said gloomily. 'She's probably trying to stop Robespierre.'

That was a strange thing to say. Josh frowned at the painted woman, and said, 'You don't know who she is?'

Essie let out a heavy sigh. 'Oh, I know all right. *À bientôt*, Mother.'

Mother? Josh stared for a moment, and then he realised what she meant. Her mother was probably an actress. That explained quite a lot, really. The eccentricity of the household. Maybe the animals were performing animals?

He could still hear parrots squawking. So far, none had made themselves apparent. He turned away from the painting of the Revolutionary woman and followed Essie down the corridor. It was wide and long, apart from the places where two corners seemed to almost meet in the middle of it, and the floors sloped up and sometimes down, and there were steps in apparently random configuration.

'Come on, this way—' She stopped with her hand on a blue door. 'Wait, is it Wednesday?'

'Thursday,' said Josh.

'Is it? The moon is waxing crescent though. But it's not as if we're really starting anything, are we? Come on, it's probably safe.'

With that bemusing pronouncement, she opened the blue door, and a sudden whirlwind blew books and dust and papers into their faces.

'Not safe then!' she yelled and wrestled with the door to pull it closed. Josh grabbed it too, and tugged hard against the wind. It wasn't cold, because the room seemed to be fully enclosed, just… fully enclosed around a whirlwind.

The door suddenly slammed shut, knocking them both back on the floor. From behind it came absolutely no sounds of a miniature tempest.

'What the hell was that?' said Josh, picking a bit of paper out of his hair. '*…newt less efficacious than snake-head…*' it read, in spidery handwriting.

'The library,' Essie said, frowning. 'Are you sure it's not a Wednesday?'

Josh fumbled his phone from his pocket and showed her the time and date.

'Hmm. Well, Avery said they were going to read up a storm…'

She got up, and pulled him to his feet with surprising ease. 'Come on. Almost there.'

'You talk like it's a trek across the Sahara.'

Essie shrugged. 'Sometimes, under a wolf moon.' She stood and squinted at the corridor. It twisted and turned and looked from this vantage point as if it was very short indeed. She began approaching doors. 'There is a shortcut here somewhere…'

'To where?' Josh saw a door with a cool egg timer motif on it, and went to try the handle. Essie's hand gripped his wrist.

'*Don't* open that one, it goes to the eighteenth century.'

'Haha,' he said, but he said it weakly. This was a very strange prank she was playing. 'Uh, where are we going?'

She opened a door, and Josh winced. But it was just a cupboard, with towels and linens. 'The conservatory, of course.' She opened another door. A cosy reading room with an open fire and an armchair. A cat curled by the fire, this one smoky grey. 'Oh, there you are, Tomkin.' She made to close the door, then opened it again and said, 'The whirlwind…?'

Tomkin hissed. Essie nodded gloomily. 'Yeah, I thought so. We really must stop Avery looking at Gammer Fidget's cookbooks. At least, not inside the house.'

She closed the door and tried another.

'Cute,' said Josh.

'What?'

He waved his hand. 'The talking cat bit.' Not to mention the whirlwind. Maybe they were stage magicians or something.

Essie gave him a patient look. 'Cats don't talk.'

'No, obviously, but you had a conversation. It was cute.'

Essie paused with her hand on the handle of a door painted sage green. 'Tomkin,' she said, 'is not cute. Tomkin once banished a banshee by screaming back at her.' She cocked her head. 'I felt a bit bad for her, really. It's not a banshee's fault when someone dies, they're just the warning siren.'

'Right,' said Josh, for want of anything else.

She opened another door, somewhat cautiously, and said, 'Aha! Success.'

The door revealed a twisting spiral staircase, wrought iron and ornate. It did not look as if it could hold Tomkin's weight, let alone theirs.

'Come on,' she said, and started up it.

Essie was – he tried to think of a polite way to put it – a substantially built woman. And the stairs seemed to have no problem holding her weight. They didn't creak or groan.

He put one cautious foot on the bottom step. It held. Nothing swayed.

Josh peered up into the stairwell. It was basically a cupboard into which a staircase had been crammed, and at the top of it, light flooded in.

'Fortune favours the brave,' he said to himself, and followed her up the steps.

What he emerged into was a jungle any botanist would be thrilled with. Surrounding the staircase, and filling his vision in every direction, was a verdant spread of lushness. Every shade of green burst upon the retina, glossy leaves throbbing with health and vitality. Spears of green thrust upwards, topped with voluptuous flowers in shades of deep blush and crimson.

Josh blinked back sweat, even though the room wasn't particularly hot. It was just incredibly horny.

'You should be glad it's not spring. Try one of these,' Essie said, handing him some kind of dry wafer. 'Avery baked them a while ago when they were in a terrible funk, and eating them tends to put the dampeners on anything.'

Josh bit into it. It was like someone had made a cracker out of pure boredom. Still, it seemed to help rebalance his libido.

'Thanks. Is there a, uh, is there some kind of pheromone working here, or…?'

'No, just Blessing. Anything that can multiply, will multiply. The flytraps got totally out of hand and we nearly had a *Little Shop of Horrors* situation. I honestly thought it was going to eat Misty, but she clawed her way out of it. As cats do. Had to feed her smoked salmon for a week to get her over it. Come on. Don't touch anything. Some of these are dangerous.'

Josh followed her along a narrow path, damp gravel crunching under his feet. They seemed to be in a huge rooftop greenhouse, far larger than it seemed the outside of the house could hold. He was sure it must be done with mirrors or something.

At intervals there were lampposts, and hanging pendulum lights, all made beautifully out of stained glass like a Tiffany lamp. They were in the shape of parrots.

Parrots that flapped their glass wings and opened their glass beaks and squawked. 'Lawyer, lawyer! Son of Hob! Son of Hob!'

'That's some clever, uh, robotics,' he said, stumbling slightly as he watched a glass bird preen itself.

'Careful.' Essie grabbed his arm. 'The sundews are particularly proactive.'

Josh looked down and saw the sleeve of his shirt was

covered with something sticky. Nearby, a plant was retracting a long, curling tendril covered with little beads of some liquid that glittered in the light. As he stared, it undulated at him seductively.

There is a plant trying to seduce me.

Maybe he was high. Maybe there had been something burning on that fire downstairs and he'd gotten high from it. That might explain the talking lampshades and the sexy carnivorous plants.

'This place is… dangerous,' he said, somewhat inadequately.

'Yes, don't worry, I'll get you a charm or something so you don't end up seduced by a plant. Pay particular attention to the flytraps,' she said, stopping in front of a display of large, wide-open pods. They looked inviting, as if he could just go and curl up in one for a nap, until he noticed they were lined with spikes and edged with teeth and the sweet scent coming from them seemed to be related to the sticky ooze inside.

'My roommate had a Venus flytrap in college,' he said distantly. 'They dissolve their prey and drink it.'

'Yes,' said Essie briskly. 'Only they do it with flies and this could probably eat a human. Over several days. You'd go for a nap and wake up to find your legs had been dissolved. Now. Blessing cut them back a bit, and it is nearly time for them to go into dormancy, but do you see the problem they caused? Up there. Blows a draught something chronic through my bathroom, I can tell you.'

Josh followed her gaze upwards to the high ceiling,

which was ornately curved and made of glass. It was less a conservatory than a royal botanical garden.

Several of the panes were cracked, with a large hole in two of them, and the metal joining them was twisted out of shape. Cold air blew in, along with the faint scent of woodsmoke.

'Do you see the problem? They're curved. I suppose it's a specialist job?'

'I guess it is,' said Josh.

'Is it something you can do? Or do you know someone who can?'

He frowned. He looked back at Essie, and then at the broken glass, and then at the plants. Then back at Essie.

'You want me to fix the glass?' he said slowly. He was wearing jeans and a plaid shirt. He guessed he could have been mistaken for a contractor, but…

'Yes.'

'Uh.' He scratched his neck again. 'Well, this is awkward.'

She gave him a narrow-eyed look. 'Why is it awkward?'

'Because – look, I know it's a landlord's duty to fix things around the house, but that does depend on the tenancy agreement, and I don't even know where to begin looking for one of those, because it's probably written on parchment, haha…'

He found himself trailing off under the pressure of her gaze. Well, it was more of a glare now. A sort of glare turned into a drill of some kind. He took a step back.

'But, uh, the thing is, there's no actual, uh, record, as it were, of you, um… paying any rent.'

Essie's eyes were like chips of flint-grey stone.

'Rent?' she said.

'For three hundred years. Almost.'

'Rent,' she repeated.

A heavy silence fell in the rooftop conservatory, in which a draught was blowing, or the air conditioning had come on or something, because Josh shivered a little.

'Who are you?' said Essie, and she seemed to be taller somehow, her face harder, and Josh was suddenly reminded that he was surrounded by giant plants that could eat people.

'Uh,' he said, and swallowed. 'I'm Josh Henderson. I just moved into Brook Manor Farm. And I, uh, apparently I'm your landlord.'

Chapter Three

'I need,' Essie announced to the kitchen, 'a very large drink.'

She had escorted Josh Henderson off the property. Once it had become clear he was not there to fix the glass in the conservatory but to collect two hundred and eighty years of back rent, she had dragged him back downstairs as fast as the house would allow her – which was fast, because it tended to expel people they didn't want there – and outside.

'So sorry, such a confusion, didn't realise who you are,' she gabbled. 'Brook Manor Farm, of course, I'd completely forgotten, it's not me who does the rent— ' It was nobody, nobody did the rent. 'I'll get that seen to straight away.'

'Right, it's just,' Josh said, as she propelled him past the umbrella stand full of broomsticks, 'I was really hoping I could talk to someone about it. Because the whole three hundred years thing can't be right, can it? Also I don't know about the inflation, but—'

'No, me neither, it's basically witchcraft, am I right, haha.'

'—but the solicitor estimated it was about ten thousand pounds a month, which—'

Which was eye-watering, but that wasn't what had caught her attention about that sentence fragment.

'Solicitor?' She stopped and gripped his arm hard. Out of the corner of her eye, she saw Avery materialise in the doorway, hands floury and incidentally gripping a heavy rolling pin.

'Yeah. The property solicitor? Keswick and Sons, in town?'

Essie forced herself to relax. She shook her head minutely at Avery, who retreated back into the kitchen.

'Keswick and Sons?' She knew of them. Blessing had delivered two of Mrs Keswick's children, and those of a junior partner, too. None of them were called Hob. They probably weren't the lawyers her dream had warned her about. But she'd check, just in case.

Anyway, it would be out of character for her premonition to give her such on-the-nose information that revealed itself nicely the same day. Usually, it took years for her to piece it all together.

It really was the least useful of her limited powers.

'Look.' Josh dug his heels in right there on the doorstep, and turned to face her.

Dammit, he was really quite handsome. Essie's well-suppressed hormones tapped her on the shoulder and reminded her how long it had been since she'd last been within breathing distance of a handsome man.

And remember what happened that time? she reminded them, and they piped right down again.

'I don't want to cause trouble. I can see there's a lot going on here. It's just, I'm new in town, and I have this house that's falling down and no income to support it—'

'We have these things called jobs here in England,' Essie said brightly. 'They're quite good for supporting income.'

His smile was tight. 'That's a sticky subject right now,' he said. 'All I'm saying is, there's got to be a reason why it seems your household is supposed to be paying me rent and hasn't.'

'Maybe the cheques got lost,' Essie said. 'Terrible thing lately, the post.'

'For three hundred years?' said Josh. 'And…' He cocked his head. 'Is that an admission you know you're supposed to be paying me rent?'

Dammit. 'I couldn't say. Like I said, I'm not the rent person. Now, if you don't mind, I'm waiting in for a glazier—'

'I hope you don't expect me to pay for it,' said Josh, with an I'm-joking-or-am-I expression.

'I do not,' said Essie crisply. She had no personal luck with betting, but hopefully Maude would be in a good enough mood to pick out a winner at Newmarket next week. 'Now, if you wouldn't mind…'

His gaze fell on the umbrella stand. 'Are those broomsticks?'

'Yes, Mr Henderson. We use them for sweeping.'

'Not for… flying around on?' He gave her a thoughtful look. 'Because… you live in this weird gothic house, which contains whirlwinds and jungles and goats and cats that obey everything you say, and like, animatronic parrots…' he trailed off. 'They weren't animatronic, were they?'

Essie sighed. He was still inside the house. 'No. They're Tiffany, actually. Avery charmed them years ago and none of us have ever been able to work out how to undo it. We are able to understand the animals in a conceptual way and they in turn understand the general meaning of our intentions in a non-verbal sense. The house, as I said, reacts to our moods and has moods of its own. If you visited another day you would probably see it as a charming country retreat. But alas, you will not be visiting another day.'

His eyebrows went up. 'Is that a threat?'

'No, just a matter of fact. When you leave this house, you will begin to forget you were here. As you walk away from it, you will find yourself thinking of other things. And by the time you reach the main road, you will have forgotten we ever existed.'

'That,' he said, 'does not sound likely.'

'And yet it is true. Goodbye, Mr Henderson. Go and find some other way to make money.'

She watched him go, and the confusion began to come over his face the moment he stepped over the threshold. He frowned up at the house, then looked around at the surrounding forest, and then shrugged and ambled off.

It was a shame. He filled out those jeans rather nicely, and with his warm brown eyes and open smile he was pretty damn easy on the eye.

But he'd forget he'd ever been here, just like everyone

did. Nobody in the house could even remember who had set the perception spell. It had just always been there, and they'd had to find ways to work around it.

Essie sighed, and fetched a broom, and swept him out of the house.

Five minutes after he'd disappeared from sight, her phone rang, and it was the real glazier at the end of the road. Essie snuck out the back way to meet him, racing through the woods to avoid Josh and arriving somewhat red-faced to find a van with the name of the glazier printed on the side. Inside it was a middle-aged man in overalls.

She'd taken him to the house – passing Josh, who by this time had an amiably dazed look about his face and barely even seemed to notice the van – and got a quote for fixing the conservatory, which she made him write down there and then in his own notebook, because he'd forget as soon as he left.

'Cor, you'll have to tell me what you fertilise them plants with,' he said as he left. 'My greenhouse is full of dying twigs.'

'Placenta, mostly,' said Blessing. 'I can get you some, if you'd like?'

He was already out the door by then, and all she got in return was a bemused look. Essie made a note to chase him on the quote, then marched into the kitchen and opened the fridge.

'I need a very large drink.'

She'd brought back two bottles of wine from the shop earlier. One remained, half full.

'I needed one too,' said Avery.

He seemed a lot calmer than he had earlier. Avery was very sensitive to the house's moods, and the problem with Avery's sensitivity was that he put his own moods into whatever he cooked. Which meant sometimes dinner would be a feast for the senses and sometimes it would be like eating old carpet that the dogs had pissed on.

'Don't worry, I didn't cook until I felt better,' he said. 'There's a lasagne ready and some dough proving for garlic bread. Pub?'

Essie looked him over.

For many years, she hadn't realised that gender fluidity existed outside of her own strange household, and that it didn't usually manifest as someone who literally and physically changed their gender as they felt fit. Avery had been female when Essie left the house this morning, and was now bearded and hairy.

'Pub,' she agreed, 'but first, maybe change out of the dress?'

Avery rolled his eyes. 'The people of this village are so parochial,' he said, but took her up on the suggestion and disappeared upstairs.

Essie poured herself the last of the wine and took a big swig.

The lawyer, son of Hob. Now she'd calmed down a bit, she was pretty sure that referred to Matthew Hopkins. Hopkins, the kin of Hop, the son of Hob. Born in Suffolk four hundred years ago and trained as a lawyer. Declared himself witchfinder general twenty years later.

The man who was responsible for the deaths of

hundreds of people accused of witchcraft in the space of just three years.

And his heaviest activity had taken place in Essex, where more people were executed for witchcraft than in any other county in England. Essie didn't know how many of his victims had really been witches. She suspected not many.

'You can keep your Jack the Rippers,' she muttered into her wine glass. Hopkins might not have been the executioner, but as far as Essie was concerned he was a mass murderer all the same.

'He was handsome,' said Blessing from the doorway, and Essie managed to swallow before she choked.

She made herself smile. 'Avery?' She wiped her mouth. 'He's gone super-masc today.'

'No, not Avery.' Blessing rolled her eyes. 'The guy who wasn't here to fix the greenhouse.'

'Oh,' said Essie, as noncommittally as she could. 'Yeah, I suppose he was.' If you liked classically handsome men with broad shoulders and lovely smiles, then yeah, she could see it…

'For a witch, you're a terrible liar. What was his name? Joshua?'

'Josh. Henderson. Moved into Brook Manor Farm, apparently.'

'Agatha Cropley's place? Oh my days, that house must be mostly mould and mice droppings by now.'

Essie nodded. She hadn't been by since Agatha Cropley died, which was some time ago now. Agatha had been a decent old stick, but something about the empty house kept turning Essie away.

She remembered the green globe hanging in the east-facing window upstairs. The witch ball. Essie had never personally found a sphere of glass to be particularly repellent in any other circumstances, but she'd never examined Agatha's either. Agatha herself had declared it a load of stuff and nonsense, and maybe that was why Essie had been able to enter the house and sit by the hearth.

But Agatha wasn't there anymore.

'Joshua, Joshua. "God is Salvation", I think,' mused Blessing. 'Anglicised version of Jesus.' Blessing's natural talents had led her to qualify as a midwife, as a consequence of which she had developed a nearly encyclopaedic knowledge of baby names and their meanings.

'I'm sure that's very nice for him.'

'Your name means "God is my oath", you know,' said Blessing, with a significant look.

'Bless, half the names in use in England have something to do with God. You might have noticed all the churches hereabouts.'

'I just think you're cute together,' said Blessing. She bent down to pet Tomkin, who purred around her ankles in the hopes of some lasagne.

'Who's cute together?' Avery reappeared, still bearded, now wearing men's clothes and all the jewellery he'd had on before.

Essie thought about the after-work crowd at the Yew Tree Inn, which usually contained various manly men still in their overalls and work boots, and then figured Avery was experienced enough at this to decide for himself if he wanted to wear glittery earrings with his Metallica t-shirt.

'Essie and our new landlord.'

'He's not our landlord,' Essie said, as she collected her handbag and they made to leave the house. 'Should we ask Maude if she wants to come?'

'She was asleep when I looked in on her,' Avery said. 'Tomkin, tell Maude we're at the pub if she wants to come down.'

The cat miaowed and wound his way off up the stairs to do secret cat things.

'Is she all right?' said Essie, as they left the house. The door swung itself shut behind them; they never locked it. Why bother, when no one could even find your house? 'She's been quiet the last couple of days, and she wasn't even interested in Ascot.'

'She's just in one of her moods,' Blessing said. 'You're changing the subject. The new landlord.'

'He isn't our landlord.' Essie chewed her lip. 'Is he? I mean, we've never paid rent to anyone. I sort of assumed we owned the house.'

The other two shrugged. Nobody else in the house ever worried about things like utility bills. Essie, who figured someone had to look after the others, conscientiously paid them every quarter, even though no one asked her to. She'd been the one to get broadband installed in the house, which had necessitated getting a phone line put in because no one else had ever bothered. She was a firm believer in employing contractors to fix things like the conservatory, because while the witches could probably figure out a way to do it if they tried hard enough, it would take a huge amount of effort, days of squabbling, and probably end up with the house being made out of spun sugar or something.

Besides. Aside from one day a year, Essie didn't have anything useful to offer the residents of Beldam House, or anyone else for that matter. She might as well pay the electricity bill and make sure the wi-fi worked.

'I know a way you could pay him rent,' Blessing said, waggling her eyebrows.

'Blessing, for the love of all that's unholy. He's already forgotten I exist.'

'He doesn't have to,' Blessing said.

Yes, thought Essie. *He does.*

They were walking through the woods, which was much faster than taking the road into the village. Like the house, the woods rather changed to suit their purpose, and no one else really went near them. Darkness had fallen, but the witches never feared anything in the dark.

'You could just remind him you exist,' Blessing added. 'Outside the house.'

'No,' said Essie firmly. 'Don't go meddling. I don't need a relationship, especially not with some American who's probably going to run off back home as soon as he can't find soy milk for his lattes.'

'They sell soy milk at the shop,' said Avery mildly.

'Not the point. If you like him so much, Bless, you go after him. Have fun.' Blessing wouldn't hurt Josh. She might accidentally cause him to become the father of octuplets, but he seemed a decent guy, he could probably cope with it.

'Ooh, no,' said Blessing. 'Not my type.'

'Tall handsome men with nice eyes aren't your type?' said Avery.

'He's just not what I'm into right now,' said Blessing airily. 'But for Essie—'

'No.'

'Come on, you haven't been with anyone since whatshisname, the one who forgot you existed and took up with someone else.'

There was a short silence. Frost crunched under Essie's feet for a few steps. Avery shivered.

'Thank you for bringing up that cherished memory,' Essie said crisply.

'I'm just saying, all you've got to do is tell him who you are outside the house and he'll remember—'

'Oh, sure. "Hi, complete stranger who I don't know from Adam. Guess what? I'm a witch and you'll forget everything that happens inside my house. I also bring the winter in and occasionally freeze things by accident, so I hope you didn't need that penis to be un-frostbitten".'

'Has that happened?' Avery asked in horrified fascination.

Essie's fingernails dug into her palm. Her breath clouded in the air. 'Let's just go to the pub and get pissed and forget all about Josh Henderson, right?'

Avery shuddered. 'Whatever you say.'

By the time he got home, Josh couldn't entirely remember why he'd set out. A nice walk around the village, he supposed. It was incredibly pretty, the cottages a mixture of eras and styles all cosied up together. Some had exposed beams, some patterns made of brick and flint, and some had intricate designs carved into the plaster. There was a very pretty pub overlooking Midsummer Common, advertising home-cooked food and real ales. He bet it even had a working fireplace.

He studied Brook Manor Farm house as he crunched up the drive. It was built of red bricks, some of which had begun to crumble, with a plain tiled roof. The doors and windows were slightly arched, and all in all it would have been quite a handsome house, if it hadn't all been hidden behind a massively overgrown creeper of some kind. Mr Humble the groundskeeper had apparently been intending to cut it back. He must have been intending for about a decade, Josh thought glumly as he trudged closer. The damn thing might look picturesque, but it was clawing the bricks out.

He wrenched open the front door, which was stuck because it was made of wood that swelled when it rained, or it was sunny, or hot, or cold, and tramped inside. He'd read somewhere that really posh people in Britain lived like this all the time, in freezing houses with no proper heating, and wore their grandmother's clothes and never spent any money. But Josh couldn't see that working for him. For one thing, all his grandmother's clothes had gone to Goodwill when she died.

He opened the fridge – another new expense – and

looked disconsolately at the contents. There was a village shop, which appeared well stocked, but Josh didn't know most of the brands and there were many words on the packaging that confused the hell out of him. Even an eggplant wasn't an eggplant here.

You don't belong here.

He did. He had to. He'd burned a lot of bridges back home, for one thing. And why would his father have left him this house if he didn't intend Josh to live in it?

All he had in Seattle was a storage unit of cheap furniture, a mother who didn't talk to him and an ex-girlfriend he'd like to keep on the other side of a large ocean. Brook Manor Farm in Good Winter was home now. It had to be.

He sighed, and peered again at the contents of the fridge, as if they might have changed in the last five minutes. Some cheese and half a pint of milk. Not much of a supper.

Home-cooked food and real ales. Josh thought about his bank balance, said, 'Fuck it,' out loud, and left the house.

Chapter Four

The Yew Tree Inn was the sort of village pub Josh had always imagined when he imagined a British pub. There was a hand-painted sign swinging from a beam that extended out across the street, and tubs of flowers surrounding the patio area out front. On top of the roof, the straw had been worked into the shape of a game bird standing there, as if about to strut across the thatch. The walls of the pub were thick and ancient, the door low, the windows diamond-paned.

Inside, the ceiling had low beams hung with horse brasses, and there was a wall devoted to large frames holding… Josh craned to see… chestnuts on strings? With rows of text beside them?

The place was pleasantly full, and whilst people looked around as he entered, he gained no particular attention. That was good, he supposed. He'd been slightly worried it was going to be one of those country yokel situations where only locals were welcome.

He stood eyeing the bar and wondered if one had to form a queue. The English loved queuing.

'What can I get you?'

The woman behind the bar looked very sensible. Josh, who had been raised in Seattle and bartended through law school, looked over the beers on offer and tried to translate them into what he wanted. There were familiar brand names, and then there was an exciting-looking array of cask ales with names like Mad Bishop and Squealing Piglet.

He decided to stall. 'Hi! I'd, uh, like to get a table? For dinner?'

'Sure, help yourself. I'll bring some menus over. And to drink?'

He was just about to go for a Mad Bishop, when the barmaid's attention shifted to someone behind him, who said, 'Hi, Sharon. Ooh, you've got the Essex Blonde back on?'

Josh turned to see a woman hanging up her jacket on the wall hooks, as if she lived there. The other two people with her did the same. Josh wondered if he should, or if this was a privilege reserved for locals.

'Yep. Going fast though, so if you want some, have it today.'

'You could sell coals to Newcastle, Shaz. Two pints, when you're ready.'

Sharon started pulling a pint of beer from a pump labelled with a cartoon of a saucy blonde. Josh smiled. He knew perfectly well blonde was a type of beer, and they were in Essex after all.

'I guess I'll try an Essex Blonde, too,' he said to Sharon,

as the newcomer came to stand beside him at the bar. She glanced at him, and an expression she couldn't quite read came over her face. It looked like slight horror. But almost instantly, it was gone, covered by a slightly doubtful look.

'Are you sure?' she said. 'It's nearly six per cent. Two pints of that and Sharon'll have your keys off you.'

'Actually, I walked.'

'Will wonders never cease. Avery?'

This was said to the large bearded man who'd come in with the woman beside Josh. He sported large sparkly earrings, and a necklace and bracelet to match. He also wore a Metallica t-shirt, biker boots, and jeans covered in chains.

Beside him was an extremely attractive young woman with long braids and the sort of figure it was hard to look away from. Her skin gleamed the same rich dark brown as the chestnuts framed on the wall. She smiled, and said, 'I'm Blessing, and this is Avery. That's Essie.'

'Hi, I'm…' He turned to look at the woman by the bar, and for a second he wondered if he'd inhaled too many alcohol fumes, because the world seemed to blur a little.

Essie was –

– well, she looked like –

– that is, she was definitely –

'You're…?' she said politely.

'I know you,' Josh said, and all three of them froze.

Just for a second, but they froze. And Josh had the strangest sensation that everything around them went quiet, before sound returned, as if his ears had just unblocked.

'Do you?' said Essie, taking a big gulp of her alarmingly

yellow beer. Nobody else seemed to have noticed the odd moment.

'Yes.' Josh frowned, because he was absolutely sure he knew her, only he really couldn't remember where from. He tried to look her over without being obvious. She was of average height and build, with average-coloured hair and eyes –

He blinked. No, that wasn't right. He took a sip of his own beer – which was like a sort of liquid food, but alcoholic – and looked again as she turned away to hand the others their drinks.

Her hair was ginger. She had it fastened into two thick plaits, from which it was desperately fighting to escape, and the exposed nape of her neck was pale and freckled. No jewellery, apart from a thin gold chain around her neck. The blue plastic arm of her glasses was just visible over her ear. She wore a purple-striped t-shirt under faded dungarees, and the sort of boots that could probably withstand having a house dropped on them.

He inhaled, and there was the sharp scent of snow, the tang of pine needles, and a smoke that had nothing to do with the fireplace.

He felt someone's gaze on him, and found Avery looking at him. And when he glanced back at Essie, she seemed entirely average again.

'What,' whispered Essie as they sat down with their drinks, 'the fuck just happened?'

'He remembered you,' said Blessing, looking shocked.

'I tried to project a quick filter on you,' said Avery. 'Make you forgettable.'

'Thanks.' Essie didn't dare look over her shoulder. 'Is he looking?'

Blessing took a swig of her beer, which afforded her the opportunity to glance over at the bar. 'Yes.'

'You must have met him somewhere else,' Avery said. The house made people forget them, but outside its grounds they were just normal people living in the village – albeit nobody could ever remember quite where.

'I'm pretty sure I'd remember,' Essie muttered. Josh Henderson was cute, no doubt about it. And there was a distinct lack of cute men around – or in vague proximity to – her approximate age, in Good Winter.

'Maybe it's fate,' hissed Blessing. 'Destiny.'

'You shut up about destiny,' Essie hissed back. 'This isn't a romance novel.'

'What's wrong with romance novels?' Avery demanded.

'Nothing, they're just not very... realistic.'

'Dear, you are a witch.'

Essie tried to ignore that, even as frost formed on her pint glass. 'I've just had enough premonitions for today.'

'Yes, but none of them about him,' said Blessing, 'and we all know you can't have a premonition about your own destiny, ergo, he must be part of your fate.'

Essie and Avery stared at her.

'That is the most terrible logic I've ever heard,' Avery said.

'Oh look, Avery,' Blessing said loudly, 'isn't that Danny

Willis, whose tattoo you were designing? Let's go talk to him.'

'But,' Avery began, glancing at Josh as he made his way over to the empty table beside them.

'But it's really important,' Blessing said, elbowing him, 'that we go over there.'

She grinned at Josh as she towed Avery past him. She practically *gurned* at him. Avery turned back to Essie, making a few quick motions with his hands. She felt her hair subtly restyle itself, and he'd probably put a lick of mascara on her too. She should be annoyed about that, but Josh's eyes warmed when he realised she was alone.

'Your friends are leaving?' he said, bemused.

Essie sighed. 'I think we're being set up,' she said. She pushed out the chair opposite with her foot. 'Stay for a drink, and if we both can't stand each other, we'll drink up really fast, yeah?'

Josh looked her over, and smiled, and Essie smiled helplessly back. He really was handsome.

'I'm Josh, by the way,' he said.

I know. 'Hi, Josh.' She watched him take a sip of his beer and make a face like he was considering whether he liked it or not.

'I'm from Seattle,' he explained. 'Home of the microbrewery.'

'Ah. Seems like they're everywhere these days.'

'They sure are.'

Wow, I'm such a great date. Was this a date? Yeah, it was. It had been so long, Essie had totally forgotten what you were supposed to do. Or say.

She didn't suppose demanding to know how he was resisting the house's perception spell was a great opener, though.

There was a sticking plaster on his thumb, sticking mostly to itself the way they always did. 'What did you do to yourself?'

'Oh.' He regarded it. 'I cut it on a… you know what, it was a great and terrible wound sustained whilst doing very manly construction work around the house. Which I am renovating myself.'

That wrenched a smile from her. The plaster covered about half an inch of his thumb pad. 'Wow. Very impressive. I'm amazed you're up and about so soon after such a devastating injury.'

'I know. I know. The doctors said they'd never seen someone so brave.'

'I expect you could easily have lost your whole hand. I once knew—' Essie began, then stopped, because this was meant to be light, flirty banter and she'd been just about to launch into the story of the time Jerry Fairlamb from down the common crushed his hand with the cider press.

Josh gave her an expectant look. Essie drank some of her beer. Silence fell between them.

'What's with the poems?' Josh wanted to know. 'In the frames? With the… are they nuts?'

Oh phew. This she could do. 'Conkers. The conker tournament,' Essie said. 'We hold it every autumn. The winning conker gets framed and Bill – Sharon's dad – writes a poem about it.'

'You are kidding me,' Josh said.

'I'm totally serious. People come from all over for the Yew Tree conker tournament.'

'All over, huh?' Josh was studying them with an adorable wrinkle between his brows.

'Once, from as far as Hertfordshire,' Essie said solemnly.

Josh smiled at that, in a manner which suggested he had at least looked at a map once or twice.

'It'll be on in a few weeks,' Essie said casually. 'Open to all-comers. If you're still here then.'

Josh Henderson said, 'I guess I will be, sure.' He took a doubtful sip of his beer. It didn't look like he was enjoying it very much. 'What even is a conker? It sounds rude.'

'It's a nut.' Her mother's voice echoed in her head and Essie winced at her own mistake. 'A seed. From the horse chestnut tree.'

'Like chestnuts that you roast on an open fire?'

'Yes. But don't eat these.'

He smiled at her easily. 'You'll have to show me how to play.'

'Sure,' Essie said. She drank some more beer, then said, 'I'll show you how to swing a nut.'

Josh had his pint halfway to his mouth. 'I'm never sure how to take it,' he said, 'when a woman says she'll teach me to swing my nuts.'

'Just one nut,' Essie clarified.

'Oh, of course.'

'Into someone else's.'

He laughed at that, and as Essie had figured, he looked great laughing. Brackets around his mouth, as if he laughed often, and great American dentistry.

I could like this man. I could like this man a lot. But not too much. There was a reason Essie didn't go on dates, and it wasn't that witching and relationships didn't go well together.

'So, how come you've bought Brook Manor Farm?' she asked, and his laughter faded to puzzlement. *Bugger, he won't remember telling me that.* 'Mrs Sockburn told me. I'm assuming you're the handsome American she was talking about?'

'Mrs Sockburn said I was handsome?' He pretended to swoon. 'And they told me I'd find dating harder in England.'

'I'd be wary if I were you. They said her first husband died of exhaustion.'

He laughed again at that. 'Well, she sure as hell doesn't put her energy into cleaning. I've been here a week now and all I've done is sweep and mop and wipe. Do you know how to get rid of mice?'

'Get a cat.'

'Something less lethal?'

'Get a lazy cat.'

Josh shrugged. 'Also there appears to be no kind of heating. Like, there's an electric shower that heats as it goes, but no hot water coming out of the sink or the tub. And there are radiators, but I can't figure out how to switch them on.'

'I seem to remember a Rayburn,' Essie said, cocking her head and trying to picture Mrs Cropley's kitchen.

'A...?'

'A big kind of stove in the kitchen?' She tried to gesture

with her hands. 'You keep it on all the time and it heats water and powers radiators. We have one.'

Josh looked hopeful. 'Do you know how to fix them?'

Essie laughed. 'Good god, no. But I'll find you the number of the person who does.' She got out her phone.

Josh gave her a grateful look. 'It will be so nice to wash dishes in warm water.'

'Yeah, all right, Tiny Tim.' Essie found him the phone number, hesitated, then said, as casually as she could, 'Give me your number so I can text it to you.'

Josh smiled slowly, as if he knew exactly what she was doing, and recited it to her. When her text arrived, he sent one in reply.

'Do you know any chimney sweeps?'

'Why, Mr Henderson,' Essie said, 'I might think you only wanted me for my local knowledge.'

Too late, she remembered he hadn't actually got around to telling her his surname, but at least it was right there on her phone now.

'That's not true. I also want you for your jokes about nuts.'

She laughed at that, and she carried on laughing all evening. Even after Blessing and Avery had left – both of them nudging and winking like they were in a Carry On movie – and she had coaxed Josh into eating beer-battered fish and chips with mushy peas, and he had coaxed her into sharing a bottle of wine.

This is nice. Dating is nice. Essie watched Josh refill her glass and speculated on how long she could spin this out before something went wrong. Like him forgetting she existed, or falling foul of one of Avery's transformations and needing years of therapy to be convinced he wasn't actually a frog, or the dreaded frostbite incident—

Stop it, Essie. Maybe nothing will go wrong. She'd just have to stop him trying to come home with her and plant some firm excuses for where she was going to be on the cross-quarter day. And then everything would be fine.

Essie pushed aside the headache-inducing premonition, the hole in the conservatory roof, the parrots who were still shouting 'Lawyer! Sonofob!' and the disturbing truth that Josh had remembered her when he should have forgotten, and smiled at his anecdote about the Seattle Seahawks.

Yes. Totally fine.

The cool evening air hit Josh as he followed Essie out of the pub, and made him realise that last glass of wine with dessert might have been a bad idea.

But there was Essie, in a light jacket, showing no signs of the cold. Josh told himself it probably wasn't much colder than Seattle, and pretended he was fine.

Should he offer to walk her home? What about when they got there? A kiss goodnight or an invitation in?

'Come on, Seahawk, I'll walk you home,' she said, and linked her arm with his. That was nice. Really nice. Essie had the sort of rounded figure it felt good to touch, even if it was only with his arm and through layers of clothing.

She felt solid like this. Josh had spent all evening looking at her and talking to her, and yet he still had an unnerving sense that he didn't really know what she looked like or even if she was actually real.

'Wait, shouldn't I be walking you home?' he said, as they set off down the middle of the road. It was quiet in the village, and he'd observed earlier that in a village as old as Good Winter, sidewalks appeared to be entirely optional.

Essie arched an eyebrow at him. 'Uh, do I want you to know where I live?' she said.

'Good point. But will you be all right going home by yourself? My house is kind of out of the way and there aren't even streetlights in most of the village.'

'Trust me,' said Essie, as a cold wind blew over them. 'There is nothing in this village that is more dangerous than me.'

He laughed nervously. 'What, are you like a ninja or something?'

'Not exactly,' said Essie, and something in the confident way she strode ahead made him drop the subject.

'I'll take your word for it. You said you've always lived here?'

She nodded. 'My family's been here centuries.'

'That must be nice,' Josh said wistfully. 'I'm not even from the same state as my mom.'

'And now you've moved continents. How come? I mean, why Good Winter?'

'Well,' said Josh, and tried to decide how much to tell her. He'd avoided the subject over dinner, but now the cool night air, wine and the warmth of Essie beside him had his tongue flapping loose. 'I inherited this house. And I didn't know what to do about it, figured I'd sell it, maybe, but then…'

Then the whole nightmare with Maya, and his job, and Siena had reminded him he had applied for dual citizenship and could live in the UK, and…

'You don't have to tell me,' said Essie.

He'd been silent for too long. Josh cleared his throat. 'Uh, I'd just quit my job, and my relationship ended… badly,' to say the absolute least, 'and I needed to get away. And I figured I'd at least come see the house.'

'And then you fell in love,' she said lightly, 'with Good Winter?'

Relieved, he nodded. 'It's so pretty here,' he said, looking around at the lights twinkling behind lead-paned windows.

'Yeah, it's not bad.' Essie sighed. 'Everyone thinks Essex is all Towie, you know, fake tans and white stilettos, but three-quarters of the county is rural. Constable painted here. Well, not here, you know, but Dedham Vale's only about half an hour away.'

'Constable?' Wow, that wine had really gone to his head. He'd understood about a quarter of what she'd just said.

'He painted the *Hay Wain*.'

'I'm sure he did.'

Essie gave him a sideways glance. 'Not an art lover, huh?'

Josh tried to come up with an excuse to cover his lack of knowledge, and eventually said, 'The only piece of art on the wall in the apartment I grew up in was a framed poster of *Raiders of the Lost Ark.*' And it had been a cracked frame, at that.

'Indiana Jones, though. I approve.'

'You like Indiana Jones?'

'Everybody likes Indiana Jones. You ever find someone who doesn't like him, run. Run fast.'

She began to turn him towards a narrow opening between two high hedges.

'Uh, speaking of running fast,' Josh said, eyeing the dark passageway nervously, 'where are you taking me?' He tried to ignore the little voice in his head, the voice that sounded a lot like Maya's, that said he was a coward. He was merely being sensible.

'Shortcut.' She indicated a signpost informing them this was a public footpath. 'Brook Manor Farm, right? It's much quicker going across the fields.'

'But,' Josh said as she tugged him down the narrow path, 'is it safe? I mean, it isn't lit. What if you trip on something?'

'I have excellent night vision.'

There were no streetlights here. Essie carried no flashlight and hadn't even turned her phone torch on.

'What if *I* trip on something?'

'I'll keep you on your feet.'

The path was just about wide enough for the two of them to walk side by side, with the garden hedges quickly giving way to a more rural setting. Trees loomed high on one side of them, with a ditch on the other side separating them from a ploughed field. The moon shone brightly, not quite full, silvering the fields and casting the copse of trees into dark shadows.

'Are there, uh,' Josh said, trying not to sound scared, 'what kind of wildlife do you have around here?' There weren't bears, he was pretty sure about that. Wolves? Probably not, although he knew there had been that one in *Outlander*. Three hundred years ago. In Scotland. In fiction.

'Oh,' said Essie, with relish. 'Well. Did you ever hear about the Essex lion?'

Coyotes? Pumas? 'The what now?'

'Terrifying beast photographed in a meadow about, oh, maybe ten years ago now. Huge maned creature.'

'A lion?' Common sense caught up with him. 'Escaped from a zoo?'

'Nah, from someone's house.' She walked in silence for a few paces more, then said, 'It turned out to be a Maine Coon cat and a zoom lens. Honestly, the most dangerous land mammal we have around here is probably… ooh, a cow.'

'A cow?'

'Yeah. Bulls in mating season. Don't worry, this is arable country. Worst that can happen to you is tripping on a bit of flint and turning your ankle, and we've already established I'll keep you upright.'

'Uh-huh,' said Josh, as they reached the end of the ditch and she turned towards another dark section of footpath under some trees. He found himself coming to a stop.

He didn't know Essie at all. He didn't know where they were, or how to get back to his house. Or the pub. Or anywhere with people.

He willed away the panic growing in the pit of his stomach.

Essie stopped too, and turned to face him. The moonlight glinted off her glasses. 'It's really only a hundred yards or so from here,' she said.

A hundred yards of pitch-dark footpath under low-hanging trees. The wind made a moaning sound, and he found himself clutching her arm even harder.

'That's what they always say in horror movies,' he said, hating the way his voice broke a little.

'You just have to trust me for a few more minutes.'

'I mean, I hardly know you,' said Josh. And he was kind of drunk. She could take advantage of him. Follow him home and break in and—

'And if our roles were reversed, you'd have to be pretty dumb to follow me down this path in the middle of nowhere, in the middle of the night,' he added, trying to make his voice sound light and failing.

She appeared to consider this.

'True, but that's mostly because you've only lived here a week and you probably would get us lost. Why don't you switch on the light on your phone? That way, it'll be in your hand in case I decide to drink your blood and then you can call the police.'

A light. Yes. He could make his own light. He had a phone, he could call for help if he needed it.

The light illuminated Essie's pale, freckled face. She was smiling in a slightly concerned way.

'You see?' she said.

Josh made himself take a breath and calm down. She

was Essie. She wasn't Maya. Essie was nice, and normal, and not about to do anything mad and dangerous.

Josh cleared his throat. 'The police around here deal with a lot of vampire attacks, do they?'

With the flashlight on his phone switched on, he could see the path ahead ended in less than the promised hundred yards, and opened up onto an unpaved road. He began walking, and Essie squeezed his arm as she came with him.

'Oh, sure. Remember those bats? They're really a vampire in discorporated form.'

'Oh yeah? What were they doing out in the daylight then?'

'They were just riled up by...'

Her footsteps faltered. Josh tugged her upright, laughing. 'Excellent night vision, huh? Now who's going to turn their ankle?'

But Essie was staring up at him, her face pale in the darkness.

'You remember the bats?' she said.

He shrugged. 'Not until you mentioned it.'

'Do you...' She paused, and looked away, chewing her lip. And Josh realised that the thing Essie had, which he hadn't even noticed until now, was a sort of iron-clad confidence. She knew who she was and where she was, and the reason she wasn't frightened of the dark was that she confidently expected it to hold nothing to be frightened of.

Except that now, that certainty seemed to have drained away.

'Do you remember where you saw them?' she asked cautiously.

Josh frowned, but he didn't really. 'Somewhere around the village,' he said. 'I went for a walk earlier.'

'Alone?' she said doubtfully.

'Well, sure. I don't really know anyone else.'

'Right,' she said. 'Sure.' She shivered. 'Come on, we're nearly there.'

She started walking again, and Josh frowned a little at the darkness but followed along with her, and in less than a minute they were on a track that looked familiar.

'There,' she said, pointing to his right, and there was the entrance to Brook Manor Farm. The five-bar gate stood open; the rotting wood being gently reclaimed by the ivy that swarmed over the low wall beside it. The unpaved road turned into what should have been a gravel track but wasn't, and beyond it, he could see the edge of the house. His house.

He looked back down at Essie. Her eyes were hidden by the reflection in her glasses of his own face.

'Go on,' she said, and he rolled his eyes.

'I shouldn't have doubted you,' he said obediently.

'You should not have doubted me.'

'You know this place like the back of your hand,' he said, and picked up the hand she had tucked into his arm.

'I do.'

'The back of your hand, which looks as if it's been attacked by one of those dangerous animals you keep saying don't exist in England.'

Essie tilted her head. 'I said wild animals. I said nothing about bad-tempered cats who don't want their flea treatment.'

He smiled. 'So what you're saying is that you know this place like something regularly savaged by angry beasts?'

Essie smiled back. She was standing very close now. Josh breathed in, and smelled woodsmoke and cold, icy days. 'Yes. But at least there are no vampires.'

'Are you sure?' His heart was beating fast.

'Absolutely positive.'

'Well, that's a relief,' he murmured, and then her other hand was touching his cheek and her face was tilting up towards his, and her lips parted.

Just for a second, her confidence seemed to dim a little.

Her face held a question, an invitation, and Josh RSVP'd eagerly. It seemed like such a long time since he'd kissed anybody, and here he was kissing Essie, or maybe she was kissing him. He really wasn't quite sure who'd started it, but it was a wonderful kiss, warm and soft, full of anticipation and excitement.

His arm slid around her to pull her closer as he kissed her back, this strange woman who walked alone in the darkness and kept goats in the hallway and had conversations with dogs –

'Josh?'

– as if she understood every word, which she might actually do because there was something very unusual about Essie, if only he could put his finger on it –

'Josh, is that you? Oh my god, I'm so glad to see you! It's freezing out here and I'm still dressed for Provence.'

His head turned slowly, as if in a nightmare. Away from the warmth of Essie's mouth and the softness of her body, back out into the cold dark night, where a figure was approaching from the house. The light it held obscured its details, but the voice was too familiar to mistake.

'You expecting visitors?' said Essie, and Josh couldn't manage to speak. He still had his arms around her as Siena approached.

Because it was Siena; nobody else had that sweet, high voice and hair that shone pale and silvery in the moonlight, and nobody else would have turned up at his door in the certainty of a warm welcome.

She and Essie would get along well, he thought distantly, as coldness rushed in where Essie had been holding him.

'Josh!' The light was lowered, and Siena threw her arms around him. 'Oh boy, am I glad to see you!'

And as Josh looked around to try to figure out a way to explain this to Essie, he realised three things. That his sister had been lying to him about her whereabouts, that she was quite heavily pregnant, and that Essie had vanished.

Chapter Five

'I should have bloody known it!'

Essie's voice rang through the deep and dark woods. She was stomping uphill now, the landscape changing to reflect her mood, which was filthy and violent.

'Handsome man moves into the village and of course he's got a secret pregnant girlfriend! Of course he has! Essie bloody Winterscale can never have anything nice or normal, can she? Because Essie bloody Winterscale is not normal!'

She kicked a puffball mushroom, and a cloud of spores erupted into the frosty air.

'My relationship ended badly,' she mimicked. 'Because she was pregnant, and you moved countries to avoid her! You moved *continents*!'

No wonder Brook Manor Farm had been repelling her. She could feel it, like a sort of force radiating outwards. Except it hadn't been the house, had it, it had been her own instincts telling her to get out.

She should have frozen him on the spot. She should

have gone to bed with him, and had her wicked way, and frozen his penis, see how he liked that!

'One day I'm just going to quit on all this,' she muttered mutinously. 'I'll get a job in a… in a… I'll get a job,' she rallied, 'and leave here, and the winters can be just as shitty as everywhere else. No snow! You can be just like the rest of Essex,' she turned and shouted in the direction of the village, 'and never have any snow bloody ever!'

'That's probably a bad idea, dear,' came a voice from up ahead.

Essie paused, and looked around. The damn forest had sent her in the wrong direction. That was how bad her mood was.

She'd arrived at the gallows tree.

She rubbed her face, and trudged along the path until she reached the clearing. Frost crunched under her boots.

'Hello, Prudence.'

'Hello, dear. Why don't you want Good Winter to be cold? It be always cold here in the winter.'

There never seemed to be any particular rhyme or reason to Prudence's appearances. Usually she wafted around Beldam House, making bitter comments about how things were much harder in her day and these young witches had better be grateful nobody was going to try to hang them. And sometimes, if you walked the wrong way or the moon was in an awkward phase or she just damn well felt like it, she appeared in the last place she'd been alive.

Hanging from the gallows tree.

Essie supposed she ought to be grateful Prudence didn't

appear as she probably had at the moment of death, with her blood vessels popped and her tongue swollen out of her mouth. Hanging was a nasty way to go, especially when you were just left to swing and choke.

'It's not that I don't want it to be cold,' Essie said. 'It's just that I had a premonition it wouldn't be.'

'Oh dear. Well, it always must be, you know. You do perform the ritual, don't you? To bring the winter in?'

Essie sat down on a tree stump and wrapped her jacket around herself. 'Of course we do. Every winter. We bring in the winter. *I* bring in the winter. There's always a white Christmas. It's always cold in Good Winter,' she recited bitterly. 'But why though, Prudence? Are we the bloody tourist board?'

They'd always done it. All the witches who happened to be present in Beldam House gathered at the cross-quarter day, the precise point where the northern hemisphere tipped from autumn to winter, light to dark, warm to cold, and performed the same ritual they'd done for hundreds of years to welcome in the winter.

There was no denying it worked. Meteorologists had studied the effect for decades, unable to come up with an explanation for the microclimate that surrounded the aptly named village of Good Winter, especially since the summer months seemed entirely normal. Even the advent of global warming hadn't dented the village's perfect reputation for white Christmases.

'The tourist what?' said Prudence, twisting gently in the breeze. 'I, personally, never liked the snow. Cold and mushy. O'course, you've got it easy these days. You don't have no boots made out of cheap pig leather and held together with no bits of string, do you?'

Essie looked down at her Doc Martens. 'No, Prudence,' she said obediently.

'And the mud! You don't have that neither.'

'Course we do. Look,' said Essie, pointing at the ground, and Prudence scoffed.

'That be not mud, that be dirt. You don't have mud so thick you sink right down into it the first step you leave the house, do you? Got all that fancy paving now. Tar-mac-adam,' she pronounced carefully.

Essie closed her eyes. 'Not that you ever worried about mud,' she murmured.

'Not that I ever worried about mud. Speciality of mine, it was, keeping out of the mire.'

'Broomsticks, too,' said Essie.

'I even had a broomstick, not that I dared use it much. Always some bugger out a-watching the sky when you didn't want him to. Not going to get caught that easy, was I?'

'Nope,' said Essie. She yawned.

Prudence sighed. It was a big, gusty sigh, containing all the woes of the world, which was all the more impressive given that she didn't have lungs or, indeed, a body anymore.

'And that's what did for me,' she recounted. 'Merely walking—'

'—across a muddy farmyard,' Essie murmured along with her, 'without getting my skirts dirty.'

'Hah! Next you'll walk on water, they said, and bugger

me but then Goodie Shilling heard it and said, only the Lord can walk on water, and I said…'

Essie had heard the story more times than she could remember. Goodwife Shilling had accused Prudence of mocking Our Lord and Saviour and that this must mean she'd made a pact with the Devil, and once the accusation had been made it didn't take long for everyone else to join in. A poor harvest, a greedy landlord, a bout of consumption picking off the weak – the village was angry and afraid, and looking for someone to blame. Why shouldn't it be Prudence?

Prudence, who delivered babies, and had a much better success rate than other midwives – well, that was probably her pact with the Devil doing that. And then one of the babies died, and that was the Devil too, extracting his price. The barley, which was being grown in the same field they'd used for several years now with no rotation, had struggled and withered, and that was probably Prudence's doing. They said she'd made Goodwife Hempe's husband ill because he'd spurned her licentious advances, and the fact he'd always had weak lungs made no never mind to the village.

No one could remember where Prudence lived, nor how long she'd been there. Prudence had no husband to curb her licentious ways, nor any children to care for in a virtuous manner. This clearly showed that Prudence was not a good, God-fearing woman.

And so Prudence, who might be somewhat forthright but only ever helped people, had been dragged to the ducking pond and held under the water until her witchcraft saved her, threw her clear of the choking weeds and onto the muddy shore. Whereupon the villagers had screamed that this proved she was a witch, locked her in the pig stye – there being no jail in Good Winter – and held a court in the Yew Tree Inn's assembly room to prove her guilt.

Prudence had been hanged two days later from a branch of the sturdy sycamore that still stood in a clearing near Gallows Lane. She hadn't been allowed to speak at her own trial. Women didn't.

Bloody making up for it now, Essie thought, as Prudence embellished the story with some exciting declamations from the courtroom, and chastised herself for being unkind. She'd probably be bitter too, if she'd been denounced as a witch and hanged by the people she'd considered her friends and neighbours.

No issue with that now, of course. They had no neighbours, and most of the village forgot they existed unless they were actually right there.

Except for Josh Henderson.

Josh Henderson, who had a pregnant girlfriend.

She shouldn't even be mad at him. She was just mad at herself, for believing – even for a single second – that she could do anything, be anything, other than a witch. On the edges of society, never joining in. Hiding who she was and what she was, because witches might not be hanged these days but you didn't exactly hear about them being stalwarts of society either.

Hadn't she left once already? Gone to university like a normal person, and got a boyfriend like a normal person, and now she was back here, not like a normal person, because normal just didn't seem to be allowed when you were a witch, even a halfway useless one.

Even if handsome American Josh didn't have a pregnant girlfriend, and even if he should happen to be interested in her, whatever made her think it was ever going to work?

Ugh. Maybe there was something to drink in Avery's stillroom.

Essie got up from her tree stump. 'Well, I'll see you around, Prudence.'

'Wait!' called the ghost as Essie started back towards the house. The frost had cleared now she'd had a little time to think. 'I hadn't even got to the bit where my gut burst open and sprayed all the maggots! Essie!'

Back at Beldam House, all was quiet. Avery and Blessing appeared to have retired, and Prudence was twisting gently from a tree. Maude was presumably in, somewhere, knitting the future and staring off at whatever era she'd currently tuned her vision in to.

Essie glared at the hall fireplace until it burst into flame, nodded, and made her way up the stairs. Marley was sprawled across the half landing, a big messy mop of a dog, and as Essie approached he lifted his head and wagged his tail hopefully.

Dog thoughts were simple, and usually revolved around food. Or, if it was springtime and an appropriate partner was in the vicinity, sex.

Essie shook her head as she passed him. 'Thank god it's autumn, eh, buddy. Is Maude upstairs?'

Marley's expression turned worried, and so did his thoughts. Maude, source of head pats and dog biscuits, was currently dispensing neither, and that was concerning.

'Yeah,' said Essie. 'I'll go and see what's wrong.'

The house was calm and quiet, and didn't manoeuvre Essie into any shenanigans as she approached Maude's room and tapped on the door. 'Maude?'

The very faint sound of knitting needles tapping came from within. That was reassuring, at least. Maude knitted constantly. She carried it around with her, needles constantly moving. In the past, she'd made scarves and blankets, but these days it was just abstract forms.

They told the future. Essie had never been entirely sure if they actually created it.

She pushed the door open and went in. 'Maude? Are you all right?'

Maude sat in her wingback chair, staring at the plain wall as if it was a cinema screen showing the best film ever. Her hair had been white for as long as Essie could remember, her face lined, her fingers knotted with arthritis. She had an old Essex accent, the kind you didn't hear much anymore, and always smelled like peppermints. She was wreathed in knitting, so much of it Essie had no idea what she wore under it.

'Yes, dear,' she said vaguely. She gestured with her head to the little table beside her. 'I made those for the baby.'

Essie looked down. There was a baby bonnet and a pair of bootees, in a dark shade of orange. Maude had known about Josh's girlfriend. Essie figured she should probably have asked – but then, why would she? *Hey, you know that handsome guy who was here earlier? Should I go for it or do you think he's hiding, say, a pregnant girlfriend?*

She sighed. 'How's the future looking?'

Maude frowned. She transferred the needles to one hand and felt at the last few inches of knitting. At her feet, Tomkin snoozed on a pile of stockinette.

They were in Maude's sitting room, and beyond it was her bedroom, but Essie had never been in there. A household like theirs only functioned if everyone had their own privacy. This room was lit by a single table lamp, and the walls were crammed with small paintings and faded photos and pressed flowers in frames. The dresser and occasional tables – of which there were many – held more frames, and glass-domed keepsakes of the kind it paid not to look too closely at. As a child, Essie was sure she'd seen human hair and teeth in some of them, and she was convinced she'd seen one move.

The fire crackled in the grate, and Maude's needles flew.

'Hard to say,' she said eventually, which was truer than she knew. Maude spoke a dialect that might have been in use in Essex a century ago, or might have been of her own making. Even Prudence looked at her sideways sometimes.

To Essie, the mass of yarn just looked like knitting. She could make out patterns in it, of course, but they were just that, patterns. It was rare to see an actual shape or recognisable form in it. It would be nice, she thought wistfully, if just once she could look at the knitting, see the shape of a plane or a boat and understand it meant they were going on a trip. But texeomancy was an inexact art, especially to someone who couldn't even read tea leaves.

'There was a bit,' Maude muttered. 'Us did mean to tell you about… hmm.' She tugged on the long rope of knitting, and her frown increased. 'It's stucken.'

'Stuck?' This was alarming.

'Mmm.' Maude ran her tongue over her teeth, which were sparse and brown. She still never took her rheumy gaze from the wall. 'It's heated.'

'The future is… hot?' Oh god, just like in her dream.

'And.' Maude's fingers skimmed over the knitting as if she was reading Braille. 'It's… squashed.'

'Squashed?'

'And gromelling.'

'Grom—' Essie broke off, and rolled her eyes. She knew that word. She'd been laughed at in the playground for using that word. 'You mean it's purring? Maude, is it the bit Tomkin is sitting on?'

Maude tugged on the knitting, and then her mouth split in a wide grin and she cackled. She had a proper witchy cackle, did Maude. She pulled again on the knitting, and Essie leaned down and picked up Tomkin. He dug his claws in, probably altering the future in some crucial way, and Essie untangled him, holding him safely away in her arms.

'It is warm,' Maude conceded.

'Is that because of the cat, or…?'

Maude's fingers flew over it. 'No,' she said.

'No?'

'Shh and let us see.'

Whether Maude could actually see, with her actual eyes, was something Essie had never been entirely sure about. She never bumped into anything or tripped over, but she also never really seemed to look at anything. For her, texture was all that mattered. The balls of yarn in the huge basket beside her were of varying colours, some completely undyed, but all had a texture that mattered to Maude in the moment.

Currently she seemed to be knitting with hot-pink acrylic. Essie had no idea if this was significant.

'You been dreamering?' she asked Essie.

'I always have dreams.'

'You knows the kind I mean.'

Essie sighed, and sat down on the other chair in the room. 'Yes. But I want to see if you can shed any light on it.'

'Hmm. Well, there do be a man.'

Essie ignored the leap in her heart, and asked as neutrally as she could, 'What kind of man?'

'Young, but also old. Older than I, and younger than thee.'

'Thanks, that's very helpful.'

Essie tried to ignore the question in her head about how old Josh was. Mid-thirties, probably. But did that matter with a prediction as gnomic as Maude's?

On her lap, Tomkin settled down to purr and knead at her knees with his claws. Maude grunted, and pulled more knitting towards her. She touched a bit of blue chenille, shook her head and moved on to some thick yellow wool.

'This I knitten double,' she said. 'Fate intertwined, that is.'

Essie ignored her foolish heart. 'Whose? Mine and this man's? Maude, is this one of those "You will meet a tall dark stranger" things because I'm really not interest—'

Maude's gnarled fingers had reached some rough, undyed wool. 'Ah. There's being a door. You got to go through it.'

'A door,' said Essie. Maude's predictions seemed to be about as useful as her own right now.

'And… still it be warmen, Essabett. 'Tis not the cat. Thou shalt not see snow this winter, unless…'

'No snow?' said Essie, sitting up straighter. 'But – there's always snow! We do the ritual. Does something interfere with it?'

Maude kept feeling at the knitting. 'Maybe,' she said.

'Is it the man?'

'Maybe. Or could be… a woman.'

Essie couldn't help the sigh that escaped her.

''Tis the vine now, and all will be well until 'tis the reed,' she said. 'Which may mean no holly.'

There were vines growing all over the house, and holly bushes outside. Reeds grew in the village pond. None of this was very helpful.

'The night, it is icumen in,' said Maude.

'You mean the daily night or the night of the year?' said Essie, leaning forward. The cross-quarter day, what some called Samhain, was when she did the winter ritual, because it was when the world turned from light to dark. It was the sunset of the year. 'Do you mean winter?'

'I can't be sayin'. Just night. It will come. And—'

Suddenly, Maude threw the knitting away from her, and it hit the wall and fell into a jumble like a snake.

'Maude?'

Her milky-blue gaze fell on Essie. Her eyes were wide, frightened and still unseeing. 'It comes, child. It is icumen.'

'What comes? What's wrong?'

Maude pointed a shaking, knotted finger at the knitting, and Essie peered at it –

– and recoiled.

For the first time, she saw a shape in the knitting. And it was a monster.

Chapter Six

Josh had bought a couple of electric heaters when it became apparent the house was an ice box without them, and now he moved them both into the kitchen as Siena sat at the kitchen table and shivered theatrically. He'd also bought a hot water bottle, which he filled and handed to her, then hesitated.

'Uh, should you be using, um, heat?'

'It's better than being cold,' said Siena, huddling into the blankets he'd brought down from his own bed. Where the hell he was going to sleep tonight he had no idea. 'Do you know, in Finland, women give birth in saunas?'

'Why would I know that?' said Josh, sitting down opposite her. He had some chamomile tea, which was about the only hot drink he felt comfortable offering Siena.

'I've been looking these things up. I didn't know if the rules in France were going to be insane, but it turns out they just tell you to avoid cheese that's unpasteurised.'

'It's a pretty good rule in life anyway,' Josh said. 'Why,

and I realise this could be a very loaded question, why were you in France?'

Siena shrugged. She had an incredibly pretty way of shrugging, he'd noticed years ago. It was sort of self-deprecating and giggly, her face turned to the side while her eyes glanced back shyly. 'Who, me?' it seemed to be saying. 'Silly little old girlie me? I'm sure I don't know, but it's a good job I'm adorable!'

'Well,' she said, 'do you remember Carmel? She was dating that tennis player? There was the tournament in Monaco in April and I flew over with her to see it, and then I remembered the yacht in Cap Ferrat, and I guess I hung out there for a while, but then I started to show and, like, I didn't really know what to do about that, so I just… kind of… hid.'

'Hid,' said Josh.

'I guess. In a villa in Provence. It's so pretty there.'

'For five months?'

'Well, four and a half, I guess. I've been practising my French,' she said. 'The locals there were very sweet.'

Josh ran a hand through his hair. He suddenly felt horribly sober, and had a nasty feeling he was about to hurtle straight into a hangover without even going to sleep first.

'Right,' he said. 'And then you decided to come here because…?'

She gave him a sunny smile, or at least attempted to. At best, it was a scattered showers sort of smile.

'Because I missed my big brother?' she said.

'Nope,' he said.

'I wanted to see the house Daddy left you,' she tried.

'Closer,' Josh allowed. Siena had always been fascinated with how Josh lived, the tiny apartment he'd had in Seattle and the marginally larger one he'd grown up in. It was as if she couldn't even remotely understand how a person could live on less than seven figures a month.

He gestured around the shabby, crumbling kitchen. Even the bulb hanging from the ceiling was bare.

'Well, now you've seen it,' he said. 'Why are you really here?'

Siena gave a very teenage flail, which by rights she should have grown out of years ago. It was easy to think of her as the teenage brat she'd been when they first met, but that had been a decade ago. She was an adult brat now.

'I didn't want to be alone,' she admitted quietly.

'Siena, you have hundreds of friends.'

She snorted. 'None of whom have tried for more than a second to hang out with me over the last six months. If it's that easy to hide this,' she gestured to her midsection, currently hidden by the blanket, 'from your closest friends then they're probably not your closest friends, you know?'

Josh nodded. She had a point. Siena had the sort of friends you went shopping with and tagged in Instagram posts. Not the kind of friends you turned to when you were about to have a baby and you were scared.

'What about…' He tried to think of a delicate way to say it. 'You know. The baby's father.'

Siena turned away. 'I don't want to talk about that.'

Great. Josh mentally braced himself for some angry boyfriend turning up at his door.

'Or your mom?' he said.

Siena shrugged again, but this was a much sadder, much more childish shrug. 'She's seeing this new guy,' was all she said, and she didn't need to say any more. Siena's mother had been on the lookout for her second husband long before the first one died.

'So,' said Josh. He looked at the sister he'd only met ten years ago, the sister he hadn't even known existed until he was twenty-five, the sister he'd believed was happily yacht-hopping her way across the world without any cares at all. 'So I'm all you've got?'

Siena looked him over in return. His freezing, shabby house, his ancient plaid shirt, his slightly drunken dishevelment. 'I know,' she said. 'It is, like, garbage.'

However garbage it was, it didn't match the day Essie woke up to.

Hungover, because she'd come home and raided Avery's stillroom, and that was always a terrible idea. Most of what Avery distilled there was for medicinal use, and very little was drinkable.

Essie drank it.

Now the house sounded like a haunted zoo, and it really wasn't helping matters that she had a vague feeling some of this might be her fault. She sat up, discovering that she appeared to have got bored halfway through undressing last night, and dragged the rest of her clothes back on to go see what the fuss was about.

Her mother's portrait at the top of the stairs had changed. Now she wore a full-skirted red dress with a large collar edged in lace. In one hand she held a broad-brimmed hat trimmed with a plumy feather, and behind her the sky was full of smoke. The red hair and the challenging, direct gaze remained.

'I don't even want to know,' muttered Essie. But she did know, all the same. She knew exactly when and where that dress was from.

Two steps down she was assaulted by a flying glass parrot, which screamed, 'Men! Men! Fucking men!' at her. The sound its glass wings made as they flapped was excruciating.

'Fun,' she remarked flatly. Her head felt dreadful. 'Avery, your parrots have got loose!'

'Oh, you think?' Avery snapped, from somewhere in the recesses of the house.

By the turn of the stairs Essie heard the clash of what sounded like swords, and braced herself as she made it down the final steps to see Marley the dog and Bob the cat on their hind legs, fencing.

'What the actual fuck?' Essie said. 'Stop it, you two! How are you even – you don't have opposable thumbs!' Bile rose in her throat. *Would they stop if I was sick on them?* She took a deep breath, and said in the best voice of command she could summon, 'Stop it. Right now.'

The swords clattered to the floor, and both animals dropped to all fours. Marley looked puzzled. Bob flicked his tail and sauntered off as if he'd totally meant all that to happen.

Essie picked up the swords and put them in the umbrella stand. She concentrated, and found Avery in the kitchen.

Surrounded by saucepans of bright-blue liquid.

'Um?' said Essie.

'Don't ask me,' Avery said tartly. 'I was trying to make jam and it turned into this. Gravy, this. Jambalaya, this.'

Essie sniffed at a pan. It smelled sickly sweet and vaguely alcoholic. 'It smells like,' she said, and scrunched up her face, trying to remember. It was not a smell that helped her hangover. 'Just, gimme a minute,' she said, and staggered to the stillroom.

The kitchen at Beldam House was large, maybe even cavernous. It had pantries and larders and little side rooms partitioned with frosted glass, where the witches made herbal remedies and mixed medicines. One of the larger rooms was used by Avery as a still, and Essie guiltily realised there was much less inventory than there had been last night.

However, one important bottle was always within reach, and it was labelled in large, clear letters *Avery's Nasty Hangover Cure*. Essie reached for it with one hand, and a bucket with the other. Nasty was an appropriate label. It worked by removing the offending alcohol from your system, usually forcibly, the way it had gone in.

Anyway, it eventually made her feel better, and once she'd rinsed the taste out of her mouth with the last of the gin, she made her way back out into the kitchen, which was still full of saucepans of blue stuff.

'It's a bloody madhouse this morning,' Avery said. She was femme today, dressed like an angry 1950s housewife with a scowl to match. 'The parrots have gone insane. I'm letting them fly it out, but they're usually done by now.'

'Bob and Marley were fighting like…' Essie said, and trailed off.

'Like cats and dogs do not traditionally fight,' said Avery. 'I know. Blessing escaped early to do her rounds.'

'Blessing has rounds?'

'She does when the house is insane. Maude,' she added with a penetrating look at Essie, 'said all would become clear in the forenoon.'

Essie yawned. The hangover cure was good, but not quite good enough. 'Forenoon?'

'Right about now. I thought I'd let you sleep it off,' Avery added. 'I take it things didn't go quite so well with Captain America last night?'

At that, Essie groaned and sank into a chair. 'Urrgh,' she managed. She dragged a pan towards her and took a slurp of the horrible blue stuff. It tasted like artificial sweetener and regret. 'Ugh.'

'I know. What happened? It's got to have some bearing on,' Avery waved an expressive hand, 'this.'

Essie sighed. There was no point pretending it was all fine. 'Josh Henderson,' she said, 'has a girlfriend.'

Avery's fake-lashed eyes flew open. 'No! He was definitely flirting with you.'

'He was more than flirting,' Essie muttered, but maybe Avery didn't need to know about the kissing. 'It gets worse.'

'How? Was she there? Did she come to the pub? Why didn't I hear about this! Did she storm in, all "How dare you steal my man, you slaaaag?" and slap you?'

Essie blinked slowly at her. 'This is Good Winter, not *Eastenders*,' she said. 'And no, she didn't come to the pub. She was at his house.'

'His – wait a minute. You went back to his place?' Avery said, waggling her eyebrows. She picked up a pan and began to empty it down the sink. The contents fizzed alarmingly.

'I walked him home. It was dark,' said Essie defensively. 'And there she was, waiting on the doorstep – eight months' pregnant.'

The pan clattered in the sink. Avery spun around, lipsticked mouth wide open. 'No!'

'Oh yes. I mean, you'd need Blessing to tell exactly how far along, but – wait a sec. Where's that doll she made?'

Avery picked up a gravy jug of blue stuff. 'Which one?'

Essie got up, marched into the hall, and found it sitting on the mantelpiece along with the poppets of Blessing's current patients. Red dress. Leather jacket. Stylish boots.

'His girlfriend is Blessing's poppet?' Avery said, behind her.

Essie stared down at the little figure in her hand. It even had that mane of blonde hair that had silvered so prettily in the moonlight.

Essie hadn't been lying about having excellent night vision. She'd seen the wide-eyed prettiness of the American girl, her full lips and glossy hair and golden tan. The red dress that clung to the roundness of her belly. She'd even had the boots and leather jacket.

'It's her,' she said, carefully placing the doll back on the mantelpiece and taking care to seat her comfortably. Beside her sat a little doll with a white face and violet hair. Essie made a mental note to bathe it in one of Avery's analgesics later. 'It's exactly her. Avery, why did Blessing make a doll of Josh's girlfriend?'

Avery looked as lost as Essie felt, but it was nothing compared to her expression when a sonorous clang reverberated around the hallway. Dust fell from the ceiling light. The parrots struck up a fresh squawking.

'What the hell was that?'

'Do we have a doorbell?' asked Essie dubiously.

They looked at the door, then each other.

Essie had never even heard anyone knock at the door before. Nobody approached Beldam House without one of the witches guiding them. The place didn't even show up on satellite imaging, and GPS tended to go haywire around it.

'Maude told me,' said Avery, 'that the house will always be found by those who need it.'

'Maybe it's one of Blessing's patients?' Essie said doubtfully.

''Tis men,' said Prudence matter-of-factly, drifting in through the closed door. 'So 'tis unlikely 'tis one of Blessing's patients.' She caught Avery's raised eyebrow. 'But not impossible o'course,' she mumbled.

'Maybe it's some nervous fathers,' said Essie, but she didn't believe it.

'Or a paternity dispute,' said Avery, who watched a lot of daytime TV.

Well, they wouldn't find out just standing there. Essie squared her shoulders and went to the door. 'You'll have to give her a call, my midwifery really isn't up to – ohholyfuck.'

The man who stood with his hand raised to knock was a little under average height but made up for it with gym-toned muscle. He had the slick hair and tight trousers of a man with a sales commission on his mind, and he wore no socks with his loafers.

'Liam?' Essie said faintly.

'Yeah,' he said vaguely. 'Do I…' He looked up at the house, then peered inside. 'Did you book an evaluation, or…?'

Essie turned in horror to Avery, whose mouth was hanging open.

'I know this one,' said Prudence, who had decided to become corporeal. She wandered up and peered at Liam, who shied away from her uncomfortably.

Liam, who she'd met at one of Blessing's christenings, who'd seemed normal and fun and low-pressure… and then she'd brought him home and he'd been so horrified by the madness of Beldam House even when it was behaving itself that he'd run away and never come back.

He used to drink those horrible blue alcopops. Just like the contents of Avery's gravy jug.

Oh buggeration, had she somehow *summoned* him?

'How did you find us?' Essie said.

'Well, you're on my…' Liam looked at his clipboard. 'I coulda sworn you was on my…'

'We didn't book anything,' Essie said, her heart beating faster, and made to close the door on him when a voice behind Liam said, 'Essie?'

'No,' she breathed.

The one standing on the drive wore paint-stained clothing and heavy work boots. He had on a hi-vis jacket and held a hard hat. His hair was receding and he sported stubble that didn't hide his weak chin.

'He's the one with the 'nesia,' announced Prudence, who had never met a modern word she couldn't mangle.

'Bradley,' Essie said, and he frowned at her for a moment.

'Essie Winterscale. I thought that was you. Bloody hell, long time no see!' said Bradley jauntily, as if he hadn't gone on three dates with her and then simply forgotten she existed, a fact she didn't discover until she saw him snogging someone else at the Midsummer fete.

People still talked about the weird hailstorm that had come out of nowhere and blasted the fete so hard the stalls had been knocked over and more than one person had suffered injuries.

Essie peered at Bradley's head, where his receding hairline made the scar from a golf ball-sized hailstone even more obvious.

'What in the name of Julia Child is going on here?' murmured Avery.

'It's like the ghosts of boyfriends past,' moaned Essie,

and then the moan turned into a groan as that triggered a memory. She'd sprawled on the floor in the stillroom last night, cursing all the men she'd been involved with. A parade of bloody rat bastards, the lot of them. Bloody Liam and sodding Bradley and even Sean—

'Oh no,' she whimpered, as a car drew up and a third man got out of it.

Prudence examined him. 'I don't know this one,' she announced.

'And I don't know you,' he replied, puzzled. But then he spotted Essie, and his gaze hardened. 'But I know her.'

'Why are all your exes here?' said Avery.

'I might have accidentally summoned them,' Essie said. 'Avery, what was in that bottle with the pink label and the glittery, you know, sparkles? Tasted like grapefruit.'

Avery said, 'Grapefruit gin?'

'You mean it doesn't have any special powers?'

Avery shrugged. 'It'll give you a hangover, darling, but that's about it. Why is the new one glaring at you?'

Essie grabbed the gravy jug and swigged the blue contents. Ugh. It was just as horrible as she remembered. Sickly and fizzy, and the sugar rush made her head spin.

'Who are all these guys?' Liam said, eyeing Bradley's dirty clothes apprehensively. 'Are you having work done?'

'You!' said Sean, pointing at Essie, and both Bradley and Liam drew back. *So much for chivalry.*

'Hi, Sean, long time no see,' Essie said bravely. She tried not to look at his crotch as he stalked up the porch steps.

'This woman,' Sean said, 'is a fucking *menace*.'

'How've you been?' Essie said weakly.

'How've I been?' Sean cast a scathing look at the other two men, who avoided his gaze. 'How have I been? Well, let's see. Since the last time I saw you I've had fourteen surgeries. I've had skin grafts and blood vessel grafts and nerve stimulation therapy. I'm in *medical textbooks,* Essie.'

'Er,' she said. 'Yay?'

'Not yay. Not fucking yay. Do you know what she did?' Sean thundered at the other two.

'No way,' breathed Avery. To Essie, she said, 'He's *that* guy?'

'What guy?' Prudence wanted to know.

'Oh, you tell your friends about me now?' said Sean.

'Hahaha no, it just sort of slipped out, look, good to see you're doing well, really nice to catch up, super-busy right now or I'd stay and chat—'

'Mate,' said Liam. 'What did she do?'

Sean's eyes burned into Essie. They had been a pleasant light blue. Now they were a resentful, angry blue. Sean had lines on his face a person in his thirties shouldn't have. He radiated bitterness.

'It was a horrible accident,' Essie said. 'Sean, I'm so sorry. You know I didn't do it on purpose.'

'How could you do it by bloody accident?'

'I didn't mean to! It was my first time! I didn't know what I was doing!'

'Essie, when you don't know how to have good sex it means you don't have orgasms, it doesn't mean you turn your boyfriend's penis into a—'

'No!' yelped Essie, too horrified by the words about to come out of his mouth. She flung her hands forwards, as if to push them back in, and Sean's mouth clamped shut as if he was about to be sick.

'Into what?' said Liam, fascinated.

'Is this like those tricks they do in those YouTube clips?' said Bradley.

'No! All of you, shut up! And go away!'

'Essie,' said Avery, sniffing at the gravy jug. 'Be careful what you say, this—'

'You're just a bunch of stupid rat bastards,' Essie shouted, and there was a horrible sound, like three men who started off screaming and ended up squeaking.

'—is a manifesting drink,' finished Avery, as Essie stared, stupefied, at the three rats on her porch.

One of them was sleek and glossy and looked down at its claws in frank distaste. One of them had thinning fur and a scar on its forehead. The third one sat up, peered down at its own genitals, then hissed at Essie and ran away.

'You made them rats!' cried Prudence, delighted.

'No no no no no!' she yelped, and froze for a moment. The air crystallised.

'Gotcha,' said Avery, grabbing the Liam rat by its tail and holding it up. The Bradley rat squeaked in alarm and ran off.

'O'course, in my day t'would have been a ducking for thee,' Prudence added, hands on her hips, watching the mayhem.

Avery looked around for a moment, then planted her hand on the gravy jug. It expanded to a size large enough to shove the rat into, and then the top closed over.

A forlorn squealing came from the spout. 'I'll get that one, you get Mr Frosty.'

'That is not funny,' moaned Essie, racing down the porch steps and beginning to search frantically around the bushes that crowded the front of the house. 'Sean! Sean, I'm really sorry, I didn't mean… Avery, can you change them back?'

'No, you have to,' Avery called. 'I can help, but she who spelt it dealt it.'

Fantastic. Essie was not great at transformation spells. They usually required a lot of effort and concentration just to happen in the first place let alone to actually remain in effect for long. But Avery had been accidentally turning everything into drinks that reminded Essie of her last ex, and then she'd drunk one and…

Witchcraft had never been an exact science. Essie knew that beyond the basic chemical properties of various herbs and distillations, most potions and poultices were just props to focus the mind and deliver the intent. It was the same with incantations. The words uttered never meant much without any feeling behind them.

Therefore, a night of cursing her exes had summoned them to her, and her drunken nostalgia had manifested in Avery's accidental drink, and the drink had combined with Essie's unwise outburst and now…

Now she was chasing a rat with reconstructed genitalia around her front garden.

Except that a house like Beldam House didn't have anything as simple as a front garden. It had overgrown grass that tangled the feet of the unwary, and tall trees that twisted like the bones of a crone, and creepers that literally crept. The garden, like the house, responded to the mood of the inhabitants. And Essie's mood was terrible.

'I didn't mean to do it,' she said, feeling tears threaten. 'I got carried away and the frost just… happened. I'm better at controlling myself now,' she added, gazing around the jungle that surrounded her.

Her shoulders slumped. 'It's no good,' she said. 'I'll have to do a finding spell.'

'Want a hand?' said Avery, holding up the wriggling Bradley rat in one suddenly large hand.

'Now, for a finding, you'll be wanting a wart from a man who died of the plague,' began Prudence.

'Like buggery I will,' said Essie, and Prudence sniffed.

The pans of blue alcopop served well enough as a focal point, as did the hastily modified crate Avery had put the two rats into. Essie fetched a broomstick and a blue crystal, and the three of them held hands over the kitchen table.

Words were just the delivery for the intention…

'I guess,' said Essie, 'find the rat bastard?'

The crystal started to glow.

Chapter Seven

He'd forgotten how exhausting Siena could be.

Josh had lived in Brook Manor Farm a week now, and had managed to get a new bed and some space heaters. Siena had been here for twelve hours and…

'Siena, why is there someone on the phone arranging delivery of a sofa, two chairs, a coffee table, a bed, a chest of drawers and an…' he squinted at his notes, 'armoire? What even is an armoire?'

'A wardrobe,' she called back. 'Aren't they sending the bed linen?'

'Apparently it's a separate delivery.' He stood in the doorway of the living room, where she had made a nest out of the furniture she'd bought that morning. This consisted of a huge bean bag, piles of blankets, a garden table and chairs, and a small mountain of cushions. She had spotted this haul in the store Josh had gone to for towels and kitchenware while she bickered over safety features at the car dealership next door.

The car, a surprisingly sensible family model, sat outside on the drive. Josh had to admit, it would be nice to have proper transport and not have to beg the local taxi firm to pick him up whenever they had the time.

Also in the small retail park Siena had Googled for, there had been a tech store where she had demanded of a hapless employee how to get Wi-Fi in a house where the phone had been disconnected since 1997. There was now a sleek Wi-Fi *thing* sitting on the kitchen counter, and it appeared to be working, as did the large TV his sister had purchased at the same time.

'It's not great for streaming,' she said critically, regarding the behemoth sitting on the slightly musty carpet in the living room, 'but it'll do until you can get full fibre installed here. They can come Wednesday.'

'But you already bought a—' Josh stopped himself. There was never any stopping Siena when she was in shopaholic mode and, right now, she appeared to have added a nesting instinct into the mix.

'Also, I'm talking to the heating and water people because, oh my god, Josh, you cannot live in a house where the only hot water comes from one frankly inadequate shower. It's unsanitary. I can't raise a child here.'

Raise a child. Josh had not, at any point, offered to co-parent with his sister, but she appeared to have decided that this was the house she was going to bring up her baby in and he was going to help her do it.

He should probably be mad about that. Right now he was just mostly confused.

'And there's a room upstairs that is full of broken glass.'

'Right,' Josh sighed. He never had got around to sweeping it up.

'Also, I'm looking up contractors for a new bathroom, because ew—'

'Hey, I scrubbed that bathroom,' said Josh. 'You could eat your breakfast off that tub.'

Siena stared at him from her beanbag. She had a plate of toast resting on her belly and jam smeared on her lip. 'I repeat,' she said. 'Ew.'

Josh rolled his eyes.

'Anyway, a second bathroom is what I meant. There are the three rooms at the back of the house, with the view over the fields? One for a bedroom and one to be split into a bathroom and dressing room, and the third one for the baby. Of course, it won't need it just yet—'

'Because it hasn't been born yet.'

'—because it'll sleep with me. But it's so much better having your own bathroom. Also, we should probably replace the toilet downstairs because that flush thing up on the wall is just insane. It's like being in the…' She cast around for an appropriately backwards era. 'Seventies or something.'

Josh scratched his neck. He'd slept on the sofa with the one blanket Siena hadn't appropriated, or at least he'd attempted to. His dreams had been full of talking glass parrots and giant plants that tried to flirt with him. The room was freezing and the sofa was lumpy, but at least he'd come out of it with a new piece of knowledge: the sofa definitely had fleas.

It was now sitting on the driveway, being gently

drizzled on. Josh had dragged it out there first thing, then walked into the village for some calamine lotion and antihistamines.

He'd been kind of hoping he'd bump into Essie, or maybe one of her friends, but there had been no sign of them. He was a little worried she'd run off last night after they'd kissed. Was it Siena's presence, or was he a lousy kisser and nobody had told him?

'Also, I'm ordering kitchen stuff because, seriously, Josh, you cannot live off of microwave meals.'

'I don't,' Josh protested, but it was a weak one. He was also living off meals you could just add hot water to and meals you could buy from the Chinese takeaway in the village. Although that had proved a confusing experience, because it turned out English Chinese food was very different to American Chinese food and he still wasn't really sure what he'd eaten.

'That huge old stove in the kitchen is really cute and I totally think it should stay, but I am not cooking any food on it and neither should you. So I'm ordering new appliances, and really you should think about getting the whole kitchen remodelled, because it's kinda got that *Downton* thing going on, but seriously I saw something move at the back of one of the cupboards and…'

Josh let her voice wash over him. Siena had immense amounts of money, he had none, and the house really did need fixing up. He'd tried to be proud about the whole thing and keep her from paying for it all, but at the end of the day it was a drop in the vast ocean of her wealth and he was down to his last metaphorical cup of water.

Cups, actually, he should buy some of those. Siena had discovered a liking for English tea.

A movement outside caught his eye. The house was surrounded by handsome, mature trees, and something was flailing in one of them.

Josh peered through the slightly grimy window. Was that an eagle? Did they have eagles here? Or a… stork? Heron? His bird knowledge was hazy.

The bird screamed, and Josh wondered what kind of fowl made a cry that sounded very much like, 'Fuck!'

'Be right back,' he said, and dashed outside.

There was something thrashing in one of the trees. Something way bigger than a bird. Something human-sized.

Josh scanned the sky, as if that would be any help. There were no planes or helicopters around, and no sign of a parachute or paraglider.

'Hi,' he called.

Something fell out of the tree and clattered to the ground. It looked very much like a broomstick.

We use them for sweeping, Mr Henderson.

He remembered her saying that, but he didn't remember when or why. Why did it always feel like there was more going on with Essie than he knew about?

He knew it was Essie. For some reason he couldn't picture anyone else crashing around in a tree outside his house.

Guiltily, he was aware he should probably have sent her a text or something last night, or at least this morning. Siena had interrupted that kiss just as it had been getting really interesting, and Josh's dreams had been interspersed with some very pleasant fantasies about Essie soothing his flea bites with her lips.

'Gotcha! I have *got* you, you bastard!'

There was a squealing sound, and then more rustling. Josh considered taking a seat on the flea-bitten sofa while he waited, but decided against it.

Finally, a pair of boots appeared, followed by denim legs, and then with a slight yelp and a scramble, Essie more or less slid out of the tree. He squinted through the drizzle, which didn't seem keen on going away.

'Fuck,' she muttered, grasping a sack in one hand and rubbing her knee with the other. There were twigs in her hair and the strap of her dungarees had come undone.

'Need a hand?' Josh enquired, and she spun around guiltily.

Her lips parted as if to say something. The last time he'd seen those lips he'd been kissing them.

'Hi,' she said, and tugged self-consciously on the string holding the sack closed. Something inside it wriggled. 'Er, how long have you been standing there?'

Josh cleared his throat and tried not to think about how soft and warm she'd felt in his arms. 'Long enough to see you fall out of my tree,' he said. He nodded at the sack. 'Whatcha got there?'

He watched the possibilities chase each other across her face. Eventually she said uncertainly, 'A rat? A pet rat. It got loose.'

'In… a tree?'

'It ran away.'

'From…?'

Her eyes darted around. 'From… me,' she said. She cast around on the ground, spied her broomstick, and marched over to pick it up.

Or at least she tried to march. Josh realised the knee of her dungarees was torn, and that she was limping.

'Are you okay?'

'Fine. Totally fine. I'm… dandy. I have to go.'

'Essie.' He crunched over the gravel towards her, and she took a step back. She held the broomstick as if it was a barrier between them. 'What's going on?' *Why did you run away last night?*

'Nothing. My rat ran away. That's all. I should get him back.'

He looked down at the wriggling sack. Then back up at her. 'Your rat ran away here?'

Her shoulders slumped. 'Yes. Apparently I'm being haunted by the ghosts of boyfriends past. All congregating together. Next up will probably be Bobby Fincher, who pulled my ponytail and ran away when we were seven.'

Josh had very little idea what she was talking about. 'The rat is your boyfriend?'

She winced. 'It's a metaphor?'

'I see.' He didn't. 'Look, about last night—'

'I don't want to talk about it.'

'Well, I do. You just left. I turned around and you'd vanished. I thought…'

He remembered the feel of her in his arms, the softness of her lips against his, the little sound she'd made when his tongue touched hers. It *had* been a good kiss.

'I thought it was going well,' he finished lamely.

Essie's eyes went wide for a second, and then she spat out a laugh. 'Well?' she said.

'You walked me home, I was terrified, we kissed, and then—'

'Yes, and then?' she said, as if he was incredibly stupid.

'And then my sister turned up, with impeccable timing, and you ran away.' The drizzle was coming harder now. Josh swiped at his wet face.

'Your,' began Essie, and the world turned a few times before she finished, 'sister?'

'Yeah. Well, half-sister actually, it's a long story, and no I did not know she was coming, I thought she was in France or something, but she got on the Eurostar and – anyway, she's here now, like the giant buzzkill she is, and… why are you staring at me like that?'

'That woman,' Essie said, as the rain began to spatter them quite hard, 'in the red dress, is your *sister*?'

'Yes,' said Josh, and realisation hit him. 'Oh my god! Did you think – you thought she was my – ew! God, no!'

'She's not your girlfriend?'

'No! I'm from Seattle, not… Kentucky!'

'And the baby is…?'

'My niece or nephew! Jesus, Essie, why did you leap to that conclusion?'

Essie stared up at him as the rain turned her hair a dark red and the sack gave an angry squeak.

'I guess all my exes have been rat bastards,' she said.

'Great. Well, good to know you gave me a chance,' he snapped.

Essie opened her mouth, then hesitated, and from the

house Siena called, 'Josh? It's really coming down! You should come inside.'

'I'm from Seattle,' he called back. Rain could not hurt him.

'Wait, does the roof leak?' Siena craned her head out of the door, as if she could see it from there.

'God, I hope not,' he sighed, and turned back towards the house. Then he stopped, glanced back at Essie, whose arms were scratched and bruised and whose dungarees were torn, and said, 'You'd better come in.'

Brook Manor Farm was probably in a better state than it had been last time Essie saw it. Back when Mrs Cropley still lived there, she'd mostly occupied the kitchen and her bedroom, and the whole house had been left to gather dust and mould. Now, although the wallpaper was peeling and there was hardly any furniture, at least it looked vaguely clean.

Essie stood in the doorway. The house had been subtly repelling her after Agatha died, but she didn't know why. The witch ball? That was just nonsense. Essie hadn't believed in it, and neither had Agatha.

But she never took it down, either.

Essie took an experimental step forward, and nothing happened except that she stepped inside the kitchen.

'Hi!' Josh's sister was far too perky for someone eight months' pregnant. 'I'm Siena. It's so nice to meet you. I'm glad Josh is making friends.'

Friends. Well, she knew what his tongue tasted like, so that was one way of defining their relationship.

'I'm not at kindergarten,' he grumped.

'What with his sunny personality and all,' Siena carried on. 'You look drenched! Come in and sit by the heater. We don't have proper heating yet, and I wanna light a fire but Josh says there are bees in the chimney.'

'I said there might be,' Josh said. Reluctantly, he added, 'Do you still have chimney sweeps here?'

'I'll get on the phone to Dick van Dyke,' Essie replied. They mostly did their own chimneys at Beldam House, but she assumed the other inhabitants of Good Winter who lived in old houses had some kind of arrangement. Not everybody could enchant a sweep's brush to fly up and down the chimney itself.

'I could have a look for you,' she offered. 'If it's bees you should really leave them. But there could be a bird's nest or anything up there.'

'You know how to clean chimneys?' Josh said. He still seemed very annoyed with her as he banged around the kitchen, putting the kettle on and poking into boxes. The whole place had a very unpacked look about it.

'Uh, kind of. I'd need to bring over a brush or something,' she said vaguely.

'Like that brush?' he said, and she realised she was still holding her broomstick.

'No, this is for… floors,' she said.

'Oh good, you can help with the upstairs bedroom,' he said cryptically.

'What's in the bag?' Siena asked, as she led Essie into the sparse living room and settled into a beanbag nest.

'Um. A pet rat,' Essie said, emphasising the 'pet' and not the 'rat'. 'It escaped. I've got it now. It's not dangerous in any way.'

Siena shrugged. 'My friend Kendall used to go with this guy who kept tarantulas. I do *not* see the appeal. But they were mostly harmless.' She shuddered. 'Mostly. Do you have spiders like that here?'

'No,' Essie said firmly, although when Avery was in one of their moods there had definitely been some hairy incidents. 'Definitely not. There is a massive lack of scary things here that can kill you,' she said, and tried to ignore the little voice in her head that said, 'Like witchfinders.'

'The most dangerous things you have here are cows,' Josh said, coming in and handing her a mug of what looked and smelled very much like tea. He gave her a bit of a smile as he did, and Essie smiled back, because maybe he wasn't really mad at her for making such a stupid assumption last night.

He didn't appear to have shaved this morning. The dark stubble on his jaw looked as though it would feel really good against the palm of her hand.

'Cows? That's random. Listen, Essie, right? Do you know how I register with a doctor around here? Like, do I just walk in and get an appointment, or have to prove my citizenship, or what?'

'Do you have British citizenship?' asked Essie doubtfully, because Siena's accent was pure California.

They both nodded. 'Our father was British,' Josh

explained, as a slight shadow came over Siena's face. 'We have dual citizenship.'

'Handy,' said Essie, who had never visited the local surgery in her life. The witches were adept at treating most ailments, and if push came to shove Blessing had undertaken actual NHS training in order to get her midwifery licence. 'I'm not sure, I think you can just register. I'll check with my sister.' She hesitated. Blessing had made that poppet after all. 'She's a midwife.'

Siena's eyes lit up. 'A midwife? Like in that cute drama series? Oh my gosh, does she wear a little cape and hat?'

'Not since the eighties,' Essie said absently. 'I'll get her to come round if you like.'

'That would be amazing.'

'You also should see a doctor,' Josh said patiently.

Essie opened her mouth to explain the British system, then shut it. Blessing would probably be breezing in of her own accord soon enough, and it was literally her job to do that kind of thing.

'Why don't I have a look at that chimney?' Essie said. 'Do you have access to the roof?'

Josh said he didn't know, so she went upstairs with him to see if there was an attic door. And also to be nosy. Witches, Essie had always noticed, were incurably nosy.

The upstairs hallway was the sort you got when a house had been adapted and extended over the years. There were little corners and doors in slightly asymmetrical places, but after Beldam House Essie could probably navigate an Escher drawing. She noticed that only one bedroom appeared to contain any furniture, and that it also contained several large suitcases and many feminine accessories.

'Siena took my bedroom,' Josh explained. 'I don't – there's only one bed, so I took the sofa—'

'What sofa?' Essie said, because the living room had contained Siena's beanbag and nothing else to sit on.

'The one outside in the rain,' he admitted. 'I should have gotten something at the store today…'

'Quite probably. Why is the sofa outside in the rain? Were you going for a *Friends* opening sequence kind of vibe?'

He smiled at that. 'Not exactly. It was more of a "yikes, my sofa has fleas" kind of vibe.' He showed her his wrist, which was pink with bites.

She took his hand and bent her head to examine them. She probably had an ointment for this at home somewhere, but actually the bites didn't look too bad. If anything, they looked as if they'd been healing a while.

The back of Josh's hand was rough with hairs. There were small calluses on his palm and the plaster on his thumb had gone. Her fingertips moved of their own accord to feel the texture of his skin.

'I did shower immediately,' he assured her, 'and my clothes are in a trash bag, cos I don't have a… is there a launderette around here?'

Essie dropped his hand.

She'd met Sean at the launderette on campus when she was at uni. He was still wriggling around in the sack she'd slung over her shoulder. Dammit, dammit, she had to get home and change him back before he was permanently damaged.

'Uh, I think maybe in town,' she said, and then she noticed something.

There was a door behind Josh, which was closed. An ordinary door, just like all the others. And yet…

'Cos there's a twin tub in the scullery, at least I think that's what it is, but when I opened it the smell was not good,' said Josh.

'No. Probably not,' said Essie, trying to find her place in the conversation. There was something behind that door…

'I guess I'll have to add that to the list of boring things Siena doesn't want to buy,' he said. 'I'm pretty sure once the baby comes she'll appreciate being able to wash and dry… not that I'm entirely sure she knows what laundry is or how to do it… okay, what is it? I swear to God I don't have fleas. I washed my hair twice and everything.'

He gave her a smile to tell her he was joking, but the tension coming from the room behind him kept sucking at Essie's attention.

'What's in there?' she said.

Josh glanced at the door. 'Nothing. Except some broken glass.'

'Broken—'

He shrugged and moved to open the door. 'There was this fishing float or something hanging in the window, and I guess something must have… uh, the string broke or something and it—'

'The witch ball.' She felt it smash in the pit of her stomach.

Of course. That was the window Agatha Cropley had hung the witch ball in. The witch ball she had declared stoutly to be 'stuff and nonsense'. Essie had never really quite been sure if Agatha knew exactly who she and her sisters were.

But now Agatha was dead, and nobody had been here for years, and the witch ball her ancestors had hung here lay shattered on the floor by the window. And the house had kept repelling Essie…

'I meant to clean it up yesterday, but with one thing and another…' Josh said.

There were scraps of paper on the windowsill.

'Careful,' said Josh, as she moved closer. 'That glass is sharp. Remember my life-threatening injury?' he joked, holding up his thumb, and Essie felt her jaw drop as her gaze turned, horrified, to the parchment on the windowsill. 'Speaking of, do you want to wash up? That tree attacked you back there.'

Essie ignored him. 'Did you…' she said, and tried to move closer, but the broken witch ball repelled her. Pushing further into the room was like wading through treacle. 'Did you read what it said?'

Josh shrugged. 'No, I…' He frowned. 'I don't remember.'

There were reddish-brown stains on the parchment. 'Did you pick it up?'

'Yes? It's pretty ancient, I wonder if it's valuable,' he said, moving past her into the room.

'No, don't! Don't. The glass,' Essie said. 'It's dangerous. You already cut yourself once.'

He paused, and gave her a curious look, as if she was acting strangely. Which she was.

Essie didn't know what the parchment said. But she knew thresholds and hearths were important. And she knew witch balls were meant to repel witches. And she knew blood sealed promises.

And she knew whatever was on that piece of old vellum made her feel queasy.

He invited you in. And Siena told you to sit by the heater. You've been invited to cross the threshold and to sit by the hearth. So whatever had been in that witch ball hadn't been a protection against witches, or else Josh spilling his blood on it would surely have had some effect.

Just because he didn't remember reading it, didn't mean he hadn't.

'Maybe,' she said slowly, 'you can take a picture of it. When you've cleaned up the glass. And send it to me.' Surely she could look at a picture of the parchment. 'I know someone who might be interested.'

'Sure,' said Josh, utterly guileless. 'Who?'

Me. 'A relative,' Essie said. 'Now, we were going to look at that chimney?'

Chapter Eight

'Okay,' said Blessing, setting down Josh's drink on the table and lowering her voice. 'The team from the Cock are on thirty-five, and the Helions are on twenty-four. That means we've just got to beat their eight-er and we'll have forty-seven. Unless the last player from Cold Christmas beats the Cock's six-er, in which case we're screwed.'

Josh took a sip of his beer. It tasted the same as it usually did, so he assumed nobody had slipped anything into it. Which meant this whole evening was real and not a drug-induced hallucination.

'Josh, you're our last player,' Blessing said.

'What? I can't be.'

Avery nodded and laid down a piece of string with a few bits of chestnut still clinging to it. Beside it were the remains of two more conkers. The fourth was a slightly battered horse chestnut, gleaming in the pub's low lighting.

It had been threaded on a piece of string that everyone insisted on calling a lace for some reason.

'That was an eleven-er,' he said sadly. 'That Beryl from Cold Christmas is a menace.'

There was much about the game of conkers that Josh didn't understand. He'd been told how to play, and the basics of the scoring – to whit, you hit the other guy's conker until it fell apart, and gained any points he'd accumulated – but the basic question of 'Why?' remained unanswered.

Still, Essie had asked if he'd like to play, and he found himself completely unable to say no. Sharon the barmaid liked to tease him he'd developed a liking for Essex Blondes, and Josh just smiled and laughed along with everyone else.

But if he was honest, he'd prefer an Essex redhead.

Said redhead was nodding at him encouragingly. 'Come on, Josh. If you win this, you can have your name immortalised in a poem on the conker wall.'

Josh glanced at the wall of framed conkers. He'd honestly thought she'd been joking a couple of weeks ago. Even when he ventured to look up the game of conkers online, he'd come to the conclusion it was a playground game, and figured the trophies were some kind of eccentric decoration, like the horse brasses that were hammered to the low beams.

But no. Here he was, preparing to swing his twelve-er at an eight-er from somewhere called Helions Bumpstead.

'Are you totally sure there's nothing in my drink?' he said, but right then Sharon bellowed, 'All right, final round!

Josh from Resting Witch Face vs Phyllis from the Helions! Everybody outside! If you get conker shell on the floor you can damn well pick it up, thank you!'

Essie dragged him from his chair even as he was trying to take another sip of beer, and he grabbed the conker on its string and followed her outside.

'Okay, champ,' she said, facing him as he stood waiting for the somewhat elderly Phyllis to join them. 'You ready?'

'I guess.'

Essie danced from foot to foot and made jabbing motions with her fists. Her hair flew about her face, red tendrils bouncing and curling. 'I said, are you ready?'

Josh smiled. 'Yeah, I'm ready.'

'You psyched up?'

'Yeah, I'm psyched up!'

'Are you gonna smash your nut against that old lady's nut?'

He sputtered out a laugh. 'Yeah, I'm gonna smash my – I can't, Essie, I can't say it.'

'Say it, champ!'

'There are people here! That guy is old enough to be my grandpa.'

As they both glanced over, the elderly chap in the flat cap grinned at them. 'Bloody slaughter her, lad!' he said.

Josh looked back at Essie. 'I understand nothing about this country,' he said.

She grabbed his shoulders in both hands and rubbed them, as if he was actually a boxer and she was preparing him for the final round of a championship fight.

At least, that was what she started out doing. But it

brought her much closer, close enough for him to see the freckles on her nose and the fullness of her lip.

It was so pink. Her lips were so pink. And so plump and soft. And they'd tasted so good. The memory of it filled up his senses, the warm scent of her skin, the softness of her hair against his hands, the little sounds she'd made as they'd consumed each other.

Just one kiss. Just that one kiss, and it had kept him up at night ever since.

She'd been friendly ever since. She'd replied to his jokey texts. She'd invited him to join their conker team tonight. But she hadn't made any reference to that kiss, and it was destroying him. If he was a braver man, the sort of man Maya told him he'd never be, he'd talk to Essie about it. He'd ask her how she felt. If she wanted to go for dinner. Maybe do some more kissing. Maybe more than kissing.

He should do it now. Maybe. Maybe when he won. Maybe she'd want to date a winner.

He looked down into her fascinatingly flecked eyes, and was sure he saw the same desire reflected back at him.

'All right, you two, get a room,' called Blessing, merging from the pub with their drinks, and Essie blinked behind her glasses. Josh's face heated.

'Uh,' said Essie, and stepped back. He was gratified to see her cheeks were turning pink, too. 'Go get 'em, champ.'

If he offers to walk you home, say yes.

Essie watched Sharon sweep the conker shards away as

the Helions congratulated Phyllis and Josh was borne back into the pub on a tide of commiserations.

'We nearly won,' she said to Blessing.

'Nearly isn't winning, Essabett,' said Blessing. She took a sip of her drink. It had a pink umbrella in it. 'You should have let me play.'

'You cheat.'

'I do not cheat! It isn't my fault if my opponents choose conkers that are unripe,' said Blessing, with the injured air of one who wouldn't *dream* of hexing her opponent's conker. 'And anyway, this is at least half your fault.'

'How is it my fault?' Essie protested, peering through the pub windows for a glimpse of Josh. 'Mrs Sockburn dropped out. We needed another player. Josh has good hand–eye coordination.'

'I'll bet he does,' said Blessing, over her pink umbrella.

'Hey, stop that.'

'Me? I have done nothing to the pair of you. All that mooning around is your own doing. You should've seen yourselves, Essie, honest. I thought you were going to start going at it right here in the car park.'

Essie turned away, but she knew Blessing would be able to tell she was blushing. Truth was, it wouldn't have taken an awful lot for her to have dragged Josh behind the bushes and had her wicked way with him. The way his eyes lit up when she said something that made him laugh, the frown of concentration when he was playing a game as silly as conkers, the feel of his shoulders under her hands – dear god, she couldn't remember the last time she'd been half as into someone.

Except that she could. The memory of those three little pink ratty noses made her shudder. And worse, the sheer fury in Sean's voice, the terror of what she'd done to him. She couldn't hurt Josh like that. She couldn't hurt anyone like that.

She couldn't be with anyone normal or have a normal life. She'd tried, and it had backfired spectacularly every time. She was running a risk even being friends with Josh, because what if she forgot herself around him?

'Do you sometimes just wish—' she began.

'What?'

That you were normal. But Blessing loved being a witch. She wouldn't understand.

Essie huffed out a breath and watched it cloud in the cold air.

'Why don't you just tell him you like him?' said Blessing kindly. 'He likes you too. When he came round the other day he was totally looking for you.'

'He came round? Again?' Essie shook her head. 'But – wait, looking for me? He's not supposed to know…'

Blessing shrugged. 'I don't mean he was literally looking for you, love. It was more a sort of… you know.' She waved her hand expressively. 'Yearning.'

'Yearning?' Essie rolled her eyes. 'Well, he can yearn off.' Before Blessing could object, she held up her hand. 'Nothing good can come of this, can it? He can't know where we live. The house is insane, we're all insane, and we owe him squillions in back rent.'

Blessing gave her a knowing look. 'And if none of that

was true, would you still want to…?' She made a crude gesture. 'Or would you find another excuse?'

'Those aren't excuses.' But they were, and she knew it. 'I have my reasons, Blessing.'

Blessing shrugged, but it turned into a shiver. She pulled her jacket about herself. 'All right, the temperature's plummeting, I can see you're in a bad mood. Come and have another drink.'

Essie glanced back through the window, where Josh was being handed a yard of ale he clearly didn't know what to do with. He was laughing, his cheeks pink, his hair flopping down onto his forehead, and he looked so handsome she couldn't stand it.

'No,' she said, and drained her glass. 'I'm going to go home. I've got a busy week coming up.'

'You have?' said Blessing. 'I've got those twins delivering on…' She tilted her head as if in thought. 'Friday, I think, but what have you got?'

Essie couldn't answer that. She could feel it at the edge of her mind, like a dark cloud on the horizon. Something tugging at her attention, but she couldn't get hold of it.

Or maybe she was just in a massive strop because she fancied the pants off Josh Henderson and couldn't damn well have him.

'I've got the house to run, while you lot fanny about knitting the future and making fertility charms,' she snapped, jamming her hands into her pockets. The words 'I might as well make myself useful' hovered in the air in front of her.

Blessing narrowed her eyes for a moment then she said,

'Fine. Tell Maude the Helions won, will you, I'm sure she knitted that last week.'

Essie nodded and turned for home, leaving the warmth of the pub behind her as storm clouds gathered.

Siena had managed, through a combination of sweet-talking, pregnancy sympathy and massive tips, to get Josh's list of white goods installed, along with full sets of bedroom and living room furniture. The ancient threadbare carpets were banished to the dumpster that magically appeared outside, and the oak floorboards sanded and varnished. New curtains replaced the old. The house had resounded with the sounds of carpentry for weeks now, and smelled constantly of paint.

They even had the chimney swept and cleaned, although Josh had a feeling that was more to do with Essie than his sister. He also suspected she was behind having the roof patched, and the Rayburn serviced, because those were things that would have escaped Siena's frivolous mind.

Essie had been helpful about things like chimney sweeps and getting someone to clear the gutters. She'd been warm and friendly when he'd met her at the pub, and outright chummy at the conker tournament. But after that moment outside the pub, when he'd been so distracted he'd gone and lost the tournament, she'd just vanished. She couldn't be really mad about that, could she? Her replies to his texts hadn't betrayed any annoyance.

He'd been inches from kissing her, and then she'd vanished.

Maya had been right. He was pathetic.

Josh kept himself busy. He spoke to the solicitor about the rents, which were eventually collected even though none of them would have covered a single delivery arriving at the house, and considered asking him if he knew of any work going for a US-trained lawyer.

But the words stuck in his throat, and he never spoke them out loud.

'Did you try this one?' the solicitor asked, from his small, crowded office in a building even older than Josh's house. 'Beldam House? We can't find it.'

Josh frowned at the papers on the desk. 'I… thought I had,' he said. 'I meant to. I've just been so busy. I'll take another swipe at finding it.'

But somehow he never did, and when the solicitor asked again he couldn't remember why. 'Maybe the house isn't there any more,' he said. 'And nobody amended the records.'

'Probably. But it's strange there's no mention of it. In villages like Good Winter, people remember who used to own what for generations back.'

Josh assured the man he'd ask in the pub, which seemed to be the repository of all local knowledge. He sent Essie a text to casually mention he might be down there this evening.

Cool. By the way, did you get a picture of that bit of parchment?

Dammit. He kept forgetting. The parchment, and the

faded note that had been wrapped around it, were in a Ziploc bag in the kitchen dresser. He hadn't known what to do with them, but somehow they seemed important.

'I'll do it when I get home,' he promised, but when he arrived home there were workmen taking out the kitchen cabinets.

'Are you kidding me?' he muttered, and yelled for his sister.

'Isn't it amazing?' she said, cosily ensconced on her new sofa with her new support pillow and her new cashmere blanket. There was a ball of yarn and some knitting needles beside her, but she didn't appear to be doing anything with them. 'It's someone Blessing knows. They just had a cancellation.'

'To take out the old kitchen?'

'Yeah.'

'And… fit a new one?'

'Duh,' said Siena.

Josh glanced back at the kitchen, which looked slightly as if it had been bombed. 'They just happened to have cabinets and things that would fit into this space?'

'Apparently.' She picked up a stick of celery from a plate loaded with it, dipped it into ketchup, and ate it with every sign of enjoyment.

'This space exactly?'

'Josh, what's your point?'

He gave up. 'Fine. Did Blessing come today?'

Siena nodded serenely. 'Not long now, she says.'

Blessing appeared to be the only means of estimating when Siena's baby was due. Siena herself didn't appear to have any idea, or even any interest in finding out. Josh desperately wanted to know why this was, and who the father of her child was, but whenever he tried to raise the subject, Siena changed it.

'I'm going out this evening,' he said. 'Just for a couple of drinks. I won't be late.' He watched her carefully. 'If you'd rather I didn't—'

'No way, I want to watch *Bake Off* and you always complain through it.'

Siena had discovered the rich treasure trove of British TV streaming services, and with them the panoply of extremely wholesome, cosy competition shows, where people baked cakes, or sewed clothes, or made pottery. Josh had nothing against any of them, but Siena watched them all day long and after seven hours of spotted dicks and soggy bottoms, he was climbing the walls.

'Great. So, you know if you have the slightest twinge…'

'I'll call Blessing.'

'Yes. And then you call me.'

'Really, Josh,' Siena mixed some ranch dressing with the ketchup, 'you don't have to be so anxious. Blessing has it all figured out.'

Yes, she probably did. Essie's sister – and given his own relationship with Siena he wasn't about to enquire into the details of that relationship – might well make grown men walk into lampposts just by swinging her hips, but she appeared to be an extremely experienced and reassuring midwife. The house was filling up with baby paraphernalia, but also with books and leaflets. Siena appeared to be more prepared than she had been when she arrived here.

Only… she still didn't seem very prepared at all. Siena still seemed to have some sort of idea that the birth would whizz by in a sort of montage which would all be over soon, and then it was straight into soft-focus cooing over a delightful infant who would never refuse to go to sleep, or cry all day for no reason, or poop out the back of its diaper—

Josh was really beginning to regret reading that particular chapter in the baby book.

He should probably have a word with Blessing. Make sure Siena wasn't relying on her too much. Maybe she'd be at the pub tonight.

He sent Essie a text to ask, then hesitated in case she thought this meant he was interested in Blessing. He wasn't, not in a romantic sense. She was extremely attractive for sure, but Essie was the one who kept drawing Josh's attention. Even if she was frustratingly private all the time.

Essie came to Brook Manor Farm fairly frequently – and, like Blessing, always waited to be invited in. Josh figured this was some polite British thing, and didn't question it. He'd tried to find out where they lived, and every time they'd waved vaguely and said, 'Oh, you know, just past Gallows Lane,' and Josh had utterly failed to find the place.

'Siena, do you know where Blessing lives?' he asked.

She shrugged, already glued to the sight of an amateur baker attempting to make petit fours. 'No, why?'

'Does she live with Essie?'

Siena made a sound that was what might happen if a person started out saying 'I dunno,' and then removed all the consonants and most of the vowels and half translated it into a shrug.

'Right. Well, you know what, I'm going to see if I can find this Beldam House that's supposed to owe us rent,' he said.

'What house?' Siena said vaguely, eyes on the TV. 'Oh come on, you haven't even put them in the oven yet!'

He backed off and fetched his coat.

The weather in Good Winter had turned decidedly chilly as September gave way to October. Now, Brook Manor Farm sported carved pumpkins outside the door, presumably for the entertainment of the small army of delivery and tradespeople who arrived every day, and the air smelled of woodsmoke more often than not.

The Yew Tree Inn was holding a Hallowe'en party this weekend, and Siena had vague plans to go dressed as 'a pumpkin or something'. Josh had bought a load of candy in the expectation of trick-or-treaters, assured by Essie that they would come even to his remote house. He'd also dusted off his tuxedo and bought a cheap pair of vampire fangs, after Essie had explained to him that his usual plan of going as James Bond wouldn't wash in England.

'Unless you're scared of James Bond,' she'd added dubiously. 'Hallowe'en costumes are supposed to be scary. Or at least spooky.'

'What are you going as?' he asked.

'Oh, we always go as witches,' she said, and her smile looked somewhat peculiar.

The people of Good Winter had lived among witches for longer than they knew. Certain things seeped into the collective memory, such as keeping the duck pond nicely kept, and never dressing as an ugly old hag come Hallowe'en. And they all knew, deep down, that if someone was in trouble, they could call on Beldam House.

It was Blessing they called for the births, and Essie for the deaths. No one had ever questioned this.

The air had turned decidedly cooler in the last few days of October, and the weather forecasters talked about areas of high pressure and cold fronts making it feel like winter. Essie knew it had nothing to do with the wind blowing in from Siberia, and everything to do with the cross-quarter day next week.

Winter would arrive at half past ten next Monday morning. She knew this because she would be the one to summon it.

She knew it in her bones.

Said bones felt tight and achy today, and not just with the impending winter. She sat on the bench outside Mrs Sockburn's house, every muscle tight like concrete, and tried to hold in the tears. In her hands was the small doll with the violet hair. Its arms were folded neatly across its chest. Later, she would bury it somewhere peaceful, and plant some winter pansies.

The old lady had called her last night. 'Would you come and sit with me, love? I feel ever so peaky.' And Essie had known exactly what was coming.

She'd gone upstairs to Maude's room, where she was passed a blanket made of knitted squares that matched the violet of Doris Sockburn's hair. As she went downstairs, Prudence handed her a couple of ancient copper coins.

'We'll speak her name,' promised Avery, passing Mrs Sockburn's poppet to Essie. It had begun to look decidedly thinner and paler these last few weeks.

'I've got to attend a birth,' said Blessing, who had her bag in hand already. 'Twins. It's going to be a difficult one.' She hesitated. 'I'll suggest Doris as a name.'

'Won't they have suffered enough?' said Essie, but she accepted Blessing's kiss and went off to do her duty.

She'd always done it. Even as a small child, she'd followed her mother as she visited the dying, made cups of tea and mumbled along with whatever prayers the patient preferred. Sometimes, family members called her in specially, but mostly it was people like Mrs Sockburn, who didn't want to be alone.

Now she sat on the bench in Mrs Sockburn's tiny front garden, in the cold afternoon air, and stared out at Midsummer Common. Most of the trees had shed their leaves now and the fierce wind was making short work of what they had left, but the old oak was still holding on, stately and grand as ever. That tree had been there since before Beldam House had been built.

Well, probably. Essie didn't actually know how old the house was. She'd tried to find out once or twice, but when she looked in the library all the books that might have been relevant disappeared or refused to open. A couple translated themselves into what was either an ancient runic system of writing, or a toddler scribbling on the page.

Essie suddenly remembered a hand nudging her crayon

out of the way, and a voice telling her, 'Don't draw on that, dear, it's four hundred years old.'

She watched a crow pecking around the grass that sloped down to the duck pond. The reeds there had turned yellow and brown now, awaiting somebody to come and clear them. Loosestrife, she thought they were called. The wind blew through them, sighing a little.

All will be well until 'tis the reed.

The wind turned colder.

'Essie?'

She looked up, and there was Josh, ambling towards her with his hands in his pockets. Damn, he was handsome. After she'd done the ritual, and after Siena had had the baby, and after she'd figured out what was going on with that witch ball and Josh occasionally remembering Beldam House... she should probably try to go on a proper date with him. Maybe one that didn't end with her running away.

She could control herself now. She could.

She'd restored the rats into ex-boyfriends, albeit with Avery and Prudence's help, and given them a few bevvies while they were still in a confused state. Then she'd taken them to the pub, got a couple of rounds in for them, and left. From the scuttlebutt around the village, it sounded like the three of them had got pissed and made plans to go to the World Cup together, so that was nice.

They would have forgotten her again. Maybe a vague memory might surface, but they'd put it down to alcohol and forget about it soon enough. They had lives to be getting on with.

As did Josh. His smile faded as he strolled closer. 'What's wrong?'

She swiped at her eyes. Her glasses had splashes of tears on them.

'Nothing. Just the wind making my eyes run.'

Josh didn't look convinced. 'Are you waiting for someone?'

Essie had seen death many times. She knew it was a natural and necessary part of the grand cycle of the world. She hadn't been particularly close to Mrs Sockburn.

None of this prevented her from bursting into tears.

'Hey!' Josh was there beside her, taking her cold hands in his warm ones. 'It's okay, it's okay.'

'I know it's okay,' said Essie. 'It's not like she was young or it was a terrible shock. Most people didn't even like her.'

'Like who?' Josh glanced up at the house behind them. It was a traditionally built affair in red brick and flint, with a tiled roof and a small porch. The windows had been replaced with double glazing, the back had been extended into a kitchen conservatory, and there was a small en suite upstairs. It would probably sell quite nicely, although a new owner would probably turn the front garden into parking, which would be a shame.

'Mrs Sockburn. Did you... no wait, she was housekeeping up at Brook Manor Farm, wasn't she? Did you know her?'

Josh frowned at the window by the front door. Essie had drawn the curtains, even though it was only mid-afternoon.

'Our paths crossed,' he murmured. 'Is she okay?'

Essie shook her head. 'I'm waiting for the undertaker,' she said.

'Undertaker? What the – what happened?'

Essie sniffed, and took off her glasses to wipe her eyes with her sleeve. 'She had cancer, Josh. She didn't tell anyone. A lot of people of her generation still think it's a dirty word.'

She put her glasses back on. Josh looked shocked. His hands were still holding hers.

'She has children, but they live miles away and they never visited that I can remember. She said I should contact them after she'd passed. I hate making calls like that.' A thought occurred. 'Do you think they'll sell this place? Maybe one of them will come to live here.'

'If they do they can pay the market rate,' said Josh. He nodded at the house number. 'Number 25 The High Street. I own this house, Essie.'

'You do?'

He didn't look very amused as he said, 'Apparently I own half the village. Do you know how much money I make from that?' She shrugged. 'About twelve pounds a month.'

'Are you kidding?'

'I am not. If I could only get tenants for Box Cottage, Willow Barn, and Number 3 Rose Buildings, I could be coining it in at a rate of thirty shillings a month.'

'Two pound ten,' corrected Essie absently.

'How did this country ever function with such… Harry Potter money?' Josh said in exasperation. 'There's one house I can't even find. It apparently hasn't paid rent since 1746.'

Essie felt her body stiffen away from him slightly. The wind whipped around them. 'It's probably not there anymore,' she said.

'But there should be some record of that, right? Some local news item or something, if it had been pulled down, or there was a fire, or it was turned into a hotel or something? I mean, there are people in the pub,' he waved an arm across the Common at the Yew Tree, 'who still talk about the time Elizabeth I came to visit.'

'She stayed at Brook Manor,' Essie said. 'That place did burn down, a hundred or so years later.'

'Brook Manor, right. There's like half a wall in a field a mile from my house, I guess that's what's left of it.'

'Is that so?' said Essie, scanning the street for the sight of the undertaker's vehicle.

'I know this because at least three people in the pub told me, and so I went for a walk the other week and I found where the house used to be. There are old maps you can see online. But you know what's not on them? Beldam House.'

Essie took her hands from his and jammed them in her pockets. 'I don't know what to tell you,' she said.

'No, and nor does anybody else. I have walked the length of Gallows Lane today and I can't find a single hint of it. It's weird, Essie. Why does no one know about this place?'

Because none of them need it. Doris Sockburn had needed Essie last night, and so she'd remembered the phone number of Beldam House. People who were sick, or desperate, remembered how to find the place. But people in the village pub didn't need it. They forgot, just like everyone else.

'I really couldn't say, Josh,' said Essie. 'Look on the bright side, you'll be able to get a new tenant for this place now, and charge them whatever you want. It's a desirable spot. The kitchen needs replacing and the bathroom is old fashioned but it should get a fair whack. Just wait for them to remove the corpse first. It's still warm.'

The sky had really clouded over.

'Hey, don't,' said Josh, immediately retreating. 'Don't be like that. I didn't mean it like that. I'm sorry your friend died. I really am. I was just saying—'

'Well, don't,' snapped Essie. Doris Sockburn hadn't been her friend. She hadn't really been anyone's friend. She'd just been part of the village, just as Essie was part of the village, and she deserved some basic respect.

There was a spell on Beldam House to make people forget it existed. There was no such thing on Number 25 The High Street and Josh had completely forgotten about it anyway.

'You don't know a single thing about this place,' she said. 'You turn up, just casually owning half a dozen properties and bitching about the rent, and what do you even know about the people who live in them? Do you know Number 3 Rose Cottages is derelict because the last tenant killed his wife? Do you know the woman who lived in Box Cottage was an agoraphobe and the house just rotted around her? Do you know Willow Barn is empty because it's where a farmhand was crushed by a tractor? Do you know any of those things?'

Josh looked appalled. Essie hadn't realised she'd got to her feet and was glaring down at him, but she didn't see any reason why she should stop now.

'And do you know why you can't find Beldam House? It's because you don't need to. Collecting rent isn't a need, especially when your sister appears to be as rich as Croesus.'

'Hey, I don't like living off her,' Josh began.

'Oh, no, I can tell,' Essie snapped. 'You hate it so much you're refusing all of the deliveries and tradespeople coming to your house, aren't you? You hate it so much you walk past my goddamn house every bloody week trying to collect the fucking rent!'

'I – what?'

Shit. Shit, she'd said it.

Overhead, the sky blackened.

'Your house?' said Josh. He was on his feet now. 'Beldam House is… your house?'

'No,' said Essie, and rain started to fall. 'It's – look, you won't find it.'

'It exists? You live there?' He was advancing on her now. The front garden was really not big enough for advancing. 'What were you doing, hiding it behind a tree? Essie, there is a rental agreement on that house. There is a contract, and unless you can prove that it has been terminated then it's still in existence.'

'Oh, what are you, a lawyer?'

'Yes,' said Josh, swiping rain out of his eyes. 'I am,

actually. Or was. I quit, because it was soul-destroying, and I like having a soul, dammit.' He seemed to realise he'd got off-track. 'Look, I know how contracts work, Essie, and I don't suppose they're that much different on this side of the Atlantic.'

A lawyer. The man who'd broken the witch ball and remembered her house was a goddamn lawyer.

The late October day was by now as cold as midwinter. Steam clouded in front of Essie's face as she breathed. 'What was your father's name?' she asked.

'What? What the hell does that have to do with anything?'

Car headlights flashed along the road. It was mid-afternoon and dark as night. Essie saw the words 'private ambulance' written on the side of a van.

She fumbled Mrs Sockburn's key from her pocket. If he was Mrs Sockburn's landlord he could damn well let the undertaker in. 'Tell me your father's name, Josh.'

The cold light of the ambulance headlights put Josh's face into terrible shadow. Rain dripped from his chin as he said, 'Edward Mason Hopkins.'

Lightning split the sky, and Josh flinched as if he'd been electrocuted. But Essie was turned to stone, staring at him in horror.

Hopkins, the kin of Hop, the son of Hob. The lawyer, son of Hob.

The premonition hadn't been warning her about a witchfinder who'd been dead for three hundred and fifty years. It had been warning her about Josh.

As if a magnet drew it, her gaze turned to the flowers

growing on Midsummer Common. Under the relentless downpour, the tiny purple crocuses battled to stay upright, their orange stamens sinking under the weight of the rain until they looked like forked tongues.

When she blinked, she saw the monster from Maude's knitting behind her eyes.

'Essie?' said Josh, and Essie threw the key at him and ran.

The downpour was torrential as Josh squelched home in the unseasonal darkness. He'd let the undertaker in, explained that he was the landlord but otherwise didn't know the deceased well, and fled as soon as was decently possible.

There hadn't been any point trying to follow Essie. The undertaker – a polite and gentle woman who had assured Josh everything was under control – had just arrived, and anyway, Essie had simply vanished into the darkness and pounding rain. Josh had been in Good Winter long enough to know that there were a dozen streets and alleys and pathways she could have taken.

She'd been hiding from him all this time, after all.

Never telling him where she lived. All this time he'd been trying to find the place and she'd been hiding from him. Laughing at him. Lying to him. How many times had she met him at the pub and silently sniggered to herself over the deception?

She knew everything about this place. That first night, when she'd walked him home, poking fun at his fear and making it clear who held the upper hand. She knew the derelict houses he owned and why they weren't lived in. She knew he was living off his sister, because once again Josh Henderson had failed to make his mark…

The lights of Brook Manor Farm glowed out at him across the driveway. Siena had every light in the damn place on, just because she could. Profligate with her money, flaunting it at him. As he stormed closer, he could make out the tarps covering building materials and the dumpster, piled high with debris. She'd moved in and immediately started making the house her own.

'Oh my god, Josh, where have you been? It's biblical out there!'

Siena stood in the doorway, wrapped in a cashmere blanket that probably cost more than his last pay cheque. Her hair was beautifully styled for just sitting at home watching TV. Her nails were manicured.

And suddenly Josh was ten years younger, standing on the doorstep of his father's huge mansion, the poor relation coming to beg for help. Because no matter what he did or tried to do, he would always be his father's unwanted son, Siena's unwanted brother—

'Josh?'

'I'm going to my room,' he snapped. Because it was his room, just about.

'Are you okay?'

He stalked past her into the kitchen. Every light was on. 'Oh my god, could you just learn how to use a light switch?' he exploded. 'They go off as well as on!'

'All right, Mr Switches Everything Off The Second He Leaves The Room,' Siena laughed.

Yes, he did. He always had. He remembered the meter whizzing around above the door of the apartment when he was a kid. 'Do you know how much this all costs? Do you even know what an electricity bill is?'

'It's all taken care of. I had it set up when I—'

'Oh, yeah, you took care of it. You're paying for it now. I can pay for my own goddamn electricity, Siena!'

She took a step back. 'I know you can,' she said slowly. 'I'm just trying to help.'

'Help? Siena, look at this place! It's like Las Vegas in here. Just turn off a goddamn light sometimes, huh?'

She looked confused, and a little hurt. Clutching her blanket, his sister said, 'But I'm paying for it, so—'

'I don't care! I don't care who pays!' Too angry to make any sense now, Josh stormed around the kitchen, flicking switches. 'It's my house, Siena, do you understand that? This is my goddamn house.'

'I know,' she said. 'I'm running things by you. If you don't like it you can just say—'

'Say? When do I get a chance to say? You turned up here and started ordering things and fixing things and installing things! What even is this?' He gestured wildly at a plastic thing on the counter top.

'It's a bottle steriliser,' she said quietly. 'For the baby's bottles. Josh, what is going on?'

He glared at the bottle steriliser, which was probably quite sensible and normal, but he was too rattled to think properly.

Essie had lied to him. She'd laughed at him. She'd controlled him. Just like Siena was doing. Just like Maya had done. Just like his mother.

'This is my house,' he said. It was his. He owned it. For some reason his father had left him this, and nothing else. Josh had nothing else. 'You could go anywhere, be anywhere, and you had to come here. To my house. And make it yours.'

'If you don't like it,' she began sharply.

'Maybe I don't!'

'I didn't see you doing anything to fix the place up,' she fired back.

'When did I have the chance! You swanned in here and took control, like I can't even fix my own house—'

'You can't,' Siena spat.

'—and just assumed I'd be fine with it! Cos I'm just Josh, huh, Josh the doormat, and you can just walk in here and tell me I'm going to help you raise this baby—'

'I did not—'

'—which you never even told me about until you ran out of options,' Josh said, 'because you don't, what, even trust me enough to tell me who the father is?'

Siena looked away. For a moment she didn't move.

Fuck. He'd said too much.

'Look, I'm…' he began, and she shook her head.

Then she went to the dresser, picked up her keys, and calmly walked out of the house.

'Siena?'

By the time Josh reached the door, she was getting into

the car. By the time he reached the car, she was already driving away.

Essie didn't even remember walking back to Beldam House. She might have run. She might have flown. The sky was dark as pitch, the rain hammering down so hard it would have hurt if she'd been less angry, and the sky flashed bright with lightning.

Josh Henderson was Josh Hopkins. He'd lied. He'd *lied*.

What else was he going to do?

The house looked dreadful when she reached it, a towering monstrosity of blackened stone, crooked turrets and lurching roofs. Gargoyles leered from every corner, spewing filthy water. Ivy coiled over the front door, and Essie had to physically fight it before she could shove the damn thing open and fall inside to stand, dripping, on the flagstones.

Avery stood on the stairs, and Essie could tell they were in some distress because they had lipstick and earrings on the left side and a beard on the right side of their face. They turned.

'Essie? Thank god you're back.'

'Don't ask,' Essie snarled. She was soaked to the skin and burning with anger. 'No wait, do ask. Do you know who the lawyer, son of Hob is?'

'Look, forget about that,' said Avery, as a shadow fell on the stairs above them.

'Forget about it? Are you insane? Maude's knitting had a monster—'

'We will contain it,' came a cool voice from the stairs above Avery, and Essie faltered.

'But,' she began, and couldn't remember any more words.

She watched, dumbfounded, as a long red skirt came into view. A dainty leather slipper beneath it. A white hand appeared on the banister.

'The monster is the lawyer, son of Hob. We will contain it. As we have always contained it.'

A tight-waisted bodice appeared, and full sleeves, and a square lace collar. Fat coils of red hair framing a white, red-lipped face.

'But we must hurry,' she said.

Essie swallowed and stared up at the only person who had ever silenced her.

'Hello, Mother,' she said.

Chapter Nine

Lilith Winterscale had always been possessed of a formidable presence. She was the sort of person who never waited for the right moment to make an entrance, because the moment she made her entrance automatically became the right moment. She carried an air about her of always being in exactly the right time and place. Kings and empresses had bowed in her presence.

'Essabett,' she said, looking over her only daughter as she stood, dripping wet in her jeans and fleece. Her voice was that familiar, dreadful mixture of disappointment and disdain as she said, 'What *are* you wearing?'

'It's the twenty-first century,' Essie said. 'I can wear what I like.'

She was a grown woman, and had been for much longer than it seemed. And yet, whenever Lilith was around, Essie felt like she was twelve years old and not mature enough to talk to grown-ups yet.

The emerald gaze swept her again. 'And you like wearing… that?'

Essie gritted her teeth. 'You look lovely, Mother.'

Lilith absently touched the fat, gleaming pearls on a ribbon around her neck. 'Yes,' she said. She descended the final few steps, and said urgently, 'What is the date? Is it the cross-quarter day?'

'No, that's next week.'

'It's not even Hallowe'en,' said Avery. They had picked up Misty the black cat, as if for protection from Lilith.

'Hallowe'en,' scoffed Lilith. 'The Christian corruption of the sacred. We must gather the evergreens. Cut the mistle. Bring in the holly.'

'But it will die before we're ready,' said Essie. She had a whole day set aside for that, on Sunday, the day before the ritual had to take place. The holly from the church grounds. The mistletoe from the ancient oak on Midsummer Common. The yew from the tree behind the pub. They all grew strongly every autumn, and nobody ever cut them until Essie had taken her crop.

She had never questioned this. It was just something else everyone in the village knew.

Lilith advanced on Essie, her face pale, her eyes burning. 'We must be ready now,' she said. 'He rises, Essabett. The monster awakes.'

'What monster?' said Essie, bewildered. 'Look, it isn't time to do the ritual yet. Winter doesn't start until next Monday. About half past ten, I think—'

'Winter?' said Lilith. 'Essie, do you really think the ritual is about winter? About snow? About white yules?'

Essie stared at her. Then she looked at Avery, and at Prudence, who had drifted in from the kitchen. Neither of them met her gaze.

'What else is it about?' she said slowly.

Lilith was about the same height as Essie, but she still managed to look down at her as she said, 'It is to contain the monster, Essabett. The ice that freezes him beneath the earth. The sleep that must be renewed. The cold that contains. For nearly four hundred years we have bound him, but now he wakes. Now the monster awakes.'

Josh had put on a waterproof coat and grabbed a large flashlight, but the night was still dark and howling and he was soaking wet already. He wasn't entirely sure why he was out on foot looking for Siena, but it was better than sitting at home trying to call her.

The location services on her phone were off, of course. He figured he'd call at the pub to see if anyone had seen her, and then try some local hotels, and then if he couldn't raise her after that he'd call the police.

Visions of her going into labour in a ditch beside a crashed car tortured him. The rain was relentless, hammering down on him like a thousand tiny punishments, so heavy he could barely hear the thunder.

He saw the lightning, though. As he arrived in the village, he realised that lightning was the only thing giving the place any illumination at all. Every house was dark, and what few streetlights existed were out too.

There was a faint glow coming from the pub. Candles, he realised. The good people of Good Winter wouldn't let something like a power cut stop them from drinking. He stumbled across the slick, muddy common and regarded the small river where the road used to be. Well, they said wild swimming was fashionable these days.

'Fortune favours the brave,' he muttered, and began wading through the water. He fell to his knees at one point, which was just fabulous because now all of him was soaked through, and then he crawled to the other side of the road and the slightly raised ground of the pub car park. Staggering upright, he hesitated, and shone his light across the cars parked in front of the pub. None of them were Siena's. Well, he might as well go in and ask.

The heat and sound enveloped him as he pushed open the door. Steam rose off his clothes.

'Come in, come in!' cried someone he didn't even know. 'The more the merrier! You look like a drowned rat.'

'Yeah,' said Josh. He figured there might be an inch or so of one of his hips that wasn't soaked through to the skin, but that was about it. His jeans seemed to weigh about a hundred pounds. 'Listen, have you seen…'

But the man had already turned back to his friends, laughing in the candlelight over their pints. Josh pushed through to the bar. There was a Jack o'lantern pumpkin there with a flickering candle in it. 'Have you seen my sister?'

'Not sure I know her, love,' said Sharon the barmaid.

'Oh, you'd remember. Blonde, very pretty, nine months' pregnant?'

Her plucked eyebrows went up. 'No, you're right, I would remember.' She raised her voice. 'Oi! You lot! American Josh is looking for his sister! Blonde, very pretty, nine months' pregnant. Anyone?'

A chorus of shrugs was his reply. A few people looked as if they'd been about to make a joke at 'blond, very pretty' and abruptly stopped at 'pregnant'.

Josh considered asking after her car, but figured there wasn't much point. 'If anyone sees her, could you call me?' he said. He took Sharon's pen and scribbled his number on her order pad. The flickering pumpkin leered at him.

'Is she all right, love?'

'I'm just worried about her in this weather,' Josh fudged, and left the warmth of the pub.

Outside, the weather seemed to be even worse. Josh hadn't thought storms like this happened in England, where rain for more than hour was treated as an exciting weather event that had to be discussed for days, and sunshine was something that had to be mentioned, as if by law, every time it occurred.

Maybe there was a law about it. *Thou shalt form a queue and talk about the weather. Penalty for failure: learn all the rules of cricket.*

Oh god, he was delirious.

Josh stood in the dark as the rain battered him sideways, and tried to take a few deep breaths. She couldn't have gone far. Maybe to the nearest spa. A luxury hotel maybe. Perhaps he should go back inside and ask where that might be.

He wished he had Blessing's number. It was written on

the fridge in stick-on magnets, but that was no damn help to him now.

He could call Essie…

Guiltily, he glanced down towards Mrs Sockburn's empty cottage. Essie had been upset because the old lady had died, and Josh had been an insensitive asshole. He deserved her yelling at him. And he should not have taken it out on Siena.

All this he knew to be true, but it didn't help very much.

He was about to go back inside the pub to ask about hotels and the like, when a movement caught his eye from the side of the building.

A flash of red. The glint of torchlight on spectacles.

'Essie?'

She didn't hear him, of course. The wind was blowing so hard it was all he could do to stay upright. He battled forwards, towards the side of the pub where there was little respite, and saw Essie and a woman in a long dress standing under the large old tree there.

'Hey! Get out from under that tree!' Josh rushed forwards. 'What if lightning hits it?'

'Oh, we be safe,' said the woman in the long dress, 'for lightning dare not hit a witch and besides I already be dead.'

At least, he thought that was what she said. But the wind was howling and the rain was hammering. Josh grabbed the sleeve of Essie's red coat. 'You can't stand under a tree during a thunderstorm,' he said urgently. 'It's a lightning rod.'

She turned, and her face in the glare of his flashlight was

something strange and terrible to behold. Her bones were sharper, her lips redder, her eyes glowing like emeralds. In her hands she held a fearsome axe the length of his forearm.

Then she moved, and she was Essie, soaking wet and scowling at him. She held a garden implement and some greenery.

'What are you doing out in this?' she said, stuffing the branches into a sack held by the other woman. 'It's dangerous. You could get hit by lightning. You're soaking wet.'

'So are you,' Josh said, but she already appeared to have lost interest. She reached towards the tree with her knife and hacked off some more small branches. 'What the hell, Essie?'

'We still need more,' she said to the woman with the sack and the strange way of talking. 'Get inside, Josh. This doesn't concern you.'

'Doesn't – that axe is metal, and you're—'

'Do not meddle in the affairs of witches,' Essie snarled, and there were harmonics in that voice that reached down inside Josh's soul and told him to run away very fast indeed. Her voice was the howl of a wolf and the roar of a lion and the scream of a crow, and what was worse was the multitudes of all those things it contained. A pack of wolves and a pride of lions and a murder, quite definitely a murder, of crows.

But Josh's feet rooted themselves in the cracked tarmac of the pub car park and he said, 'Siena is missing.'

Essie froze with a fair-sized branch in her hand. 'Missing?' she said.

'We have not time for this,' said the woman with the sack.

'Missing how?' said Essie.

Josh shrugged helplessly. 'We argued. It was dumb. I said stupid stuff and she got in the car and drove away, and now the weather is…'

He gestured at the road running past the pub. Running was the operative word. The damn thing was like Splash Mountain.

'Essabett,' said the other woman. 'We must gather the yew and return. The monster wakes.'

'It's not time yet,' Essie said uncertainly. She glanced at the dark village, then back at Josh.

'Canst not thou feel it? I taste it in the air and I have not a living tongue!' cried the other woman. Josh realised she was wearing some sort of period costume, a long skirt and apron and tattered linen cap. Maybe she'd got the wrong day for the pub's Hallowe'en party.

Only she didn't seem to be very wet.

'She's overreacting,' Essie said. 'The storm is just my bad mood.' She didn't look at Josh.

The costumed woman scoffed. 'Now who's fancy about herself?' she said. 'Were it you there would be blizzards and I expect a crying man with gaying instrument of ice turned to a rat. This man here, comely as a fancy man, be in plump current.'

'Please stop,' said Essie.

'What?' said Josh, and decided to ignore her. 'Essie. Can you help me or not?'

Essie looked at the mad woman in the costume, then at the tree, and then back at Josh.

'All right,' she said. 'You'd better come with me.'

The ritual was sacred. The ritual was always done.

The ritual never happened early.

Essie had participated since before she could remember. The witches in a circle of yew, holly and mistletoe, candle flames soaring high, invoking the winter. Without it, she'd been told, the winter would not arrive on time. The winter would not be cold enough. The earth needed its sleep, and the blanket of cold, in order to rise again in the spring. The winter was necessary, and Essie was necessary to bring it in.

Her mother had done it, and her mother before her. Winterscales had always brought the winter. Always. But Essie had a special talent for it. Essie brought the winter without breaking a sweat. Essie was the Winterscale of Winterscales. Essie could do the winter ritual in her *sleep*.

And now she had to perform the damn thing early, unprepared, during a bloody hurricane, with a… a civilian in the way. What was she supposed to tell him? 'Long story short, turns out there's an ancient evil sleeping beneath Good Winter and we have to perform a ritual to keep it trapped in ice every winter. This year, for some unknown reason, it's stirring early and we have to get the ritual done before it bursts forth and… I don't know. Burns the world down or something.'

Yep, that oughta do it.

The crocuses. The dying reeds. The world on fire…

And Doris Sockburn's face made of bones. She should have known. She should have *known*.

'Where are we going?' Josh wanted to know as they hurried across the muddy Common. She had his hand in hers, since the wind was trying to push them both over, and leaned on her broomstick as a walking stick. The yew branches stuck out of the heavy sack strapped across her back and poked through her thick coat. They did not make for aerodynamic travel.

Prudence, of course, wasn't bothered by such things as weather unless she chose to be. She wasn't even wet.

'My house.'

'Your house? Am I so honoured?'

'Don't,' said Essie wearily. She did want to help him find Siena. It was probably at least partly her fault that Josh had argued with her – Josh, who was always so easy-going and nice! And she'd managed to upset him to the extent that he'd upset Siena's equally sunny disposition and now she was out alone in the worst weather Essie could remember.

As they neared the huge, creaking oak tree that sheltered the common, she made out the figure of Avery, stuffing mistletoe into a sack. 'Avery! Can you take this back to the house?' she yelled.

Avery looked taken aback at the sight of Josh clinging to her arm. 'You've picked up a stray,' they said.

'We have a problem,' said Essie. She glanced at Josh as she unstrapped herself from the yew sack and handed it over. Releasing Josh's hand felt like letting go of a tether.

Leaning in, she explained the situation to Avery as quickly as she could.

'Have you tried calling Blessing?' Avery said.

Essie gave them an incredulous look. 'Oh yeah, like that hadn't occurred to me! The phones are down,' she said. 'Besides, Blessing's out Hertfordshire way, delivering twins. I need you to take this all back to the house,' she said, giving Avery's broomstick a meaningful look. Flying wasn't a good idea in this weather, but the broom could at least carry the load. Avery had a much faster turn of speed than Essie anyway and wasn't burdened with a civilian who couldn't see in the dark and kept losing his balance.

'Are you sure?'

'Why are you all out in this weather?' said Josh. His whole face was screwed up against the rain.

'I'll explain later,' said Essie. She leaned in to Avery, and said, 'Can you do a finding spell on Siena? Use the poppet.'

Avery nodded reluctantly and turned to go. Prudence floated after them, barely bothering to appear mortal anymore.

In seconds, they had disappeared into the darkness.

'We shouldn't let them go alone,' Josh shouted over the rain.

'They're faster than us. They'll get things ready.'

'Ready for what?' Josh yelled.

There was still a fair way to go before they reached Gallows Lane and the border of the witches' property. Essie racked her brain for an explanation.

None came.

She'd been up most of the night watching Mrs Sockburn

take her last breaths, which was an emotionally draining thing even if you weren't particularly close to the patient. She'd fought with Josh. Her mother had appeared…

And now she had to do the ritual in a hurricane and Siena was missing and Blessing wasn't around to help and there was a *monster* –

She pressed her hands to her face.

'Essie?'

She looked up into Josh's concerned face. He was having a terrible day too, and now he was soaked to the skin and probably freezing cold and he was still managing to be concerned for her.

'I need you to trust me.'

He almost physically withdrew from her. All the muscles in his face tightened.

'Josh.' She took his freezing hands in her own. 'Please. I promise to help you find Siena. I promise I'll do everything I can. I swear to you I won't rest until she's safe.'

Thunder boomed around them, so loud she thought her eardrums would burst, and lightning lit the sky like a floodlight for several seconds.

And Essie felt the vow travel down into the earth and take root. A promise was a promise, but a promise made three times was physically binding.

She could see the reluctance on his face. What had happened to this sweet-natured man that he found it so hard to trust?

Finally, he said, 'Okay. Like I have any other choice. I guess, lead on.'

It was hardly the rallying cry she'd been hoping for, but

it was good enough. Essie smiled, linked her arm with his, and set off towards Beldam House.

The fastest route took them through the woods. She felt Josh's body tighten with fear as they walked into the darkness, but under the tightly packed trees the rain abruptly lessened and the wind was reduced to an eerie howling.

'It's not much further,' she said, because she could have found Beldam House with her eyes cut out.

'Why is it quieter in here?' Josh said. His voice wasn't quite steady.

'The trees are keeping out the storm. They're pines, see? The branches grow into each other and form a sort of canopy. Can't rule out some fierce drips, though,' she added, as a massive splat of water smacked the top of her head.

'The wind is, uh,' said Josh, as it whirred and moaned around them.

Essie nodded. 'Uh' was about right.

'So what's with the greenery?' he asked, in the tones of a man desperate for distraction.

'Oh, it's for an important ritual.'

'Ritual?' She could feel him scrabbling to remember things he'd been told in the pub. 'Like… when you do the bonfire thing next week? Will it have dried by then?'

'It's not for a bonfire,' Essie said. 'That's Guy Fawkes Night and it's… different. This is a different kind of ritual.'

Josh was silent a moment, then he said, 'What was that you said earlier about witches?'

Fuck. She had said that, hadn't she. Essie glanced

around and decided they were close enough to the house for the perception spell to work. As much as it ever worked on Josh.

'Only, there were Wiccans when I was at college, and—'

'It's not the same.' Her voice came out flat.

'Hey, each to their own faith,' said Josh.

'It's not a faith. Well, it's not quite a… Look, it has nothing to do with scented candles and silly chants and burning herbs,' she said.

'Okay. So what do you do in this ritual?'

Essie winced. 'The candles aren't scented,' she said.

To her surprise, that brought a laugh from Josh. 'And the chants?'

'Are very solemn.'

'And the herbs?'

'Holly isn't a herb. And we don't burn it.'

'Holly? I saw you cutting yew and Avery collecting… what was that, mistletoe? Like at Christmas?'

'Yes, exactly like at Christmas.' She shot him a look in the darkness. 'You see too much, Josh Henderson. Or should I say Hopkins.' The cold wind blew.

She felt his sigh as much as heard it. 'I have my reasons for taking my mother's name,' he said.

'So do I. Look, the house is just through there.'

If anything, Beldam House looked worse than when she'd left. The gargoyles had multiplied, horrifying faces appearing in every flash of lightning, and some of them appeared to have already begun to collapse. The walls were black and grey, streaked with moss and slime and the skeletal remains of ivy. Tiles flew from the turret roofs and the battlements crumbled.

'We have battlements now,' she murmured. That was a new one.

Josh was staring at the house in bemusement as they reached the edge of the woods. 'I have been here before,' he said.

'Four times this month,' Essie said. 'Twice you came inside.'

'I did? I did,' he said, as she tugged him back out into the rain to hurry across the cracked and puddled paving to the front door. 'There was a goat,' he said, as she dragged him up the steps. There were rather more of them right now than there were usually. Several flights, it seemed.

The house was in a towering mood today.

'Goat, cats, dogs, parrots—' Essie wrenched open the door, and was faced with Lilith's tight-lipped fury. 'My mother. Lilith, this is Josh. Josh, Lilith.'

She heaved him inside and slammed the door shut. The sudden cessation of wind and rain was like sinking into a warm bath, and for a second Essie just stood there and enjoyed breathing air that wasn't mostly water.

'Ma'am,' said Josh, holding out his hand as if all this was perfectly normal.

Lilith looked him over as if he was something Essie had just scraped off her boot. 'What,' she said, her voice icy, 'is this?'

Josh's gaze darted to Essie's. His hand remained outstretched.

'A friend,' she said firmly. 'I promised him help. Where's Avery?'

'In the kitchen,' snapped Lilith, 'despite my orders.'

'Orders?' said Essie, and at her tone, Josh stepped meekly back. 'We do not give orders. All are equal in the coven.'

'I have crossed time to bring you this warning,' said her mother. 'It is of vital importance.'

'I have a prior promise,' said Essie. She felt slightly giddy. 'A vow thrice stated.'

Lilith's nostrils flared. Essie half expected smoke to stream from them. 'What vow?' Her voice crackled.

'His sister is missing. She's heavily pregnant. The weather—'

'The weather that is caused by the rise of the beast!'

'The weather that could kill her,' Essie said, and saw Josh flinch. 'I promised to find her. Avery said they'd start a searching spell. It won't take long.'

Lilith looked beyond furious. Her jaw worked in a multitude of unpleasant ways. But she knew as well as Essie that a vow thrice stated had to be fulfilled.

'Why don't you go and start the ritual,' said Essie.

'You know full well the winter is your responsibility—'

'And I know full well you did it before I was born.'

Essie had never known anyone as proud as her mother. She knew it absolutely burned her that Essie had a greater affinity with winter and therefore was much better at bringing it in than Lilith.

The conflict chasing across her face was like the storm outside.

Lilith nodded very tightly and stalked away towards the back of the house.

Essie blew out her breath. 'Come on, Josh.'

She started towards the kitchen and assumed he followed her. Avery stood at the table, holding a pink crystal in one hand and Siena's poppet doll in the other.

'Oh good,' they said. 'I've started it going, but it'll be better with you here. We should probably get a move on though. Your mother is not happy.'

'When is she ever? Come on, Josh.'

He stood in the doorway of the kitchen and gaped.

Like the rest of Beldam House, the kitchen was wont to change a little every now and then. As it was Avery's favourite place and seat of power, it most closely reflected their moods, but in every iteration it was a cavernous room, with high vaulted ceilings and many side chambers. This evening, as Avery appeared to be a little anxious but nowhere near as overwrought as Essie and her mother, the place had just a touch of Victorian Gothic about it, the dark beams festooned with blackened pans and candles flickering in lanterns.

'Whoa,' Josh said.

'You should see it on a good day,' said Avery, holding out their hand.

'Siena would freak,' said Josh, gazing at the huge dresser stacked high with cracked and stained earthenware. On the massive stove, large copper vats bubbled.

'Well, I'm sure we'll all enjoy that,' said Essie. She took his hand and pulled him towards the table. 'Now, you take the doll—'

'This looks exactly like her,' Josh said, turning it over in his hands.

'That's the idea.'

'Wait, is this a voodoo doll?'

'Are we in an inaccurate and culturally appropriating Hollywood movie?' Essie said crisply. 'No? It's a poppet doll. We use them for good.'

Josh's eyebrows creased in a way she tried not to find adorable.

'The doll represents her. It has a connection to her. We keep it safe, we treat it as if it was actually Siena.' Only yesterday she'd watched Blessing examine the doll's ankles before bathing them with iced cypress. 'We use it to care for her.'

'Gently, now,' said Avery. 'Think about Siena. Close your eyes if you need to. Think about her laugh, and the way she smiles. Think about her being happy and content.'

'Wrapped in her blanket,' said Josh. 'On her beanbag.'

Avery hurried away and came back with a little sack of dried chickpeas and a towel. They wrapped the poppet up and posed her on the bag.

'You got any celery and ketchup?' said Josh.

'Any what?'

'Or a baking show? Siena loves baking shows. Never mind.' He regarded the swaddled doll with his head on one side. 'It really does look like her.'

'Okay, focus on the doll. Tell her she'll be safe and we'll take care of her. Hold this crystal.'

Josh darted her a look, and then gave a hopeless shrug and said, 'Siena? You'll be safe. We'll take care of you.'

Essie sighed. 'Try to mean it,' she said.

Josh looked doubtfully down at the doll, and said, 'Is this some kind of spell?'

'Oh my god,' muttered Avery.

'Yes,' said Essie, as patiently as she could. 'It's a spell. But it won't work unless you believe in it. Do you want to find your sister?'

'Yes.' That was firm and sincere.

'Then say it. And mean it.'

Josh took in a deep breath and blew it out. 'Siena,' he said. He stared hard at the doll. 'Please be safe. Please be found. I care about you. Please come back.'

The crystal started to glow.

'Keep thinking that,' said Essie. 'Just repeat it over and over, in your head if you want. Tell her to come here. She'll be safe.'

Josh closed his eyes and muttered the words over and over. Essie met Avery's gaze, and they shared a nod. The crystal was beginning to move in Josh's hand, and apparently without realising it he followed it, away from the table and back into the hall.

'She's close,' said Avery in surprise.

'Really close,' said Essie, as the crystal glowed brightly.

The loud, frantic banging of the door knocker made them all jump.

'No way,' breathed Josh, his eyes opening.

Prudence, appearing from nowhere, opened the door, and caught Siena as she tumbled inside. 'You be right good now, child, fret no more,' she said, and then her eyes went wide.

'No *way*,' said Josh, gaping like a fish.

Siena looked up at Prudence, and then at Josh, and then at Essie and Avery. She was in leggings and a huge sweater and her hair was bedraggled, her make-up smudged from crying.

'What are you guys doing… where exactly…' She looked up and around at the swords and skulls on the walls, the reliquaries of gold and bones, the rows of poppets on the mantel, and whimpered, 'Where am I?'

With sudden presence of mind, Essie rushed to take the crystal and poppet from Josh before he dropped them to throw his arms around his sister. She carefully placed them on the mantel above the fire, the little doll still wrapped in her blanket towel. The doll's eyes were smudged with mascara.

'Thank god. You're okay. You're okay.' Josh hugged her tight. 'I'm so sorry. I shouldn't have yelled. I didn't mean it.'

Essie smoothed the doll's hair and gently closed the blanket around its rounded belly, and then she froze. Her eyes met Prudence's.

'Is this a… where is this? I was trying to find a hospital, or…' Siena trailed off.

'Oh dear,' said Avery quietly.

'Why?' Josh was all concern as he held Siena by the shoulders and looked her over. 'Are you okay? Did you have an accident?'

'Not exactly,' said Siena, and suddenly she gasped and clutched at her belly.

'*No*,' said Josh.

'I believe the babe is coming,' said Prudence placidly.

Chapter Ten

'Is she here? Good. Essabett, you are needed,' rang a commanding voice from the stairs. It was the sort of voice that demanded you pay attention to it, so Josh did, despite the fact that his sister appeared to be going into labour right in front of him.

I just summoned her here with a crystal and a voo— a doll, he thought giddily. Essie said they were witches and they had to do some ritual and then they'd done a spell. A *spell*.

He'd been prepared for English eccentricity. He hadn't been prepared for *actual witches*.

'Mother, we're a little busy,' said Essie.

'The babe be on its way,' said Prudence.

Lilith, still dressed in her dramatic red costume, swept down the stairs and took Siena squarely by the shoulders.

'Uh, hi?'

Lilith peered at Siena. Then she said, 'Your first?'

Siena nodded.

'You have hours. We do not. Essabett. Come.'

Essie chewed her lip. She looked guiltily at Josh and Siena. He could see her wavering.

'Are you sure?' she said to her mother. 'It must be done now?'

'If I could do it yesterday I would.'

'Then go back through the door and—'

'Essabett! The baby will not come for hours. We have ample time. Blessing, take this young woman to a bed and make her comfortable.'

There was a short pause, as they all looked around as if expecting Blessing to materialise from the sheer force of Lilith's will.

Josh glanced at Essie. Her lips were tight and white.

'Blessing isn't here,' Avery said eventually. 'She's out delivering twins.'

'She isn't?' wailed Siena.

'Did you,' Essie addressed her mother, her voice like an icicle, 'forget which one Blessing was?'

Lilith's face was rigid, the same way it had been when Essie had challenged her to do this ritual. Josh knew that look. He knew it from his mother, and he knew it from his ex. It was the look of someone who knew they'd been caught out and were mentally rearranging the world so that this was someone else's fault.

'Siena, honey,' said Avery, moving forward. Josh noticed for the first time that Essie's friend looked a little strange today, but Siena didn't seem to care and that was more important. 'Come with me and have a nice sit down. I'll get a bed ready for you. Maybe a nice warm drink, yes? And something clean and dry to wear.'

Siena nodded gratefully. 'Are you a midwife too?' she said.

'In a manner of speaking,' said Avery, and Josh winced. As Avery led his sister slowly up the stairs, he hesitated, reluctant to get between Essie and her mother.

'Will Blessing be back any time soon?' he asked.

'Probably not.' Essie didn't take her gaze from her mother.

'Is Avery medically qualified? Are any of you?'

'We have delivered more babies than you have ever met,' said Lilith.

'It's true,' said Essie.

'I knows my way around a birthing,' volunteered Prudence, which didn't exactly fill Josh with confidence. She looked like an escapee from a Thanksgiving pageant. 'Come with me, young man, and we shall take care of things.'

'Fetch Maude,' Essie said quietly, as Prudence escorted a reluctant Josh up the stairs.

He had no idea what was really going on. This house, this huge gothic cavern, seemed at once familiar and totally alien. Essie said he'd been here before, he'd been inside, and some things about the place did seem familiar now he was looking at them. The twisting staircase, that split and meandered off in odd directions, and the tree growing halfway up it. The banister and wood panelling were carved and painted with intricate little symbols that seemed to shift and shy away when he tried to look at them.

Prudence led him upwards, and he tried not to stare as he picked out increasingly weird details in her smoke-grey dress. Her skirt was narrowly pleated and very full, topped with a sort of narrow-waisted jacket and a long apron from the waist. Around her shoulders was wrapped a long, filmy shawl, tucked into the front of her bodice. Here and there he could see careful darns and rows of tiny handmade stitches. The fabric was worn, and stained around the hem and under the arms. Her hair straggled loose from beneath a lace-trimmed cap that had seen much better days.

And her neck…

'Prudence, right?' he said. 'Did you hurt your neck?'

Her hand went to the nasty burn at her throat. 'It does not pain me,' she said after a moment, and continued up the stairs.

When Josh reached the landing at the top, an impulse made him turn. Hanging in the stairwell was a huge painting, the frame massively ornate. It depicted a smoky landscape scene, trees blasted to stumps. In the distance, he could make out what might be a cannon on huge wheels. To the left was a church, its tower crumbling.

In the foreground was an empty wooden chair.

Josh narrowed his eyes. He'd seen this painting before, only he hadn't.

'I've seen this whole house before, only I haven't,' he said to himself.

''Tis true enough,' said Prudence. 'The house does change itself but while it stays the same.'

'That doesn't actually make any sense,' he said.

'No,' she conceded. 'But yes. In any case, you have forgotten what you saw until you came back, when it had changed.' She gestured to the painting. 'My lady's portrait is now empty, of course. Yesterday and tomorrow we will not see it the same.'

Josh pressed the heels of his hands to his eyes. He was tired, he was cold, he was wet, and literally nothing made sense.

'Can you just please take me to my sister?' he said, and Prudence nodded and opened a door nearby. Josh, who had a sudden memory of a whirlwind behind a door exactly like it, braced himself, but it was just an ordinary bedroom. *It must have been a dream.*

The bedroom was large, and had the slightly plain, unlived-in look of guest bedrooms everywhere. Siena sat on a huge beanbag, calmly watching a large TV on the wall, whilst Avery made the bed.

Josh opened his mouth to talk to his sister, then something registered in his brain and he glanced back at the bed. At first sight it had appeared normal, and now Avery was pulling up hospital rails at each side and fiddling with some contraption at the foot of it that had a distinct look of stirrups about it.

'This is a… birthing suite?' he said.

'It is now,' said Avery.

'You just happen to have a birthing suite in your house?'

Avery shrugged. 'The house provides what we need. Now then, dear. Are you timing the contractions?'

Siena nodded, her gaze glued to the screen where people were glazing pottery. 'Uh-huh. The last one was forty-five minutes ago.'

'Then we've got plenty of time. I'm just going down

to check on the others. Call us if you need anything. Prudence?'

Prudence bobbed a curtsey – a *curtsey* – and the two of them left. And then Josh was standing in a home birthing suite in a house that seemed to defy the laws of physics, time, and common sense.

'I'm having a *Stranger Things* experience,' he muttered.

Siena sipped from her mug. 'Sit down, Josh. You're making the place look untidy.'

Josh looked around the room. Untidy was really not the word. The walls were papered in a cool, calming blue, and the rug by the bed was a pretty pale green. There was a wardrobe and chest painted white, with a jaunty frieze of apples or something on it. In the large bay window, there was a freestanding bath and a collection of fluffy towels and robes. The place looked so much like a spa retreat Josh expected to hear harp music and a tinkling fountain.

He twitched aside the long, heavy drapes at the window. Rain streaked the window, and lightning lit up the dark forest beyond.

Which was very strange, because he didn't recall there being much in the way of forest anywhere around the village. He'd walked the length of Gallows Lane more times than he could remember, and he figured a full-sized forest was the sort of thing he'd recall. But then apparently he'd been inside the house several times already and he didn't remember that either.

'Siena?' he said slowly.

'Hmm? Oh, no, she's messed up the handle.'

He glanced at a fretful potter on screen, nobly trying to

smooth a clay handle back onto a pot. 'Bummer. Listen, does anything about this place seem… weird to you?'

Siena shrugged. 'I mean, kinda. But Avery said Blessing isn't the only one who delivers babies so it makes sense, I guess.'

Josh looked around the room again. There were frosted lamps on the walls, with what looked like very realistic flame effects. A fire burned merrily in the grate, and the smoke smelled faintly sweet. There were some framed prints on the walls, which looked like ancient woodcuts of women holding babies. The pattern on the wallpaper appeared to be snakes.

'I've been here before,' he said.

'Hmm?'

It was like remembering a dream. The details twisted and slid away from him, combining and confusing his memory. 'There was a goat on the stairs.'

'A goat? You mean, like a picture of a goat?'

'No. I mean a real one. And the cats were fighting bats. Or – no. There was this tree…'

'There's a cool tree in the hallway. I don't know how it grows there when there's no natural light.'

'Light,' said Josh. He stared at the frosted lamps on the walls, and strode to the nearest one to peer at it. There was a sort of brass key at the base of it, and the glass had an etching of… was that a pomegranate? He could feel the heat coming off it.

He used his sleeve. Inside the frosted glass dome was a naked, pale-blue flame.

'Gas,' he said.

'Huh?'

'It's a gas lamp.' Josh carefully replaced the glass. 'There's a power cut all over the village. No lights anywhere.'

'Yeah, I noticed that. I didn't think they got storms like this here.'

'They don't,' Josh said. 'Siena, if there's a power cut all over the village, how are you watching TV?'

Siena went very still with her mug halfway to her lips. Then she shrugged. 'They must have a generator. It's pretty remote out here.'

A generator just for a TV in a birthing suite they just happened to have ready?

Josh sat down on a wooden chair and tried hard to remember. There had been a portrait of Essie's mother hanging above the stairs. He'd assumed she was an actress in costume, but now the painting was empty of people, and the woman with the disturbingly direct stare was in this very house, having some kind of tense argument with Essie.

There had been doors that contained whirlwinds. A step that would send him into the middle of next week. A cat that seemed to converse with Essie, and some elderly relative who knew the results of the test cricket in advance.

Josh had encountered test cricket on the television. He was still unsure if it was all an English prank.

There had been a huge conservatory, bursting with lush green life, the air heady and fragrant with fecundity. And the parrots that appeared to be made of glass but didn't realise it. He remembered that pretty clearly. The plants had been horny, which in itself was really damn weird.

Do not meddle in the affairs of witches.

She'd brushed off his comment about Wiccans. Josh remembered those girls at school, wafting around with flowers in their hair and lots of pentacle jewellery. They'd been big into scented candles and incense sticks, probably to hide the smell of weed.

They hadn't been anything like Essie and her friends.

'I don't like this,' he said.

'But she worked so hard painting all those individual grapes,' said Siena, and Josh blinked at her a couple of times before he realised she was still talking about that damn pottery show.

'Siena, there is something very strange about this house. Can't you feel it?'

But Siena was prevented from answering by the howl that shook the whole house and made every hair on his body stand on end.

The ritual had to be done outside. That was the simple way of it. Most years, the weather was perfectly pleasant for the time of year: a little chilly, but dry. Sometimes a light drizzle. Nothing the right protective clothing couldn't cope with.

The weather this year would have defeated an armoured tank.

The witches stood in a rough circle with Essie at the centre, the rain blowing in from every conceivable angle, and even some that weren't. They had dressed the circle with mistletoe taken from the oldest tree on Midsummer Common, and holly from the ancient church. It nestled on boughs of yew cut from the tree that had witnessed the magistrates court held in the upper rooms of the inn, the same court that had sentenced Prudence to her death.

Essie had changed into a white dress, the colour of snow and ice, and Avery had quickly fashioned her a crown of the greenery they had collected. White for ice. Red for blood. Green for renewal.

She knew, as she'd always known, that all of these things were props. That no matter how much she scoffed at Josh's Wiccans for their scented candles and silver jewellery, her greenery was just a different kind of accessory. But just as the words were a vehicle to deliver her intent, so the dress and the greenery were props to set the scene.

There were no candles, scented or otherwise. Even the witches would have had a job keeping them lit in this weather.

'Bind the creature,' said her mother, her eyes blazing emeralds in the darkness of the storm. 'Use your will to lock it in slumber.'

Oh yeah, and some kind of ancient evil monster was about to rise and kill them all or accelerate global warming or really mess up Good Winter's record of white Christmases or something.

When this is over, Mother, you and I are going to have a hell of a talk.

Essie took a deep breath, which nearly drowned her, and raised her arms.

'I call on winter to rise from the earth. I call on snow to

darken the sky. I call on ice to still the water. I call you by mistle, and holly, and yew. I call you by the force of my own will.'

She felt the cold rising from the earth. She'd always loved that feeling, the ice cooling her veins, spreading like crystals over her skin. Winter brought sleep, renewal, peace. And no one was better at bringing it in than Essie.

As a child she'd enjoyed the snowflakes. As a teen she'd understood the winter must be welcomed.

And only now, after decades of bringing in the winter, had anybody bothered to tell her about the ancient freaking evil below the earth!

But now she knew about it, Essie felt it, waking from its slumber and raging beneath. How had she never felt it before? Never felt the rage, the sheer murderous heat of its hatred? This was an ancient evil, and it wanted to kill.

The thought crossed her mind that there was little wonder she'd been so out of sorts lately, before she forced herself to concentrate.

'Come ice and snow and hear my words. I call you with the force of my will!'

She was shouting the words above the howling storm. The rain that stung her face was hard as ice.

'Come blessed winter, sacred dark, come cherished sleep and soothe the earth!'

Something wasn't right. The rain should have ceased by now and turned to softly falling flakes of snow. The ground should be frosted, not sodden and squelching. The sky was lit with the constant, sickly yellow flashes of lightning, and thunder boomed so loud it drowned her words.

'I call the winter with the force of my will!' Essie roared. 'Come sacred ice and bind the evil that sleeps below!'

The ground trembled. From the corner of her eye, Essie saw Avery and Prudence exchange a glance.

'Come sacred ice and bind the evil!' Essie screamed again. With her outstretched hands, she desperately beckoned the other witches to join in. 'Come sacred ice and bind the evil!'

They began to repeat it with her, and Essie felt the spell begin to take hold. The cold rose up through her, turning her to ice, and then spread out around her. The ground crystallised, spikes of ice growing rapidly outwards, and the familiar cold calm settled in Essie's veins.

The ground shook again. Essie concentrated harder, chilling and calming it. The cold flowed through her body and into the ground, soothing the ancient evil, binding it—

'Bind the evil that sleeps below!' she screamed.

This time the tremor knocked her off balance. Essie fell to one knee, squelching in the mud, and yelled the words louder.

She felt the sound before she heard it. A great keening wail, like the howl of a wolf but with a serrated edge. It sawed at her nerves.

'Call winter,' she snarled through gritted teeth. 'Force of my will!'

She'd just got back to her feet when the earth rebelled, exploding upwards in a spray of mud and water. Essie felt the force of the creature slam through her, like a hard wind made of needles and fire. And hatred. So very much hatred.

It robbed Essie of speech and breath. For a hideously

long moment all she wanted to do was hurt, to kill, to wreak a painful and terrifying revenge. To inflict dreadful suffering, to be feared and reviled, to grow powerful from hate—

And then it was gone, and Essie stood retching as the thing flew around the circle of witches. She would never be able to describe it. Somewhere between a cloud and a swarm, if a swarm could be made of pain and anger. It glittered blackly, as if absorbing all light, and at the same time oozed like a pustulent wound. It knocked them all to the ground, until it reached Prudence, and then the dark and terrible cloud developed a mouth and laughed. Prudence, who had no corporeal body. Prudence, whose soul it could absorb.

'No!' shouted Essie, and threw herself at it. This time it was like the wasps went through her, stinging and buzzing as they did, and she screamed. The creature screamed.

'What the *fuck*?' came a voice from the house, and she looked over, panting, to see Josh in the doorway.

The creature turned, interest flowing in Josh's direction, as if it had found a much more interesting kind of prey.

Its voice arrived in her head like a migraine. '*Hopkinnsss…*'

'Josh, run!' she gasped. 'Run!'

She made it to her feet, retching and coughing, and stumbled towards him. 'Go. Inside. The house will protect…'

But would it? She didn't even know as she ran towards him, pushing past the creature. It didn't seem interested in her anymore, which was just as well as she put all her remaining energy into blasting it with binding ice.

That slowed it down long enough for her to push Josh inside. The others could take care of themselves, but he was vulnerable, and she had to protect him.

'Go! Run!'

'What is that thing?' Josh yelled, as he ran towards the stairs.

'Evil!' She didn't know what to do. It had never escaped before, ever. How could they contain it? Where could they run to? 'Where are you going?'

'Siena!'

'It's following you! Go back—'

But he was halfway up already, and there was nothing for it but to chase him, and turn and try to slow down the creature as it oozed evilly after them. It wasn't even rushing. Almost as if it was playing with them.

'Don't go to Siena's room,' Essie yelled as she raced after Josh. He hesitated at the top of the stairs. 'Turn left! Turn left!'

Maybe she could send it to the conservatory, and one of Blessing's plants would eat it. Maybe trap it in the library. There was always the middle of next week—

Heat suddenly shot through Essie like a thousand hot knives, and she went to her knees as the creature flowed through her. She thought she heard it laughing.

And then it was swarming towards Josh, backing him into a corner, and Essie forced herself forward.

'By my will I bind you,' she snarled, or at least tried to. It came out as more of a whimper. She watched in horror as

Josh flattened himself against the wall, and as she ran towards him his groping hand found a door handle.

'No,' she began, but she had no breath left to shout as she threw herself at the creature, which threw itself at Josh, just as the door opened.

The three of them fell through it.

Chapter Eleven

Josh opened his eyes to sunlight, the pleasant sound of birdsong, and the even more pleasant sensation of Essie in his arms.

Pleasant but very confusing, since a moment ago he'd been running for his life from a special effect. The… *thing*, buzzing and cackling like a swarm of malevolence, that had passed straight through Essie and come for him.

'Where'd it go?'

He tried to sit up, but Essie was sprawled on top of him. 'Essie?'

He was lying in long grass that smelled of summer. A butterfly fluttered overhead. The sky was blue, with a few wispy clouds. There was nothing here to suggest the hideous creature was still around.

'Mmm?'

'Are you okay?'

She stirred against him, which Josh tried not to enjoy. Essie, as he remembered from that single kiss several weeks ago, was round and soft in all the right places. Her dress was damp and clung to her curves. Her vivid hair was drying into curls that tickled his chin.

She lifted her head, and her eyes were a greener green than Josh had ever imagined. Her gaze travelled over his face, and for a moment lingered on his lips. Then she cleared her throat and rolled away, a blush stealing over her cheeks.

'Yeah,' she said. She cleared her throat again. 'Yep. Yeah. Fine. Are you?'

Josh sat up. 'I think so.' He looked around. They were in a summer meadow, all long grass and wildflowers. A small wood was visible in the near distance. Some hedgerows. Very little else.

A buzzing sound made him flinch, but it was just a fat bumblebee coming into land on a tall flower nearby.

Several questions chased themselves across his mind, but the one that made it to his mouth was, 'What the hell just happened?'

Essie sat up, brushing herself off. Her dress was white, and not as opaque as it might have been. Josh ordered his eyes not to linger below her collarbone.

Essie took off her rain-stained glasses and attempted to clean them on her dress. 'At a guess,' she said, popping the smeared glasses back on and looking around the meadow, 'we went through Lilith's door.'

Right. All the crazy doors in her house. Josh had thought he must have dreamed them, or exaggerated their effects in his mind. Or maybe she'd drugged him.

He looked around exaggeratedly. The meadow was entirely empty of doors. 'Okay. Where to start here?'

Essie sat up, and looked around carefully, like a meerkat. Then she turned back to Josh and said, 'There probably isn't any point in pretending any more, is there?'

'Pretending about what?' said Josh.

She gave him a frank look. 'Listen, I can't see anyone, but I'm going to need to keep this conversation quiet in case there's anyone listening because I don't know exactly when and where we are. Okay? Right. Well… we're witches.'

This did not have the effect on Josh that she appeared to be expecting. 'I got that part,' he said. 'You told me on the way to your house this… yest…' He looked up at the bright sunny sky. 'Recently.'

'I don't mean like burning herbs and fannying about dancing in the nude,' she said, and as Josh battled against that image in his head she went on, 'I mean we're real witches. We do things ordinary people can't. Like… I can understand animals, sort of. I can make a fire start at will. I can put one out, too,' she added quickly. 'Every witch is different. We all have things we specialise in.'

Josh figured he might as well go along with this, if only to stop himself thinking about her dancing in the nude. There were various bits of Essie he was sure would jiggle delightfully.

'Such as?' he managed.

'Well…' Essie fiddled with the long blades of grass nearby. 'Maude – you haven't met her, I don't think – she knits the future. By which I mean what she knits shows the future, like tea leaves or something. Texeomancy, she calls it. None of us have ever been sure if what she does actually… affects the future. After a while, it's impolite to ask.'

'I guess it is,' said Josh, for the want of anything else. He watched Essie begin to plait the grass.

'And Avery specialises in illusion and perception. And also manifesting inner desires. Haven't you noticed that sometimes they're very masculine and sometimes very feminine and usually somewhere in between?'

Now that she mentioned it, Josh had. But he hadn't really remembered it until now. Which was weird, really, because it was the sort of thing he supposed would usually stick in a person's mind.

'But you probably don't remember, because Avery is also very good at making people think they've seen something entirely different to what they have seen. Most people in the village think they're twins.'

'Both called Avery?'

Essie shrugged. 'Like I said, people forget. Also, I think most people just sort of… rewrite the bits that don't make sense. You tell yourself you can't have seen what you think you've seen, and then go about your day. You know?'

Josh raised his eyebrows. 'You mean, like I couldn't have seen that mad buzzing cloud thing that chased me up the stairs? Where did it go, anyway?'

Essie frowned a little. 'I don't know. It followed us in here. Or… out here. And then I'm afraid…' She looked a little embarrassed. 'I might have fainted. I've never travelled through time before.'

Josh nodded, and went on nodding as he tried to work out what to say to that. 'Haven't you?' he said.

'Not that I recall. But that's what Lilith's door does. It goes to a different time and place. She's the only one who can control it really, and even then it's sort of erratic.' She snorted. 'You know how we say some people live in the past?'

'Yeah?'

'With her it's literal. Still, it's handy for making investments. You wouldn't believe what Apple stock is worth these days.'

Josh rubbed his face again. They were sitting here in a pleasant meadow talking about time travel as if everything was perfectly normal and they hadn't just been chased by a haunted swarm of wasps.

'Okay,' he said. 'So. You're a witch—'

'Voice down!' she hissed. 'I don't know when we are yet. Unless you see an aeroplane up there,' she jabbed a finger at the blue sky, which was entirely free of jet trails, 'consider "witch" to be a dangerous word.'

He nodded. 'Sure. Why not. And we've just… fallen through a door into another century, right?'

'Possibly.'

'And a different place,' he added, because they had definitely been inside before.

'Ye-es. Unless this is before the house was built.'

'Then we'd have fallen down a storey,' pointed out Josh, because he felt logic might help, 'and I don't feel bruised enough for that.'

'Good point. Well, Mother uses the door for place as well

as time. She spent half my childhood in 1930s Berlin, trying to kill Hitler.'

Josh felt his eyebrows go up. 'Did she succeed?'

Essie's features lapsed into sarcasm. 'Did you learn about the Holocaust at school?'

'Of course.'

'Then I'd say she failed.' Essie sighed. 'The working theory is that some things just can't be changed. She tried pretty much everything. Right back to his childhood and beyond. Tried killing his mother, but even for Lilith, pushing an innocent child in front of a horse is a bit much. So she gave up, and put her efforts into other things.'

'Such as?'

'Well, have you ever heard of the Franco–British War of 1858?'

'Uh, no.'

'There you are then.'

Josh rubbed his eyes. 'Look, this is all fascinating, but what's really happening here?'

Essie looked annoyed. She got up, her damp dress clinging to her in interesting ways, and gestured around. 'What do you think? Do you have a better explanation for this? We were inside the house, and now we're – oh, bollocks.'

'What?' But Josh could hear it too. People talking and giggling. The hedgerow parted, and through it burst a young man and woman in very strange clothing.

'More costume drama?' he muttered, although he was very much beginning to doubt this was the case.

Essie looked him over, and then herself, and swore under her breath.

'I don't know when we are,' she hissed, dropping to her knees, 'but your clothes will not pass muster and I look like I'm wearing a nightie.'

Josh looked down at himself. He wore the dark jeans and t-shirt and plaid shirt he'd had on all day. The denim was still slightly damp from running around in the rain earlier.

He looked up at the couple loitering at the edge of the meadow, kissing hungrily. She had on a long, full skirt, and a sort of jacket thing that came to her hips, and a linen cap covering her hair. Her swain – he'd never used that word before, but there was no doubt it fit – had on a short coat, tightly buttoned up with a lacy collar showing at the top, and some form of… culottes was the closest word Josh could think of. He also appeared to be wearing ladies' woollen tights, and a tall, brimmed hat.

Josh looked back helplessly at Essie.

'We could say we were robbed?' she offered.

'And they took our clothes? And left me with… I don't know, when were jeans invented?' Was he really agreeing with her that they'd travelled through time?

'Not whenever this is,' she said. They both peered over the long grass at the trysting couple, who were starting to dispense with bits of their clothing.

'I guess it looks kinda like the first Thanksgiving,' said Josh, trying not to blush.

'Lot of making out went on at the first Thanksgiving, did

it?' Essie snapped. Her cheeks were pink. 'Remind me what year that was?'

'Uh, 1620, uh, something,' Josh said vaguely, trying not to stare as the girl's corset came into view. 'Holy shit.'

'Well, we can use that as a baseline,' said Essie. 'Um. You know there's really going to be only one way to do this, don't you?'

'Do what?' said Josh, although he was beginning to suspect he knew.

Essie smelled of pine, and the sharp scent of snow, and of smoke even though there was no fire nearby.

'Explain what we're wearing. Or not wearing. Um. Remember how we kissed that one time?' she asked, as if it was of very little importance and not something Josh thought about whenever he looked at her mouth.

'I mean, I guess,' he said as offhandedly as he could.

'Well,' said Essie, with a meaningful look. She took off her plastic-framed glasses. 'Take your shirt off.'

He gaped at her.

She wants to fake kiss. Not a real kiss. She didn't want to actually make out with him. Josh tried frantically to think of another way to get out of this as disappointment crushed him.

Essie glanced frantically over her shoulder. 'Look, I'm sorry, this isn't exactly how I wanted to start kissing you again, but unless you can conjure up doublet and hose from somewhere it's all I can think of.'

And the sun suddenly came out for Josh Henderson. He felt himself smile. 'You want to start kissing me again?'

'Oh, so that's the relevant part of the conversation here,'

muttered Essie, and then her mouth was on his and her hands were pushing at his shirt and Josh didn't even try to resist.

He kissed her back enthusiastically, which seemed to surprise her, and he felt her lips curve against his as her eyes sparkled. She cupped his face in her hand and slipped her thigh over his.

Oh boy, she felt good. Last time Josh had kissed her both of them had been fully dressed with jackets on, and now she was wearing a damp dress with not a lot under it. He allowed his hand to slip around to her back, and Essie made a pleased sound and pressed herself against him.

Oh well, if that was the way it was going to go…

He stopped thinking about things and just did what he wanted to. Which was to touch Essie, a lot, to explore her lush curves with both hands and get as much of her body pressed tight against his as he could. Her legs wrapped around him, and his fingers touched her bare thigh as her skirt rode up.

He liked the sound she made when he stroked her there, so he did it again. Her own hands were making short work of his t-shirt, her cool fingers leaving behind trails of shivering goosebumps. She kissed his neck, sucked gently on his earlobe, and made him whimper when her fingers brushed his nipple.

'Josh,' she breathed, and even the way she said his name was a turn-on. Then she was kissing him again, and Josh forgot everything but sensation.

'Devilry!' someone suddenly shouted, and Essie froze.

The fear that came into her eyes was nothing to do with

being caught half-naked and well on the way to becoming fully naked.

'He has tempted thee to licentiousness! Repent! Repent!'

'Papa-a,' lamented a female voice, and Essie unfroze just a tiny bit.

'We mean no harm by it,' said the young man. They both sounded terribly close by. 'We both will take hands by the church soon enough.'

'And will the church cast thee out?' thundered the voice of the girl's father. 'For fornicating with others in the broad light of day?'

'Others?' said the girl, bewildered.

Josh's eyes met Essie's. It wasn't hard. They were about an inch away.

She cleared her throat and sat up.

'Um,' she said, and waved at the dishevelled lovers a few yards away. 'I don't suppose you'd believe we were robbed?'

Essie had heard of people being run out of town, but never into it. She and Josh were herded like errant sheep into the village, trailed by the two young lovers who had taken the opportunity to gain the moral high ground, because at least they both still had their clothes. Even if they hadn't exactly been wearing them when the girl's father found them.

'Fornicators!' the older man shouted. He wore a short cloak and a hat with a tall crown, and his doublet was too short and strained across his belly. But the sword he carried looked quite real, and he was using it to prod them ahead of him along a track beside the hedgerow. Essie's wrists had been bound with a belt and Josh's with his own shirt.

'We found them naked,' shouted the young woman.

'Cavorting for all to see!' added her lover.

'Hypocrites,' Essie snapped back at them, and not just because they'd been out gathering nuts in May. Something about that young woman drew her attention. *No wonder she wants to deflect attention. She's got power, I'm sure of it.*

But Essie wasn't about to drop anyone else in it. Her mind raced. What could she do? Her magic was not very useful in this situation, and even if it was she'd be sent straight to the ducking stool.

The village opened up ahead of them, and Essie didn't immediately recognise it, especially since her glasses were lost in the meadow. *That'll be fun for some future archaeologist.* Sheep grazed the open land that sloped down to a large, muddy pond, and the cottages that surrounded it had a distinct air of 'hovel' about them. The road was dried mud, heavily rutted from wheels and hooves. The people who came out of their houses to watch the entertainment wore the same kinds of woollen dresses and doublets as the two lovers who were now decrying them as fornicators.

'Just checking,' Josh muttered, as he trudged along beside her, 'but fornication is bad, right?'

'Not if you do it right,' muttered Essie. *Hah, as if you'd know,* said a spiteful little voice inside her.

'They are ungodly!' shouted the stout man. 'And incite others to join their licentiousness!'

''Tis true,' shouted the younger man. 'They made us join their filthy games.'

'We are but goodly people, and I a maid,' the young woman added hurriedly.

Essie snorted.

'Do you know any Bible verses?' Josh said from the corner of his mouth.

'It may surprise you to know that wasn't high on my mother's list of priorities,' Essie replied.

'Call the witchfinder!' shouted the stout man, and Essie stopped dead.

'The witchfinder?' she said.

His piggy little eyes gleamed malevolently. This was the sort of man, Essie recognised, who was still alive and well in the twenty-first century, complaining to the council about litter louts and young people who played their music too loud. Only here and now – whenever now was, and she suspected she had an idea – he had an awful lot more power than merely complaining.

'Oh aye,' he said, waving his sword at her. 'For he be nearby in the Rodings.'

'Shit,' Essie said. Panic lanced through her. The Rodings were a collection of villages and hamlets less than ten miles away from Good Winter, assuming that the vaguely unfamiliar surroundings actually were her own village. 'Fuck.' How long would it take someone to cover ten miles in the seventeenth century? 'Bugger.'

'Be thou a witch?' thundered the stout man, and Essie tried to summon her most withering scorn.

But Josh got there first. 'Of course not,' he said, in such

reasonable tones the stout man wavered. 'My wife told you we had been robbed.'

'Wife?' said the younger woman.

'Yes. They took our jewellery,' said Josh.

'And my dress,' Essie said. 'It was an expensive one,' she added, when the onlookers looked sceptical.

'But you are dressed most strange,' said the younger man, waving at Josh's t-shirt and jeans.

'Well,' he said, and glanced at Essie. 'Yes. But I put it to you—'

'He's—' Essie began, and desperately tried to remember her history. America had probably been settled for about five minutes. Scottish? No, probably a war on. Dutch? Maybe. French? Almost definitely a war on. 'Irish,' she said. 'They wear different clothes. Because of the… rain.'

'Uh-huh,' said Josh, and attempted a smile. 'Top of the—'

'No,' said Essie, kicking his ankle.

'And we were travelling,' Josh went on, warming to his theme, 'to visit family.'

'What family?' said the stout man suspiciously.

'Good question,' Essie said, shooting Josh an evil look.

'Why, they have come to see me,' said a woman's voice, and the two of them looked up in astonishment as a well-dressed woman pushed her way through the crowd. Her gown was made of some kind of brocade, and the large collar covering her shoulders was several inches deep in lace. Her hair was dressed in ringlets and her eyes were shrewd.

Her dress, Essie realised, was more or less a blue version of the red one her mother had appeared in.

'We have?' Josh said.

'We have,' Essie said firmly. Whatever this woman was offering had to be better than being witch-hunted. 'My dear aunt,' she said, forcing a smile.

'My dear niece,' said the older woman. 'All the way from Ireland to meet with such villainy! To be robbed and then paraded naked through the streets.' She tutted. 'You will untie them at once,' she said to the stout man.

'But what if they be witches?' he said.

'They were fornicating,' said his daughter, without looking at her lover.

The woman in the blue dress said, 'Ha! Stuff and nonsense. Do not fall prey to those tricksters, Master Godwin! For they will take all our coin in promise to root out evil and, having taken it, determine to find what they seek. ''Tis a devilry of its own. Put up thy sword, and release my kinswoman, or you will be paying the witchfinder, and you still owe me the quarter's rent.'

Stuff and nonsense. Essie peered at the woman as Master Godwin gestured reluctantly for their wrists to be unbound. She couldn't be an ancestor of Agatha Cropley, could she?

'Now, you will come along of me,' said the forthright woman, 'and these good people will go about their business, and we will have no more of this un-Christian nonsense. For shame, Master Godwin,' she added, and Essie fancied her eyelid flickered in a wink as she swept them away.

Essie waited until they were out of earshot, striding

across the Common, before she said, 'Uh, my thanks to you, madam. Do you, er, know us?'

The woman snorted. 'Nay, but I will wager I know thy kinswoman. Be you her sister? Cousin?'

Essie exchanged a glance with Josh, who looked utterly lost.

'Would you be speaking of Lilith?' she ventured.

'Aye! You look much like her. The hair, the eyes.' The woman stopped and peered at Essie in a penetrating manner. 'The chin. You will take no nonsense either, I see.'

'Well, I try not to,' said Essie, running to keep up as the woman set off again. 'I, er, didn't catch your name?'

'Mistress Hopkins,' said the woman. 'Of Brook Manor. But you may call me Agatha.'

Chapter Twelve

Essie had, by virtue of arguing that they were newlyweds, managed to stick with Josh. He was grateful for this, because so far the seventeenth century was proving both terrifying and confusing.

Mistress Agatha had confirmed the year to be 1647, which had made Essie's mouth set in a grim line. The older woman didn't seem perturbed by being asked for the date, remarking that Mistress Winterscale often needed reminding.

'This is where my mother's been,' Essie hissed as they were shown to a room in Mistress Agatha's mansion. 'She must have given up on Robespierre and gone after Matthew Hopkins again.'

'Who?' said Josh. The mansion wasn't quite what he'd expected, being little larger than his own house and mostly comprised of small, oppressively dark rooms that all ran into each other. The maid they followed past dark carved panelling and gloomy tapestries had pockmarked skin and missing teeth.

Mistress Agatha had led them briskly out of the village to Brook Manor, a large building made of brick and decorative timbers. Josh had tried in vain to see which part of it might be the crumbling wall that remained in the twenty-first century as part of the border to a field, but given the lack of ivy growing over it and winter barley in the background, he'd been unable to place it. His own house wouldn't have been built yet, and that was an even stranger thought.

'I'll tell you in a – oh, lovely, is this us?' said Essie, as they were shown into a room with a towering four-poster bed. It had thick, heavily carved pillars supporting an even more carved canopy, and more carving on the head and footboards. The drapes looked as if they could withstand a small siege.

'My mistress begs ye will take fresh linen and doth sort her clothes for lending,' said the maid. At least, Josh guessed that was what she said. Her accent was thick, and she mumbled through rotten teeth. She bobbed a curtsey and left through another door.

Essie shut it behind her, and leaned against it.

'Holy shit,' she said.

Josh found himself nodding vigorously. 'Yeah. Exactly.' He sat down on an ornately carved wooden chair that was not remotely comfortable, and said, 'What the fuck is going on?'

Essie blew out a breath. 'At a guess? Lilith has come here to try to kill Matthew Hopkins, which she does when she's bored, and has befriended Mistress Agatha here in the course of it. Mistress Agatha Hopkins,' she added, with a significant look at Josh.

'You can't be suggesting she's my ancestor,' he said, as Essie straightened and went over to the window to peer out. The panes were tiny, diamond-shaped lumps of thick glass welded together with lead, and gave very little view of the outside world. 'Hopkins is a pretty common name.'

Essie sighed. 'Sure it is,' she said, 'but it's also the name of one of the most prolific serial killers in English history, a man with a particular grudge against witches, who happened to also be a lawyer and who, oh yes, I had a premonition about the day you walked into my life. You,' she advanced on him, 'Josh Hopkins Henderson, who seems to have some resistance to the perception spell on Beldam House that makes everyone else forget it even exists.'

'I really don't remember it well,' Josh began.

'You inherited a house with an ancient witch ball hanging in the window, which just happened to break almost immediately, whereupon you bled all over the parchment inside it, and then somehow forgot to send me the photo of it you promised.'

'I…' He had forgotten. 'I was busy?'

Essie made a sound like a game show when a contestant gets the wrong answer. 'I don't suppose there's the remotest chance you have your phone on you right now?'

Josh felt his pockets, then closed his eyes. 'No. It's in my jacket in Siena's room.' His eyes flew open. 'Oh my god, Siena. Do you think she's all right?'

'She won't be born for three hundred and fifty years. Concentrate. There are too many coincidences here, Josh. The day you turn up in my life I have a premonition of the world ending because of the lawyer, son of Hob. The ritual I have done every autumn without a hitch suddenly fails and it turns out there is an ancient evil lurking beneath the earth that I have to bind with the winter. An evil that has just broken free in the form of a swarm of bees or something. And do you know what it said when it came after you?' Josh shook his head, mutely terrified. 'Hopkins. Meanwhile we end up in the heart of witchfinding country in the final year of Matthew Hopkins's reign of terror, in the company of a woman who shares both his name and yours. Now I ask you, again, do you really think any of this is a coincidence?'

Josh swallowed. Essie was leaning over him now, and her eyes blazed green.

'Who is Matthew Hopkins?' he breathed.

'He is the self-proclaimed witchfinder general,' said Essie. 'He takes advantage of a desperate, fearful and war-torn country to torture and murder hundreds of people in the name of God. For profit. He is a mass murderer, and a psychopath, and he is about ten miles away from us right now.'

'And you're a witch,' croaked Josh.

'And you're his descendant,' said Essie.

Mistress Agatha had clothes sent to them, which proved so complex neither Essie nor Josh could get into them without help. After the manservant had finished with Josh, the poor guy looked traumatised.

'I am hooked into these clothes,' he hissed to Essie, lifting the tabs at the base of his doublet. There were indeed hooks connecting it to his breeches, which were a baggy sort of knee-length trouser over some long woollen stockings. 'I have no idea how to even take a leak. Or…' he glanced around fearfully, as if the realities of Jacobean plumbing were only just dawning on him, 'where.'

'Oh please, come back when your clothing contains whalebone,' said Essie. 'I am wearing four hundred layers here.'

The clothes looked clean enough, but they had a faint smell of ammonia that made Josh wrinkle his nose. Essie found it weirdly comforting, however, and she couldn't figure out why. Sometimes her mother's clothes smelled of it, but Essie had never found any particular comfort from her mother.

The maid had offered them water to wash their faces, but seemed to think no more than that was required even when Essie was covered in mud. Instead, she had rubbed Essie down with a linen cloth, vigorously, as if she was a horse, and then dressed her in layers of clothing that somehow failed to include any knickers. All this had taken place in the same bedroom where Josh was protesting his own invasion of privacy, and the two servants had seemed to find it hilarious that either of them required privacy. Essie had managed to convince them to draw the curtains on the bed and used that as a barrier, but the knowledge that Josh was naked behind it had made her far warmer than the fire.

Their modern clothing was taken away by the mystified servants, who peered in confusion at Essie's underwired bra and exclaimed aloud that the Irish were strange people indeed.

Feeling somewhat draughty, she followed Josh and the dour manservant down to the lower level of the house, where more gloomy panelled rooms were traversed before they stopped in one that held Mistress Agatha.

'Ah,' she said, looking up from an embroidery frame. 'Much more suitable attire. Mistress Lilith does often arrive in the very strangest raiments. What manner of kinswoman is she to you?'

'Lilith?' said Essie. 'She's my mother.'

Agatha laughed delightedly. 'Ah, she enjoys a jest also! Sister, perhaps? Cousin?'

Essie exchanged a look with Josh as they took seats on hard wooden chairs. Both of them were wearing so many layers of clothing, however, that this didn't matter much.

'She does look younger than you'd expect,' he said.

Essie sighed. It was true. Witches tended to age slowly, and Lilith especially had little regard for the usual progression of time. 'Sister,' she agreed, through gritted teeth. 'My older, very bossy sister.'

'She is a woman who knows her mind, which I respect,' said Agatha. 'Such women be afeard to speak their minds in these parts, and so I relish her company. But she did leave under much haste.' She gave Essie an enquiring look.

'Family emergency,' Essie said. 'Which, actually, is why

we're here. Did my m— did Lilith ever mention a house called Beldam House?'

She'd been giving this some thought. If Beldam House existed in 1647, which to the best of her knowledge it did, then surely the time door existed within it? She and Josh might have to contrive a reason to get inside, but once they did then maybe, hopefully, they could get back? Otherwise they were stuck here waiting for her mother to retrieve them.

The possibility that she couldn't or wouldn't do that was simply not something Essie could allow herself to entertain.

'Beldam?' This seemed to amuse Agatha. 'T'would be boldness indeed to name a house such as that in these times! Did not you hear Master Godwin threaten to call the witchfinder?'

The witchfinder. Yes. It had not slipped from Essie's mind.

'I have heard they did hang a witch in High Roding,' said Agatha, looking carefully at them in turn.

'That's terrible,' said Josh.

'Aye. And she no more a witch than you or I,' Agatha said.

'Indeed,' said Essie.

Dust motes danced in the sunlight that came through the leaded panes. The fire crackled in the huge brick fireplace. Outside the room, footsteps made the floorboards creak. None of them spoke.

'I do not hold with the actions of my kinsman,' Agatha said eventually. 'He stokes fear in a town that any small evil is caused by a witch, then charges good coin to rid them of it. In Ipswich, taxes had to be raised to pay for his villainy. For when a man is paid to find a witch, a witch he shall find, aye, and hang. Defenceless women, simple-minded men. Do you know, my house is overrun with mice because I dare not keep a cat for fear of accusation that I consort with it in the name of the Devil?'

'Yeah,' said Josh beside Essie. 'Who would hold a conversation with a cat?'

Essie kicked him from beneath her voluminous skirts.

'Did you say kinsman?' she said.

Agatha sighed. She fiddled with the metal tankard beside her, then took a sip from it. 'Matthew Hopkins,' she said, 'is my kinsman by marriage. He hath turned all else of his family against him, and no wonder. Were I not the widow of his uncle, and raising his ward, I do wonder that he would send me to the gallows.'

'His… ward?' said Josh.

'Aye.' Agatha's expression was wry. 'He is a sweet child, with none of his father's madness. His mother died in the birthing.' The older woman's eyes darkened. 'Hopkins said 'twas the work of a witch, and took the midwife and beat her 'til she confessed to lying with the Devil, when all must know the poor child was scarce old enough to be a mother. Such a man is he, to blame the whole world for the ills he has made. Ye must make certain sure never to cross paths with him, good sir and lady, for if any are touched by the Devil, 'tis Hopkins himself.'

The fire crackled and spat. Outside, there was the distant sound of horses' hooves and tack jingling.

Hopkins had a son. Essie was well-versed enough in

classic literature to know that a 'ward' was usually an illegitimate child. Hopkins had a motherless son, who he'd sent away to be raised by a distant relative while he raced around the place having innocent women tortured and hanged.

'But we must not say so,' Agatha added, shaking herself. 'We must serve God in every good way. Such is the fear of witches in these parts that every cottage has a witch bottle buried 'neath the hearth or over the door.'

'A witch bottle?' said Josh. There were raised voices somewhere else in the house.

'Is that like a witch ball?' said Essie sharply. She leaned forward.

'Aye, like a ball, I suppose. ''Tis all stuff and nonsense. I time and again have chastised the servants for such superstition – what is the commotion?'

She got up, but had barely taken a step when the manservant in his plain doublet opened the door and said apologetically, 'Mistress, there be without a visitor. He claims you harbour witches.'

Essie's stomach clenched, which was an impressive feat given the layers of boned and stiffened clothing restricting it, and felt Josh's hand in hers.

'Stuff and nonsense,' said Agatha stoutly, but the servant was already being swept aside by a man in a very fancy outfit indeed.

He wore a short cloak over one shoulder, and it was trimmed and lined with fur. His doublet had a lot of decoration on it, piping and buttons and lace at the cuffs, and his tall boots had spurs and turnbacks on them. His hat sported a wide brim and a tall crown, and at his hip he carried a sword on a shiny leather belt.

Everything he wore was black, but it was a theatrical black, a fancy black, a black that wanted you to notice how expensive it was.

Essie took all this in, and then she let herself look at his face.

He was young, and that came as a shock. He might even have been handsome, with a small beard and moustache, except for his eyes. His eyes were blue, and blazed with absolute hatred. Essie felt a buzzing in her ears, and saw the witchfinder general turn into a pustulous swarm in front of her eyes—

'Essie?'

Josh caught her as she fell, and she blinked up dazedly into his concerned face. 'Are you all right?'

She couldn't speak. Her mouth and nose were full of the stench of evil.

'She can't breathe,' said Josh. 'Loosen her clothing. Help me!'

Agatha hurried to her side and began unfastening the ties at the front of Essie's bodice. Josh laid her down on the floor, which was the only flat surface around, and tugged at the lace collar around her neck.

'I will not be swayed by thy pretence,' said the witchfinder. To Essie, his voice was the buzz of a hacksaw.

'You scared her to death,' snapped Josh. 'Essie? Can you hear me?'

She nodded, and took in a breath. The air stank of rotten meat. 'I'm all right.'

'The innocent have nothing to fear of me,' said the witchfinder. 'Such a swoon is proof of guilt.'

'Nay, or every woman with her bodice laced too tight would be a witch,' snapped Agatha.

'Licentiousness is the work of the Devil,' replied the witchfinder. His face appeared above her, and Essie's hand clutched Josh's. 'See how she bares her flesh to tempt me?'

'I did that so she could breathe,' Josh said.

'Then you are her accomplice! You were right, Master Godwin, they are a pair.'

'I'm not an accomplice to anything,' Josh said. He seemed to attempt a smile. 'Listen, I'm sure we can sort this all out if we—'

But the witchfinder ignored him, and thundered, 'Be thou a witch?'

'I'm really not,' said Josh.

'I say thou art. Take them from this place,' he said to someone in the doorway, and booted feet sounded on the flagstones.

'Good sir, I beg of you,' said Agatha. 'She is my kinswoman, and a God-fearing soul, and—'

Hopkins smacked her across the cheek and both Essie and Josh sucked in a breath. Agatha rocked on her feet and said nothing.

'The assizes can try two, or they can try three,' the witchfinder said softly. 'You are of use while you rear the whelp, but it does not have to be so.'

'Sir, they are not witches,' Agatha said quietly.

'Then they will be proven innocent. Come, to Godwin's house. His cellars are stout.'

Essie wanted to fight, she really did, but the presence of Hopkins made her feel so sick she could do very little but be led, half-dragged, from the room, with Josh's protests ringing in her ears. They were tied by the wrists to the saddle of Hopkins' horse, and led through the village, across the common, so everyone could see them.

And then they turned up a narrow, sunken lane lined by trees, and Essie suddenly felt laughter bubble up inside her.

'What's so funny?' said Josh.

'I know where we are,' said Essie. She nodded at the tall stone building looming ahead of her. 'Beldam House will always be found by those who need it.'

Chapter Thirteen

'So,' said Josh, pacing up and down. 'To summarise: Beldam House is currently called Godwin House, and is owned by a man who really doesn't like us and called in the witchfinder general, who is my ancestor by way of an illegitimate child, who is being raised by an ancestor of Agatha Cropley who left her house to my father, and who also seems to own this house.'

'I think so,' said Essie.

'The witchfinder has locked us in this cellar while he sits at banquet with his buddies, in advance of taking us to Chelmsford assizes – which are the court sessions?' he queried.

'Again, I think so. Although Prudence was tried by the local magistrates,' said Essie. She knelt on the floor, her hands feeling at cracks between the stones.

'Prudence? Your housemate Prudence? In the…' Josh stopped pacing as he realised. 'Is she a time traveller too?'

'Prudence? No. She was hanged in the mid-eighteenth century though. About a hundred years from now. Only she decided to stick around.'

Josh stared at her. 'She's a ghost?'

'Sort of. Sometimes she's quite solid. Mind out if you walk through the woods on Gallows Lane though,' Essie said. 'Sometimes I come across her literally hanging out. I mean, I don't think anyone else has ever seen her there, but… you can remember things about us, Josh. I wonder why that might be.'

She looked up at him with a calculating expression.

'I swear to God I have no—'

'Seriously? Josh, come on. Can't you feel it? Hopkins is the monster. That thing that chased us back in our own time? It's him. He's the thing the witches bound in ice all… those… years… holy shit.'

'What?'

Essie stared at her own hands. 'All this time I thought we were doing a ritual to welcome the winter in, and nothing more. Like dancing round a maypole or something. And now I find it's actually a binding ritual, only no one ever told me this, and my ancestors have done it for centuries to bind an ancient evil below the earth.'

'About this ancient evil,' Josh began, but Essie wasn't finished.

'Only it wasn't started by my ancestors, was it? It was started by me.' She looked up at him. 'I bound him in ice. Me. I did it.' She laughed mirthlessly. 'I thought it was something that had always been done, since the beginning of time, but Hopkins is the monster and the reason I have to do it is because I always did it.'

'You're losing me,' Josh said.

'I'm the one who stops him. Don't you see? Hopkins had a really short reign of terror, and it ended in 1647 shortly before his death.'

'You're going to kill him?' said Josh. So the guy was evil, anybody could tell that – but was she really going to try to kill him?

'I'm going to stop him,' Essie said firmly. 'Josh, he isn't human. Not any more. He's so full of anger and hate, it's destroyed whatever soul he had.' She knelt up, and reached out to him. Josh took her hand reluctantly. 'You know those people who snap and go mad and take a gun into church? He's like that. In our era he'd be some kind of terrorist. He's wound up on hatred and rage.'

'Well, even I can see that,' said Josh, because it was clear the man was a sadist. 'But why witches?'

Essie shrugged. 'Easy target. People have hated witches for a very long time. Trust me on this. At this point in history, we've had a hundred years of religious warfare and bishops being burnt at the stake for being the wrong kind of Christian, and now we're in a state of civil war that will result in the king being beheaded in a couple of years' time, and people are afraid. They're uneducated, they only know what they're told and they're too scared to question it. And then you get someone like Hopkins, a con man with incel tendencies, who sees an opportunity for his hatred of women to be weaponised. For profit.'

Josh gazed at the dark, dank walls of the cellar. They'd

been left a candle, and a small amount of light came in through the high windows as the sun began to set.

'Four hundred years and nothing changes,' he muttered. 'Okay, so how do we stop him?'

'We don't. I do.'

Her face was determined. Her hair had long since fallen out of the style Agatha's maid had attempted to put it into, and the lace collar that had covered the low neckline of her dress had been left behind. Her bosom – there was no other word for it – heaved.

Maybe it was the impending danger, but Josh had never wanted a woman more in his life.

'How?' he managed, and Essie smiled.

'Remember I said most witches have a speciality?' He nodded. And suddenly noticed his hands were becoming very cold. Very cold, very quickly. Gasping, he pulled them back, and shoved them under his arms.

Essie looked smug. 'Now imagine what I can do to Hopkins.'

They decided to wait until the house had settled down for the night, which wasn't hard to determine because the house creaked with every footstep. Doors slammed and voices called out, and frequently, a light showed under the edge of the cellar door as someone came down to listen at it. All they had to do was wait until all activity ceased.

Essie had heard that Hopkins employed sleep deprivation on his victims, and also that he liked to find a 'devil's mark' and prick it with a pin to see if it felt pain or not. Since she was covered in freckles, she wasn't really looking forward to this. Best to head it off at the pass.

She had never used her powers to hurt anyone before. At least, not on purpose. But Hopkins was a monster, and had to be stopped.

She told herself that, and almost believed it.

Beside her, Josh suddenly laughed.

'What?'

He looked down at his woollen stockings and baggy breeches. 'Go to England, they said. See the historic sights, they said. Well, I'm seeing them now.'

Essie smiled. 'Yep, it's a highly immersive experience.'

'I don't recommend the hospitality though.'

'No, or the catering.'

There wasn't a lot of light now. The summer sun had eventually set, and their candle was guttering out. Essie leaned against Josh in the gloom.

'Why did you come to England?' she said.

'I inherited the house.'

'Yeah, but… you could have sold it. Rented it out. You didn't have to live in it.'

Josh sighed. 'I… there wasn't a lot for me in Seattle anymore.'

'Oh?'

It was a leading question. She quite expected to be told to mind her own business. Josh was silent for a long while.

Eventually he said, 'I told you who my father was. Back in… in the storm. You asked his name.'

'Hopkins.'

'Yeah. Edward Mason Hopkins.'

Essie shrugged. The name rang a very vague bell, but she didn't know where from.

'You really don't know who he was?'

'Should I?'

Josh's shoe scraped on the ground as he shifted his weight restlessly. 'When he died,' he said, 'he was the forty-third richest man in America.'

Essie turned towards the pale shape of his face. 'Seriously?'

'Seriously. The bulk of it going to Siena, mostly in assets, with hefty bequests for his second and third wives, a couple of cousins, various friends.'

Essie didn't know how much wealth the forty-third richest man in America might have, but she suspected it was an eye-watering amount. And yet Josh had barely been able to afford a new roof until Siena moved in.

Her curiosity itched like a rash.

'My mother got nothing. I used to be angry about that.'

'Used to?'

Josh sighed. 'My parents met in college. She was the daughter of blue-collar workers and scraped herself up by her bootstraps. He inherited wealth and enjoyed slumming it. I guess opposites attract, at least for long enough to get married and have a kid. And then, probably sometime around the rent being due and the baby teething, he got tired of slumming it and went back to the warm, loving bosom of his billionaire family.'

'Leaving you and your mother to fend for yourselves?'

Josh's fingers plucked at the lace on her sleeve. 'That's

what I always believed. My mother loved to tell me how my father's family had tried to pay her off, but she said no, because money isn't everything. She told me that so many times I almost believed it. She said she didn't need his money, which left me with the impression he'd never offered her any.'

'An impression that was proven wrong?' Essie guessed.

'You know when you're a kid, and you just accept what your parents say, and it's only much later on you realise something doesn't add up?'

Essie looked around the dank cellar as it sank into darkness. 'Speaking as someone whose mother spent most of her time in a different century,' she said drily, 'please tell me more.'

'Right. I guess… sure.'

'What did you mother lie to you about?'

Josh made a sound that was almost a laugh. 'Do all parents lie?'

'Seems like it.'

Josh said, 'I put myself through law school. Scholarships, second and third jobs, ramen noodles for dinner. It was hard. I spent all of it resenting my father, who could have paid for it all. And my mom always said, look what you've achieved all by yourself, you don't need him. Until she got sick and… and I did need him.'

Essie, who had grown up with the NHS on hand if she should ever need it, said, 'Medical bills?'

'You have no idea. The numbers were terrifying. Even with insurance, she'd be in debt for the rest of her life.

Assuming she even lived long enough… and she was my mom, you know? I couldn't let her just…'

Essie squeezed his arm. She could write the book on difficult mothers, but she understood nonetheless.

'I know,' she said.

'So I did the only thing I could think of. I had an address for him, you see. He'd reached out when I graduated high school, offered to buy me a car. I said no, being the proud idiot I was. But he left an address, in case I ever needed anything. So I got in my car – which was cheap and crappy, as was my apartment – and I drove from Seattle to LA, and – oh, did I tell you at this point I had no idea Siena existed?'

'Really?'

'No. I refused to learn anything about my father as a point of pride. So when I was buzzed into the compound and I drove up to the front door, this teenage girl came out and said, "Daddy never told me he had a son" and we were both pretty flabbergasted.'

'Wow.'

'Yeah.' His fingers brushed her arm. 'I thought I'd be angrier, to be honest, but Siena is just one of those people… it's hard to dislike her. She went to bat for me against her father – our father – and said he should give me some money, and he said, "Well, Son, I tried."'

'He did?'

Josh sighed. 'I didn't believe it until I confronted my mother, who was mad as hell that I'd even gone to visit him. She said he'd been trying to buy her off for years. He'd been sending her child maintenance payments, large sums, and cheques for my birthdays and Christmas. She said it was guilt money, and sent it back. And I remember looking around her kitchen, where the cabinet doors were coming off and the linoleum was cracked and there was a water stain on the ceiling, and thinking, how could you be so selfish?'

The light had almost completely gone now. Essie had excellent night vision, but nobody could see in total darkness.

'I worked myself to the bone getting through college. I nearly burned out several times. I used to lie awake and worry about not being able to afford my textbooks. And all the time she was turning down money. She was choosing to be poor. And – like, I guess I get it, kind of, because I don't really like Siena paying for everything in my house, but come on. It's cutting your nose off to spite your face.'

'To spite *your* face, too,' Essie added quietly.

'Yeah.' Josh cleared his throat. 'She was so angry about me getting him to pay off her medical bills we barely spoke for a year. We haven't been close since. The trust has gone, I guess.'

He said it very simply, but Essie heard the ache underneath it. Josh, the kind, smiling man who made silly jokes and accepted insane facts like time travel and was also a really good kisser, was still in pain from an argument with his mother, how many years ago? A decade, if Siena had been a teenager.

'I'm sorry,' she said, leaning into him.

'I know, I don't have the monopoly on weird relationships with my mother,' Josh began.

'Hey, don't apologise. It's still shitty.'

After a moment, his arm came around her shoulders and he gave her a brief hug. 'Thanks.'

It felt good to be held by Josh. A different kind of good from the kissing they'd done earlier. There was trust here, and companionship, and understanding. Of course, the red-hot lust was something she was keeping in mind for later.

Maybe… maybe if it's red-hot enough it will thaw me out?

She cleared her throat. 'So that's why you came here? Fresh start?'

'Well, kinda. I mean, that was years ago. I threw myself into my career. Climbed the corporate ladder. Made a lot of money for a tech firm who liked my ability to find legal loopholes whenever they screwed someone over. It's soul-destroying work, Essie,' he sighed. 'And you spend your time with soul-destroying people.' He hesitated. 'Like Maya.'

'Maya?'

But he was prevented from saying any more by the sound of footsteps coming down the stairs towards the cellar door.

'One last victory taunt before he retires to sleep on a bed of blood money?' Essie muttered, bracing herself. Josh squeezed her shoulders.

The sudden light of the lantern was dazzling after the darkness. 'Behold their licentiousness!' declared Hopkins.

'We were hugging,' said Essie.

'Hah! Is that what you call it?'

'And did we mention being married?' Essie could think about the warmth that thought gave her later.

'Fornication!' thundered Hopkins. He stank, but Essie

could distinguish it now. It wasn't a physical stench. It was the foulness of a rotten soul.

'Who are you trying to prove this to?' Essie said, because there was no one with Hopkins.

'Do you hear voices?' Josh said sympathetically, and Essie had to hide a smile.

'Silence! The Devil hath taken you,' spat Hopkins. His eyes glowed with madness. 'I will root him out!'

'Dude, we don't know any Devil,' said Essie.

'We really don't,' said Josh.

'He hath touched you,' said Hopkins. His eyes darted to his left. 'There be a witch's mark on you where he hath suckled.'

'Ew,' said Essie.

'Nobody is suckling anybody,' said Josh.

'Not without proper consent,' Essie added, and maybe the Devil did make her say that. Josh barked out a laugh.

'You think this a jest! You will not find it so when you are hanging from a rope,' Hopkins threatened. 'They all cry and repent. Even you!'

Once more, Essie had the feeling he was talking to someone else. She craned to see into the darkness beyond the flickering lantern.

'We've got nothing to repent of,' she said calmly. In an hour or so, she'd bind him with her magic. He was younger here, weaker. He hadn't spent four hundred years festering in his own madness.

The thought occurred to her that she'd still have to deal with it when she got home, but that could wait. Here and now was all that mattered.

'Thou liest! The Devil lies with thy tongue,' muttered Hopkins. His eyes darted again.

'Again, no one lies with any part of me without consent,' said Essie. 'Master Hopkins, who do you talk to?'

'What?'

'Is there someone else in here?'

''Tis a distraction!' shouted Hopkins. Spittle flecked his mouth. 'A lie! The Devil is in you!'

'He really isn't,' said Essie wearily.

'We're gonna need proof,' said Josh.

'I shall prick thee! In front of witnesses,' Hopkins said.

'The innuendoes just make themselves, don't they,' said Essie, and could swear she heard a faint giggle.

'Whatever happened to innocent until proven guilty?' Josh said. 'The writ of habeas corpus? The right to a fair trial?'

'I don't think they have the Bill of Rights here,' Essie said.

'Right. Magna Carta?' said Josh.

'Did we mention he's a lawyer too,' said Essie. Not that it would do them the slightest bit of good against Hopkins and his foam-flecked rage, but it was fun to wind him up.

'I will see you dance the Tyburn jig,' spat Hopkins. 'I am the witchfinder general, and I will see thee hang!'

With that dramatic statement, he swept out, and they heard the key turn in the lock.

Essie peered into the darkness, willing her eyes to adjust, but before she could make anything out, Josh started laughing.

'Holy shit,' he said. 'Essie, my god. You're magnificent. I could kiss you.'

Essie said, 'Yes,' before she even thought about it.

And he kissed her. His hand cupped her cheek and guided her to him in the darkness, and his mouth found hers in a kiss that was becoming thrillingly familiar.

She moved closer to him, at the same time cursing all the layers between them and delighting in the sensation of his doublet against her exposed bosom. She was tired and she was filthy and she was scared, but Josh was kissing her, so there was still some hope in the world.

The sound of a giggle had her head whipping round.

'Is someone there?' she said.

'Wha'?' mumbled Josh. His hand gripped her bare shoulder.

'Canst thou hear me?' said a small voice.

'I can,' said Essie, reluctantly drawing away from Josh and his wonderful kisses.

'Wait, who is that?' said Josh.

'You can hear it too?'

'Very faintly. Is someone there?'

It appeared as a glimmer, as if light reflected off something that wasn't even there. The very faintest suggestion of a white arm and face, the merest idea of a wisp of hair.

'Few hear me,' said the voice.

'Is Hopkins one of them?' said Essie.

The giggle came again. 'He pretends he can't. That I am sent by the Devil to torment him.'

'Are you?' asked Josh fearfully. His hand found Essie's

in the darkness. It went by way of her nearly exposed breast, but she didn't mind that.

'Nay! I am sent by Hopkins.'

'He… sends you himself? To torment… himself?'

The voice made a noise that was a verbal shrug. ''Twas him slew me. 'Tis him tormented.'

Into the silence that followed, Essie said, 'Hopkins killed you?'

'Aye. He does not like it when you laugh at him. Or tell him no.'

Essie closed her eyes. A picture was being painted behind them. 'He killed you because you turned him down?'

The glimmer of light bobbed and flickered. 'Heads do not like it when they strike stone,' it whispered. ''Tis red and bloodsome. He said next day he had not seen me. He said 'twas villainy. Witches, said he. But 'twas him.'

Essie turned to look at Josh, even though she couldn't see him.

'And you've been… haunting him ever since?'

'I suppose I have.'

So. Hopkins had killed a girl who laughed at him and turned him down, and he'd gone on killing. So much for incels being a modern problem.

'And he can see you?' said Josh. His hand gripped Essie's.

'He hears me. I do not know if he sees. Do you see me?'

'We see you,' said Essie softly.

'What's your name?' Josh asked.

The ghost appeared to have to think about it. 'Mary,' she said eventually.

'How long have you been like this?'

'I know not.' The light flickered again. 'I was young. I thought I would move on. They said I would go to heaven.'

'I'm sorry,' said Essie.

'And I am dragged around with him. Am I real? Or just his memory of me?' asked the ghost suddenly.

'I don't know.' She didn't look or sound like Prudence, but then Prudence had been a witch. Essie hadn't encountered many other ghosts, and most of the ones she could recall were just faint, drifting echoes. 'Mary?'

'Aye?'

'Can you tell us if anyone is still awake in the house?'

The light bobbed around. 'I could. I can. Why?'

Essie took a deep breath and let it out. She honestly didn't know if what she said next was true or even possible.

'Because I am going to bind Matthew Hopkins so that he can't hurt anyone else,' she said. 'And I'm going to set you free.'

The light bobbed closer. 'Truly?'

'I swear.'

Mary giggled again and flew away, the faint light disappearing through the door.

'Can you do that?' Josh murmured.

'Let's hope so,' said Essie, who had no idea. Surely, if Mary was tied to Hopkins, and she bound Hopkins, or even killed him—

Could she do that? Should she?

The light flowed back into the room. 'They all do sleep but the fornicators in the attic,' she reported.

'The…?'

'I did not know two men could do that,' mused the ghost.

Into the following silence, Essie said, 'Is either of them Hopkins?'

'Nay. He be sleeping.'

Essie took a deep breath and let it out. 'Right,' she said. 'Okay then. Uh, stand back. Or float back. Josh, I might need you ready to catch the door. But cover your hands.'

'Why?'

'Because I'm going to freeze it.'

She heard rather than saw him unbutton and remove his doublet, and concentrated her will. The door, a plain rectangle of planks nailed together, was cool and slightly damp under her hands. Damp was good.

'All right,' she said, and willed it to freeze.

After a moment, Josh said, 'Should something be happening?'

'It is,' Essie said. The wood grew cold as stone under her palms.

'Such as?'

'Just be ready.' It was cold as ice now. The hinges began to crackle.

'For what?'

'Will you shut up? I'm trying to concentrate.'

All the moisture in the wood began to evaporate as the temperature rushed past freezing. Frost rippled over it. The planks contracted, and the hinges snapped. The door was shrinking.

'Cover your hands,' Essie whispered. 'And be ready…'

The door wobbled, and collapsed in a heap of wood and metal shards. A faint light slipped in from the stairwell beyond. Essie winced at the noise.

Josh stood with his hands wrapped in his doublet, arms outstretched, waiting.

'I was ready,' he said. 'Fuck, it's cold in here.'

She put her finger to her lips. Josh silently slipped back into his doublet, and Essie picked up a piece of frozen wood. She inched forward.

'There be a man,' whispered Mary, and Essie raised the piece of wood. As a pair of feet came down the stairs, she swung at them, and when he fell she grabbed him and pressed her hand to his mouth.

'I'm sorry,' she whispered, as his skin turned faintly blue with cold. He was just doing his job. 'I'm sorry.' The man slithered to the ground and lay still. Essie stared for an awful moment until she saw his chest rise and fall.

Then she turned back to Josh, and said, 'Come on!'

'Is he dead?'

'Unconscious. He'll be fine.' She held out her hand, and Josh hesitated before taking it. 'I won't hurt you,' she said impatiently, and very much hoped that was true.

'Right.' He swallowed, and took her hand, and Essie led the way with her frozen club in one hand.

The cellar steps opened onto the kitchen, a vast stone-built space that barely resembled the one Essie was familiar with. She stilled at the sight of people sleeping on straw mattresses near the huge fireplace, which glowed with faint heat. She and Josh crept as silently as possible across the flagstones to the door, the wispy light of Mary almost invisible behind them.

The layout of the house was entirely different. The kitchen door gave onto a stone walkway, bordering a small courtyard Essie wasn't familiar with. They had initially been brought straight to the kitchen and then down to the cellar. She had to think.

'Essie, what the fuck?' whispered Josh, and she opened her eyes to see the courtyard changing. A staircase appeared on the far side of it, as if it had always been there.

'The house changes with our needs,' she breathed.

'Those steps,' Josh began. His hand clutched hers tightly.

'They're where we need to go.'

She pulled him across the courtyard to the steps. They began outside and ended inside, with no actual entrance along the way. When Essie glanced back, the bottom of the stairs was in a large, almost familiar hallway with a fireplace.

'The time travel I could deal with,' Josh whispered, 'but this is freaking me out.'

'He be this way,' announced Mary, drifting through an antechamber, and Essie knew she was entirely right. She knew where Hopkins was. And she knew what she had to do.

She glanced the other way, towards a door that pulled at her attention. Yes. The Godwin girl had power, all right. Should she ask for help?

No, there was no sense in that. There was too much risk whether the girl helped her or not. And Essie didn't want to change the course of history. She just wanted to go home.

She glanced the other way, to where she could fell Lilith's door calling her. Best not to let anyone else know it was there.

'Let's do this,' she said.

Chapter Fourteen

Josh had rather been expecting a dramatic entrance, perhaps another door crumbling to its constituent parts and exploding across Hopkins's bedroom. But Essie just lifted the latch and walked in.

'Matthew Hopkins,' she said, as the moonlight illuminated a figure beneath the heavy blankets. 'I bind thee to my will.'

The figure jerked, and Hopkins's eyes opened.

'I call on winter to rise from the earth. I call on snow to darken the sky. I call on ice to still the water. I call you by mistle, and holly, and yew. I call you by the force of my own will.'

Josh knew that, in 1647, it was a mild summer night, and that long grass and flowers grew in the meadows. He knew that, but he smelled winter. He smelled the cold crackle of frost, and the gentle freshness of pine.

From three feet away, he felt the cold radiating from Essie.

'Begone,' gasped Hopkins, but his voice was frail.

'I call on ice to bind this evil,' said Essie, and her voice grew stronger. 'Bind the malevolence of Matthew Hopkins, freeze it in time and let it rise no more.'

Her voice contained multitudes. Josh suddenly felt that Essie wasn't alone, and that he could hear other voices joining hers, slithering around it, creating harmonics that sawed at every nerve he had.

He glanced at the faint light that was Mary the ghost. She had drifted closer to Essie, and now he could make out the faint outline of a woman in a bloodstained shift. Frost crackled on the windowpanes.

'I cast your evil down beneath the earth,' Essie said. Her eyes glowed green. 'By my will, I bind you.'

And Josh realised that Mary's was not the only ghost.

'Matthew Hopkins,' they all said, whispers that slipped into Essie's voice. 'No more shall ye walk the earth. No more shall ye lie and cheat. No more shall ye kill!'

The voices grew stronger and stronger, and Josh didn't dare move, not even his eyes. He stared resolutely at Essie, whose outline seemed to be of more than one person.

'Matthew Hopkins,' they vowed, voices rising to a howl, 'I bid thy ghosts to peaceful rest! I bind thee beneath the earth to never rise again! As I will so will it be!'

And with a sudden sucking sensation, the combined force of Essie's will and the ghosts that crowded the chamber surged towards Matthew Hopkins, whose body jerked almost off the bed, and then with a great gasp, lay still.

Essie wavered, and Josh caught her as she fell.

The room was abruptly empty. Whatever spirits had filled the air had vanished, and now it was just the two of them, kneeling on the cold flagstones. From the bed came the sounds of laboured breath.

'Is he dying?' Josh said. He wasn't sure if he felt good about that or not.

'His soul is gone. He's just a shell,' gasped Essie. 'We have to go. The door. The time door.'

'It's here?'

She nodded. Her skin was a bluish white. Her fingers had no strength as they clutched at his. She jerked her head to his left. 'That way.'

He somehow managed to get her half to her feet, and pretty much dragged her from the room. As he did, another door seemed to close somewhere else, but there was no one there, and Josh was too worried to think about it.

'That way,' Essie murmured, but Josh could already *feel* the door. Through this room, and then the one beyond it –

Startled faces looked up at him from pallets on the floor. These goddamn rooms that led into each other!

'Excuse me,' he said, and dragged Essie through the room to the door beyond.

It was red. There was a motif of an hourglass on it. It seemed to glow around the edges. Josh reached out, and their combined hands lifted the latch, and as a voice came from behind them, the door opened and they tumbled through it.

'Thou art a witch,' breathed the Godwin girl, her voice fading like a breeze.

Josh kicked the door closed, and then there was silence.

He and Essie lay on a wooden floor in darkness. The only sound he heard was her breathing, hard and ragged as if she'd just run a marathon.

'Are you okay?' he said.

'Yes.' She panted. 'I just. That took. A lot out. Of me.'

Josh felt for her in the darkness and pulled her close. She was cold, but not deathly cold. Her head lolled against his chest. She was exhausted.

'I've got you,' he said, although it seemed horribly inadequate. She had just banished a soul to Hell or something, and all he'd done was open a door.

'Are we back?' she said.

'I don't know. No one's chasing us.' He tried to peer into the gloom. He could make out a window, through which very little light came. 'I figure someone would be chasing us. There… was a voice?'

'The Godwin girl. I think she was a witch.' Essie shook her head. 'She didn't follow us?'

'No. I don't think so. No.'

A pale-blue light suddenly appeared at the end of what seemed to be a corridor. Josh felt Essie brace herself, which given her exhaustion was probably the bravest thing he'd ever encountered. Footsteps sounded on a staircase.

Then more lights, suddenly bright and blinding, as lightbulbs popped into life, and around the corner came Avery, phone in hand.

'The electricity's back on,' they remarked. 'Come on, Josh, you don't want to miss the baby being born.'

Essie woke hours later, in her own bed, with her phone charging on the table and Tomkin the cat purring on her chest.

'Oh god, twenty-first century, I love you,' she moaned.

She reached for her phone, gasping as her muscles protested. She couldn't remember the last time she'd felt this exhausted, not even after the first time she'd performed the winter ritual by herself.

Had it worked, then? Had going back in time and redoing the initial ritual worked? Essie wasn't entirely sure about the quantum mechanics of the last twenty-four hours. Had she always been the one to create the ritual and banish Hopkins? Or had she changed history?

Her phone said it was early afternoon, the day after they'd fallen through the time door. She had little recollection of what happened after they'd got back last night. She and Josh had stumbled into Siena's delivery room, where Blessing was thankfully in attendance, and then Maude had said something like, 'You need your rest, child. There's more to come,' and Essie had somehow made her way to bed.

'Is everything all right?' she asked Tomkin, who indicated with a flick of his ear that it seemed to be. 'Did Siena have the baby?'

His disdain told her she had, and that it was noisy, and that he wasn't impressed. Under all this, however, was the impression that everything was all right, and nobody in the house was upset or concerned.

'Is it a boy or a girl?' she asked, and Tomkin made a

bored noise and batted her fingers. He didn't care enough to know.

Essie shifted a grumbling Tomkin and dragged herself out of bed, realising as she did she was still wearing the linen shift Agatha had given her. On the floor was the stained bodice and skirt and all the petticoats and corset.

She stepped over it all, took a very long hot shower, and got dressed. Oh god, she'd never take a pair of knickers and a bra for granted again. Or trousers. Trousers were just the best thing in the world. There was such a lack of draughtiness.

Finally, she picked up her spare glasses and perched them on her nose.

'Right then,' she said, and left her room.

The house certainly seemed calm. There was even some cautious sunlight filtering in through the windows. Essie found her mother's portrait, currently empty of human figures. In the background of it was the house she now recognised as the old Brook Manor, where Mistress Agatha had sheltered them. She wondered what had become of that lady. Had she been the one to set the witch ball in Brook Manor Farm?

Her footsteps took her down to the kitchen, which was a bright, warm room utterly unlike the smoky cavern where Master Godwin's servants had slept. What had become of him, too? Had he known his daughter was a witch? Had she been the one to rename Beldam House?

'There you are, dear.' Avery was at the stove. 'Are you hungry?'

Essie's stomach growled. 'I haven't eaten in nearly four hundred years.'

Avery nodded. 'Bacon and eggs, then?'

'Thanks.'

There was a pot of tea on the table. Essie poured a cup, and sat down. The clock ticked. All was quiet. 'Is everything okay?'

'Looks like it. Your mother's gone out paying calls, because apparently she thinks it's the eighteenth century or something.'

'Seventeenth,' said Essie.

'Whatever. Maude kept muttering darkly about her knitting, Prudence has gone off to hang out in the woods, and Blessing is doing…' Avery waved a hand, 'baby things.'

'Is Siena okay?' Essie realised guiltily she should have asked sooner. Tomkin hadn't exactly been forthcoming. 'The baby?'

'Oh. A boy, no name yet, mother and baby doing well.'

A boy. Josh had a nephew.

'No complications?'

'None whatsoever. It was a funny thing, as soon as Josh got in there she calmed right down. He was like a sort of hand-holding epidural. Very calming presence.'

A plate of food was put down in front of Essie, who began shovelling it in with indecent haste.

'You're eating nearly as fast as your American. I had to lend him some clothes.'

Essie looked up, and said through a mouthful of eggs, 'Is he okay?'

Avery shrugged. 'I'm sure he will be. A bit bruised, no more.'

They had been jolted around quite a bit in the past. *The past*. Already, it felt like a rather terrible holiday she wanted to forget. 'Did he go home?'

She wouldn't really blame him. Even for a witch, it had been a terrifying and baffling period. She couldn't imagine how Josh felt. He was probably on a plane back to Seattle.

'No, he's upstairs. In the library. Don't worry, Marley is keeping an eye on him.'

'Marley the dog?'

Avery shrugged. 'He promised to howl if any of the books try to eat him.'

'Marvellous.'

Essie finished her plate of food, threw a piece of Avery's chocolate cake down her throat just because she could, and downed some Coke for the same reason.

Then she set off upstairs. Her stomach fluttered a bit. She and Josh had kissed a couple of times in the past, and they had been good kisses. Really good kisses. Essie wanted more kisses like that.

She thought she wanted more than just kisses, too, but… was she ready for that? Would Josh understand?

But the library was empty, apart from a large book open on a stand. Essie scanned the pages. It appeared to be a genealogy of the Hopkins family, which she hadn't even known they possessed. Well, the library had secret dimensions of its own. Essie skipped back to the start of the book – which was too far, beginning in the Middle Ages – then forwards to find Matthew Hopkins, born 1619.

'"Died 1647, after suddenly contracting a chill." You don't say,' said Essie drily.

Beneath Matthew Hopkins was an entry for John Hopkins, born 1644, mother unknown. The child had grown, married and had children of his own. And the line then passed on, and on… until it reached one Edward Hopkins of London, who married Martha Mason of New York, and their son was Edward Mason Hopkins.

'"By his first wife, a son, Joshua. By his second wife, a daughter, Siena. To Siena, a son, born 29 Oct 2022, father unknown."'

The book was printed and bound. The ink was dry and old.

Essie stared at nothing for a while. Then she said, 'What, you don't already know his name?'

She tried to turn the last page, but it suddenly became hot under her fingers, and she yanked her hand back, staring in astonishment as the page turned to flames and ashes in under a second.

'All right, I won't ask,' she said. She stepped back and frowned at the book. The ashes had already blown away, although there was no breeze. 'No more of that, you hear?'

The book said nothing.

'Just don't call him Matthew,' said Essie, and left. Behind her, the word 'Matthew' glowed briefly in the air.

Some instinct took her upwards, to the first place she'd taken Josh in this house. The rich, earthy scent of the conservatory hit her as soon as she opened the door, and a chill she hadn't realised she was feeling dissipated in the warmth.

Josh sat on a bench amid the giant pitcher plants and fecund flytraps. He wore his usual plaid shirt and jeans, because even though Avery had lent him clothes, they wouldn't have dreamed of doing so without altering them to first.

There were smudges under Josh's eyes, and as he lifted one of Avery's anaphrodisiac biscuits to his mouth, Essie saw that his hand was bandaged.

'What happened?' she said and he looked up.

'Oh. Hey.' He waved his hand at her. 'Uh, I told Siena she could hold my hand.'

'Ouch.'

'Yeah. I mean, she was probably in more pain, but still. I survive being accused of witchcraft in the seventeenth century, only to break my hand when I get back to the safety of the twenty-first.' He regarded it, and waggled his fingers. 'Your mom is a dab hand with a splint though. And I should probably not ask what was in the special drink she gave me.'

'Probably not,' agreed Essie.

She moved closer. Josh looked tired, and thoughtful, and all the more handsome for it.

'Congratulations on being an uncle,' she said.

Josh shrugged nonchalantly. 'Oh, it was nothing.'

Essie smiled, and he smiled back, and patted the bench beside him. She sat, and he put his arm around her, and there was the comfort she'd found from him in that cellar four hundred years ago. Josh had seen her weirdness laid bare now. He'd watched her perform the winter ritual, he'd seen her freeze wood, he'd travelled through time with her for heaven's sake.

And he'd kissed her a couple of times. A couple of blistering hot times.

Essie reached for the plate of biscuits, and crammed one in her mouth.

'Did you sleep?' he asked, and she nodded, chewing and swallowing. The biscuits were like cardboard.

'Yeah. For half the day. And I still feel like I've been hit by a bus.'

'You were witching pretty hard there.'

'Witching? It's a verb now?'

His eyes were warm. 'Is there one you'd prefer?'

'Witching works for me.'

'It sure does.'

The conservatory was warm and fragrant, and Josh's arm felt exactly right around her.

'You saw the ledger?' she said.

'Yeah. Matthew Hopkins, self-proclaimed witchfinder general, is my ten times great-grandfather.' Josh stared at the tall, dramatic flowers of the sarracenia, which were beginning to smell like cat piss. 'That sucks.'

'Hey. You're not him.'

'He murdered hundreds of witches.'

'He murdered hundreds of people. Probably very few of them were witches,' corrected Essie.

'Witches would fight back?'

'I don't suppose any of his victims gave in without a fight,' Essie said. 'But how could any of us fight back without revealing ourselves? If I'd tried to freeze him when anyone else was watching, don't you think someone would have noticed?'

'Damned if you do, and damned if you don't.'

'That's about the size of it.'

Josh said, 'I looked up Mistress Agatha too. She raised the boy in that house until there was a fire, maybe ten years later. Then they moved to Brook Manor Farm.'

'Your house?'

'My house.'

Essie thought about the witch ball in the upstairs room of Josh's house, the one that had smashed and broken just after he'd moved in.

'Did you ever take a picture of that parchment inside the witch ball?' she asked.

He seemed surprised she'd asked. Essie knew it wasn't coincidence that made him keep forgetting.

'Uh, sure. Hang on.'

He dug his phone out of his pocket and scrolled through it. 'Here. I can't make out the words.'

Essie could. She wasn't an expert in reading old handwriting, but the words leaped off the page at her in a way that had nothing to do with her eyes.

> *I, thee right and goodlye Hopkins, do swear withall to abjure thee Devil and all who worshipe him and more I will see clearlye those beldams who are so ungoodlye and they never will cross this threshold or seat at my hearthe and never will I fall prey to they tricks and knavery this I swear.*

The words made bile rise in her throat, and she had to look way for a moment.

'Essie?'

'Yeah.' She swallowed. 'Yes. I'm fine.'

'Does it mean anything to you?' Josh asked.

Essie frowned at the screen. There were bloodied fingerprints in a cluster at the bottom, like a terrible finger painting. One of them, she was fairly sure, would be Josh's.

'One of your ancestors wrote this,' she said. 'I-I can't read it out loud. I physically can't,' she said, looking up at him. 'It won't let me. Honestly, it makes me feel a bit sick.'

'Then I'll delete it,' said Josh, and she shook her head.

'No. It's important you know what it is so you can decide what to do with it.' Essie took a couple of deep breaths. 'It says, basically, that you reject the Devil and his followers, and that you wish to be able to see witches clearly. That we're never to be allowed across your threshold or to sit at your hearth.'

Josh was silent a moment. 'That's why you had to ask to be invited in?'

'Yes.'

'Every time?'

'Yes. It also says you will never be deceived by any of our tricks.'

'Well, I haven't been,' said Josh. 'I don't think I was deceived by you doing that binding spell, or moving us through time, or freezing the door…'

'And the house's perception spell has never worked fully on you,' Essie said. 'You kept remembering me, right from that very first day.'

Josh frowned down at her in honest bewilderment. 'Essie,' he said. 'How could anyone ever forget you?'

Essie's heart leaped.

'When we were in that cellar, I swear to God I didn't know if we'd ever get out. I had no idea what to do. And you were just so... cool.'

Essie laughed. 'I have never in my life been called cool.'

'Then everyone you know is an idiot. You were *taunting* Hopkins. It was amazing.'

'It probably wasn't wise,' Essie said. She wouldn't have been very surprised if he'd snapped and turned on them in the cellar. And then she'd probably have had to freeze him to death, which wouldn't have been ideal.

'It was fun though,' said Josh. His eyes crinkled at the corners when he smiled.

She smiled back. 'Yeah. It was.'

His arm was warm on her shoulders, and just the right weight. His bandaged hand cupped her shoulder, thumb stroking gently. Essie could feel his breathing, the rise and fall of his chest, the beating of his heart. Around them, the conservatory was heavy with the scent of plants ripening and bursting into life.

She wasn't a witch who had any particular affinity with seeing the future. The odd premonition, sure, and the feeling after an event that she'd known it was going to happen.

But right now she could see the future very, very clearly.

Josh cleared his throat. 'That first night you walked me home. You were so confident. Like you were exactly where you should be, all the time.'

'Well, I know this place pretty well.'

'It was more like it reshaped itself around you. Like if

there was a stone that was going to trip you up, it just moved instead.'

She laughed. 'I don't have that sort of power.'

'Don't you? I'm pretty sure you could do anything.'

She'd turned towards him at some point. Her breasts against his ribcage. Her hand on his chest. His heart was beating fast.

She wanted him. And this time she was sure it was going to happen right. This time she could be herself, and she could have what she wanted. This was Josh, and he knew who she was.

'And then you kissed me,' he said, in what was probably supposed to have been an off-hand tone.

'I thought you kissed me,' she said. A cluster of butterwort flowers nearby seemed to throb with colour.

'Well, I was going to, but you got there first,' Josh said, slightly exasperated.

'Because I knew what you were planning.'

'Another witchy power?'

Essie laughed and looked up at him. 'No. Josh, it was written all over your face.'

'It was?' His voice was hoarse.

'I'm pretty sure it was written all over mine too,' she said.

His eyes met hers. His heart was really pounding under her palm. 'It was a really good kiss,' he whispered.

'Yeah?'

'And… that one in the meadow…'

His face was so close to hers they were sharing the same

breath. Heat rose between them. A sundew tendril snaked over Essie's foot.

'That wasn't a good kiss,' Essie breathed, and the joy suddenly slid from Josh's face. She felt the shock ripple through him, and the shame, and he turned his face away from her, his whole body stiffening.

Essie cupped his jaw and turned him back to face her. 'Firstly, it was an amazing kiss,' she said, and his eyes reluctantly swivelled in her direction.

He swallowed. 'And secondly?'

'And secondly,' Essie said, moving so more of her body touched more of his, 'it was much more than a kiss.'

Her lips touched his, and Josh groaned and kissed her back. The arm he had around her shoulders curved around, pulling her closer, and when she slid her thigh over his he ran his other hand all the way up it.

'Yes,' gasped Essie. She needed him to touch her. All of her. All that time she'd been sitting beside him in that terrible cellar, all the time she'd fought and argued with him, all the jokes and flirting over the pub table – all of it had been leading to this and she felt as if she'd always known it.

Josh pulled her on top of him, the bench creaking under their weight. Essie wouldn't have cared if it collapsed. His hand was on her back, pressing her closer to him, as if she needed any encouragement. Her fingers burrowed into his thick hair, the sensation of it against her fingers making her shudder. He was like fire under her hands.

She was wearing too many clothes. Josh's hand was on her back but there was too much in the way, she needed to feel his hands on her bare skin. She fumbled with the catch of her dungarees and released the straps, and Josh growled in approval as his hand found the bottom of her t-shirt.

Yes. That was what she needed. His fingertips on her spine sparked a wave of shivers that had her trembling against him. Heat pulsed through her.

'Yes,' she mumbled against his lips. 'More.'

His eyes smiled at that, even as his hands were pulling her t-shirt up, and Essie tore her mouth from his long enough to toss the offending garment over her head, where a giant flytrap snapped shut over it.

Josh stared at her bra and swallowed. Essie hadn't intended to put on a pretty bra today, but maybe she really had known what was going to happen because it was a nice one, with lace and a little flower between the cups.

'Yesterday,' he said hoarsely, gaze glued to the rise and fall of her breasts, 'in that corset. I thought I was going to go blind every time you breathed.'

Essie trailed her fingertips over the slight roughness of his cheek. 'I still have it in my bedroom,' she said, and Josh made a whimpering sound and dived in to kiss the slopes of her breasts.

Essie decided to assist him in this by reaching back and unfastening her bra. Josh mumbled something that sounded like, 'Oh god, the freckles go all the way down,' and took her nipple into his mouth.

'Yes,' she breathed. 'Josh. Yes.'

'I have been fantasising about these,' he said, looking up at her with unfocused eyes. His hands cupped and shaped her breasts. 'They're even better than I hoped.'

Essie laughed, which made her breasts jiggle, which made Josh moan softly.

'Your turn,' she said, plucking at his shirt, and he nodded and grabbed clumsily at the fabric. His eyes were still glued to her breasts, however, and he didn't really seem to be concentrating.

Essie climbed off his lap and let her dungarees fall to the floor, standing there in just her knickers, and Josh pretty well clawed his own clothes off. He stood up to get rid of his jeans, and nearly tripped over his own feet.

'Careful,' said Essie, steadying him. 'I need you in one piece.'

'You've got as many pieces of me as you want,' Josh promised, and took her in his arms to kiss her again. But now his chest was bare and so was hers, and her thigh brushed against the hairs on his leg and made her breath come faster, and her hips—

'Oh, fuck,' said Josh, and drew back.

'What?' He had a lovely chest, well-defined without being overdeveloped, dusted with dark hairs that felt really good against her skin –

'I don't have... anything,' he said. If she'd thought he looked crestfallen before it was nothing to his expression now. 'There's probably an expired condom in my wallet, which is in my jacket in Siena's room—'

Essie silenced him with a kiss. She wanted to tell him they didn't need anything, that she'd be a poor witch if she couldn't sort out her own contraception, but she knew that wasn't the point. 'Look in your pockets,' she said.

'But these aren't my clothes—'

'Avery altered them for you. To give you what you need.' And Avery was very good at manifesting exactly what was required when it was required. Essie thought about their knowing expression in the kitchen. She hadn't been the only one who'd known this was coming.

Josh looked highly sceptical, at least right until he produced a condom from the pocket of his borrowed jeans.

'But?' He looked up, and saw Essie had taken off her knickers.

'Ask and ye shall receive,' Essie said, and pushed down his boxers. 'And boy, did I ask for the right thing,' she said, grinning up at him.

Josh went a bit pink, but he let her take the condom from him and roll it on, and then she was pushing him onto the bench and climbing on top of him, and Essie looked down and saw the same hunger on his face she knew was on hers.

'Yes?' she said, rocking her hips against him. This time would be good. This time she'd get it right.

'Yes,' breathed Josh, and Essie took him inside her. 'Oh, christ, yes.'

She kissed him as she rode him, licked the sweat from his skin and gasped as he tried to kiss as many of her freckles as he could. Heat rose around them, a dense fog of lust, and Essie laughed as she discarded her steamed-up glasses.

Josh laughed back, sweaty and dishevelled and absolutely gorgeous. Essie tasted that laugh, drank it down and fed on it. She didn't know if she'd ever laughed with a lover before. She was getting drunk on it.

'Essie, I'm close,' he murmured, and she nodded,

because she was too. The tension was building inside her, and any minute now it would snap –

– snap and freeze, and then he'd scream and she'd cower and sob and –

'Essie?'

But this wasn't Sean, and she wasn't in some dingy student digs, she was with Josh and she could control herself now. She was in control.

'Yes,' she gasped. 'Josh, yes.'

'Are you?'

'I'm almost there,' she told him, and she was, or at least she nearly had been. She closed her eyes, but then she saw Sean's horrified face, and opened them again. There was Josh, gorgeous and sweaty and right there inside her, and if she just…

'Essie,' he gasped, and she willed herself to go with him.

But the moment was lost, and while Josh tipped over the edge, gasping her name, all she could do was hold him and curse herself.

A sticky plant tendril grasped her ankle, and she kicked it away, irritated and miserable.

She could still feel the tremors running through his body as he lifted his head and said, 'Are you okay?'

Essie smiled and lied. 'I'm great,' she said.

'But you didn't…'

'It's fine.'

'But I thought—' Josh slid his hand over her back, and she shivered pleasurably at his touch. Her body reminded her he was still right there inside her, and maybe there was something they could do with that. 'Okay, so how about if we—'

'No.' She flinched away, and Josh frowned up at her. She saw the last of his pleasure fade away, and hated herself for it.

'What's wrong?'

The heat of the conservatory felt suddenly oppressive, the heady scent of the plants oppressive. 'There's something I should probably tell you,' she said.

Chapter Fifteen

Essie's bedroom was surprisingly normal. Josh didn't know exactly what he'd been expecting, but it wasn't floral wallpaper and Ikea bookshelves. There were several half-drunk mugs of tea going gently mouldy on the table by the bed, and teetering piles of paperbacks everywhere.

She picked a large grey cat up off the bed and hugged him as she gestured to Josh to take a seat. The cat eyed Josh smugly. *See which one of us is getting the hug.*

Her t-shirt had ended up being eaten by one of the rapacious plants, so Josh had offered her his shirt as they left the steamy conservatory. She'd refused it, all of a sudden distant and tense, and crossed her arms over the front of her dungarees instead. Josh realised he'd never seen her this unsure before.

He had no idea what had gone wrong. Everything had been going extremely well – more well than he could ever remember it going before, as a matter of fact – and then right at the finish she'd suddenly withdrawn from him, shut down and given up.

He sat down on her bed, which had a duvet cover patterned with cats wearing sombreros, and looked up at her.

'Essie,' he said. 'We've travelled through time together. We've survived a witch hunt. And we just had what was nearly the best sex of my life. Can you please tell me what's going on?'

'Nearly?' she said. The cat grumbled, and she let him go. Josh realised she was trembling slightly.

'Well, yeah. Right up until the end,' he said. He held out his hand to her. 'Did I do something wrong?'

She shook her head vehemently. 'No. It wasn't you. You were… you were perfect.' She sighed. She looked near tears. 'You are perfect.'

'I'm really not,' he assured her. 'Come and sit down and talk to me. Please.'

She took a step forward, then hesitated, her fingers twisting around each other. Finally she sat beside him, then immediately moved further away.

Ten minutes ago they'd been gloriously naked together, as close as two people could physically be, and now she couldn't even look at him.

'Essie?'

She nodded, and swallowed a couple of times, and said, 'So you saw what I did with the door. In the cellar.'

'You froze it,' said Josh. 'I guess… the wood contracted as it got colder?'

'Yes. And then I used my magic to bind Hopkins in ice.'

'It was,' Josh tried to think of a word that wasn't *terrifying* and came up with, 'impressive.'

'Ice is the thing I do,' Essie said glumly. 'Blessing nurtures things and brings them to life. Avery manifests things into reality. I make things cold.'

Essie, who smelled of snow and pine and performed a ritual to welcome in the winter. She was basically the Snow Queen. But she'd never made him cold. Josh vividly remembered the heat of her mouth, the slick sweat on her skin, the warmth of her surrounding him.

'I can do it when I want to, but sometimes it happens without me trying. The weather suddenly goes bad, or there's a ground frost in June. When I'm upset, or excited, or just not really in control of myself.'

She gave him a meaningful look. It was the first time she'd looked directly at him since she'd put her clothes on.

'You mean,' Josh licked his lips nervously, 'like when you're having sex?'

She nodded rapidly, gazing at her hands again.

'But it didn't happen with me,' he said. He'd have remembered that. He was pretty sure he'd have remembered that.

'No.' To his horror, a tear trickled down her cheek. 'Because I stayed in control.'

Realisation swept over him. 'Essie. Are you telling me you deliberately stopped yourself from coming because you didn't want to freeze things?'

'Not things,' she said, swiping at her eyes. 'You.'

He tried to reach for her, to reassure her, but she shied away from him.

'I'm not being paranoid,' she said. 'It happened. It was… bad.'

Josh couldn't stop himself from asking, 'How bad?"

Essie shuddered. 'Like, call an ambulance, loss of circulation, frostbite, reconstructive surgery bad,' she said. The tears were falling fast now. 'It destroyed his life. I destroyed his life.'

He was building up a terrible mental picture. 'You gave a guy frostbite? Just from touching him?'

Essie looked at him like he was stupid. 'Not just from touching him, Josh, christ. We were having sex. I… look, most people don't orgasm their first time, so I figured it was going really well, and then he started screaming and…'

Her gaze darted to his crotch, and this time the realisation was both swift and appalling.

'You froze his dick?'

The words flew out before he could stop them, and if Josh could have recalled them he would, because Essie started crying properly, big ugly sobs that shook her body. He wanted to hug her, but to his terrible shame he was a little afraid to.

'I didn't mean to!' she wailed. 'I didn't know it would happen! He went around telling everyone on campus I had some hideous sexually transmitted disease, it was a nightmare, I had to quit and go somewhere else. And I was so scared of hurting anyone else, I took Avery's perception potions all the time and made myself unnoticeable and didn't date anyone.'

Josh's horror began to fade into something that felt a bit

like pity. 'All the way through college? You didn't date anyone else?'

She shook her head miserably. 'Since then I've been with two other guys. By the time I got the courage up to go to bed with anyone I was too scared to do it again so I just held everything back. I did a lot of faking,' she added. 'And eventually decided it wasn't worth it.'

'Oh, Essie.' Vibrant, smart, glorious Essie, who walked through pitch-dark woods without fear and faced serial killers with the courage of a lion.

'And then you came along,' she sniffed, 'and you were so… I thought maybe I could try again. I'm older and wiser and all that, and you were…'

'I was what?' said Josh.

She hiccupped out half a laugh, and said, 'Oh come on, Josh. You're all gorgeous and funny and kind and you didn't freak out about the witch stuff and you're a really good kisser, and I thought, maybe…'

She hadn't wanted to hurt him. She'd held back for him, denied herself the pleasure she'd let him have.

'Essie,' he said, and touched her shoulder. She stiffened. 'You didn't hurt me. You'd never hurt me.'

'I might,' she said. 'Do you really want to risk it?'

Yes. 'Look, how old were you?'

She shrugged forlornly. 'I was a late bloomer.'

Okay, she didn't want to tell him. 'And now you're…?'

Essie gave him a sideways look. 'Older than I look,' she said.

Mistress Agatha had thought Essie's mother was her sister. Josh realised Lilith really hadn't seemed quite old enough to be Essie's mother, and Essie herself looked less than thirty.

'I'm thirty-five,' he said. 'Older or younger than that?'

'Older.'

She didn't appear to be inclined to tell him any more than that. Josh nodded, and said, 'But since you were a student, haven't you gotten better at this witchcraft stuff? Essie, I watched you bind a man's soul in ice and send ghosts to heaven, all by yourself, with no props or support. Could you have done that when you were younger?'

'It's not quite the same,' she said.

Josh thought for a minute. 'Okay. All right, I don't know anything about witchcraft. When we did that finding spell for Siena, you used that little doll thing, right? And a stone of some kind?'

'Yes?'

'And for the winter ritual, you were gathering all that holly and stuff.'

'They're just props. To focus the mind.'

'So witching is focusing the mind? Like it's… force of will?'

'Sort of.' Essie wiped her eyes and sat up a bit straighter, apparently on safer ground now. 'I guess it's like an innate skill. Like being really good at the piano or being able to run really fast. We can just sort of… do things most people can't. But you have to practice, and concentrate pretty hard, especially for the big stuff.'

'Big stuff like the winter ritual?'

'Yeah. Like, I can light a fire without really thinking about it.' She glanced at the fireplace, and Josh very nearly *felt* the small effort run out from her, like a tiny shockwave. The coals brightened into flame.

'That's amazing,' said Josh gazing at it. 'And you're an ice witch? You can make fire and you're an ice witch?'

She shrugged. 'Everyone can do that. Everyone witchy, I mean.'

'Sure. Sure. You can just make fire by thinking about it?'

'Yes.'

'And can you stop it?'

The flames died down very quickly. 'I mean, that's only a small fire. I couldn't put out a towering inferno, before you ask.'

Josh thought about the cold that had radiated from her in Hopkins's bedroom, the frost that had crept over the windows, the ice on the floor. She probably could, if she wanted to.

'So you can control that, but not the ice?'

'Of course I can control the ice,' Essie snapped, and then she stopped. She slumped. 'All right, I see what you're doing,' she said.

He smiled. 'You do?'

'If I can control the fire why not the ice. Things don't burst into flame when I'm angry,' she said.

'Were you angry when we were having sex?' Josh said.

'It's the same thing. Losing control.' She shrugged away from him. 'I can't do it. I don't want to hurt you.'

She stood up and paced away from him. Josh watched her, frustrated. It had been so good between them. When Essie abandoned herself, she was wild and delicious. And she had been enjoying herself, and she had been hot and slick and perfect, and he simply didn't believe that could suddenly turn into frostbite.

'What feeds magic?' he asked.

'What?"

'What causes it? Where do you get your power from?'

Essie looked bewildered. 'We just… have it.'

'But you have to practice it, right? You have to learn? I mean, you weren't born knowing how to light a fire, were you? Were you?' he added, because the thought of an infant pyromaniac was terrifying.

'No, of course not. You learn how to focus on what you want,' she said.

Josh said nothing. He waited for the cogs to turn, and watched her shoulders slump.

'Hey look,' he said, and tried not to smile, because he knew he had her. 'If you're too scared to try—'

'Don't even start with that,' she warned.

'I'm just saying, practice makes perfect. You could almost certainly learn not to freeze my penis.'

She rubbed her face with one hand. 'You're not taking this seriously.'

'Or fingers. Or tongue,' said Josh, because really, there were plenty of possibilities.

'You could deal with a frostbitten tongue, could you?' Essie said.

'I could learn sign language,' said Josh.

'With your frostbitten fingers?'

He waggled them at her. 'I'm very versatile.'

Essie began to roll her eyes, and then she stopped, and a totally different expression came over her face.

'Do that again,' she said. 'Wiggle your fingers.'

Josh did, a little bemused.

'Josh, you said you broke your hand last night. You said Siena broke it.'

He looked at the bandage on his hand. Lilith had splinted his hand and wrapped it up, but somewhere along the line – *probably while we were having sex* – it had loosened and he'd been more or less using his hand normally.

'Well, Avery gave me some special tea,' he said uncertainly.

Essie sat down suddenly beside him, took his hand in hers and carefully worked each finger. 'Any pain?'

'No.'

'But you can feel it? You can feel me touching you?'

'Essie,' said Josh. 'I can always feel you touching me.'

Heat flared between them. Heat, not ice.

'Can I take the bandage off?' she asked, and he nodded.

He'd never really thought of bandage-winding as erotic, but when Essie did it, it was. Pretty much everything she did was erotic. Josh had never been so turned on by a woman in his life.

He was watching her face, not his hand, and so it was Essie who reacted first.

'It's bruised,' she said. Her fingertips traced the back of his hand, then pressed lightly. 'Does this hurt?'

'A little.'

She carefully manipulated his fingers and thumb. 'This? This?'

'It probably wasn't as bad as it seemed,' he said. He

didn't know what the big deal was. 'Whatever Avery gave me helped it.'

'When did you drink it?'

'Last night.'

Essie shook her head. 'Avery's tea can't heal bones,' Essie said. 'And it doesn't last more than a few hours. They can make you forget it hurts, but they can't actually fix it. Only time helps broken bones to heal. Josh, this isn't even swollen. It should be agonising.'

'Then it wasn't as bad as I'd thought,' he said. 'I over-reacted.' Things had gotten pretty intense there last night.

Essie cocked her head. 'Have you ever broken a bone before?'

He shrugged. 'No.'

'Sprains? Pulled muscles?'

'When I was fourteen I got hit in the head playing basketball,' Josh said, 'but there was no concussion. I got off lightly.' Everyone had been surprised. He remembered that.

Essie was frowning in a way he didn't like. 'When was the last time you were ill?' she said.

'I don't really get ill. I exercise and I eat right,' he said. 'Why are you asking?'

Essie's thumb was still stroking the bruise on the back of his hand. 'Avery said last night, as soon as you held Siena's hand she calmed down. Like a sort of hand-holding epidural.'

Josh winced. His memories of the birth were somewhat hazy, because he'd just travelled through time to escape a probably gruesome death, and he was exhausted and he had no idea what was happening. He'd just held Siena's hand and told her everything would be all right, and she seemed relieved to have him there.

Essie was looking at him now as if she was a zoologist and he was a monkey that had just started reciting Shakespeare.

'You could see the ghost,' she murmured.

'You mean Prudence?'

'I meant Mary. But Prudence too. Josh, that piece of parchment. That shouldn't have had such an effect on you.'

'Not even after I accidentally got blood on it?'

Essie took his thumb and inspected the pad of it. 'How quickly did that little cut heal?'

'Like a normal amount of time,' he said impatiently.

'What's normal?'

'Less than a day. Essie—'

'Less than a day isn't normal. Josh, broken bones healing in a day aren't normal. Never getting sick isn't normal. And you eased Siena's pain…'

She got up, went to her dresser and came back with a small pair of scissors.

'Essie,' said Josh warningly. He didn't like how sharp they were.

'Nothing ventured,' said Essie, and scored a line across the back of her hand.

'Fuck! Essie,' he yelped, grabbing hold of the hand that held the scissors and flinging them away. 'What are you doing?'

Essie regarded the blood welling up from her skin. 'Do you want to heal it?' she asked, as if she was offering him a plate of biscuits.

'Heal – what are you talking about?'

Essie held her hand under his face. 'Make it better,' she said. 'Will it to be better.'

She'd gone mad. Or he had. 'Essie…' But she wasn't backing down, so for the sake of it Josh took her hand and closed his eyes and said, 'I will this cut to heal.'

'Hmm,' said Essie.

Josh opened his eyes. The cut was still oozing.

'You see? Nothing. Essie, for the love of god promise me you won't do that again.' He carefully wrapped his hand around hers. 'Please. Don't ever hurt yourself like that.'

Essie looked up into his face, and with her other hand she gently touched his cheek. 'All right,' she said. 'I won't. But, Josh, the next time you hurt yourself, a shaving cut or whatever, just tell me how long it takes to heal.'

He bought her hand to his mouth and kissed it. 'You think I have healing powers?' It was a ludicrous suggestion.

'I think there's more to you than the eye can see,' she said cryptically. She glanced down at her hand, and smiled. 'See? Already stopped bleeding.'

'Like normal,' Josh said, but he wasn't quite so sure anymore.

'Not really,' said Essie, and then to his surprise, she kissed him. She smelled of pine and ice and smoke, and she kissed him with her soft warm lips, and for a moment he forgot everything that had just happened. Essie was soft and warm, and under her dungarees she wore a lacy bra and not much else. His fingers simply adored touching her.

'I have a deal for you,' she said, when she let him go.

'A deal?' He'd probably agree to sell her his house for a handful of beans right now.

'If you promise to take my suggestion seriously, that you can heal things – even if it's just yourself – then I promise to try not to hurt you.'

Josh narrowed his eyes and tried to think beyond her fingers caressing his neck. 'Because you think I can heal myself?'

'No. I mean… you need to learn to focus your will. And so do I. And that takes practice. So,' she took a deep breath, which drew his gaze downward, 'will you help me practice?'

Josh felt a smile begin to spread as he realised what she was asking.

'Are you asking me,' he clarified, 'for orgasm practice?'

Essie blushed a little. 'I guess. Yeah. Maybe.'

'Essie.' Josh's smile widened into a grin. 'I thought you'd never ask.'

Chapter Sixteen

Shortly after midnight on Hallowe'en, all the printed flowers on Essie's wallpaper burst into life, showering petals and pollen all over the carpet.

This might, she later conceded, have had something to do with the oral talents of Josh Henderson, whose lips and tongue remained unfrozen and whose warm hand clasped hers tightly as she came back down to earth.

'Holy fuck,' she gasped.

'Not holy,' Josh said, 'just really good.'

Her head spun. Her fingertips tingled. Her muscles seemed to be completely unresponsive and also wound up like springs at the same time. Every bit of her skin felt like one giant nerve ending.

'Even the bedsheets feel awesome,' she murmured. She raised herself up on her elbows and looked down at him. 'Are you sure you're okay?'

He touched his slick lips. 'I feel great.'

'No… like, numbness, or tingling?'

He appeared to consider this. 'There's tingling, but it's the good kind.'

Essie sat up anxiously. 'Are you sure? Because frostbite—'

He put his finger on her lips. 'Essie. I'm pretty sure frostbite doesn't feel this good. Or if it does then it's awesome.'

He kissed her, and she tasted herself on him, and wow that was because he'd just made her come her brains out and everything was fine. He was fine, she was better than fine, everything was way better than fine…

'Whoa,' she said, noticing the petals all over the floor.

'Whoa,' Josh agreed, and she followed his gaze to the wallpaper. There were flowers growing out of it. Little blue and pink ones, the petals painted with brushstrokes.

'Did we do that?'

Josh nuzzled her neck. 'Looks like it. I like it. 3D wallpaper. You know where this would look good?'

'Mmm.' Essie buried her fingers in his hair. 'Where?'

'My house.'

She laughed. 'What, like in your bedroom, or…?'

'I think,' he grinned up at her, eyes sparkling, 'maybe we start with the bedroom and then see how we like it elsewhere.'

'Yeah?'

'Yeah. I have plans for that beanbag.'

She laughed, and fell back against the sheets with him in her arms. His skin was damp with sweat, his mouth hot on hers, and joy surged through her at the pure sensation of it.

She could have this. She could have Josh, and laugh

with him and roll around naked with him and have orgasms with him. He knew about her witching and didn't mind.

As she dissolved into pleasure with him, she didn't notice the petals on the carpet turning to ash.

There was a definite chill in the air as Josh and Essie left Beldam House, but it was a good chill. The air was clean and fresh, with a hint of woodsmoke, and the trees were still showing the last of their fiery autumn leaves.

A warm jacket had been located for Josh, who wasn't surprised any more to find it fit perfectly. He'd been given a scarf, too, but he'd been too busy kissing Essie as they left to put it on.

He held her hand as they walked down the drive. That felt exactly right. Her pace easily matched his, as if they'd been walking together for years. And every now and then she'd glance up at him and smile, her cheeks going an adorable pink.

The last few days had been… well, they'd been nothing short of spectacular.

Essie's crippling fear of orgasm had proved to be more or less unfounded. One terrible moment when she lost control so many years ago – and she wouldn't tell him how many – had been eating at her ever since. Josh had simply taken his time, so that nothing crept up on her unexpectedly, and she learned to control herself bit by bit. It had been simple.

And very rewarding.

She nudged his shoulder as they walked along, apparently for no reason other than to remind him she was still there. As if he could forget. Whatever perception spell the house had on him seemed to have worn off completely, possibly because he'd spent several days within its walls naked with Essie.

'Was Blessing really mad at us about the plants?' he said.

'Nah.' Essie pushed her glasses back up her nose. Her red hair sprang out from beneath a knitted hat and she looked absolutely adorable. 'Served that mutant flytrap right for eating my t-shirt.'

'And the parrots?'

Essie shrugged. The glass parrots that had flown, squawking, around the conservatory, were now sitting sedately on their lampposts, and barely moving unless Blessing poked them with a broom handle. Nobody could figure it out. None of the house's inhabitants had done any specific magic that might have affected them.

'Apart from you making all the paintings burst into flower,' Avery had noted.

'They went back to normal after,' Essie protested.

'It was alarming though, dear.'

'And what did you do to my flytraps?' Blessing complained. 'They've been thriving all year and now they're all turning black.'

'They do that every winter,' said Essie. 'Don't they? Like a hibernation?'

'Yes, but not all in one go,' grumbled Blessing.

Josh had tried to sympathise, but inside he couldn't care

less. He and Essie had spent several days exploring the hundred and one ways he could make her come her brains out, and he was way too pleased with himself to care about some mutant plants.

'Do you know where we are now?' said Essie, her hand tightening in his a bit.

Josh looked around at the woods. He hadn't really thought they went in for deep dark forests in this part of England, but the footpath was surrounded by one anyway.

'Uh, somewhere spooky where the Essex Lion is going to eat me?' he said.

Essie's green eyes glowed. 'If there's any eating of you going on,' she purred, 'it'll be by me.'

He grinned. 'I'll look forward to it.' He curved her towards him and kissed her, something he still hadn't got tired of and didn't think he ever would.

'Mmm,' said Essie, keeping her arm around his neck. 'We're just off the edge of Beldam House's property border. Do you…' For just a second, panic flashed across her eyes. 'You remember who I am, right?'

'Hmm,' said Josh, pretending to think. 'Hot stranger who kisses like the Devil. Pleased to meet you.'

'Josh,' she said quietly. 'It's important.'

'I know who you are, Essie.' He kissed the tip of her nose. 'I know every part of you. I'll always know.'

She smiled at that, and kissed him again, and then said, 'Just checking, but you remember about the house and everything that's happened?'

'Everything?' Josh groaned. 'Like, Essie, about a month's worth of stuff has happened in the last week. My sister had a baby in a hurricane. You and I time travelled. We had sex in a horny conservatory. A painting on the third landing winked at me.'

'It did?'

'Yeah. Some lady with hair like a spaniel. I told her I was very flattered, but I have a girlfriend.'

A smile crept across Essie's face. 'You do?'

'Yeah.' He smoothed back a bit of hair that kept blowing across her face. 'Hot girl who kisses like the Devil.'

'She sounds amazing,' said Essie, against his mouth.

'She really, really is.'

They kissed again, for longer this time, and Josh was just wondering how private the woods were when a voice said, 'I would not wish to interrupt thy loving, dears, but you did promise to fetch back the baby carriage for Miss Siena before it falls dark.'

Essie's eyes flew open, and Josh began to turn towards Prudence's voice. 'No,' hissed Essie. 'Don't look.'

'At Prudence?' He'd somehow become used to the idea that Prudence was sort of a ghost. She was just another person around Beldam House, really. No stranger than the others.

'We're on our way, Prudence,' Essie called. Her eyes were full of warning.

'The babe be thriving,' Prudence said fondly. 'He looks so handsome in the arms of his uncle.'

Josh, who still wasn't sure what to do with the baby other than hand it back to Siena in short order, turned to thank her, but Essie shook her head rapidly and put her hand on his face to stop him.

'No. Don't. Let's go this way. Don't look. Please.'

Josh, of course, wanted only to look, but Essie practically dragged him away as Prudence's cackle faded on the breeze. He couldn't help himself, though, and glanced back just for a second –

– like Orpheus turning back to Eurydice –

– and saw a woman swinging by the neck from a rope.

She waved at him.

Josh stumbled, his heart nearly exploding with panic. 'The fuck?'

Essie glanced past him, and carefully turned his back to the ghastly sight. 'I told you not to look.' She was pretty much holding him up.

'She – was she – that was Prudence?'

'Yes.'

'*Hanging*?'

'Yes. Sometimes she just goes back there. I don't know why. Maybe to get some peace from the living.'

'But she's…' Josh couldn't get the image of Prudence waving out of his head. 'She *likes* it?'

Essie shrugged. 'Prudence is an odd duck. I suspect that's what got her hanged in the first place.'

She made him keep walking, and this time Josh forced himself to keep his eyes ahead. 'Was she, uh, hanged by Hopkins?'

'No. She'd have been about a hundred years after that. Hah, she was probably the last person who paid you rent.'

'She was?'

Essie shrugged. 'I suspect none of the other residents of the house were what you might call official. And with the perception spell and all, I guess your ancestors just completely forgot about the house. Just like you kept doing.' She nudged his shoulder again. 'Until I hammered it back into you.'

Josh glanced down at her, some of his good humour restored. 'If we're going to be technical, I think I was the one doing the hammering,' he said, and Essie grinned.

Then it faded, as footsteps rounded the corner, and Lilith came into view.

'Hello, Lilith,' said Essie.

Lilith had discarded her seventeenth-century dress, with some considerable reluctance, for what she kept calling 'unstructured leisurewear'. Currently, her idea of leisurewear seemed to be a wasp-waisted vintage Dior suit and shiny, cherry-red high heels. Her immaculate hair was topped with a hat that sported both a feather and a little veil.

'Essabett.' She was shorter than Josh but still managed to look down her nose at him. 'And Joshua.'

Josh thought about correcting her. He couldn't be bothered.

'I have been to see Mrs Sockburn's family,' she said. 'They have agreed to clear the house by the end of the week. Do we know who the landlord is?'

'Uh, yeah.' Josh waved at her. 'Me.'

Lilith looked him over as if trying to work out if he was telling a joke.

'He owns half the village,' Essie said. 'Did you say you went to see her family? Don't they live in, like, Manchester?'

'"Like"? Essabett, really, I despair of this modern vocabulary.' Lilith straightened her gloves.

'We can't all live in the past, Mother.'

Lilith shrugged, as if to say it had never been a problem for her. 'I do hope you caused no problems back there. You said you performed the first binding of Hopkins?'

'Yes.' Essie shivered, and Josh put his arm around her.

Lilith frowned, a tiny wrinkle in her porcelain forehead. 'It was traditionally done by Elless Godwin,' she said. 'The daughter of the house. One can only assume she continued to repeat your ritual.'

'But did she even see it?' said Essie. 'I thought I heard someone, but...'

'Maybe she did,' he said. 'But look, someone has been performing the ritual, right? Ever since the 1640s?'

Lilith sighed. 'Up until last week, someone had been performing the ritual ever since the 1640s,' she corrected. 'This does not mean that the ritual has always been performed since the 1640s. Why do people find temporal thinking so hard?'

'I can't imagine,' Essie said. 'But look, we fixed it. I performed the first ritual, it's been done ever since, we did it early this time and everything is fine.' She cocked her head. 'Why did we do it early?'

Lilith looked, for the first time, as if she was a little mystified. 'I felt compelled to return, and immediately felt him stirring. The Earth... rebelled. I don't know how you didn't feel it.'

'I just bring the winter,' Essie said, as if it was a minor talent and anyone could do it.

'And a very nice winter it is too,' said Josh. 'If you'll excuse us, ma'am, we're going to pick up the baby seat so we can take Siena home.' The car was still skewed across the drive of Beldam House, but both he and Essie had felt like a walk. 'Can you imagine? The first Hopkins born on British soil for generations.'

'Two generations,' Essie said drily. 'Your grandfather was from Chelsea.'

'Generations,' Josh repeated firmly, and she rolled her eyes at him and grinned.

But Lilith's pale face had gone rigid. 'Hopkins?' she said.

'Yeah. Turned out Josh is a great-great-whatever grandson of the old monster himself. Did you know he had a son?'

'Yes, he was being raised by Agatha so that he might learn some goodness and humanity,' whispered Lilith. 'Essabett. I must speak with you.'

She dragged Essie a little way away, towards the lane that bordered the woods, and turned her away for a furious conversation. Josh caught very little of it, but the tone was clear. Lilith was horrified that Essie was dating a Hopkins.

Well, she'd just have to be. Josh knew he wasn't a monster, and in fact Essie even seemed to think he had a little magical power. He disagreed, but he'd be willing to play it up if it placated her terrifying mother.

He scuffed his feet in the dirt. Funny how Lilith's red heels were completely immaculate. He bet dirt was too frightened to land on them.

'...completely unreasonable, Mother...'

It was getting pretty cold now. The wind whistled down

the lane and through the trees. Josh recalled the scarf he'd been given and dug it from his pocket to wind around his neck.

'…only making you think that…'

He sighed. Was he going to have to break up this argument? Granted, he was not the poster boy for excellent family relationships, but he didn't think it was right that Lilith spent so much time in the past and just appeared to randomly mess up Essie's life. Not that Essie wasn't doing a brilliant job of standing up to her…

Josh scratched at his neck. What was this scarf made of? It prickled and tickled at his skin. It was like horsehair or something. He'd never worn something so uncomfortable.

'Ow!' He yanked the thing from his neck and held it at arm's length, but the wire wool or whatever it was seemed to be scraping his fingers. He flung it to the ground.

'Josh?'

'See how he rejects our gifts? Maude knitted that for you,' Lilith said accusingly, as Essie bent to pick up the scarf.

'From what? Barbed wire?' He rubbed his neck. It felt scoured.

'It's just normal wool. Do you have an allergy?'

'No.' He could feel Lilith's stare on him, as she stood there with her arms folded.

Essie came closer and peered at his neck. 'It looks fine. I told you, you heal fast.'

'Maude knitted that,' said Lilith.

'Yes? It's just a scarf, Mother.'

Lilith made a dismissive sound. 'Show me.'

With bad grace, Essie did. Lilith examined it as Essie fussed over Josh's neck, which felt fine now the scarf was no longer touching it.

'Any exciting portents there in the knitting and purling?' Essie asked archly.

Lilith glowered at them. 'Perhaps it is because he is a Hopkins, wearing a witch-made garment.'

'He's wearing Avery's clothes!' Essie protested. 'This is nonsense, Mother. We've got things to do. I'll see you later.'

She grabbed Josh's arm and towed him away down the lane, leaving the scarf in Lilith's hands and his neck somewhat draughty.

'What was that all about?' he asked, as the cold wind swirled around them.

'Ugh. My mother being absurd. She thinks because you're a Hopkins you'll cause harm to us all!'

Josh said, 'Well, you all know that's not true. Right? I mean, look at me. I can't even kill spiders.'

'I know! And Avery and Blessing and Prudence and everyone knows!'

'And Maude?' Josh scratched his neck.

Essie frowned. 'I don't know what was up with that scarf. Maybe you do have an allergy.'

'Maybe. Look, Essie.' He stopped and took her hands. 'You know the whole Hopkins thing means nothing, right? So he's my million-times great-grandfather, so what? It doesn't mean anything. Who was your million-times great-grandfather?'

Essie raised an eyebrow. 'Francis Godwin.' She nodded

in the direction of Beldam House. 'The man whose cellar we were locked in.'

Josh faltered. 'What?'

'Yeah. I looked it up. The one who the village was named after. His daughter Elless inherited the house. Remember? The one gathering nuts in May?'

'The one who accused us of being witches?'

Essie sighed. 'You know what witchphobia really says about you, right? We're descended from her. Me and Lilith, anyway.' She shook herself. 'She was just being a paranoid old besom about it. She's always been like that. Controlling.'

Josh hugged her, because he could tell her a thing or two about that. Maybe he should.

They started walking again, hand in hand. 'And I know she's wrong about you,' Essie said. 'That's the important thing, right?'

'Yeah.' He smiled at her. 'I really mean you no harm. I love witches.' *Well, one of them anyway.*

The thought didn't surprise him as much as it might. He was in love with Essie. Of course he was. Essie was amazing.

'Well, I'm glad to hear it.'

They walked on together for a while, the sun warming the fine autumn day, and as they skirted the edge of the Common, Josh said, 'There is maybe something I should tell you though.'

'Oh god. Do you have a pentagram tattoo I haven't found yet? Actually, scratch that, if it was there I'd have found it.'

He smiled at that, but it was a tense smile. 'It's not a tattoo. I'm too chicken for a tattoo.'

'Josh, you are not in the slightest bit chicken.'

He sighed. 'Well, that's not what Maya would say.'

'Who's Maya?'

Josh took a deep breath. 'My ex.'

He ended up telling her everything, from the first time he'd met Maya at a corporate event, with her high-maintenance hair and rock-hard nails and lipliner that didn't budge even when she stuck her tongue down his throat at the buffet.

He thought he'd been impressed by her. It had taken him a long while to realise he was actually terrified of her.

He didn't remember ever actually agreeing to date Maya, just being told when and where to pick her up and being ridiculed for his car. Maya earned more than him, but she expected him to pay. Maya hated his apartment, but she moved all her stuff into it. Maya told him he should be more ambitious, dress better, push harder at work. Maya coached him on interview techniques, mostly by shouting at him until he cried.

Maya made him throw out his Nirvana CDs and cherished vintage tour t-shirt. 'And I loved that shirt,' he told Essie sadly. He'd got it on eBay. They went for hundreds these days.

Maya made Josh into a different person, a person he'd never really wanted to be in the first place. She moulded him into her dolly and stuck pins in him to make him comply.

'Oh, Josh,' said Essie, as they turned down the path towards his house. 'She sounds awful.'

She put her arms around him. Funny, they were on the footpath Essie had led him down that first day, when he'd been so unsure of her. And for what reason? Essie wasn't going to walk him down a dark path so she could laugh at his terror. Essie wasn't going to try to change him to suit her.

'But you left her in Seattle, right? She can't follow you here.'

'Oh, I left her. "Took all my stuff and moved into a motel" left her.' He hadn't had any friends to count on. They'd been something else Maya disapproved of. All the people he socialised with were her friends, and he'd come to realise they were just as unpleasant as she was.

'Good. Did she come after you?'

'Not until I cancelled my rent and the landlord evicted her,' said Josh. It was a shame. It had been a nice apartment. 'I was honestly terrified she'd find me. I didn't know if she'd scream at me or try to – to seduce me.' He shuddered, and Essie's expression turned concerned.

'Josh?'

Essie's arms around him were warm and comforting. Her hand cupped the back of his neck. Her eyes promised he could trust her.

'She, ah, she liked, to, uh, look, you think you're the only one with hang-ups around sex?' Josh said. 'Why are we talking here? It's really public. Anyone could hear.'

Essie glanced around. There was no one within eyesight and hadn't been since they started talking. But she said,

'You're right. Let's keep going. And, Josh?' she added as they went.

'Yes?' His hand trembled in hers.

'You don't have to tell me anything you don't want to.'

The sun was setting over the newly ploughed fields as they walked along the narrow footpath. Sunlight filtered through the trees with their last handfuls of bright red and yellow leaves, setting the world on fire. The sky was ablaze with hot pink and orange clouds.

Dead leaves crackled beneath their feet. Overhead, a crow cawed.

'It's probably nothing,' Josh said eventually.

'Well, if it's nothing, you can just say it,' said Essie reasonably.

His heart pounded.

'You're so confident about everything,' he said.

She laughed. 'I'm really not.'

'You walk around these woods like nothing frightens you.'

'Oh. Well, that's because there's nothing in them that does frighten me. No bears, remember,' she added, nudging him.

'What about murderers or rapists?'

Essie snorted. 'Listen, I can freeze the bollocks off someone I *do* like.'

'You see? You're not afraid.'

Essie gave him a curious look. 'Josh, I'm afraid all the time. Do you not remember what the last few days were about? I was terrified of hurting you.'

He clung to that. 'You were. But I knew you wouldn't.

Back in the seventeenth century, you asked me to trust you, and I… I guess I do.'

She squeezed his hand. 'I trust you, too.'

Josh took a deep breath. 'You'd never try to have sex with me while I was unconscious, right?'

For a moment the only sound was their footsteps crunching on the fallen leaves.

Then, 'She did what?' Essie said. Her voice was dangerously low.

It was a few months after his father had died. Josh had told himself he wasn't affected by the death of a man he barely knew, but maybe he had been, because he'd thrown himself into work and done everything Maya told him to and hadn't entirely realised how bleak his life had become until…

He swallowed. 'I was asleep. She…' His voice stopped working.

'She fuck she did.' Essie sounded furious. 'Right. Get me on a plane to Seattle, because your ex-girlfriend is going to learn in detail the exact meaning of "colder than a witch's tit".'

Josh exhaled, too shaken to make a joke about the relative temperature of Essie's tits. 'You don't think,' he tried to remember how his colleagues had put it when he'd tentatively raised the subject in a purely theoretical way, 'it would be just, like, a really awesome way to wake up?'

'Are you kidding? That is *not* consensual. If I woke up and a man was having sex with me, whether or not he was my boyfriend, I'd freeze more than just his dick, I can tell you. She really did that to you?'

Josh nodded, kind of relieved. If she'd reacted like his co-workers, he didn't know what he'd do.

Essie hugged him, there on the edge of the frosty field. He wasn't sure when it had become frosty, but he figured Essie had something to do with that.

'I'm sorry,' she said. 'I'm so sorry that happened to you. And I'm so glad you got away.'

Josh hugged her back, relief filling every part of him. Essie understood. He could trust her.

They started walking again, and Josh had never been so glad to hold someone's hand in his.

'Everyone thought I was crazy when I quit my job,' he said. 'I'd been chasing a promotion I realised I didn't even want, and I realised I hated everyone I worked with, and the company I worked for. So I quit. I quit my job, and my relationship, all on the same day, called it a sick day, packed up what very little I still owned into the car Maya had nagged me into buying, and drove away.'

He could remember the dizzying sense of freedom as he'd left. He'd felt giddy for the first time in his life. He had no plan and nowhere to go, and that was still better than where he'd been.

'I spent the rest of the day cancelling my rent, and changing all my passwords, anything she had access to. Sold the car. Had a panic attack about getting a new apartment with no job. Realised I didn't want to go back to law.'

'Ah. Hence Siena's suggestions falling on deaf ears.'

'Yeah.' He smiled. 'It's funny, though. Siena was the one

who gave me a route out. I don't think she has any idea how much she helped me.'

For a second, he could almost feel Essie trying to work out what the impressively self-absorbed Siena could possibly have done to help someone else. He took pity on her.

'She called to ask something really weird about whether I had any family history of diabetes or high blood pressure – and now I realise why,' he groaned. 'This was probably three or four months ago. She'd have been doing all her antenatal stuff, right?'

'I guess.'

'I don't know why I didn't realise. It was a really weird conversation.'

'Well, I assume you had other stuff on your mind,' Essie said drily.

'Yeah. True. I guess. Anyway, I said something about the motel's terrible cell reception, and then I had to explain I'd left Maya – Siena doesn't know any of the stuff I just told you, by the way,' he added in sudden panic. His sister did not need the burden of his relationship trauma right now.

'Understood.'

'She said – and my god, it was the most Rich Person thing I've ever heard her say – she said, "Don't you have somewhere else to stay?" Like yeah, I'm just living in a motel for the fun of it, sure.'

'I suppose she just has mansions all over the place?'

'Yes,' said Josh simply, and Essie burst out laughing. 'Essie – you wouldn't believe how rich she is. Like, she had shares and dividends and stuff before, but our father left her the bulk of his money and it's… well, it's a lot. It's a *lot*.'

'Wow, I picked the wrong sibling,' Essie said, nudging his shoulder.

'Yeah, all I have is this falling-down farmhouse,' Josh said, as it came into sight. 'She had a whole empty beach house in Malibu which, and I quote, "You'd really be doing me a favour by staying there."'

'I always thought you had a kind soul,' Essie teased.

'That's me. Favours for everyone. So I went to stay there, get myself back together again, and then one day she says, "Hey, Josh, did you ever go check out that house in England?"'

'This house?'

'This house.' It was looking better now, he had to admit. Siena's army of workmen had finished the roof and the kitchen, and he'd been assured the suite of rooms she wanted upstairs had been completed.

'So I've got Siena to thank,' Essie said, squeezing his arm.

'For what?'

'For you, dummy. You might still be in Malibu if she hadn't told you to come here.'

'That's true.' Josh looked up at the handsome red-brick farmhouse that was now his home, and groaned. 'Great, something else I have to thank her for.'

The baby, like all babies, was a tiny squashed-looking creature who slept most of the time and screamed the rest of it.

'Please come back to the house with me,' muttered Josh under his breath, eyes full of panic. 'I don't think I can do this by myself.'

'You won't be by yourself,' Essie said, folding a baby blanket. 'You'll have Siena.'

Siena was rocking the baby in her arms, apparently oblivious to its screaming.

'Essie.' He'd never looked more desperate, not even when they were locked in the cellar. 'I'm begging you.'

She grinned. 'Of course I will. I'll even rustle up some earplugs, how about that?'

'Oh my god, I love you,' said Josh, and kissed her, and then looked a bit stunned.

'Sure, you would say that,' said Essie lightly, trying not to let her elation bubble.

All right, so they hadn't been together very long. She still didn't know exactly what parameters they were operating under. But she knew him now, knew him bone deep. She'd exposed her truest self and her worst demons to him and he'd done the same, and neither of them had run screaming.

She'd like to freeze the tits off his evil ex-girlfriend, but that was about the extent of it.

They drove Siena back to Brook Manor Farm, marvelled at all the changes the workmen had made, picked up a takeaway and settled down to watch Siena's beloved cosy crafting shows.

'That is the worst concealed zip I have ever seen,' Essie said, crunching on a prawn cracker.

'I know,' said Josh, his arm around her as they lazed on the new sofa. A fire burned cheerfully in the newly cleared fireplace. 'How hard is it to align the seams?'

Essie raised her eyebrows at him.

'I have watched way too many of these,' he sighed.

She snuggled into his body. 'You can help Avery with their next sewing project,' she said.

'Hah. As a "What not to do" example, maybe.'

A snore came from Siena's direction.

'We could put something else on?' Essie suggested.

'No way, I want to see if the girl with the nose ring can pull off that pattern matching,' Josh said, and Essie thought that might have been the moment she realised she was in love with him.

She was so in love with him, in fact, that she dismissed the shapes in the flickering fire as just a draught in an old house. Tomorrow was the cross-quarter day, the day she would traditionally perform the winter ritual, but she'd already done that, so she didn't pay any attention to the moaning of the cold wind outside the house, or the scratching of the branches on the windowpanes as she followed Josh to bed.

As she peeled off his clothes, kissing hotly, she didn't see the piece of parchment on the windowsill twitch and burst into flames that burnt out as soon as they'd started. She didn't think any more about the scarf that had scratched Josh, or about the flytraps that had turned black and died.

She fell into the heat and glory of Josh's lovemaking, ravenous for him, oblivious to everything else.

She fell asleep in his arms, supremely content with the world, and it wasn't until the screaming started that she realised something had gone terribly wrong.

Chapter Seventeen

Josh dreamed that he was being chased by the Devil.

The Devil had a nasty little beard and glinting evil eyes, and he sent demons to torture Josh in the form of his ex-girlfriend. Maya, dressed in some flimsy négligée, seduced him in a field and laughed at him when he begged her to stop.

The Devil locked him in a cellar where ghosts tormented him with their weeping. It sounded like the desperate cries of a baby. He saw a woman hanging by her neck from a tree and felt the noose close around his own throat, a prickling and scratching sensation that choked and choked him –

'Josh? Josh! Wake up, you're having a bad dream.'

He scrabbled desperately at his throat.

'Josh!'

A light flicked on, and Josh gasped back to life, flinching from the brightness for a second.

'Are you all right?'

And Josh screamed and scrambled from the bed,

because there was a complete stranger stroking his arm, leaning over him naked, her bare breasts against his chest.

'Josh?'

The sheets tangled around his legs and he stumbled, crashing to the floor. 'Who the fuck are you?'

'Are you all right?'

'Get away from me!'

He cast around desperately for a weapon, but for some reason when furnishing his bedroom, he'd neglected to place any baseball bats, sidearms, or planks with nails in them by his bedside.

Outside, a sudden crackle of thunder made him scream again, and he grabbed the nearest thing and threw it at her.

She looked down, bemused, at his sock. 'Josh? It's just a thunderstorm. Are you all right? Are you still asleep?'

'No, I'm not asleep, and how do you know my name?' He scrambled away from her across the floor, horribly aware he was naked too, and grabbed at clothes. 'I'm going to call the police.'

The naked woman in his bed drew up short at that. 'Okay, this isn't funny,' she said. 'What is going on?'

'You're asking me?' He looked around – this was his room in Brook Manor House, with the bare floorboards and the low windowsills, and the rug Siena had bought for him.

Holy shit. Siena. The baby!

Josh struggled into his boxers, a difficult feat whilst backing towards the door, and tried to remember what the situation was with the phone line. His own phone was on the bedside table, but he didn't dare go back for it, not with a naked stranger so close. Maybe he should go into Siena's room, get her phone. But he didn't want to draw attention to them…

'Josh, it's me. Essie. Essie Winterscale.'

That name sounded so fake. Probably her English accent was too. 'Who?'

Thunder crashed again, and lightning flashed through the curtains.

She was a total stranger. Nothing in her frankly unremarkable features was familiar to him. She held the bedclothes up to her breasts now, as if she'd suddenly realised being naked in his bed was inappropriate.

'How did you get in? Are you armed?'

'No, of course I'm not.' She looked worried now. 'And I came in with you. A few hours ago. Don't you remember? We brought Siena back with us.'

'Stay away from Siena.' He edged towards the door.

She raised her hands, or at least tried to. The sheet began to slip.

'Don't you even think about it,' said Josh, glaring at her. He realised he was trembling. 'You can't just seduce me like that. You think I'll wake up with a naked woman and be so horny I won't even care who she is? That's assault. I'm calling the police.'

The woman appeared to be a good actress. She even managed to get some tears in her eyes. 'Josh, please. I don't know what game this is, but I need you to stop it.'

'This is not a game,' said Josh. This was the most serious he'd ever felt in his life. He opened the door, and eyeballed Siena's room. Her door was still shut.

'I'm Essie. I'm your… we've been sleeping together for a

week. Don't you remember?'

'No,' said Josh. He glanced back inside his room, and nodded at a pile of fabric on the floor. He felt braver now. 'Those your clothes?'

'Yes—'

'Good. Now put them on, and get the fuck out. You've got five minutes.'

Josh had never owned a firearm in his life, which was probably just as well if he had one right now, he'd probably be aiming it at her.

Should he let her go, and then call the police? Or keep her here? How was he going to do that?

Across the hall, Siena was asleep with her new baby. His nephew. Siena, who was extremely wealthy and very vulnerable. That decided it for him.

'Toss me my phone,' he said, and she did, looking somehow heartbroken.

'Josh, please.'

'Get dressed,' he snapped, catching it and trying to remember through his fog of terror what the emergency services number was in England.

'Look, if you want me to go, I'll just go,' she said, although she cast a doubtful glance at the curtained window, where the lightning flashes and crashing thunder were making themselves well known. 'If you've changed your mind about us—'

'Us?' said Josh. 'There is no goddamned us.' He glanced back at Siena's room again. 999, that was the number! He dialled it and waited for the answer. 'Yes! I need police, now. There's an intruder in my house.'

But when he looked up, she was gone.

The storm was raging, even worse than on the night they'd performed the winter ritual. Essie was soaked through to the skin, not least because she'd climbed out of the window in just her knickers and got hurriedly dressed once she'd reached the treeline.

Her arms and legs were covered with scrapes, her feet were bleeding all over because she'd left her shoes behind, and she'd banged her knee landing on the bay window beneath Josh's bedroom. But none of that hurt quite as much as the look on his face when he'd told her, 'There is no goddamned us.'

There had to be some explanation. She told herself this as she hurried home through the woods, the dark trees whipping in the wind and lashing at her face and arms. There had to be some reason the sweet, loving man she'd gone to bed with had woken up accusing her of being a stranger, an intruder – a danger to Siena and the baby.

The way he'd looked at her. It was the way Hopkins had looked at her, four hundred years ago.

The storm was deafening, the sky full of lightning that only served to illuminate the masses of dark clouds boiling up the sky. Essie realised she should have been freezing but she was hot, although maybe that was just sheer rage and fear.

I should have stayed. And done what? Tried to reason with him? Josh had looked like he was half a second from finding a baseball bat and beating her with it. Essie had no magic that would work against that. What was she going to do, freeze him in place until his memory started working again?

Memory. He'd kept forgetting the house before all this, but he'd never forgotten her before. Even before they went through the time door, he'd known exactly who Essie was whenever they met in the village or at the pub. He remembered every detail of their meetings outside the house, and his memory of the house itself had seemed to be getting stronger. Ever since he'd read that parchment…

Her steps faltered. Mud oozed between her toes and a branch smacked her in the back.

The parchment. Did she still have the photo of it on her phone? Where was her phone?

It wasn't in her sodden pockets. Dammit, dammit, dammit, she must have left it behind! If she could just get Josh to read the parchment again, maybe he'd remember her. Maybe she needed to gather the coven and get them to run some kind of perception spell on him so he wouldn't keep forgetting.

The coven. The spell.

The rain pelting Essie's face turned to ice.

Lilith had been so angry when she found out Josh was a Hopkins. Furious that Essie was fraternising with him. Desperate to prove he was evil. And she'd always been so protective of the perception spell on the house.

'Mother,' said Essie, as the sky turned yellow and the rain froze in the air. 'What did you *do*?'

Snow shouldn't have covered ground soaked by a

storm, but this snow did. The earth froze, and the sky with it, and the snow came so thick and fast it was impossible to move through.

Impossible for anyone but Essie, that was. She stalked through the woods, the trees giving way and the snowflakes sizzling on her skin. Her bare feet left melting footprints behind, pink with blood,

The house was wreathed in snow, drifts of it obscuring the front steps and the porch. Essie strode grimly up them, threw open the door, and shouted, 'Mother!'

She glared at the fireplace and it burst into pale, bluish flames. On the stairs, the worried face of Marley the dog appeared.

'It's all right, the storm won't hurt you,' she assured him. 'Mother! I know you can hear me.'

Marley crept down the stairs, tail between his legs. From the passageway came a frightened bleat, and one of Blessing's goats poked her long nose around the corner.

'A private dispute between humans,' Essie answered her unspoken question. 'Go back to your stable. You will be safe.'

Tomkin and Bob wound around her ankles, their fur smearing her wet jeans. Steam rose from Essie's skin.

'Lilith Winterscale! I command you to come here at once!'

The house shook with the force of her voice. Essie had never felt anger like this.

From corners of the house Blessing, Avery and Maude appeared. Prudence floated in through the still open door.

'It be blowing a hoolie out there,' she observed, as the snow swirled through her.

'It's freezing,' said Avery. He was bearded and wore paisley pyjamas.

'It's the middle of the night,' said Blessing. Her silk bonnet slipped from her braids.

'It is the monster,' said Maude.

Essie strode towards the old woman, who stood in a nightshirt, clutching a shawl about herself. In one hand she held a candle in an old-fashioned chamberstick.

'That scarf you gave Josh,' she said. 'What was it made from?'

'Yorkshire wool,' said Maude promptly. 'Knitted on bamboo in moss stitch.'

'It scratched his neck to nearly bleeding,' Essie said.

Maude was silent a moment. Her milky eyes gave nothing away. ''Tis not he but him,' she said.

'I don't have time for riddles,' Essie said.

'It scratchen not he,' Maude said urgently. 'But him. The othern.'

Essie glanced at the others for help, but they simply shrugged.

She shoved up her sodden sleeves and stormed up the stairs.

'Mother,' she shouted. 'If you've gone back through that bloody door, you *coward*—'

'What did you call me?'

Lilith appeared in front of her painting. Essie sometimes suspected it concealed the door to her bedroom, which she'd never visited. Which in itself was a strange thing.

Essie trembled with rage. 'I said you're a coward. You disappear through that door into the past instead of ever spending time in the present. Your own present. My present.'

Lilith stood on the landing, more beautiful than anyone had a right to be in a nightdress, her hair bound with a red ribbon. 'It might be yours, but it isn't mine,' she said. 'I go where I can do the most good, Essabett. You were never neglected.'

'I haven't seen you for years!'

'You're a grown woman.'

'A grown woman,' Essie advanced on her mother, her feet bleeding all over the carpet, 'who just got kicked out of her boyfriend's bed because he thought she was a stranger.' Furious tears burned her eyes.

Lilith said calmly, 'You know there is a perception spell on this house.'

'Don't you give me that. He knew me perfectly well outside the house. You were *there*. You *saw us*.'

Lilith was silent for a moment. Essie was aware the others filled the staircase behind her.

'I merely strengthened the existing spell,' Lilith said quietly.

'Bollocks,' Essie spat. 'He forgot me completely. He called the police on me. He thought I was a – a burglar, or a rapist—'

Horror slammed into her as she remembered what Josh had told her about his horrific ex. Maya forcing herself on him in his sleep. No wonder he'd been so appalled. She'd just triggered a harrowing memory for him.

'Do you have any idea what you've done?' she wept.

'He is a Hopkins,' snapped Lilith. 'You shouldn't go anywhere near him. What his family did to us—'

'Hundreds of years ago! Mother, get over it!'

'It might be hundreds of years ago to you,' said Lilith, 'but it was a week ago to me.'

'And me, you stupid woman. I was there. I saw him. I bound him—'

'The bounden be false,' mumbled a voice from behind her. Maude's voice.

Essie felt herself go still as the terror spread through her body like concrete. 'What did you say?'

'The bounden. 'Tis false.'

Essie turned slowly and stared at the old woman.

'Him be bounden not in ice,' explained Maude, her gnarled fingers twisting together anxiously. 'I seen it. The ghosten be banished, but the monster he slipt away. Him did creep the door through.'

Essie's gaze flew to her mother. Lilith looked as horrified as she felt.

'Hopkins followed them?' she said. 'Back here?'

'Ayes.'

'Why didn't you say something!'

Maude shrugged. 'I gived thee the scarf,' she said, as if it was obvious.

'Oh my God,' said Essie. 'Are you telling me the scarf scratched Josh because – ew, because Hopkins is *in* him?'

'Ugh,' said Blessing.

'And you two have been—' Avery began.

Essie felt suddenly sick. It couldn't be possible.

Every time Josh had touched her, kissed her, every time

he'd been inside her, god*dammit*, that was Hopkins. Hot tears froze on her skin.

'No, him be a shadow 'pon he,' said Maude.

'He's haunting Joshua?' said Lilith.

'The word be good as any other.'

'I thought you could feel Hopkins,' accused Essie, turning on her mother. 'You said you always knew.'

'I didn't know he was haunting your bloody boyfriend, Essie,' Lilith said, but she looked shaken.

'Maybe that's why you can't sense him?' ventured Blessing. 'He's being… masked by Josh?'

Essie swiped at her face. Was that why Josh had forgotten her? Hopkins had taken him over? But that couldn't be right. The man who'd leapt out of bed just now hadn't been a raging, hate-filled misogynist. He'd been Josh, frightened and appalled but never violent, and he'd known exactly how to call the police, too, which a seventeenth century ghost surely wouldn't. He'd been trying to protect Siena and the baby, she could see it.

'Oh my god,' she said, as an even worse realisation came over her. 'The baby.'

'You think he's after the baby?' said Blessing.

'Then why didn't he try something here?' said Avery.

'There be powerful protections 'pon the house,' said Prudence.

'And we'd surely have noticed,' said Essie. '*I'd* have noticed.'

There was a small diplomatic pause.

'What, in all that time you spent fully dressed and discussing the topics of the day?' said Blessing.

Essie felt her face burn.

'It's been all I could do to keep the floorboards from bursting into leaf,' Blessing muttered. 'We get it, you can have orgasms now.'

'Oh my god,' Essie muttered.

'You didn't have to be *so* vocal about it,' said Avery.

'*If* we could move on,' said Lilith, and Essie looked at her mother with something like gratitude for what might have been the first time. 'Do you think Hopkins is going after the baby?'

'Over my dead body,' growled Blessing.

'It's logical,' said Avery. 'Look at the facts – the same day Siena arrived in Good Winter was the same day Lilith told us Hopkins was waking early.'

'Which was also the same day Josh first came here,' Essie pointed out.

'Yes, but only to Beldam House. He'd been in the village a week or so, right?'

'And the day you did the ritual was the day she went into labour,' Blessing added.

'And the day he followed us back through the door was the day the baby was born,' agreed Essie. 'But why has he come back today? It's been a week.'

'Maybe because Siena took the baby away from the house's protection?' suggested Lilith.

'Mayhap she named him,' said Prudence.

'She said she hadn't decided on a name,' Essie said. 'The book didn't seem to like it when I asked.'

Essie felt – actually felt – every eye come to rest on her.

'What book?' said Lilith.

Chapter Eighteen

The wind screamed in what seemed to be a constant howl, the thunder beneath it a growling basenote. Snow flew at the house from every direction, lighting up in terrifying shades as lightning flashed and crackled.

Helpfully, the newborn baby in Siena's arms joined in the cacophony, which made it rather hard for Josh to hear the police on the phone, especially given the interference on the line.

'No, I don't know how she got in,' he shouted. 'All the doors and windows were locked.'

'Do you have… camera… anywhere?'

'No, we don't have security cameras,' Josh said. He frowned at Siena and tried to move away from the baby's fretful screaming, but she followed him through the downstairs rooms. 'They're coming next week.'

He'd checked all the doors, including the ones to the cellar and attic, and they were all securely locked. The windows were all latched shut, the curtains undisturbed. He'd found nothing broken or missing.

But there had been an extra phone lying on his bedside table. Josh wondered what kind of idiot his home invader was.

'Josh,' Siena began.

'…outside the village, what seems to… snowstorm like this. Are you sure she's gone?'

'Yes,' said Josh grimly. 'I tried looking through her cellphone for any clues, but it's locked.'

'Well, we… the GPS. Keep hold of…'

'Josh, where is she?' persisted Siena. The kitchen door rattled as a blast of snow hit it.

'She's gone, we're safe,' he told her. 'I'm sorry, officer, my sister is anxious. She has a newborn baby. I'm sure you can understand.'

'…course, we'll keep trying…'

'I'm not anxious,' Siena snapped, 'I'm worried. Josh, listen to me, because this is important.'

'Excuse me a moment.' He held the phone away from his ear. 'What? Siena, I know you're scared—'

'Scared? Yeah, that's a better word. I'm scared of you.'

He blinked at her. Nobody had ever been scared of Josh in his life.

'Your girlfriend is missing,' Siena said slowly, deliberately, 'and you don't seem to care.'

'What?' He went cold at the thought Maya could have found him. 'I don't have a—'

'Whatever you two are calling yourselves! You spent the

week in bed with her, you literally can't even look at anyone else—'

Oh god, she'd gone mad. Maybe it was some kind of post-natal psychosis.

'—and now you're telling me there was a strange woman in your bed, Josh, don't interrupt me, she was here last night –

'Nobody was here except you and me. And the baby.' His heart was still pounding at the idea anything could have happened to the baby. Even if its screams were currently making it impossible to think.

'She was here! We ate Chinese food! Don't you remember, she'd never heard of General Tso chicken and she ate a whole bag of those prawn cracker things? Look.' Siena shifted the baby to one arm and wrenched open the fridge. There were piles of plastic cartons in there. 'The… uh, look, quarter crispy duck. I didn't order it, you didn't order it—'

'They make the pancakes differently here,' said Josh, reluctantly moving closer.

'Right! You kept saying that! And the wineglasses, look.'

He glanced over at the sink, where two wine glasses stood waiting to be washed. 'So?'

Siena gestured madly to the baby. 'I'm not drinking, am I? Josh, Essie was here last night. She was. Her toothbrush is probably still in the bathroom.'

He shook his head. 'No. That's not right.' Nobody had been here but him and Siena. She must have been drinking juice or something from a wine glass. And ordered some new food for a change. How was he supposed to remember every detail with the baby screaming like that?

'Sir?'

Josh glanced at the phone in his hand. 'Yeah. I'm sorry, my sister is making up some weird—'

'I am not making anything up! Right, I'm going upstairs to look in your bathroom right now—'

Josh sprinted after her. Siena deliberately blocked him from trying to get past her, stood in the doorway of his bathroom, and said, 'Look. Two toothbrushes.'

Josh stared at them. The bathroom was only half finished, and he'd been using a coffee mug to keep his toothbrush and paste in. And now there was another toothbrush beside it.

'And,' Siena said, marching over to the bin, 'given the noise the two of you were making last night… Yep. If there was no one else here last night, please tell me why there is a condom wrapper in the trash?'

The bathroom window rattled. Lightning lit up the snow.

'Sir, did you say there was someone with you last night?' asked the voice from the phone.

Josh began to wonder if this was what going mad felt like. 'No. No, there can't…'

'I am *not* looking for the used one. You can get goddamn Forensics in here if you want.'

Siena looked furious. He'd woken her up to tell her there were police on the way because of an intruder and now she was telling him… but that couldn't be right. How could he not know he'd brought a woman home? Was this all some kind of prank? Had she got a friend to pretend to do all this?

But Siena didn't have any friends in this country. Unless she'd been lying about that, but then why would she…

'I don't know,' Josh said bleakly into the phone. 'I don't know what's happening.'

'There,' said Essie, storming into the library and pointing an accusing finger at the book on the stand. It was large and old, the pages yellowed at the edges, and open towards the end.

The others crowded in behind her. Lilith said, 'I have never seen that book before in my life.'

'That's because you're never bloody here,' Essie snapped. She strode over and glared at the page. 'Here. Edward Mason Hopkins. "By his first wife, a son, Joshua. By his second wife, a daughter, Siena. To Siena, a son, Matthew Edward Hopkins."'

Her voice trailed to nothing halfway through the name. The words seemed to glow on the page. Essie thought she could smell something burning.

'What did you say?' whispered her mother, sweeping up beside her.

'She called the baby Matthew?' said Blessing, behind her.

Essie stared hard at the page, as if she could will the words to change. But there they were written in faded ink as if they'd always been there. Matthew Edward Hopkins, born 29th October 2022, father unknown.

''Tis the monster,' gasped Maude, and there was a sudden flurry of movement as she slipped to the ground and the others rushed to help her.

'Maude? Did you see this coming?'

Blessing eased her back against a bookshelf. Avery found a cushion. Maude's milky eyes flickered. 'The monstren. Over and over in the yarn. Monstren. So many.'

Her fingers moved as if she was feeling a pattern in wool that wasn't there. And Essie realised something that made her shiver. For the first time she could remember, *Maude wasn't knitting*.

'Maude,' she said, kneeling beside the oldest member of the coven. 'Where's your knitting?'

Her fingers moved helplessly. ''Tis ended,' she whispered.

The witches looked at each other in horror. 'Prudence, go and fetch it,' Essie said. What did Maude mean, it had ended? The knitting? Or the future?

Maude knitted the future. None of them knew if that meant she saw it or created it. Essie wasn't even sure if Maude knew herself.

'You mean, the piece you were knitting has ended,' Avery said, as if trying to convince themselves.

'All of it,' said Maude. Her breathing seemed shallow. 'The future has… stopped.'

The words reached inside Essie and twisted her stomach. She glanced at the others. Even her mother looked horrified.

'There be no knitting,' said Prudence, flying back in through the door. 'There be a pot of needles all neat, and baskets of yarn. But of knitting there be naught.'

Maude had been there as long as Essie could remember. As long as any of them could. And she was old, for sure, but she couldn't be dying, could she?

The old woman slumped back against the pillow, supported on either side by Blessing and Avery. Blessing had her fingers on Maude's wrist. Essie had never seen her look so worried.

'Go and bring her something,' she commanded. There were tears in her eyes. 'Some needles and yarn. Quickly, Prudence!'

'I don't,' Prudence began, but Lilith snapped, 'Quickly, child!'

'Child?' Essie muttered when Prudence had gone. 'Mother, she's three hundred years older than you.'

'She's younger than you,' Lilith said.

'Technicality,' Essie said. 'Maude, open your eyes. Please.'

Maude sighed. 'Essabett,' she said, eyes still closed. 'I cannot tell ee what will come. Only what may. Fate intertwined, did I not tell ee?'

Essie nearly groaned. 'And you said there would be a door.' The time door. What else had Maude told her? 'That there would be a man, or maybe a woman—'

'You mean me?' said Avery.

'No, I think she means Josh or Siena. She made a baby hat in burnt sienna, didn't you. Wait! That doesn't mean there will be a fire, does there?'

'The world be warmen,' murmured Maude, eyes still closed.

'Like, global warming?'

'The ritual, child. 'Twas done too early.'

Essie shot her mother a look.

''Tis the day today, and must be done. Or all the days be stopped.'

Maude's hands suddenly gripped Essie's. 'In fire it began, Essabett. In fire it must end. The son of Hob…' Her voice trailed off.

'You mean Josh?'

A tiny shake of Maude's head. Prudence appeared again, this time with a ball of yarn and some needles, but Maude paid them no attention. Essie's gut clenched.

'Please Maude, knit what you mean.'

Maude said nothing for a moment. Her hands squeezed Essie's.

'What burnt must burn, there where 'twas done. 'Tis ee must. Always.'

Then her hands went slack.

'Maude? No. *Maude*?' Not today. She couldn't lose Josh and Maude. *No*.

'There's still a pulse,' said Blessing, and Essie exhaled hard. 'We should get her to bed.'

'We should get her to hospital!'

'In this weather?' Blessing gestured at the tall library window, where snow was still battering the panes. 'No one's going anywhere.'

'It's not me! I mean… the snow might be,' Essie

conceded, 'but I can't really help that right now, and the storm was already here!'

Avery and Blessing were picking up Maude. She seemed to weigh very little. Essie held the door open for them, helpless to do anything more. Blessing had medical training and Avery was skilled at making exactly the right drink or food to make a person better. But she didn't know what food or drink could help Maude right now.

She turned back to the library, where maybe a book could help, but her gaze fell on her mother. Lilith, so beautiful in her elegant nightdress with her hair in glossy curls over one shoulder. She looked like she belonged in a classy old horror movie, tempting Dracula, although she'd be the sort of woman who staked the old bastard in the end. And her hair would still be perfect then.

Essie shoved a hand through her bedraggled curls and tried to clean her glasses on her t-shirt, but it was soaked through. Her feet, now she was no longer running on adrenaline, stung and ached all over. She felt like a drowned rat and probably looked worse.

Josh wouldn't care, she told herself, and her heart broke a little bit more.

'What do you think Maude meant by all the fire business?' said Lilith.

Essie wanted to shout at her. She wanted to scream that it was all Lilith's fault that she'd lost Josh, and maybe that was true but it wouldn't actually help right now.

Her shoulders slumped and she made it to the nearest sofa before she collapsed. 'I don't know,' she said. 'I do ice and snow, remember? I don't do fire.'

'Then light the one over there,' said Lilith, gesturing to the fireplace.

Essie glared at her and said, 'That's not the same and you know it.'

'Do I? Essabett,' her mother came to sit beside her. 'I might not have gone to university like you, but I know that ice and fire are opposites. One is the absence of the other.'

'That's really not how physics works.'

'Who mentioned physics? We're witches. And besides, if fire is all that's needed, any fool with a tinderbox can make it.'

'And then control it? Fire isn't like ice, mother, it doesn't melt away. It spreads. It feeds. That house back in the seventeenth century? Made of wood. Lined with wood. And a fire in every room. Madness.'

'Yes, no wonder it burned down,' said Lilith, and Essie felt her head come up all by itself. She stared at her mother.

'Brook Manor burned down,' she said slowly. 'In the late seventeenth century.' She couldn't remember when. A hundred years after Good Queen Bess had visited, was all people said.

'And then the family moved to the Home Farm,' said Lilith.

The Home Farm which was now called Brook Manor Farm, and even the thought of Josh's house made Essie want to cry.

She bit back the sobs. 'The family,' she said slowly. 'Which was Mistress Agatha and her ward.'

'Hopkins' son,' said Lilith.

Their gazes met. 'What burnt must burn,' Essie said.

'But the boy must have survived the fire, because he had children. Josh's ancestors.'

At the same time, they leapt to their feet and rushed to the book still open on the stand. Essie heaved the heavy pages back, flipping through the ancient parchment without any care for it.

'There. "John Hopkins, born 1644, mother unknown. By his wife Dorothy, a daughter, Constance, born 1669, a son, Jeffery, born 1671..." a son, a daughter...' There was a smudge on the page. Essie skimmed past it to read, '"Died 1680 in a house fire."'

For a moment mother and daughter both gazed at the old ink on the page. Matthew Hopkins's son had died in a house fire. The same fire that burned down Brook Manor, where he'd been raised by Mistress Agatha.

'In fire it began, in fire it must end. The son of Hob.'

'The monster,' murmured Lilith.

'The monster you never told me about,' Essie reminded her. 'Bloody winter ritual! You let me think it was about snow, and white Christmases, and – and winter wonderlands!'

Lilith shook her head. 'Life is not a Bing Crosby movie, dear. I didn't tell you because I didn't want to frighten you. You were so good at the ritual it didn't seem necessary.'

'And if I'd got bored of winter and just decided to let it drizzle a bit instead? And the monster had awoken?'

Lilith sighed. 'I'm sorry, Essie. I was trying to protect you.'

'You?' Essie snorted.

'Yes. Me. I know I'm not terribly good at it, but I am

your mother.' Lilith's hand touched hers, very briefly. 'I wanted to protect my little girl from the monster.'

Essie blinked back unexpected tears. 'Ignorance isn't protection, Mother.'

This time Lilith's sigh was gusty. 'I know that now,' she said. 'Well – here we are then. Hopkins is a monster, and now you know. I thought we'd bound him safely. I don't know how he's come back.'

'You think he lived on through his son?' Did that mean Josh had inherited some of Matthew's evil? No. He couldn't have. Not Josh.

Lilith shook her head. 'I think you bound him in ice that first time, and Elless Godwin continued the ritual, and he's been frozen ever since. Until a child with his name was born right here in this house where he was bound.'

'So why the fire?'

Lilith shrugged. 'Sometimes a fire is just a fire, Essabett.'

Essie dealt her a look. 'Ice and fire and binding monsters and the place where it all began and "a fire is just a fire?" Give me a fucking break.'

Lilith laughed, which wasn't something Essie had seen much of before. 'All right,' she said. 'What do you think happened?'

Essie spread her hands. 'I don't know, but it cannot possibly be a coincidence. Look, what's under that smudge?'

They both peered at it. 'We could use Avery for this,' Essie muttered.

'Or a handkerchief,' said Lilith. She produced one from

the recesses of her negligee, spat on it, and dabbed gently at the page. 'It's just dirt.'

'It's probably blood,' said Essie, and frowned as a memory came back to her. That parchment Josh had found in the witch ball, the one that had broken through the perception filter for him. It had worked because he'd accidentally got blood on it.

And she had a photo of it on her phone. Which was at Josh's house, dammit, but if she could somehow get him to read it out, then maybe…

Hope swelled, but burst sadly when she remembered the look on his face when he'd told her to get out of his house. He wouldn't let her near him.

'It's the names of John's children,' said Lilith, 'and look at the last one.'

Essie knew what it would be before she looked at it. 'Matthew?'

'Born shortly before the fire.'

'Hopkins came back for his namesake?'

'And burnt the place down.'

'Or maybe not.' Essie tapped her finger on the page. 'John Hopkins was being raised by Mistress Agatha. You met her.'

'She was a good friend of mine,' said Lilith.

'She despised Hopkins.'

'She very much did.'

'Maybe she burnt the place down.'

Lilith was silent a moment. 'She would have been very old by then.'

'We both know there's witch blood in that family.'

Lilith gave her a sharp look. 'You felt it?'

Essie shrugged, internally feeling somewhat smug. 'I figured a few things out.' Like Hopkins seeing ghosts, for one thing – and his absolute hatred of witches for another.

And then there was Josh, so many generations later, able to read a spell without knowing it was a spell, who healed minor wounds in a matter of minutes.

She squeezed her eyes shut. She would fix things with Josh. She would.

But first, she just had to stop the world from ending.

Chapter Nineteen

At about ten o'clock on a Monday morning, two witches landed in Josh's back yard.

He'd spent an awful sleepless night trying to figure out why the hell Siena thought the intruder in his room was his girlfriend, and being tortured by the possibility that she was right and he was the one going mad.

The snow finally stopped falling some time after dawn. Although falling was really the wrong word for a substance that seemed to be hurling itself at his house in an absolute fury. But the storm didn't abate. The snow turned to rain, the thunder and lightning continued to crash, and the memory of the naked stranger in Josh's bed continued to spin around his fevered nightmares.

He was just about dozing off again when Siena tapped on his door and said, 'Uh, Josh? You should probably come see this.'

He groaned. He was so tired he felt sick. 'See what? Did the police finally get here?'

'Just come with me. Right now.'

He dragged himself out of bed, stumbled after her like a zombie, and peered blearily at the bassinet by her bed. The baby appeared to be sleeping peacefully.

'Is he okay?'

'Matthew? Yes. He went right back to sleep after you stopped… whatever that was last night. But look. Up there.'

She was pointing out of the tall window, pointing up at something in the bruised sky. Josh blinked and yawned. 'What is that, a couple of birds?' They looked large. Herons. Storks. Fucking phoenixes, he didn't care. 'You did not get me out of bed to see birds.'

'They're not birds. Look properly.'

Josh yawned again and peered through the old glass. He blinked. He rubbed his eyes. He blinked again.

'What the fuck?' he said.

Siena said calmly, 'It appears to be two women on broomsticks.'

She was right. It really did appear to be two women on broomsticks. Actual broomsticks, like you bought at Hallowe'en, with the bundles of twigs tied to one end. And each of them held a woman, one in a long red dress, her hair streaming dramatically behind her, and the other in dungarees and glasses.

'They've been circling the house for a couple of minutes,' Siena said, as if she was indeed reporting on the actions of some exotic birds. 'Blessing told me to look out for them.'

'Blessing?'

'My midwife. Josh, don't tell me you forgot her too!'

'Why would I know your midwife?' Josh said, but his attention was only half on her, and half on the woman in dungarees. She swooped low over some trees, wheeled around closer to the house, and looked right at him.

Against the bruised and stormy sky, her hair flamed red and her glasses flashed lightning at him.

He went cold. 'It's her. The woman who was here last night!'

Siena sighed. 'Please don't start this again.'

Josh pointed an accusatory finger at the – well, the witch – who was even now coming into land in the long meadow behind the house, in the shelter of the ruined, fire-blackened walls of the old house.

'That's my property. She's trespassing. I'm calling the police.'

'And telling them what, that a witch just landed on the lawn? Josh, listen to yourself.'

He hesitated. She had a very good point.

He rubbed his hands over his face. Maybe he was having some kind of breakdown. Maybe everything – Maya, his father, moving from one country to another, Siena and the baby – had finally broken his brain.

Or maybe he was on drugs. That woman last night could have – could have…

He sank down on Siena's bed. 'I think I'm going mad,' he told her.

Siena put her head on one side. 'Why don't you come outside and talk to them?' she said. 'Blessing said we should.'

'Who is this Blessing?' Josh groaned, his head in his hands.

'She also said we should take Essie her phone back because there's something she wants to show you.'

Josh turned his head and glowered at her. 'You're still sticking with this whole Essie thing, are you? Siena, we're in a county called Essex. Are you sure you haven't just made it up or something?'

Siena just fixed him with a glare and said, 'Get dressed, we're going outside.'

And Josh did, mostly because he couldn't think of anything better to do. She was right, he couldn't call the police again. They clearly hadn't believed him last night, what with Siena shouting that the stranger was his girlfriend and they'd been having sex all night. They'd clearly thought it was some kind joke or lover's tiff, and reluctantly agreed to send someone round later when the rain eased.

And now what? The rain was still hammering down and the girl that he had – according to the evidence in his bathroom trash – been having sex with last night had just *flown in on a broomstick.*

He really ought to be calling an ambulance and having himself checked for evidence of a brain tumour or psychotropic drugs. Instead he was putting on his raincoat, in the vain hope he wouldn't get drowned from above the moment he stepped outside, and slipping the stranger's phone into his pocket.

'You're not bringing the baby?' he said, disbelieving, as he found Siena in the kitchen, zipping some kind of kangaroo pouch to the front of her coat where the baby lolled in a sling.

'Well, I'm not leaving him,' she said, fussing with a hood over the baby's head. 'Bonding time is very important in the early weeks.'

Josh stared in disbelief. Maybe they'd both gone mad.

'It is *biblical* out there,' he said. 'I think if you go down the road there's a guy with a big boat collecting pairs of animals.'

'You're so funny,' said Siena, slipping her feet into gumboots that had cost more than he ever thought gumboots could. 'Did you bring the phone? Hand it over.'

Josh got it out of his pocket, and hesitated. 'Siena,' he began, and looked at the edge of the baby's face, just visible under all the waterproofing. She wouldn't take him if the women outside really were dangerous, would she?

He shoved a hand through his hair. His brain felt like fog. When he tried to remember the last week he could only think of Siena and the baby, but he couldn't quite remember where the baby had actually been born. He remembered a room that looked like a luxury hotel suite, with a roaring fire and claw-foot bathtub, but that couldn't be right, could it?

Siena's determined expression softened at his obvious confusion. 'Josh, whatever's going on here, we'll fix it. Even if it's some kind of weird amnesia. I'll get you the best doctors. But come on. We'll be late.'

'Late for what?' said Josh, but Siena was already taking the phone from his unresisting hand and sailing out the door. He didn't feel he had much choice but to follow.

The rain hit him like a fist the second he stepped out the back door. The hood of his coat did nothing. Josh turned to lock the door – he wasn't going to let somebody sneak in while those women distracted him! – and the wind slammed him against it.

And then suddenly it gentled. For a second the rain ceased its pounding. And then, inevitably, it came back.

Well, that was weird. He pocketed the key and went after Siena, leaning into the wind and swiping the hard rain from his face. She didn't seem to be having any trouble with it, strolling along as if there was no more than a slight drizzle in the air.

'This is what going mad feels like,' Josh muttered to himself, and struggled over the cracked and broken terrace, down the steps to the massively overgrown lawn, and through the knee-high wet grass.

Unlike Siena, he hadn't put gumboots on. His jeans soaked up the water like a sponge.

Grumbling, he forged ahead, towards the charming architectural feature he'd been told was a ha-ha. Josh didn't find it so funny, consisting as it did of a concealed wall abruptly dropping away at the end of the garden, into a ditch below. Apparently it was to keep grazing wildlife from getting into the garden. In reality it looked like a lawsuit waiting to happen.

Siena stood at the edge of it, frowning a little, and Josh was about to suggest climbing down and helping her across when a broomstick swished to a halt in front of her.

A broomstick. In mid-air. In the pouring rain.

Sitting on it was the woman in red, looking like a pre-

Raphaelite painting. She held her hand out to Siena, who took it before Josh could shout a warning, and sort of skipped across the ditch.

'What the fuck?' he whimpered, as she turned and waved at him.

'Come on, Josh!'

'Yes, do come on, Mr… Henderson, isn't it?' said the woman on the broom. She held her hand out to him. There was a glint in her eyes he didn't like one bit.

'You must be kidding,' he said, and made his own way over the ditch by the totally masculine and sportsmanlike method of sitting down on the edge of one side and scrambling inelegantly up the other.

'My way was faster,' sighed the woman on the broom. She floated along beside him as he trudged after Siena. 'I must say, you're displaying a lot of courage here,' she added.

Josh's feet were squelching inside his boots and the rain had soaked through to his underwear. 'That's me,' he said. 'Captain Courageous.'

'Following your sister like this, when you've no idea what's in store.'

Josh watched Siena reach the low piles of bricks that marked out some of the previous manor house. She waved at the woman in dungarees, went forward and pulled aside the baby's hood to show him off. The other woman grinned and waved her hands about, but her smile faded when she glanced over at Josh.

He glared at her, and then at the woman flying beside

him. *There is a woman flying on a broomstick three feet from me,* he thought. *I'm not courageous. I'm insane.*

'What is in store?' he asked the broomstick woman.

'We're going to raise an ancient evil and then destroy it,' she replied calmly.

'Cool,' said Josh. 'That happen a lot around here?'

'More often than you'd think.'

'You know what, lady, I don't even know what I think any more.'

She shrugged as if to concede the point. 'Tell me, Mr Henderson, did you ever find Beldam House?'

He stopped dead, and wondered for a second if lightning had struck him. 'Beldam House?' he said.

'Yes. Essie tells me you had trouble finding it to begin with. Don't feel bad, most people do…'

She prattled on, still hovering a couple of feet above the air, as Josh stood and tried to work out why he knew that name. Beldam House. He had tried to find it, hadn't he?

For a moment he could only think of gothic towers and giant plants and, for some reason, parrots, and then he shook himself. A bad dream, probably. He'd had enough of them last night in the short hours of sleep he'd snatched.

'Come on, Josh,' called a voice from ahead, and he looked up to see the woman in dungarees, the woman who had either broken into his house and sexually assaulted him, or else was his girlfriend who he'd been happily boinking all night, standing in the lee of the low wall, beckoning to him.

Beside her stood a rusted cauldron.

'I'm going to need you to trust me,' she said.

Essie thought she'd had her heart broken before, and maybe she had. All those years ago when Sean leaped out of bed screaming and she realised what she'd done, for one. When she'd seen Bradley snogging someone else at the summer fete, for another. When her mother used to leave for weeks, sometimes months at a time and Essie had sat outside the time door, wondering when she'd come back.

But none of them, absolutely none, hurt nearly as much as the way Josh looked at her when she asked him to trust her.

Rain dripped off his face as he said, 'I don't even know who you are.'

The pain in her chest was almost physical.

'But my sister trusts you. And what's more she trusts you with her son, so.' He glanced at Siena. 'I guess I'm gonna have to trust you, too.'

Relief left Essie in one hard breath. 'Thank you,' she said. 'Oh, thank you, Josh. You have no idea…'

Lilith glared at her, tapping her wrist. She didn't wear a watch, but Essie did, and she saw it was just after half past ten. Not that she needed a watch to tell her what every nerve was screaming.

The cross-quarter – the exact half point between the autumn equinox and winter solstice, the sunset of the year when light tipped towards darkness – was in about two minutes.

'Right. Thank you. Do you have my phone? Thanks, Siena. Can I get you to—'

'Essabett,' said her mother. 'We do not have time.'

Essie glanced down at her phone frantically. She had to get Josh to read what was on that ancient parchment so he could break the perception spell. That would take less than two minutes. But she'd also need him to seal it with blood, and persuading him to do that when he wouldn't even come closer than ten feet was going to take significantly longer.

'All right,' she said, tucking the phone into her pocket. She'd do it after the ritual. Unless the ritual failed and then there would be no point, because they'd probably all be dead.

I don't want to die with Josh hating me.

But she didn't have much choice in the matter right now.

She nodded to Lilith and lit the fire under the cauldron. For a moment, she was worried the wood had got too wet, but she concentrated hard and flames whooshed up from it.

The cauldron contained a potion Avery had cooked up for them overnight, in between tending the various broths they were making for Maude. Neither Avery nor Blessing wanted to leave the older witch, and Essie couldn't entirely blame them.

Besides, she knew that this was something that had to be done by herself and Lilith. This whole thing had begun between the Winterscales and the Hopkins. It had to end that way too.

'In fire it began,' she said. 'In fire it must end.'

'Fire?' said Josh nervously.

'You'll be fine. I won't do anything to hurt any of you. I promise. I promise. I promise.'

He didn't look much relieved, and neither should he. Essie might not hurt them, but she couldn't speak for Hopkins.

The contents of the cauldron began to bubble. It was a prop, just like everything was a prop, but into it Avery had added clippings of all their hair, plus some stray ones collected from Josh and Siena's pillows. Essie couldn't be entirely certain there weren't some cat and dog hairs in the mix too, but she figured they were all part of the family so that counted.

Besides, it was the intention that counted. Essie had asked Avery to make something to strengthen her will and her power, and Avery had smiled and said, 'Just think about who you're doing this for as I make it.'

And Essie had thought of the other witches, of the village of Good Winter, of all the witches who had come before her and would come after. And then she'd thought about Siena and the baby, and mostly she'd thought about Josh.

'And we have power,' Avery had murmured, as the potion changed from a murky brown to the green of the shirt Josh had been wearing on their last day together.

She dipped a cup in and took a sip. It tasted of cold, crisp snow and smoky autumn mornings. It tasted like spring blossom and warm summer grass.

Fire and ice, she told herself. What was one but the absence of the other?

'Matthew Hopkins!' she shouted. 'I summon thee!'

She grabbed her broom and walked in a rough circle around the cauldron, sweeping.

'My Matthew?' murmured Siena, cuddling the baby protectively. Essie saw Lilith shake her head.

'Matthew Hopkins. Son of James Hopkins, father of John Hopkins,' clarified Essie. 'I summon thee to this time and place.'

She made the circle wide, and made sure Siena and Josh were inside it. Her mother she didn't worry about. Lilith knew what was expected of her.

'Matthew Hopkins, murderer of witches. I summon thee to this place and time.'

She closed the circle and banged her broom on the ground.

For a terrible moment nothing happened, and not for the first time Essie reflected that being a witch would be a lot damn easier if spells were things you learned and memorised instead of making them up every time.

'Uh,' said Josh, and then suddenly the fire roared and the earth trembled.

'Are you sure this is safe?' said Siena. She had both arms wrapped around the baby in its sling.

'We will not harm *you*,' said Lilith, and there was something very definite about that last syllable.

From the sodden earth something like ashes rose up, forming as they did the monstrous shape of a man. It wasn't the well-dressed, handsome young man they'd met in the seventeenth century, but more like what would have happened if his corpse was preserved in ice for hundreds of years. Twisted, emaciated, the face a sunken gargoyle.

It lifted its head and roared, and ash fountained from its gaping mouth. Where the rain hit its blackened skin, it sizzled. Rage poured off it like dry ice.

'Matthew Hopkins, son of James Hopkins. I bind thee to my will. I bind thee to my will. I bind thee to my will.'

The monster paused, and turned its hideous face towards Lilith, because it was Lilith who had shouted the words.

'Your will, hag?' Its voice whined like a cold wind under an ill-fitting door.

'I will thank you not to insult me,' said Lilith sharply.

The monster that had been Hopkins laughed, a nasty grating chuckle. 'I know you,' it said.

Essie began to move closer to Siena while its attention was diverted.

'Aye?'

'I know you of old. Lilith Winterscale.'

Lilith's chin came up. 'What of it?'

'Even thy name speaks of congress with the Devil,' spat Hopkins. His voice boiled with hatred.

'Bind it to your will,' Essie murmured to Siena.

'What?' Siena looked terrified, as well she might.

'Repeat those words my mother said. Say it three times.'

'But my son is called Matthew—'

Yes, and thanks for that. 'Was his father called James?'

'Uh… I don't… um, actually know.'

'Cosmic,' muttered Essie. In front of her, Hopkins traded insults with Lilith, the shade of its body hissing and spitting in the rain. 'Call him the witchfinder general. Do it now, please. Quietly.'

Siena looked like she'd rather be anywhere but here, but she repeated the words Essie had told her. Essie nodded, and crept closer to Josh.

'I need you to bind him,' she whispered, as loudly as she dared. Josh might just be in Hopkins's eyeline.

'What?' Josh looked stunned and terrified, which was fair enough. There was a sort of ice mummy ghost shouting insults right in front of him.

'Strumpet!' shouted the monster that had been Hopkins. 'Putrid whore!'

'Hey, less of the insults, buddy,' said Josh, just as Essie reached him, and she could have shouted at him. Fantastic timing to draw his attention!

Hopkins swung around, his desiccated face a few feet from Josh's.

'What say you?' he grated.

'Just,' Josh swallowed, and leaned back but stood his ground. 'Less with the whore, okay? She's a lady.'

'I thank you,' said Lilith.

But Hopkins made a sound like a snort. 'She is a whore,' he said. 'I have seen her puling brat and yet she be unwed.'

'Puling brat?' Essie said. Did... had her mother had another child? Four hundred years ago?

'Not the time or place,' said Lilith quickly.

Essie figured time and place were rather mutable things for her mother, but she agreed they had more important things to do right now. Hopkins was leaning closer to Josh, and inhaling. She saw a look of recognition come over his face.

'A whore I may be, but I am no blasphemer,' said Lilith loudly, and Hopkins swung back to her.

'Blasphemer!' he roared. 'Not just a whore but a lying one!'

'You take the words of the scripture and twist them to your own ends,' shouted Lilith. 'For profit! You sell your soul for silver!'

Essie darted to Josh and whispered urgently, 'Say, "Matthew Hopkins, witchfinder general, I bind thee to my will," three times.'

He looked at her like she was mad. 'Lady, I don't know what it is you're doing here—'

'Trying to save the world, and I need your help,' Essie hissed. 'Just do it, Josh. Please.' She felt tears burning in her eyes. 'I know you can't remember me, but do it for Siena, for the baby. Please. For the people you love.'

He glanced over at his sister, who huddled against the ruined wall of the old manor house, cuddling the baby close.

He looked back at Essie. His brown eyes were narrowed against the rain but against her too.

He glanced at the monster, who was screaming Bible verses at Lilith as if they were arrows or bullets.

'Fuck it,' he muttered, and then slightly louder, 'Matthew Hopkins, witchfinder general, I bind thee to my will.'

'Thank you,' whispered Essie, as he repeated it. 'Thank you, Josh.'

He gave her a wary nod, but kept his eyes on the monster.

She waited until the last of Josh's repetitions had faded into silence, and then murmured her own. She felt it take hold, the link between her and Hopkins. His filthy, rotten soul bound to her.

She took in a deep breath, and reminded herself of the smell of winter and of summer. Then she raised her voice and shouted.

'Matthew Hopkins who calls himself the witchfinder general! We bind and abjure thee!'

His face whipped around, and his horrible dried-up eyes swivelled in her direction. The force of his malevolence was horrifying.

He peered at her. Then he laughed that merciless laugh. 'It is the puling babe,' he said.

'The…' began Essie, put off her stride. What did he mean by that? Had he met her as a baby? When?

'Whore's whelp,' sneered the spectre. 'Fornicator!'

Concentrate, Essie. 'We bind and abjure thee,' she repeated, but Hopkins swooped closer and breathed ash all over her.

'Foul hag born of a hag,' he said. 'I remember thee. Froze thy mother's tit as a mere suckling babe. Like Midas,' he jeered, 'but a weak, artless woman.'

I froze her? Essie's gaze darted to her mother, who avoided her gaze. *I hurt her, just like I hurt Sean, just like I'd hurt Josh if he ever remembered me –*

'Hey.' A hand touched hers, a warm human hand, and she looked up, astonished, to find Josh beside her. 'He's trying to distract you. Concentrate.'

'Useless hag who freezes all around her!'

'Let go,' begged Essie, tugging her hand away. 'I don't want to hurt you—'

The corner of his mouth quirked. 'You promised not to.'

From her other side Siena said, 'You said it three times. That has to mean something, right?'

Essie looked from one to the other of them. 'It means an oath that can't be broken,' she said.

'Well then,' said Josh, and his hand took hers firmly. 'I guess that means you can't.' Siena took her other hand. Josh said, 'What did you come here to do?'

Essie's fingers tightened around Josh's. He couldn't remember her, but he could trust her. He was still her Josh, the one she'd fallen in love with. And that was more powerful than any magic.

Essie looked at the monster taunting her, and lifted her chin. 'I came to burn you,' she said.

Hopkins cackled. 'Burn me? With that pathetic fire? Thou hast the warmth of thy mother's tit.'

Lilith came to stand on Siena's other side, and took her hand. 'And what would you know about the warmth of a woman's tit, Hopkins?' she said.

'No one's ever let you touch one,' Essie said.

'Lies,' hissed Hopkins. 'I have fathered a child.'

'Within wedlock?' said Essie.

'Even on a woman who gave you her consent?' said Lilith.

'What woman would give you consent?' said Siena, with the full force of withering scorn only a girl from Beverley Hills could summon.

'Are you sure you're not just angry at the world because a nice girl said no to you?' said Josh.

Hopkins screamed and flew at them, but he was insubstantial, no more than a stinking shadow.

'How did you know a nice girl said no to him?' Essie muttered.

'Look at him,' said Josh. 'He's every angry guy watching porn in his mom's basement.'

'You want a nice girl, you gotta be a nice guy,' agreed Siena.

'Nice girls owe you nothing,' Josh said to the raging spectre, and Essie felt a glow of pride.

'Hagridden whoreson!' roared Hopkins, surging forward.

'Fire is the opposite of ice,' Essie said to the others. 'When I say so, concentrate as hard as you can on burning him—'

But Siena wasn't listening. 'You stay the hell away from my baby,' she snapped, recoiling. Essie and Lilith held her firm.

Hopkins inched in closer, his hideous face sniffing like a rabid dog. 'Another Hopkins whelp,' he rasped.

'That's Matthew E—' Siena began, and Lilith's free hand slammed down over her mouth.

'Don't give him the name!' she snapped.

'Never give him his name!' Essie cried.

Siena's hand trembled in Essie's. But she rallied. 'You're not fit to speak it,' she spat.

'Good girl,' Josh murmured.

'Blood of my blood,' crooned Hopkins thoughtfully.

'You keep your filthy hands off him,' Siena said.

'Off him?" Hopkins was nearly purring now. 'How about in him—'

'Now!' yelled Essie, as Hopkins oozed closer to the baby in its sling. 'We burn thee with fire! We send thee to Hell!'

'You will burn for all eternity,' shouted Lilith, as the raindrops hitting Hopkins began to steam.

'You never will rise again!' Essie roared with all the force she could.

'You'll never hurt anyone,' Josh yelled.

'You'll never work in this town again,' screamed Siena, and despite herself, Essie nearly laughed.

The thing that had been Hopkins began to wail.

'With fire we burn you! We condemn you! We destroy you!' Essie shouted. The rain came harder and harder, but it was a hot rain, and where it hit the monster it burned like oil. 'We cleanse you from this earth forever! As we will it, so will it be!'

The words were a vehicle for her intent. Essie concentrated with everything she had, beaming out her will as hard as she could. To take away the ice that had bound him, preserved him, all these years, remove every atom of cold there could be, and burn him to ashes and fine powder.

And as the screams of the others joined the scream of the storm, they turned the monster that had once been a man into flames, and watched the ashes turn to mud.

Ice merely held things in place. It was fire you needed to kill it for good. In the end, Hopkins was just like bacteria.

Essie let go of Josh's hand, which she hadn't realised she'd been gripping quite so hard, and Siena's, and marched over to the cauldron. Her head felt light. Her vision blurred, but that might have been the rain on her glasses.

She grasped the cauldron in both hands. The heat of it didn't burn her.

Then she poured its contents all over the ground where the monster's ashes had fallen. Hopkins had thrived on hatred, and Essie knew perfectly well what the opposite of that was.

'You,' she said to the steaming ground, as the rain ceased and the wind dropped, 'can just—'

'There is a child present,' warned her mother.

'—love yourself,' finished Essie. The ground tilted a little beneath her feet.

'Is the baby okay?' said Josh.

Siena bit her lip. She looked a bit guilty. 'I hope so,' she said. She glanced back at the house. 'I left him in his crib.'

Josh sort of stared dumbly. Essie started laughing, and wasn't really sure if she could stop.

'Then who…?' Josh said, indicating the kangaroo pouch zipped into Siena's jacket.

Siena pulled back the hood, and showed him the doll she'd shown Essie earlier.

'I wasn't going to bring him out here where there's a monster,' she said.

Josh looked utterly bewildered. 'But… how did you know there was a monster? How did you know… any of this?'

'Did you read the parchment?' said Lilith. A weak sun began to shine.

'What parchment?'

'It's on my phone,' murmured Essie, who could really use a nice sit down around now.

Siena shrugged. 'Essie said it would be okay,' she said. 'And I trust her.'

Essie smiled at Siena, who was going in and out of focus.

'Whoa, are you okay?' said Josh, rushing to catch her as the walls and the trees swung in the wrong direction.

Essie blinked up at him, not sure how she'd come to be lying in the mud with Josh's arms around her.

'She's exhausted,' said Lilith briskly. 'I daresay we could all do with a nice cup of tea.'

'Tea?' said Josh incredulously. Tenderly, he brushed Essie's sodden hair away from her face.

'Sometimes the British are so British,' agreed Siena.

Essie tried to focus on Josh's beloved face. He was so handsome. His eyes were so kind.

'You were brilliant,' she told him. She felt about four hundred years old. Maybe she was.

He smiled. 'I was just following your lead.'

'You don't even know me,' she murmured.

'Well, no,' said Josh, 'but I figure I'd like to.'

Essie smiled, and closed her eyes just for a moment.

Chapter Twenty

'Of course Essie isn't four hundred years old,' said Lilith. 'What an absurd thing to say.'

'Right,' said Siena, after a short pause. 'Of course.'

'She was just born four hundred years ago.'

Josh glanced up at the ceiling of the kitchen, as if he could see through it to the bedroom where they'd left Essie sleeping. Lilith had picked her up as if she was a child, put her to bed in Josh's own room, and come down with a pile of sodden, dirty clothing that she appeared to expect Josh to wash.

The washing machine was churning away even now in the scullery. *I still have a scullery.*

Siena had given him a look like she expected Josh to object to Essie being put in his own bed, but he found he didn't have it in him. Besides, it wasn't as if they had an abundance of guest bedrooms all readily made up for her.

Lilith herself perched at the kitchen table like a duchess in the servants' hall, sipping politely at what was probably a terrible cup of tea. She kind of looked like a witch should look, he guessed. Dramatic, haughty, beautiful in a terrifying kind of way. Her hair and dress appeared to be no more than slightly damp, and after a few minutes nobody would even have been able to tell she'd ever been in the rain. Her broomstick was propped in the corner beside Essie's.

Essie, who had turned up to save the world in dungarees and boots. He kind of liked that.

'See, this is where I get confused,' said Siena, as if they were discussing the difference between a sidewalk and a pavement, and not the quantum mechanics of time travel. 'How was Essie born four hundred years ago, but is not four hundred years old?'

Lilith shrugged as if it was obvious. 'Time travel, dear. The time door. Josh has been through it.'

He blinked slowly at her. 'I have?'

'Yes. Hopkins chased you through it about a week ago. Thus, Essie was the first person to bind Hopkins in ice, a technique which sufficed to hold him until you two returned to England.'

'So we called up Hopkins?' Josh said blearily. This woman thought he'd travelled through time. Well, hell, given the events of the morning that didn't seem so far-fetched.

'Don't interrupt,' said his sister. She had baby Matthew in her arms and was rocking him gently. He appeared blissfully unaware of the terror he'd escaped. 'So Essie was born in…?'

'Good Winter,' said Lilith, smoothly sidestepping the

question. She gave them a wry look. 'But the seventeenth century was no place for a child. Infant mortality…' She shuddered. 'Smallpox reared its ugly head and I'm afraid I fled back to the safety of the twentieth century, antibiotics and vaccines. And she was so much happier here. Beldam House had just acquired a midwife with the full training of the NHS, and I can't tell you how relieved I was about that.'

'You mean Blessing?' said Siena. Her forehead wrinkled.

'Yes, of course. A very apt name, I've always thought. Avery helped me with the records, and as far as the world knows, Essie was born about three hundred and eighty years after the fact.'

'So she's… how old?' Josh said. Essie looked about thirty. But then again, so did Lilith.

'It is very rude to ask a lady her age,' she told him severely, and tutted. 'Americans.'

'How old is Blessing?' said Siena, who appeared to be trying to count on her fingers.

'What did I just say?' Lilith sipped her tea, and said, 'We age slowly. It's best not to ask. You have very good skin,' she said to Josh.

'Uh,' he resisted the urge to touch his face, 'thanks?'

'But then you are a Hopkins.'

'I'm a Henderson, thanks very much,' he said. He'd been saying it for years, whenever anyone discovered who his father was.

'No,' said Siena. 'You're a Hopkins.' She cut him a look as she rocked the baby. 'No disrespect to your mom and all, but it's kind of time you acknowledged Dad. He was proud of you, Josh. He loved you.'

Josh didn't know where to look, so he stared at the scarred and battered kitchen table that had been here when he moved in.

If his father had loved him and been so proud of him, why had he left everything to Siena? Why was this house the only thing Josh got? A dilapidated pile in a cursed village on the other side of the world.

'Daddy left me money,' Siena went on, apparently absorbed in the way baby Matthew sucked her finger, 'because he knew I'm helpless without it. When I have a problem, what do I do? I throw money at it. When you have a problem, Josh, you figure it out.'

'Am I still under the influence of magic or did you not pay for this whole renovation?' he asked.

Siena waved her hand as if that was nothing. 'Well, I did turn up here out of the blue,' she said, 'it was the least I could do. But you'd have figured it out. You put yourself through college,' she went on, over his protestations. 'All the way through law school. Good job with a good company.'

'They were assholes,' Josh said, and sipped his tea.

'And when you figured that out, you quit,' Siena continued smoothly. 'You made it here, you made this place liveable, you'd have fixed it up by yourself. And hey, you found the house that owes you ten grand a month in rent, backdated, over a period of two hundred and eighty years which, adjusting for inflation, is…' She pretended to count on her fingers again.

Lilith rolled her eyes. 'We paid Agatha Cropley,' she said.

'You did?' This was news to Josh. 'The solicitors didn't know that.'

'Well, of course not. We paid her in racing tips. Maude —' Her face clouded. 'I should check on Maude.'

Josh glanced at his sister, who shrugged. 'Maude?'

Lilith stood. Her hair and dress appeared to have dried to a perfectly well-groomed state. In the background, the washing machine tumbled on. He and Siena had thrown their sodden, filthy clothes in as well, but Lilith had declared she had no need for it, and appeared to be right.

That's a hell of a mother-in-law you're getting there, said a voice in his head, and he was so startled by it he almost missed Lilith leaving.

'Essie will probably sleep for a while longer,' she said. 'I think she's just exhausted.'

'She's not the only one,' said Josh, who after all had barely slept last night.

'Yes, but you didn't just send the Devil back to Hell,' said Lilith, as she picked up her broomstick. 'Helping to do the thing is not the same as the thing. Let me know when she wakes up.'

She paused right at the door. The storm had cleared to a mild, cool day.

'Oh, and the parchment. Avery facsimiled a copy.' She reached into the bristles of her broomstick and withdrew an ordinary envelope, which she held by her fingertips as if it might poison her. 'I thought they might have to manifest it, which would have been painful, but apparently they have a "printer" now, so there's that. Anyway.'

She laid it on the table and stood back quickly.

Josh and his sister regarded it for a while, but it didn't do anything.

'What does it do?' Siena asked, as Lilith opened the back door.

She smiled. 'It lets you see clearly. Up to you if you want to use it. A single drop of blood should help.'

And with that, she was gone.

Essie woke in an unfamiliar bed, aching all over and with what appeared to be twigs in her hair. The room was in darkness, with just a little moonlight showing between the gap in the curtains. She fumbled around until she found a bedside table, and then her phone, which said it was just after half six in the evening. And that it was still 7th November, the cross-quarter day. They'd banished Hopkins about eight hours ago.

Only eight hours. And it had been less than twenty-four since Josh had forgotten who she was.

She breathed in, and stopped. She'd figured she was in Josh's house, but not that she'd be in his actual bed. But his scent was all over it. His soap, his shampoo – and hers too, because it had only been last night she was here.

Cautiously, she reached for the bedside lamp and turned it on. Yep, this was Josh's bedroom. Piles of boxes everywhere, a half-restored fireplace and curtains held up with bits of wood. Hanging from a hook on the back of the door was his Seattle Seahawks baseball cap.

She ran her hand over his pillow, her heart breaking a

little. The way he'd looked at her, as if she was a stranger – a dangerous, threatening stranger at that. He'd hated her. Worse, he'd been frightened of her.

She took in a shaky breath and let it out again. He'd trusted her this morning though, hadn't he? Even when he'd believed Siena had brought the baby out with them. Whatever Maya had done to him, she hadn't broken the kind, sweet man he was inside.

There was a pile of clothes on the chair by the window. Her dungarees, her t-shirt. Her underwear, even. They looked freshly-laundered, and when she crept closer, they smelled it too.

When they'd left the house this morning, Lilith had scolded her for not dressing more appropriately. But Essie had always put on a long dress for performing the winter ritual, and had always felt a bit of a fraud for it. In her old dungarees and t-shirt, she was herself. And she had to be herself to pull off the ritual they'd managed this morning. She had to be more herself than ever before.

The mirror propped up on the dresser told her that her hair was a bird's nest of tangles and twigs, and her glasses – neatly left by the side of the bed next to her phone – were smudged. Yes, she was definitely herself again.

Essie took a deep breath, and left the bedroom. This time, she did it through the door and not the window, and she did it fully dressed.

At Brook Manor Farm, the stairs came right down into the kitchen. She smelled something savoury as she descended, and heard someone moving around. Her heart leaped.

It was Siena. She had the baby in a sling and was poking at a dish of what looked like shepherd's pie.

'Oh! Hey, Essie. Do you know how ovens work?'

Essie blinked at her. *This morning we banished a monster to Hell.* Had Siena forgotten that? Had Lilith been up to her tricks or something? But no – Siena knew who she was. She didn't seem appalled by Essie's presence.

'Uh, I guess. Avery never lets anyone near the Aga usually, but I don't suppose electric ovens have changed much since my uni days…'

She crouched down in front of the oven to peer at the controls, which looked fairly straightforward. That is, straightforward if you'd ever used an oven before. Siena looked as if she needed reminding which appliance it actually was.

'Avery sent this over, by the way.' Siena gestured at the large dish. 'They said it would make you feel better. Uh,' Siena added apprehensively. 'What *is* shepherd's pie?'

'Minced lamb in gravy with mashed potatoes on top,' said Essie. 'Not a shepherd in sight, I promise you.'

'Oh.' Siena swiped her hand across her forehead theatrically. 'Phew. That sounds yummy, actually. Essie, Avery also said Maude is doing much better.'

Essie looked up, relief relaxing muscles she hadn't realised she'd tensed. 'She is?'

'Yeah. Something about the future restarting?'

'No more monsters?' Essie said, remembering the yarn full of them.

'No more monsters. I guess we did it,' said Siena, who looked very pleased with herself. 'Uh, but I forgot to ask about the oven, because I don't know what all the symbols and things mean…'

Essie looked back at the oven. It was pretty obvious to her, but clearly Siena hadn't grown up doing a lot of self-catering.

'Right, so this knob is function, like grill or fan assist, and this knob—' Essie looked up, right into Josh's crotch.

Her face flamed.

'Yeah?' said Josh innocently. 'What does that knob do?'

'Uh, temperature,' muttered Essie, and nearly fell on her arse in her attempt to scramble to her feet.

He held out his hand, and she hesitated a moment before she took it. He had good hands, did Josh: strong and capable, a little rough around the edges, capable of extreme tenderness and passion. Heat flared through her, and she lost her breath for a moment.

'Whoa, are you okay?'

Essie nodded, and steadied herself on the kitchen counter as she got her feet under her. She stared at him. Josh stared back, and for a moment they both stood locked like that, the entire world vanishing around them.

'Oh my god, Essie,' Siena cried, and suddenly darted in to grab Essie's hand off the counter. Essie didn't quite realise why until she saw the panic flare in Josh's face, and realised she'd put her palm down on the electric hob, which was glowing orange.

'Holy shit, are you all right?' Josh grabbed her hand and carefully turned it palm up. 'Siena, quick, get some ice—'

'I'm fine,' said Essie, because it didn't hurt.

'Yeah, but burns are terrible things, sometimes you don't even… realise…'

Josh gazed at her palm in bewilderment, and then looked up at her. The skin wasn't even red.

'I really am fine,' Essie said. She flexed her fingers to prove the point.

'But—' Josh began, then seemed to run out of words. He glanced in confusion at Siena, who frowned and deliberately put an ice cube on the stovetop. It sizzled and melted right away.

'That should have burnt you,' she said.

Essie took a deep breath. Josh was still cradling her hand carefully in his. 'I'm the winter witch,' she said. 'I control ice. And what's the opposite of ice?'

'I don't think that's how physics works,' Josh began.

'It's how magic works,' said Essie. 'It's how it worked this morning. You… do remember this morning, right?'

Josh nodded slowly.

'I don't think I'll ever forget,' said Siena.

Essie sighed. 'You say that,' she said.

Josh and Siena exchanged a look. Then Siena went to the table and picked up an envelope. 'Your mom gave us this,' she said. 'She said if we read it and sealed it with blood, then we'd be able to remember you and your house and everything.'

'That we'd be able to see you clearly,' said Josh. He was still holding Essie's hand in his. His eyes were looking right into hers. 'I can see you clearly now, Essie.'

'But we wanted to wait until you were up,' said Siena.

'In case we messed up or something and then both forgot who you were and everything.'

Essie couldn't bear it. She pulled away from Josh, and wrapped her arms around herself.

'What is it?' said Josh.

She stared at the back door. Presumably, Lilith had needed to ask permission to come in with her earlier. *They never will cross this threshold or seat at my hearthe.*

'You don't actually know what you'll be reading out,' she said. 'And I can't ask you to… to consent to magic when you won't actually know what it's going to do.'

Josh frowned. 'You don't trust your mother?' he said slowly.

The laugh escaped Essie before she could stop it. 'Not as far as I could throw her!'

The siblings exchanged another glance.

'Well, I guess we both know a little about untrustworthy parents,' Josh said.

'Yeah, like how he never told either of us the other one existed,' Siena said.

'Why don't we open the envelope and read it?'

'Because,' said Essie, 'I can't guarantee it wouldn't work the moment you looked at it. You told me the first time, Josh, that you didn't actually know what any of it meant. Your brain just translated it, in some weird Hopkins-y way.'

'So the blood is for—'

'Surety, I guess. There aren't exactly… absolutes in witchcraft. It's not like following a recipe or something. You kind of have to make most of it up as you go along.'

Josh folded his arms. He looked at the envelope Siena held. He said, 'Huh.'

'Huh?'

'Well.' He cocked his head to the side, frowning a little as he thought. It was devastatingly cute. 'I guess it's kind of like the law, then.'

'Josh,' said Siena patiently. 'You do not get to make the law up as you go along. I know I didn't go to law school but I'm pretty clear on that.'

'No, I mean… it's all about intent. Wording can vary, so long as the meaning is clear.'

'Well,' said Essie, 'I mean kind of. As long as you mean what you say.'

'That's where law and magic differ,' he said gravely. 'Listen. Do I have to read out these exact words? Or could I… write my own? If I really meant them?'

Essie blinked at him.

'I mean, someone wrote these once, I guess? So… what's to stop me from writing my own? Or Siena?'

Essie moved to the table and took a chair. She thought about the winter ritual, where she'd mostly learned by repeating the words her mother used to use. She thought about the way she'd bound Hopkins, first in ice, and then destroyed him with fire. She'd made it up then, and everything had more or less worked out.

'Did Lilith explain to you what those words meant?' she said. 'That it wasn't just about seeing clearly and remembering things. It was about… making magic not work on you. It was about repelling witches from the house. I expect she had to ask to bring me in earlier?'

They both nodded. 'I thought it was just some British politeness thing,' said Siena.

'It was a witchcraft thing. Look. If you want to do this… you're basically writing a spell to undo another spell that you weren't even aware of until I told you about it. Josh, I really could be a mad stalker who broke into your house and climbed naked into your bed.'

Josh laughed. 'No, you couldn't. C'mon, Essie. I might not remember you, but I'm pretty sure I know you.'

I know you.

Essie couldn't speak. That might have been the most romantic thing anyone had ever said to her.

'That doesn't even make any sense,' Siena said, but Essie got to her feet and went over to Josh, whose smile faded when he saw her expression.

'Did I say something wrong?' he said.

She shook her head. 'You said it exactly right,' she whispered. 'Write your spell. You'll do it right.'

Josh figured something as important as getting his memory back and understanding witchcraft ought to be done with some ceremony, whatever Essie said. But his house was pretty low on witchy supplies, so he had to make do with a sheet of notebook paper and a ballpoint pen, writing at the kitchen table as Essie made cups of proper tea and Siena fed the baby.

'I figure there should at least be a candle,' he said, looking around the half-finished kitchen. The walls hadn't been tiled or painted, the lighting was one bare bulb, and he still couldn't get anyone in this country to understand what a toaster oven was.

'I can probably get a candle app on my phone,' said Siena.

Josh rolled his eyes. 'Some kind of potion?'

Essie put down a mug in front of him.

'There you go,' she said. 'Magic potion.'

'It's tea,' said Josh.

'You make mock, but we've fought wars and built empires on this stuff. Drink up.'

Josh looked at her, and then Siena. A month ago he hardly knew his sister, and now she was just part of his everyday life. And a few hours ago he'd thought Essie was a stranger, and yet here she was, in his kitchen, somehow making it feel like home.

I know you. He didn't know why he'd said it, but it was true. Essie, who strode around the place in her dungarees as if she owned the whole world, and sent demons to Hell, and didn't burn even when she put her hand on a red-hot stovetop.

He felt as if he'd dreamed about the way she felt and smelled and tasted. About the scent of winter on her skin and the heady heat of a jungle, and of flowers bursting into life.

And with every minute he spent with her, he was more and more sure that what she said was right, that he did indeed know her very intimately, and that someone had stolen that from him.

'We're going to have to talk about your mother,' he told her.

Essie sighed. 'Tell me about it,' she said. 'Are you done?'

Josh reread what he'd written, and nodded. 'I think so. Siena, you okay with this?'

She hesitated. 'Won't reading it make it, you know, happen?'

'Not if you don't want it to,' Essie explained patiently. 'When you're ready, just project your will into your words. Oh, hang on, one thing first.'

She strode over to the back door, where her broomstick leaned against the unpainted wall. Josh would never have believed, until he'd actually seen it, that she could fly on it. He still wasn't sure he believed it now.

Essie picked up the broom, opened the door to the cold night, and swept the ground vigorously. 'You,' she said. 'Old spell. Whoever set you, whatever their intent, begone from this house and the people in it.' She swept towards the back door, as if trying to clean dirt from the floor. 'Go on,' she said, 'piss off, and don't come back.'

Josh was sure he felt a sort of sucking sensation as she said that, and then she nodded, closed the door, and propped up the broom again.

We use them for sweeping…

'Ready?' she said, and by the light of the flickering candle app on Siena's phone, Josh read out the words he'd written.

'I, Josh Henderson Hopkins – ' he heard Siena's intake of breath, and continued on, 'being of sound mind and body, do solemnly promise that I will never hunt or harm a witch.

I promise that they will always be welcome in my home. I wish to see witches clearly and not be afraid of them. I also swear that no witch's spells will ever take effect on me without my consent,' he added firmly. 'And that I will always remember the witches of Beldam House, and any others that I meet. As I will this, so will it be.'

The overhead light flickered. His heart pounded. Josh picked up the knife he'd washed and dried, and cut a small nick in his thumb. He pressed it to the piece of paper, and willed his words to take effect.

And he remembered:

- *Essie's arm in his, leading him down a darkened path and teasing him about lions*
- *Essie's lips on his, a hesitant and tender kiss*
- *the goat eating the tree in her damned house, and the portrait of Lilith that changed depending when and where she was*
- *falling into the long grass with Essie round and lush in his arms*
- *the ghost in the cellar, four centuries ago*
- *that wasn't a good kiss, it was an amazing kiss*
- *the flowers on her wallpaper bursting into life and showering them with petals*

'Josh?'

Dimly, he was aware of Siena repeating the same words he'd just said, but all he knew was Essie standing hesitantly beside him, her hand on his shoulder.

He looked up at her, Essie, his Essie, the woman he'd

travelled through time with and confessed his darkest secrets to and made love with until neither of them could speak or move any more. Essie, who he trusted with his life, and Siena's and the baby's, and who he was so in love with it hurt.

'Oh god,' his chair toppled over as he rushed to his feet to wrap her in his arms, 'Essie, my God. I love you. I'm sorry. And I love you.'

She sort of crumpled against him, and he could feel the relief coming off her in waves. Her tears soaked through his shirt. His soaked her hair.

'Whoa,' said Siena.

Josh couldn't do much more than turn his head towards her. The idea of letting go of Essie right now was as impossible as flying.

Well, that was – flying for anyone but Essie.

'I gave birth in your house?' said Siena, looking down at the baby in astonishment.

'Wm db— ' Essie wriggled herself loose enough on Josh's arms to be able to speak without a mouthful of his shirt, and tried again. 'Where did you think it had happened?'

'I don't know. Like, a hospital maybe? A nice one?' She faltered. 'With a fireplace and a… bathtub?'

'You broke my hand,' Josh remembered, looking down at it. It was completely fine now. Even the tiny cut he'd just made on his thumb had vanished.

'Oh, yeah, we might need to talk about that,' Essie said.

'You think I can heal people,' said Josh.

'Maybe just yourself.'

'Because I'm a witch?'

She made a so-so motion. 'Maybe.'

'Can men be witches?' Josh said.

'I'm going to pretend I didn't hear you say that,' said Essie.

'Does that mean I'm a witch?' said Siena.

'I don't know.'

Baby Matthew started crying. Siena sniffed.

'Well, let's just hope my magic powers include diaper changing,' she said, and carried him off up the stairs.

Josh stood with Essie in his arms. Essie, magnificent Essie, who banished a demon by pouring a cauldron of love on it.

Essie, who he'd accused of being a dangerous stalker who'd broken into his house.

He flinched at the memory.

'What?' Essie said.

'I have to apologise to you,' he said.

She was already shaking her head. 'No, you don't. Josh, you didn't know me from Adam, and you found me in your bed—'

'I said awful things to you,' he said, shame flooding him.

'Yes, but you didn't mean them. Or at least – if my mother hadn't meddled with your memory, you wouldn't have meant them.'

'Yeah, but I could've…' He swallowed. The what-ifs were too appalling to contemplate.

'Could've what? You wouldn't have hurt me. You know how I know that?'

'How?' Josh asked miserably.

'Because you didn't. And because I know you, Josh. I know you.' She put her hand on his face and made him look down at her. 'I know you, Josh Henderson Hopkins.' Her other hand touched his chest. 'Right down in the core of you. You don't hurt people. You'd never hurt me.'

All he could do at that was hold her closer.

'And by the way,' she added, 'I'm completely in love with you, too.'

His heart leapt. Oh, he didn't deserve this.

'This would be a really good moment for you to kiss me,' she whispered, and Josh couldn't believe he was allowed to, but he did, and Essie kissed him back, and sort of sighed against him, all her lovely round softness. She had twigs in her hair and her clothes smelled like laundry detergent but under that, there was the crisp scent of snow and the warmth of smoke. *It was there all along*. She was never just about ice.

He wanted to fill his hands with her, peel off those dungarees and kiss her freckles all over, and he probably would have if Siena's footsteps hadn't sounded on the stairs.

'Oh good, you two made up,' she said.

Josh cuddled Essie close, unable to stop grinning. 'I guess we did.'

'You guess?' said Essie. Her green eyes gleamed up at him. 'I'm gonna need more than guessing here, mate.'

'Okay, okay. I'm sure we made up. We definitely made up.' He murmured in Essie's ear, 'And I'll definitely make it up to you tonight.'

He heard the smile in her voice even as he nuzzled her ear. 'That a promise?'

'I could make it three times if you like,' he offered.

'What, the promise, or the making-up?'

'Hey, you guys, children present,' said Siena, laying the baby down in his bouncer chair with its array of brightly coloured educational toys. 'Speaking of, do you think he'll inherit magical powers?'

The baby blew bubbles and waved his chubby fists.

Essie shrugged. 'It's not always as simple as heredity,' she said. 'Sometimes it skips generations, sometimes it comes out of nowhere.'

'Is yours generational? I mean, apart from your mother.'

'I don't know. I never knew my grandparents. Sometimes… look, most of the witches at Beldam House came there because they weren't welcome somewhere else. We don't always ask. Avery doesn't like talking about it. Blessing just says they'll drag her back to Peckham only when she's dead. And my mother… has never mentioned where she came from.'

'Or when,' said Siena, poking at a jingling bell above the baby's crib.

'No, she was born in the twentieth century. She can't go forward, you see, not further than she's already lived. The door only goes back. You know, like *Quantum Leap*.'

'Are you sure?' said Josh, unsure how much Essie remembered of Hopkins's accusations.

'Yeah. Pretty sure. It's Maude you want for futures.' Essie sighed. 'And now we discover I may have been born four hundred years ago.'

Josh kept his arms around her and watched her frown.

'Do you remember it?' Siena asked doubtfully.

'No. Although, now you mention it…' Essie's gaze drifted to the baby in his bouncer. 'I remember being swaddled. Like – quite tightly. Which isn't something we do now. I mean, you wrap a baby, sure, but not so tightly they can't move. And I remember that.'

'That sounds horrible,' Siena said.

'No, it was nice. Comforting. Like the smell of lye.' Her expression brightened. 'I knew I remembered it! When we were back there! It's what they washed their clothes in.'

Josh, who vaguely remembered the ammonia smell of the clothes he'd been given four hundred years ago, wrinkled his nose.

'So… you think your mother was telling the truth?'

Essie nodded slowly. 'Probably. But she must have brought me back here when I was quite small, because that's really all I remember.' She cocked an eyebrow at Josh. 'How does it feel to be a toy boy?'

He laughed. 'Pretty good. And you know what? You don't look a day over three hundred.'

Chapter Twenty-One

Weeks passed, and turned into months. Spring arrived, and this time, Essie felt none of the sadness she usually did at the end of winter. Snow had fallen over Christmas, because she'd wanted it to, but not as much as usual.

Siena's baby grew, and was mostly called Matty by the family. Essie spent more time at Brook Manor Farm than Beldam House, but never feared Josh forgetting anything when he left the place. Maude told him to place his faith in 'the hawk that kicks the ball' and nobody had a clue what that meant until Blessing spotted a listing in the Racing Post for a horse called Seahawk.

Josh's winnings were enough to renovate Mrs Sockburn's cottage and let it for a decent amount.

He and Siena decided to renovate the old barn and derelict cottages on the Brook Manor estate, and Essie suggested using the long meadow for glamping. At Josh's suggestion, they built an outdoor hearth there, used it for making pizzas in the summer, and kept it stoked year-round.

The ruins of the old manor house, burned down by Hopkins's son, were tidied up and turned into an outdoor wedding venue. Love soaked into the ground, helped along by Avery's immensely popular cocktails.

'You know what I think?' Josh said, as he sat beside Essie on a bench by the outdoor chimney. They had a bottle of champagne beside them; nobody ever needed an ice bucket when Essie was around.

'What's that?'

It was a beautiful late spring day, the grass growing long, flowers erupting everywhere. The air was full of the sounds of insects busy pollinating, and birds loudly showing off. May in England wasn't quite warm enough to sit outside… unless you were capable of keeping an outside hearth burning continuously, that was. Essie didn't need a sweater over her dungarees, and Josh had stuck faithfully to his plaid shirt.

He pointed to Siena, who was enthusiastically showing a young couple around the luxury yurts in the long meadow. 'I think she does have magic.'

Essie squinted at Siena. She certainly had sparkle, her blonde hair shining in the sun, her dress twirling as she spun around laughing. 'How do you mean?'

'Well, remember how I said she called me up one day, just after I'd left Maya, and she told me to come house-sit for her in Malibu? And then it was her idea for me to come here?'

'Yes?'

Josh nodded at the couple to whom Siena was extolling the virtues of Brook Manor Farm Weddings. 'Look how the moment John and Giovanni got out of their car, she said, "I bet you guys want an outdoor feast," and she was right. She knows what people need and how to give it to them.'

Essie rolled her eyes. 'Power of suggestion, Josh, yikes.'

Josh shrugged. 'Okay, have it your way. Avery said she asked yesterday if they could roast a pig on the hearth.'

Essie gazed at Siena. Well, it was possible. Stranger things had happened.

'By the way, that muscle in my back is fine now, thanks for asking,' Josh went on.

Essie blushed a little, remembering what they'd been doing when he'd pulled it. 'Glad to hear it. Hey,' she shouted at a large crow that had landed near to baby Matty as he rolled on his blanket. 'Piss off!'

The crow ignored her, wandered over to the baby, and just as Essie and Josh leapt up, Matty reached out and clumsily petted the bird.

Who let him.

They both stared.

'The bird likes him,' said Essie. Bird thoughts were fast and mad, little more than bright scribbles across the retina, but she could get the general gist of it. The bird *liked* Matty. It was responding to the child's own communication that he wanted to pet the bird.

'Holy cannoli, my nephew is Doctor Doolittle,' said Josh, as the bird allowed itself to be fussed, then wandered away.

'We can all communicate with animals a bit,' said Essie.

'Yeah? Feral corvids?' Josh drew Essie back onto the bench beside him, and said, 'I wonder if his father was a witch.'

Essie shrugged. 'I guess we'll never know.'

Siena had confided, eventually, that she wasn't exactly sure who Matty's father was. 'There was kind of a wild period after my dad died, and I… spent a lot of time at parties in the Valley,' she said.

'We could probably find out,' Blessing had offered doubtfully.

'I don't want you to. Trust me when I say none of those guys were father material. I guess that was kind of the point.'

Right now, Siena was smiling and laughing as she showed the happy couple back to their car. She gave Josh and Essie a huge thumbs up as she did.

Josh hugged Essie and said, 'Open the champagne then.'

She turned away to do that, giving it an extra chill as she did.

'I bet June,' Josh said, as the car drove away.

'Nah, July.' Essie untwisted the wire basket over the cork.

'Well, so long as it's not the cross-quarter day.'

'We passed that,' Essie said. 'Two weeks ago on Friday. Don't you remember? Siena suggested a Beltane dance in the nude and Prudence had to go and hang in her tree a while to calm down.'

'No,' said Josh, and she could hear the smile in his voice as she turned back with the champagne bottle in her hands, ready to ease the cork out. 'I mean the one in November.'

He was kneeling by the bench, and had something in his hand. It glinted in the sunlight.

Essie's mouth went dry.

'Maude told me to book the seventh,' he said. 'Around four in the afternoon, she said.'

'Four eighteen,' whispered Essie, who could calculate a cross-quarter day in her sleep.

Josh's smile widened. 'Four eighteen on the seventh of November. Will you marry me then, Essie?'

The exact point between the solstice and equinox. A year exactly after they'd banished Hopkins.

Essie swallowed, and gazed down at the ring Josh held out to her. 'Well,' she said roughly, and cleared her throat. 'I suppose, for the benefit of making sure there's love on this ground on the right anniversary…'

Josh's eyes warmed. 'Essie. Open that bottle before it explodes.'

She looked down. There was frost forming on it. 'But I haven't said yes yet,' she whispered.

'Are you going to?'

The cork suddenly shot from the bottle as Essie nodded. 'Oh my god, yes!'

Josh grinned, and slipped the ring onto her finger as champagne cascaded over them. And then he kissed her, as the sun set and the birds sang and the flowers grew, very vigorously, all around them.

'Hey,' she murmured against his lips. 'I just realised something.'

'Yeah?'

Essie smiled. 'You're a witchfinder after all.'

'What do you mean?'

She snuggled into him, and watched Siena pick up Matty and come over to them. 'Well,' she said. 'You sure found me.'

Acknowledgments

Thanks must go as always to the magnificent witches of the Naughty Kitchen, you glorious encouraging bastards.

The Boscastle Museum of Witchcraft and Magic, which is a wondrous place: compassionate, informative, and delightfully weird.

Jan Jones, for the sort of friendship and support that just goes on and on.

The RSPCA, for my own Tomkin (and Billy).

And everyone else who's listened to me becoming Random Facts Girl: the Witch Edition.

Author's Note

ON THE BURNING OF WITCHES; POPPET DOLLS; AND WITCHFINDERS

Before I started researching this book, I'd assumed witches were burned at the stake. It's the classic image, isn't it? Except it's not true. Not in Britain, or in any part of the world belonging to Britain at the time of witchmania (roughly the late sixteenth to mid eighteenth century, peaking in the mid-seventeenth). This of course includes the American colonies and Ireland.

In England, people convicted of witchcraft were hanged, as witchcraft was considered a felony, and not heresy as you might imagine. This was usual in most other British territories, too. In Scotland, strangling was the norm, sometimes followed by burning (a disturbing amount of thought went into how to achieve this without having to cut the body down). But it's important to note that even with convicted Scottish witches, the burning was done after death. Being burned alive was reserved for the most heinous of crimes, such as coin-clipping or being the wrong kind of Christian. Brr.

Of course, before being hanged, most people accused of witchcraft were tortured in some way. Many who were acquitted suffered terribly afterwards, sometimes crippled and usually shunned by society. Every way you look at it, it was a terrible thing to happen.

However, it is true that in other parts of Europe, burning was used as a method of execution for people accused of witchcraft. The Holy Roman Empire (much of Central Europe) has a particularly dark history in this regard.

As for poppet dolls: these have a long tradition in British and European witchcraft. They could be made from almost anything, and in fact the excellent Museum of Witchcraft and Magic in Boscastle, Cornwall, has a large display of poppets made from wax, cloth, clay, string… anything you could get your hands on.

Many of the existing poppet dolls appear to have ill intentions. Some are stuck full of pins, or hanged by a rope. Some have their bellies trimmed with pins to induce a miscarriage (these are often thought to be self-sought, as in the case of the pregnant WWII nurse doll). Some consist of a glove or a shoe filled with burrs.

However, not every poppet is intended to cause harm. Some are made as love charms, and some to break an unhealthy infatuation. In more modern usage, the poppet is usually intended for protection and healing. I have used them myself to bless a marriage, or even convince a shy kitten to trust me!

Of course, in Britain, 'poppet' is often used as a term of endearment, especially to a child—like 'sweetie' or 'love'. I used to call my dog 'poppet', and I never stuck pins in her (insulin needles were another matter). It's with this in mind that I had my witches create poppets of people they wanted to protect and keep safe, or whose suffering they wanted to ease.

There is often confusion between the poppet doll, which is a real thing used by European witches, especially in Britain, and the voodoo doll, which is largely a Hollywood invention with very little relation to the voodoo/vodou practised by some African diaspora communities in the Americas and Caribbean. A doll with pins stuck in it is almost certainly of European origin, and it might not be as evil as you think.

As to witchfinders. Matthew Hopkins was, regrettably, a real person. Very little is actually known about him, and there's no record of him being married or having children, but we do know that he died in 1647 when he was less than thirty years old. He mostly operated in East Anglia, and especially Essex—where more people were hanged as witches than in any other part of England. The actual number of people he persecuted, and the number who died as a result of his actions, is not something we know for sure. Estimates vary, but the number of deaths he was responsible for is probably in the hundreds.

There's some speculation he was trained as a lawyer, but no proof. What he certainly was, was a con man.

He operated during the English Civil War, a time of tremendous fear, change, and loss, and preyed upon the credulous fears of a disenfranchised, uneducated, and terrified population. With his associate John Stearne and various female assistants, he styled himself the Witchfinder

General, and convinced village after village that pretty much any problem they might be having had been caused by a witch. Bad harvest? Witch. Outbreak of plague? Witch. Impotent husband? Witch. He made money out of fear and ignorance, and as a result, hundreds of people died. In the end, he became rich enough that people began to become suspicious of him, and quit after only three years, whereupon he promptly died, and good riddance.

YOUR NUMBER ONE STOP
ONE MORE CHAPTER
FOR PAGETURNING BOOKS

One More Chapter is an award-winning global division of HarperCollins.

Sign up to our newsletter to get our latest eBook deals and stay up to date with our weekly Book Club!
Subscribe here.

Meet the team at
www.onemorechapter.com

Follow us!

 @OneMoreChapter_

 @OneMoreChapter

 @onemorechapterhc

Do you write unputdownable fiction?
We love to hear from new voices.
Find out how to submit your novel at
www.onemorechapter.com/submissions